She stepped back from the verandah, terrifyingly aware that the noises she heard were not in her mind but on the path coming up from the mill. There was a jangling of horse bridles and the stamp of marching feet.

She gasped, clasping her hand to her mouth to still her shriek of fear. A troop of men seemed to spring from the darkness, filling the garden in front of the villa.

Behind her, Bart and Kumara were banging on the locked parlour door. She turned to let them out but it was too late. The men were at the verandah step.

BLOODHEART FEUD

Richard Tresillian

SPHERE BOOKS LIMITED

SPHERE BOOKS LTD

Published by the Penguin Group
27 Wrights Lane, London w8 5TZ, England
Viking Penguin Inc., 40 West 23rd Street, New York, New York 10010, USA
Penguin Books Australia Ltd, Ringwood, Victoria, Australia
Penguin Books Canada Ltd, 2801 John Street, Markham, Ontario, Canada L3R 1B4
Penguin Books (NZ) Ltd, 182–190 Wairau Road, Auckland 10, New Zealand

Penguin Books Ltd, Registered Offices: Harmondsworth, Middlesex, England

First published in Great Britain by Century Hutchinson Ltd 1987
by arrangement with Sphere Books Ltd
Published by Sphere Books Ltd 1988

Made and printed in Great Britain by
Richard Clay Ltd, Bungay, Suffolk

For
K. A. 'Podi' Premaratna

CONTENTS

Book One

Raven
1821

CHAPTER ONE

Brushing aside the vines, Raven left the heat of the sun blazing down on the canefield and entered the jungle trail. She paused, her dark eyes lingering on its lushness. Trees were festooned with orchids and creepers, their leaves so dense the harsh sun was transformed into a soft, shadowy glow.

She was surprised to discover she was trembling. She swallowed, catching her breath to still her nervous shaking. Bart's warning that she should not walk alone in the jungle echoed ominously in her ears.

'Why not?' she had demanded when she was facing him only minutes before on the verandah of his villa that was more her prison than her home.

'Because I say so!'

She had stared at him in disbelief. Was this the same considerate man she had married? He was called Bloodheart by the Ceylonese because of his warm heart and reckless courage, yet she experienced only his overbearing attitude when she wanted to do something by herself.

'I'm not your slave,' she had replied rudely. The memory of her defiance brought a flush of shame to her cheeks. She bowed her head and hastened along the trail, heedless of the exotic beauty of the jungle around her.

Bart had grimaced, the opal blue of his eyes darkening with anger. He could be obstinate and act rashly. She knew by the tightening of his jaw and the clenching of his fist that she had offended him. If she were his slave, he would have struck her.

'You are my wife, Raven.' He sounded puzzled. 'Why don't you behave like it?'

'If you want me to stay meekly at home all day, I won't. I want to walk. I want to go down to the sea and stroll along the shore. I want to pick flowers, I want –'

'Very well!' He was struggling to keep his anger under control.

'So you shall. But you must not go alone. Take one of the boys with you.'

'I don't need a chaperon.'

'It's for your protection . . .'

She had run off the verandah then, across the canefields into the jungle. She was unwilling to listen to the objections he always raised. She knew the jungle was dangerous but it was only a short walk through it to the sea.

Leopards no longer lurked in the trees because deer no longer grazed on the plain. Sugar-cane grew on the land now, and on the plantation boundary there was a settlement of native labourers whose noisy presence scared off dangerous animals.

Of course, there were snakes. Raven had learned they were as frightened of her as she was of them, and should slither out of sight if she made enough noise to disturb them. She slowed her pace and began to sing to make sure any snakes would hear her coming and take fright.

She was shielded from the sun by the jungle's thick foliage yet the heat was making her perspire. There was no breeze on the trail; it was humid and the undergrowth reeked with the smell of rotting vegetation.

For a moment, her courage faltered. Perhaps Bart was right; she ought not to walk in the jungle alone. She was determined to prove she could.

She had been married to him for nearly a year. This was the first time she had disobeyed him despite her dislike of his often domineering manner. His attitude surprised her for Bart was known in the town for his devil-may-care approach to life.

Raven wanted to show him that she was as much entitled to her independence as he was. She loved Bart and her dash from the verandah had been a wild impulse. She half-expected him to call her back. When he did not, she kept on running.

She stopped singing and halted on the trail to listen. She heard the whistles and whoops of birds and the rustling of the undergrowth. Behind her, she could hear the *salagamas*, the natives Bart employed in his canefields, shouting to one another. She was not being followed.

Her pulse calmed and she no longer shook with nerves at defying him. Bart would understand. His reluctance to let her wander off by herself stemmed from his love.

He had risked his life to save her when she was threatened by the odious Marcus Van Dort and his gang of Caffre slaves. She was

4

nearly raped by one of them that night and Van Dort had died for it, crushed to death in the grinding stones of the sugar-mill.*

She took a deep breath and the stench of the jungle chased away the memory. She glanced around apprehensively, wondering how far it was to the sea. Her feet were aching; her skirt was stuck with burs and its hem mired with mud. She touched her hair in her anxiety and realized how dishevelled her tresses had become. If only she had stopped to don her bonnet.

It was too late to regret her action. She sighed and reached for an orchid, tugging it towards her so she could smell it. The flower was a lustrous violet colour, five exquisitely formed leaves enveloping an open bud with a touch of yellow at its centre. She held it to her nose and was disappointed that it had no scent to disguise the aroma of decay around her.

She sauntered along the trail with less haste now she was sure she was alone. She liked being in the open. When she lived in Galle with her father she loved to spend the days strolling under the frangipani trees in the garden of their official residence.

Her father, Thomas Radley, was the Collector of Customs for Galle. He was a pompous man who was a stranger to her when she arrived from England to join him. That was five years before, when she was fifteen.

She had seen Bart for the first time soon after her arrival. She was intrigued by the dashing young man with the resolute jaw, fair hair that flopped over his forehead whenever he tried to brush it back, and a sensuous glint in his dark blue eyes.

That he was ten years older did not dull his attraction. She had to fight her own battle of personal restraint because he was married. Even when his wife was killed by a Kandyan prince, Raven saw no chance for romance between them.

Her lips tingled in remembrance of his first touch as they became friends. He was gentle and caring then. Eventually they reached the point where their relationship had to be resolved and, with her father's blessing, she became Bart Taylor's bride.

As Mistress of his vast sugar-cane plantation in the hills over-looking the southern coast of Ceylon, five miles from the main port of Galle, Raven expected to find happiness. Instead, a permanent sorrow weighed her down.

After the flush of the first days of their marriage, she knew only the raw sores of an aching heart. Whenever she gazed at Bart she

* See *Bloodheart Royal*

was deeply affected by the sexual magnetism that made him such a forceful personality. She yearned to share her own passionate feelings with him.

For some reason, after the night on the river bank when he pressed the priceless pearl of ivory between her breasts and took her virginity, swearing to cherish her for ever, her glowing youthful happiness faded. He no longer made love to her with the savage ardour of that night. His touch became restrained, his manner muted.

She wanted to tell him she was not a fragile doll to be handled gently. Her body craved his strong arms holding her instead of the respectful touch of his fingers. She longed for his lips to devour hers so she could yield to the searing need which had been building up for months.

Bart behaved towards her like a man scared of desire. When he made love it was without warmth and he seemed to be performing a duty solely to give her a child. She wondered if he looked elsewhere for his pleasure. The very first time she had set eyes on him he was emerging from Madam Gudde's bordello in Galle.

The blood began to pound in her temples as she thought of it. She was glad she was alone on the jungle path where no one could see the flush in her cheeks and suspect her deep sense of shame. The idea of Bart in another woman's arms caused her a misery so acute it was a physical pain.

She was distracted as she sauntered on the trail, careless about where she trod. The path was sloping downwards and she missed her footing on its slippery surface. She grasped frantically at the trunk of a huge tree, unable to stop herself falling.

The wet path with its carpet of moulding leaves and loose pebbles was like a slide. She slithered down its incline in a flurry of twigs and stones, her dress rucking up to her hips. Her backside was sore and numb as she scrambled to halt her descent.

'Ho!' a voice cried in the gloom and suddenly she tumbled against a man's body, coming to rest at his feet.

She gazed at him in dismay. His feet were bare, anchored firmly in the mud. His legs were brown and sinewy and he wore nothing more than a scanty madras-check loincloth. He bent down and offered her his hand, pulling her to her feet.

He was slender rather than tall. His stance emphasized the strength of his thighs and the slimness of his hips. He looked tough and lean, although his face was young, even timid. He smiled nervously.

6

'Thank you!' she gasped, smoothing her dress down and trying to brush away the leaves and twigs that clung to it. 'I must look a fright!'

The youth backed away, bowing his head. His hair was black and bristly. He put his palms together at chest height, his long fingers straight, in the respectful greeting of the Ceylonese.

'Don't you speak English?' Raven was curious, wondering what the youth was doing in the jungle. He was unlike the natives from the settlement. He had an air of independence about him and exuded the confidence of being at home among the trees.

He bent down to pick up a covered wicker basket that lay beside the path. His check loincloth gave her a clue.

'Are you a Tamil, from the north?' The youth looked blank. 'Tamil?' she repeated.

He grimaced nervously again and edged away from her.

'Don't go!' She held out her hand, hoping to detain him. 'Why don't you walk with me? I'm going to the shore.' The sight of the youth's innocent smile restored her confidence. He was younger than her and probably overwhelmed by her questions.

'What's in your basket?' she asked in an attempt to make him relax. She touched the lid.

His eyes flashed with a hint of amusement. He lifted the cover and plunged his hand in.

She screamed.

A snake reared up from the basket's depths, its eyes blinking evilly as it began to coil around the youth's arm. He grinned when the snake's yellow mottled mouth opened and its tongue darted out.

'Put . . . it . . . back!' she cried, stepping away in horror, realizing that the youth was the plantation snake catcher. 'Thank you . . . for helping me,' she stammered and rapidly resumed her walk.

The ground was firmer and she glanced back when she was away from the youth. He had returned the snake to its basket and was watching her with a bemused expression. She waved and rounded a bend in the trail.

She was shaken by the encounter and looked more carefully where she stepped. Thoughts of Bart had flown from her mind and she thought only of getting to the sea so she could rest and be soothed by the waves lapping the shore.

Bart's plantation had been given to him under a grant from the British governor when it was decided to allow settlers to develop

7

the colony's hinterland. The British had wrested control of the littoral of Ceylon from the Dutch over twenty years before. Cinnamon and coconuts were the main crops then and the plantation's boundary beyond the jungle was marked with a palm grove.

As the path levelled out, the jungle thinned until Raven found herself strolling through clumps of tall, swaying palm trees. The sea glistened enticingly beyond them.

Coconuts thrive on sea air; they require a light and sandy soil and the constant presence of water in large quantities. The seabelt by the plantation, lying between the ocean on the one side and the fresh water lake formed by a river on the other, was ideal for them.

There was a native superstition that coconuts will not grow out of the sound of human voices. Since there were hamlets along the shore, and the road from Galle to Matara passed along its length, there was plenty of human company for the trees.

Raven peered anxiously along the road where the trail emerged from the jungle. Her present state of *déshabillé* would provoke comment if she were seen by anyone journeying to Galle. If her father heard that she was on the road without an escort and in a torn and muddy dress, he would be insulted.

Fortunately, there was no one in sight. The nearest houses were over a hundred yards away, hidden from view by the bushes and shrubs which grew in their gardens. She darted across the road, inspired by her survival of the jungle trail and by her desire to bathe her aching feet in the sea.

Holding up the hem of her dress so her legs were free, she ran delightedly through the trees down to the beach. At the edge of the palm grove she paused and kicked off her shoes, sinking her bare feet into the soft sand. Her toes tingled as they touched the powdery granules, burning with the sun's heat. The pain was oddly soothing and she concentrated her thoughts on her pleasure at being alone on the beach with the sea splashing the shore only yards from her.

She moved in a daze towards it, relishing the cool breeze at the water's edge. She was sticky under her clothes and longed to remove them so she could plunge into the inviting embrace of the crystal clear sea and cleanse herself. She glanced around.

She was in a small cove, a sheltered bay indented into the main strand of beach that swept along the south coast. At either side, shielding her from the view of passers-by, were outcrops of rocks. Behind her was the thick grove of coconut trees.

She hesitated only a moment before shedding her clothes. She was volatile by nature and untamed by convention. Ladies did not bathe in the sea, and they certainly did not remove their clothes in a public place. Yet the bay was totally secluded, she was alone and she was hot and wanted to cool off in the water. No one would know; what harm could there be in it?

She lay her clothes neatly in a heap beyond the tide's reach and stepped towards the sea, smiling as the sun caressed her nakedness.

She had firm, uptilted breasts, a narrow waist and hips that tapered to long, straight legs. The apricot and milky colour of her skin seemed to glow and her thick dark hair tumbled in ringlets down her back. Her heart sang with delight and she danced with a surge of joy towards the surf, plunging into the water with a gasp of contentment.

It was shallow where the beach shelved gently downwards and she frolicked without fear. She lay on the wet sand and let the waves roll her over as they swept up the beach. She forgot about time and place, about Bart and his ridiculous strictures, and dwelt on the sensuous delight of that moment.

The sky was cloudless, the blue of sapphire. She gazed from it to the palm trees and the jungle-clad hills beyond.

For the first time, she noticed the twin ropes of coconut fibre that were stretched from the top of one tree to another. They were used by toddy tappers, the men who drew the sap from the coconut's flower to make toddy, a fermented liquor.

To her horror, she saw a man walking from the top of one tree to another, supporting himself by the top rope while he trod the lower one. She ducked below the waves, hoping he would not see her. He looked small so high up, a copper skinned man with an indigo cloth wrapped around his thighs.

The waves splashed over her shoulders as she watched him run with a surprising swiftness to the end of the rope where it was tied around the top of a tall coconut tree. When he reached the tree he began to clamber down its trunk, using his feet as a brake and his hands for support.

She marvelled at his strength and how his well-muscled body moved with an easy grace. Too late she realized his descent would bring him down on the beach where she had piled her clothes.

There was no way to escape being seen by him. Her only hope was that he would be embarrassed, avert his eyes and move politely away. His shout as he jumped from the tree and strolled confidently across the sand towards her drove that hope from her mind.

'Good afternoon, Raven!' he called familiarly.

She stared at him aghast. As far as she knew, she had never seen him before.

Her eyes froze on his long, lean form. Sunlight struck his black curly hair and it gleamed like polished onyx. His handsome, bronzed face was kindled with a sort of passionate beauty while the shadow of a beard stamped him with a manly aura. His eyes glowed with a savage inner fire; they were compelling and devilish.

'Who are you?' she asked in a weak voice that didn't sound like hers.

'Kumara.' His eyes glinted as he contemplated her bare shoulders when the sea coursed away from her. She sank deeper into it, trying to hide her nakedness in the waves.

'It means Prince.'

'Go away!' she said, choking with embarrassment. She was humiliatingly conscious of his scrutiny.

His firm, sensuous lips spread in a sardonic grin. Despite her anger at his presence, she noticed how his teeth were even and white, contrasting pleasingly with his bronze skin.

'Perhaps you need my help?' he asked mockingly, extending his hand.

'I don't!' She spoke in a broken whisper, torn between the shame of her situation and a desire to know more about this lithe young man who was watching her so intently.

He radiated a vitality that drew her like a magnet and she felt a lurch of excitement within her. His features were so perfect, so symmetrical, that any more delicacy would have made him too beautiful to be mortal. He exuded a toughness that was vaguely frightening.

'Turn your back,' she said, 'and close your eyes. I want to dress.'

He chuckled lightly and the sound of his laughter reassured her. As he turned away to face the coconut trees, she emerged from the sea with the water cascading from her shoulders in droplets that sparkled in the sun. Before she could reach her clothes, he spun around.

His eyes raked boldly over her, dropping from her face to her shoulders to her breasts. Slowly and seductively, his gaze slid downwards.

She opened her mouth to protest. Her heart jolted under the impact of his eyes and her pulse raced. The noise of the surf on the beach drowned out the thudding of her heart. He took a step towards her, standing so close she could feel the heat from his half-naked body.

His nearness overwhelmed her and, to her dismay, her fingers itched to reach over and touch him. She tried to ignore the strange aching in her limbs.

'Raven!' he whispered in an insistent voice that was as smooth as velvet.

She was suddenly aware of his touch, firm and persuasive, on her hand. Her resistance collapsed. She relaxed, sinking into his embrace and welcoming his arms around her.

His lips pressed against hers, covering her mouth. She clung to him with trembling limbs.

Her own eager response to his lips shocked her. Heat rippled under her skin and she recognized the rush of yearning that had bedevilled her for months.

His lips were hard and demanding as his hands explored the soft lines of her waist. Shivers of delight followed his touch; her knees weakened. She began to sink down into the sand, and he slid down with her.

'Raven!' The shout was Bart's. It penetrated her brain rudely with its fearful warning.

The stranger released her and she fell limp in the sand. Guiltily she glanced in the direction of the shout. Bart was hidden from view in the next cove. He called again and she sighed with relief that he hadn't yet seen her.

She turned back; the man had gone. She peered into the palm trees, desperate for a last glimpse of him. There was only the tangled undergrowth and clumps of red bougainvillaea waving in the breeze.

Bart's voice calling her name grew louder.

Hurriedly, she pulled on her dress, trying to smooth down her hair and to still the passion that was soaring through her. She was conscious of where the man's warm flesh had touched her, and in her mind she relived the velvet warmth of his kiss.

She heard a whistle and looked up. Bart was standing on the outcrop of rock, beckoning her. She looked beyond him, up into the trees. There, at the top of the tallest one, almost hidden out of sight in the palm fronds, was Kumara.

She stared at him in disbelief at what had happened. Bart had saved her, but she wasn't sure if she had wanted him to. She turned away reluctantly to face him.

She wondered as she walked slowly across the sand towards him, if she would ever see the handsome toddy tapper again.

CHAPTER TWO

'Toddy tapper?' Bart's expression was one of puzzlement.

His eyes flickered over her enquiringly and Raven could see he was trying to fathom the reason for her unexpected question. Seated at the opposite end of the refectory table to him, with the empty tureens and plates of their finished dinner between them, Raven had asked her question casually.

Nimal, the houseboy, glided around the table removing the dirty dishes. Romulus, a Caffre slave, stood almost invisible in the shadows at the side of the room gently pulling the rope that swung the punkah suspended from the ceiling over the table. Its cool draught fanned her face but she could feel a flush stealing over her cheeks under Bart's probing stare.

'Yes.' She repeated her question to distract his scrutiny. 'What is a toddy tapper? I heard one of the boys mention them.'

Bart pulled the lobe of his ear and leaned back in his chair. His anger at her running off had taken a day to subside, despite her attempt to mollify him when he had found her in the bay the previous afternoon. He was peevish towards her the whole day while she feigned girlish innocence lest he discovered about the man in the cove.

'We don't have any here,' he said with a wave of his hand, dismissing her question as of no consequence. 'They come from a low caste tribe. They climb coconut trees with mallets and knives in quest of the sap. They tap the spathes of unopened flowers and sell the juice they draw off to be distilled into arrack.'

'That's why arrack is called coconut brandy,' she said with a smile of understanding. 'I often wondered.'

'The fermented sap gives it a distinctive flavour and aroma. It's totally different from molasses-based spirit like the rum we produce at the mill from our sugar-canes.'

The danger of him divining the reason for her question had passed. He began to talk about sugar, a topic that was never far

13

from his thoughts. Nimal placed a dish of diced fruit salad in front of her. She ate it slowly, savouring the sweetness of the pineapple, the texture of papaya and the sharp taste of mango. While Bart talked, the memory of Kumara's burning kiss came back.

She wondered how a low-caste toddy tapper could have gained such a hold on her thoughts. His face haunted her with its unruly black curls and dark eyes that sparked with an amber light in the sunlight. She had run to Bart and hugged him when Kumara vanished into the heavens. She loved him and was touched by his concern in coming to search for her. Why, then, had she let the toddy tapper kiss her?

'Raven, you're not listening!'

She was caught off-guard by the sudden vibrancy of his voice. She stared wordlessly across the table at him, her heart pounding.

'I said, let us go to the verandah. You seem to be affected by the heat. Your cheeks are quite red. It becomes you.'

'Oh dear.' Her fingers flew to her face. 'Yes, I am hot.' She smiled apologetically and glanced in the direction of the slave. 'Don't punish Romulus. The punkah just isn't cool enough in these hot evenings.'

She rose to her feet as Nimal pulled back her chair, then dutifully followed Bart from the dining room. She walked behind him across the parlour and through the doorway to the verandah. She felt Bart eyeing her as she sat down on the edge of her chair.

She took her time to arrange herself comfortably before raising her eyes to meet his. 'Won't you sit down too?' she asked, smiling an invitation.

He slapped the whitewashed column supporting the verandah's roof and twirled around so he was looking into the night. There was no moon and in the darkness he could not see beyond the arc of light cast by the lantern's glow on the lawn. Beyond it were the bushes and flowers planted by his first wife to keep the canefields out of sight.

'I don't know what's wrong with you these days,' he said to the night. 'Is it something I've done?' His voice cracked with an odd note of pleading.

She appreciated how he was swallowing his pride to hint that he might be to blame. 'Of course not,' she said warmly, longing for him to sit by her side. 'I've been a little moody, Bart, that's all. It's the heat.'

'The monsoon season!' he said, not bothering to hide his loud sigh of relief. He turned and sauntered over to her. 'It affects some people that way.'

'Yes, you must be right.' She settled back in her chair and gazed up at him, smiling ruefully. 'You are very understanding.'

'I learned to be that through having slaves. They are humans too. You have to understand their moods . . .'

He was off again, speaking about his problems as a planter and completely ignoring her own feelings. Yet she could not help admiring him as he stood before her, his opal eyes glinting excitedly in the lantern light and his rugged face vital and alive.

He loved his plantation with the intense passion other men reserved for their mistresses. He had created the canefields out of the virgin forest and built the villa and the mill through his own sweat and toil. He had overcome every obstacle put in his way by jealous enemies and survived the deaths of his sister, mother and his wife to make the plantation great.

His energy and determination had moulded his body and character. He was less than six feet in height yet he had the bearing of a tall man. He had a wide-shouldered, rangy body. His open shirt revealed his broad chest and the hair that grew across it down to the hard muscles of his stomach. His thighs and legs were firm, formed by years of riding and walking over the acres of his domain.

With his tousled hair flopping forward over his brow and his strongly etched features, his face exuded a force that commanded respect. Looking up at him, Raven felt a tug of shame at her behaviour. Why had she defied him and caused him hurt by running off?

Bart's diatribe on slave problems was interrupted by the grunts and scornful exclamations of Mammy Sobers arriving on the verandah. She stalked towards a chair and flung herself on to it, her weight causing it to skid backwards across the verandah's polished tiles.

Raven watched the old lady with awe. Her chubby face with her tongue a striking pink against the crow black colour of her skin, was wreathed in concern.

'I'm tellin' you, Bart,' she said, hitching up her huge bosom and glaring at him defiantly. 'I ain't goin' to leave you here wid dat chit of a girl as housekeeper. No, sah!'

Bart laughed, responding to her challenge with a sense of glee. He loved Mammy Sobers. She was from Barbados, given to his mother as a wedding present by his own father. His father was

15

American-born and owned the most successful sugar plantation in Barbados until his untimely death by drowning when Bart was eighteen. His mother had brought Mammy with them when they moved to Ceylon a year later.

Mammy was like a wise old owl, the grumpy matriarch of the plantation. She had been granted her freedom on his mother's death and inherited some of her wealth. Now she was an eccentric figure given to dressing in emulation of the wealthy ladies she had seen in London, and only happy when she had something to complain about.

She plucked at a cotton that had worked loose on the tight-fitting sleeve of her crimson evening gown. She snapped off the thread irritably and let it flutter to the floor, as she raised her face to glare at Bart. She completely ignored Raven.

'Daisy is perfectly capable of looking after us. You trained her yourself.'

'An' I train you too!' Mammy retorted. 'An' you still need me.'

'Of course I do, Mammy. I need you to take Garth to England. No one else can do it.'

Mammy scowled and looked at Raven suspiciously. 'You de one tellin' him dis! Ain't seem right to me.'

Raven put out her hand and patted Mammy on her arm. The touch calmed her. 'Garth can't get much education here, Mammy. My aunt in Bristol will look after him.'

'What goin' to happen to me?'

'Why, you shall come straight back here to be with Bart.'

'Whoo!' A gust of protest exploded from her lips. 'He knows I don't like de sea voyage.'

'You're quite the lady of quality,' said Bart soothingly. 'You'll be waited on hand and foot.'

Mammy lapsed into a disgruntled silence, broken only by snorts that seemed to ejaculate from her body of their own accord.

Secretly, Raven was pleased by Bart's scheme to send his son by his first wife to England. Garth was seven. He was impulsive and impatient like Bart himself. He had a sharp eye and an intelligence that was wasted without proper schooling. It was the custom of the British in Ceylon to send their children to England to be educated. Since they were unable to find someone going on leave, sending Mammy with him was the obvious solution.

There were two other children at the villa. Ranita was Bart's niece by his dead sister. Tissa, his headman, was the girl's father and she showed Singhalese traits in her golden complexion,

16

straight hair and almond-shaped eyes. The other child was Kirti.

Raven felt sorry for Kirti. He was only four and Bart's dead wife was his mother. Everyone assumed Bart was his father except Raven, Tissa and Malika, the boy's nurse, who shared the secret. Bart had been cuckolded by a pretender to the Kandyan throne, Prince Gamunu, and Kirti was the dead prince's child, not his own.

Bart interrupted the uneasy silence. 'It's all settled, Mammy. Collector Radley will let us know of the next sailing. It could be in a few days.'

'I want a cabin of my own an' I takin' my victuals wid de captain an' all dem white ladies.'

'How else would you travel, Mammy? You are worth more than all of them put together.'

'Flattery ain't goin' 'suade me, Bart Taylor!'

Raven's spirits rose when she saw Bart wink at her for support. 'I'll look after Bart properly, Mammy,' she said, hoping he understood the longing for him that tugged at her heart.

His expression hardened. 'Don't wait up,' he said brusquely. 'I'm going to the mill.'

'Whatever for, at this time of night –'

'Hush, Raven.' Mammy's stern rebuke squashed her protest. 'Bart's a planter. You don't want to concern yourself wid his problems.'

'But I do –'

Before she could finish speaking, Bart stepped off the verandah into the night. She gazed after him as he disappeared beyond the lantern's glow. She wondered why it was that whenever she expressed a need for him, he took umbrage.

At times he stayed away from their bedchamber all night, saying he had plantation matters to deal with. On other occasions, when her body ached with need for him and she tried to rouse him with a tender caress, he would mutter an oath and leave the bed to sleep on a mat on the floor.

'Ain't you wise to de man yet, Raven?' Mammy's tone changed from scolding to a soft whisper of solicitude. 'Bart born a master. Ain't no woman can change dat. No use you tryin'.'

She bit back her anger and stared at the grotesquely dressed old lady in surprise. Mammy's hand patted her affectionately and her rheumy yellow eyes were moist with concern.

'I don't want to change him,' she said.

17

'Dat good!' Mammy beamed. 'What you need is a rum.' She clapped her hands loudly. Nimal, who had been waiting patiently behind the door of the parlour until he was summoned, glided on to the verandah. He nodded his head as Mammy instructed him to bring a jug of old rum from Bart's private supply.

'I love him so much, Mammy,' Raven blurted out, astounding herself for exposing her feelings so openly. 'I wish he loved me even half as much.'

'Oh my lawd!' Mammy splashed rum into a glass and passed it to her. 'Don't you un'stand one piece of de man?'

Raven frowned before she tasted the rum. It was fiery to her lips and she was amazed when Mammy drained her glass in a single gulp.

Mammy belched contentedly then wagged her plump finger at her. She continued speaking in a low voice: 'Dey call him Bloodheart 'cause he warm an' carin' an' forgives his en'mies. But he 'fraid dat people will think him weak.'

'It isn't a weakness to love your wife. Mammy . . .' she took a deep breath to summon up the courage to make her confession.

'Mammy . . . he never relaxes when he's with me . . . in bed. He hasn't made love to me the way he did on the night of our marriage. He was wild . . . like a savage then. Now he seems scared of even squeezing me in his arms.'

'Whoo!' Mammy threw back her head and laughed heartily, startling Raven and making her feel ashamed for what she had said. Yet her laughter was warm and friendly and carried no sense of criticism.

Perplexed by Mammy's reaction, she found herself smiling back into the old slave's tired eyes.

'Whoo!' said Mammy again, her jowls shaking with merriment. 'You does be one lucky white lady for sure.'

'I am?'

'Of course. You ain't been brought up wid planters so you don't know de ways. Bart loves an' respec's you as his wife. So he won't make love to you like you're his slave wench or a whore.'

'I don't understand.'

'Bart been brought up to believe pleasurin' only for men. He don't know women like it too!' She giggled. 'He 'shamed to ax you to do wid him what a slave wench or whore does do. He wants you as de mother of his chil'en, not for *pleasure*.' Her voice swooped to a husky tone.

'Ain't you proud he does choose you to bear his child?'

18

She squirmed in her seat under Mammy's penetrating gaze. 'Well, yes . . .'

'What happen, girl?'

There was no hiding her doubt from the old slave. Bart was right, she was like an owl, with a head that swivelled and eyes that saw everything. Raven coloured as the heat stole into her face.

'Am I wrong to want Bart so much, Mammy? He can take his pleasure with me. I can't bear to think of him lying with a . . . with a whore.'

'Lawd, what a thing to say! He needs a wench to drain de poison from him. You ain't s'pose to *enjoy* de ruttin'. You don't know what yo' does be sayin'.' Mammy wagged her finger in Raven's face.

The gesture irked her and she regretted giving credence to the old slave's wisdom. She drew a deep breath so her temper did not show, and brushed nervously at her hair with her hand. She placed her glass of rum on the table, declining to finish it, and prepared to stand up.

'You an' he on de same page,' said Mammy. 'Too stubborn. If you don't get what you want, you sulk.'

'I'm not sulking,' she declared emphatically, her anger at Mammy's presumption becoming difficult to control. 'I'm tired. I'm going to bed.'

'I know! When Bart come to bed, you touch him an' rouse him an' he get scared 'case he shock you wid his lust so he jump out an' sleep on de floor.'

She stared at Mammy in amazement. 'How do you know that?'

Mammy tapped the side of her broad nose with her finger and snorted with scornful laughter. 'Buckra, white men, dey all de same if dey hon'ble. Listen.' She lowered her voice so Raven was forced to return to her seat to hear what she said.

'Be carin' an' kind to him. Let him be de master in de bedchamber. When he want you, he goin' take you. So wait for him. He make love . . .' she paused and sniffed at the word Raven had used, '. . . savage, if he think you does be a prize.'

It sounded odd to her. Bart went with whores to protect her from his desire yet when she made advances like a loose woman, he spurned her. She shook her head.

'Men does be simple, like chil'en, Raven,' said Mammy, clucking her tongue at her distress. 'When you give dem what dey want, dey don't want it no more.'

She felt a curious swooping pull at her innards. A recollection of the toddy tapper's fiercely demanding eyes as he pulled her naked body to him suddenly filled her thoughts.

'You does be dreamin' of him, I can tell,' chuckled Mammy happily as she filled her glass with more rum from the jug. 'You goin' find happiness wid your man, for sure.'

The verandah was peaceful as Raven stared wistfully into the night. The children were asleep in the nursery while Malika, their nanny, sat in the courtyard outside the room with Jagath, her boy friend. Nimal was nodding his head in sleep as he waited for Mammy and Raven to leave the verandah so he could close up the villa.

The calm silence of the night was comforting. Raven sighed, giving way to a dreamy contentment.

Without warning, the euphoric atmosphere was shattered by a bloodcurdling shriek. Panic welled in Raven's throat. She leapt to her feet and found herself being crushed to Mammy's ample bosom.

'Oh my lawd!' the old woman cried squeezing her in fright.

She broke away and stepped to the verandah's edge. There was another scream, the long drawn out cry of a man suffering terrible pain. Icy fear twisted in Raven's heart.

'That's Bart's voice!' she shouted, unable to stop herself as she dashed off the verandah into the night. 'I must help him.'

CHAPTER THREE

The knife was as sharp as a razor. It sliced into Bart's ear and cut through almost before he felt it. The massive hands clasped across his chest from behind pinned his arms to his sides. He was powerless to resist.

He kicked back with his heel and connected with the shins of the man holding him. Then he was lifted off the ground and his feet secured with a noose. It was pulled tight, hobbling him, the rope scuffing against the soft leather of his boots. A cord was bound around his wrists.

Only seconds had passed since shadows rose from the ground and seized him. He carried no flambeau to light the way along the path he often walked in the pitch black of night. He had no weapon either. Now, with his hands and feet bound so swiftly and the moist stickiness of blood oozing over his cheek and down his throat, he was at the mercy of his attackers.

He screamed at the unexpected agony when a fist pounded into the side of his head. Fingers fastened onto his ear and it was ripped from him where the knife had failed to complete its brutal cut. He tried to stanch his scream but the pain set off a primeval cry that mocked his famous bravado.

A hand clapped over his mouth, forcing something in to it. He retched into silence, realizing as a wave of nausea gushed through him that he was choking on his own ear.

Summoning a reserve of strength, he thrust backwards into the crotch of the giant who was holding him. The man's stubborn grunt showed there was no escape from his clutches. The other attacker silently pounded his fist into Bart's body, just below his heart. Sweat from the man's brow splashed onto his face and he caught the scent of arrack and spice from the man's breath.

Pain scorched his mind when another blow punched the bleeding flesh where his ear had been. He croaked, unable to speak or see, desperate to identify his attackers before he blacked out. His head was filled with a terrible noise, the ringing of Hell, and he longed for it to ease.

He felt himself plunging downwards. He jolted against the muddy surface of the path with a squelch. He was alone.

'Bart! Bart!'

The howling in his ears yielded ungraciously to the cry of his name. He swallowed, tasted the flesh in his mouth and hastily spat it out. He opened his eyes and tried to raise himself off the ground. Firm hands clasped his shoulders and he saw Raven's anxious face, pale with fear, staring at him.

'Bart,' she cried, pulling his head to her breast as she kneeled beside him.

His severed ear smeared against her bodice. He winced. The pain roused him and he gazed on her lovely features, deeply grateful to be alive and in her arms. She was clinging to him, heedless of the blood spouting on her dress.

A commotion heralded the arrival of bearers with flambeaux that dissolved the night's mean shadows and threw light on to his gruesome injury. He saw the horror in Raven's eyes. When she laid her fingers on the stump where his ear had been, he drew comfort from her touch.

He felt the prick of a knife in his back as someone cut the rope that held his wrists. He pulled his hands apart and placed his arms around Raven's shoulders. Someone loosened the rope at his ankles. Strong hands gripped him under his arms and he was hoisted to his feet. The wailing of the women and the shocked chattering of the men in rapid Singhala stirred him into action.

'Did anyone see them?' he demanded. 'Chase after them!'

'They are making their escape in the darkness.' The musical lilt of Tissa's voice was calm compared with the uproar around him. 'Who could have done this thing?'

'What does it matter now?' said Raven, steering him in the direction of the villa. 'You must come home. Tissa, send a boy to Galle for the doctor.'

'I'll be all right, Raven.' He held his hand to his ear. The pain numbed him.

Tissa, his headman, looked at him for confirmation of what he should do.

He frowned to countermand Raven's order. 'The doctor won't come until daylight.'

'De ear?' asked a deep voice from the darkness. 'I make a

22

poultice wid mud and jungle leaves. It soon heal.' The tall figure of Daisy, his slave housekeeper, loomed over the Singhalese scurrying around him as he walked up the path to the villa. He had faith in her medicine.

Raven looked worried. 'Only for tonight,' she said. 'To stop the bleeding. Tomorrow, the doctor –'

He wanted to reassure her with a smile but the pain creased his face into a rictus of agony. Raven's voice died at his grimace and she clung to his hand in a manner that said more about how she cared for him than any words.

He felt the strength ebbing from his limbs when she helped him on to the verandah. Mammy Sobers's fierce black face passed briefly before his eyes as he was ushered through the parlour to his chamber.

Tissa and the houseboys lifted him on to the bed. He closed his eyes, surrendering to the roaring ache that overwhelmed him. The last thing he remembered was Raven's hand pressed to his brow and her soft, loving call of his name.

Tissa had served Bart since the day he landed in Galle from England twelve years previously. He was the slave then of Marcus Van Dort, the Registrar, who became an implacable opponent to his attempts to settle in the colony. Tissa was part of the spoils of his victory over Van Dort. He was freed from slavery and now served Bart as the master of his mill and the overseer of the natives.

Tissa was a slightly built man whose grace and humility concealed a strength and tenacity that had won him respect as a natural leader of his people. He was a year younger than Bart although his age did not show in his smooth, pale gold features under the long straight black hair he wore proudly in the Galle style, with a top knot and combs to secure it. His usually bright smile was dimmed as he sat beside Bart's bed, his intelligent eyes misty with concern.

'Well,' demanded Bart impatiently, 'what have you discovered?'

'That is what is so puzzling to me, Bloodheart.' Tissa frowned. 'I am discovering nothing.'

Bart tugged at the pillow supporting his back. The movement sent a spiral of pain down the side of his neck. He tightened his lips so Tissa wouldn't see his suffering.

'Dammit!' he said, letting his eyes express his anger as he couldn't move. 'You know everyone in the settlement. Surely you can find out who attacked me?' He paused, giving way to bewilderment. 'And why . . .'

'That is because they were wanting to kill you, Bloodheart.' Tissa's head nodded from side to side.

'I disagree.' For two days he had lain in bed, reliving every moment of the attack. Daisy's mud poultice had been replaced – to Raven's obvious relief – by the dressings and bandages of Dr Chisolm from the army barracks in Galle. His protests at being confined to bed were useless against the combined opposition of Raven, Mammy Sobers and Daisy. He was dismayed how feeble he felt and grumbled out of habit although he welcomed the chance to rest and recover.

'I disagree,' he said again. 'If they had wanted to kill me they would have waited until I got further from the house where no one could hear me shout. Anyway, the knife that cut off my ear could easily have been plunged into my heart.'

'Then why did they attack you?' Tissa spread his hands wide in a gesture of helplessness.

'As a warning.' He spoke cautiously, gradually expounding the idea that occurred to him. 'The loss of my ear doesn't amount to much. They were warning me what they can do, if they want.'

'Who are these people?'

He looked at Tissa shrewdly, wondering what was going on in his headman's mind. 'I expect you to tell me that.'

'No one is knowing anything, Bloodheart. The men were not from the settlement.'

He wanted to nod his head in agreement but the bandage prevented him. Instead, he pursed his lips thoughtfully. He was not ignorant of the enemies he had made while he fought local laws and prejudices to establish his plantation.

There were the Caffres he had imported as slaves from Mozambique and Madagascar. They had been joined in an uprising against him by a band of renegades from the Kandyan kingdom. Tissa had saved his life then and lost three fingers of his right hand for his pains.*

A war between the British and the King of Kandy followed which resulted in the hill kingdom being conquered and the British gaining control over the whole of Ceylon. Bart's friendship with the exiled Prince Gamunu ended when he castrated the prince as he was escaping to lead a rebellion. The prince died and

* See *Bloodheart*

the rebellion was crushed but there were still Kandyan warriors in hiding who might seek vengeance on him.

In addition, Bart was the guardian of two talismens that Kandyan malcontents could be expected to kill for.

One was Prince Gamunu's own son, his stepchild, Kirti.

If ever the Kingdom of Kandy were to be revived, the people needed someone to call king. If Prince Gamunu had divulged the secret of his heir to his followers, some day they might come for Kirti. He would be the figure-head in any new rebellion.

The other talisman was just as valuable: the *gaja mutu*. This was the priceless pearl gouged out from within the tusk of a royal elephant and passed down over the centuries from king to king. It was beyond reckoning in worth.

By legend the elephant pearl blessed its possessor with victory, children and good health. The legendary properties were no myth. Bart had felt the force of its power when he clutched the pearl in the palm of his hand. It was the *gaja mutu* that nestled between them when he first made love to Raven, on the night of their wedding.

His arch enemy, Marcus Van Dort, knew he possessed the pearl. He died trying to steal it. He was only keeping it in trust for Kirti. Perhaps his attackers were after that?

'It's Van Dort's doing,' said Tissa emphatically, interrupting his thoughts.

'How can it be?' Bart tried to laugh until the pain stopped him sharply. 'He's dead.'

'His spirit has returned to take revenge.'

'That was no spirit who struck me.' He rubbed the bandage ruefully. 'Someone hired those men.'

'Were they Caffres?'

Bart considered. The British, following the example of their Dutch predecessors, had imported African slaves to aid the army. Caffres had built the fortifications of Galle. Some of them escaped and joined the Kandyans, forming the Kandyan king's own Caffre regiment. Others drifted from slavery as the army released them and lived by doing menial tasks in the town. Some were renowned as ruffians for hire, desperate men who would perform any evil for a piece of eight or a bottle of arrack.

'I'm not sure.' He remembered the pungent odour of the breath of the man who had punched him. 'They were well built and muscular, skilled in what they were doing.'

'If I go to Galle,' said Tissa, 'I might get a clue. I can ask in the boutiques. The Street of Moorish Traders sells secrets as well as baubles and gems.'

'Aye.' He sighed. Madam Gudde's bordello was on that street. He yearned to regain his strength so that he could visit her whores again. How would they regard him with only one ear?

'If this is the start of a feud,' he said thoughtfully, 'I must know who is my enemy. They won't surprise me again!'

Tissa's smile emerged from the dour expression that restrained it, like the sun coming from behind a cloud. Satisfaction showed in his eyes, and it cheered Bart to look at him.

'Now you sound like Bloodheart,' he said, rising from his seat and nodding his head. 'I'll help you, Bloodheart. You will have your revenge.'

Raven waited for an hour after Tissa left Bart's chamber before she eased open the door, careful not to let its hinges squeak or its edge grate on the tiled floor. She peeped into the room.

Bart's head lay back on his pillows and his eyes were closed. The cup of herb tea that Daisy had prepared to make him sleep was empty on the table beside the bed.

She tiptoed across the floor, drawn by the deep breathing to his side. Lowering her head, she studied him closely, her heart full with sorrow at the pain he had suffered. When she was finally convinced he was asleep, she backed out of the room, pleased that Daisy's tea had taken effect.

She posted Jagath, the houseboy, at the door, giving him strict instructions that no one was to enter the chamber.

'If the master asks for me,' she said, smiling persuasively, 'you must say I am visiting a sick child in the settlement. I'll be back within the hour.'

Jagath's indeterminate shaking of his head made it seem he was disagreeing with her. It was the Ceylonese gesture which really meant: yes, I understand. She smiled at him again and hurried out of the house.

She was unable to rid herself of the feeling that the attack on Bart was her fault. It was intuition, a sense of apprehension she could not put into words.

She felt secure on the plantation. There was no animosity towards her from Daisy, Little, Romulus or Mark, the Caffre house slaves, nor from Nimal, Jagath and Malika, the Singhalese ones.

Her contacts with Tissa were infrequent. He lived with his

recently acquired bride in the settlement and came to the villa only when summoned by Bart. However, his gracious good manners showed no sign of a lingering resentment.

The threat seemed to come from beyond the plantation, not from within.

She loosened her bonnet as she picked her way cautiously along the path through the canefields towards the jungle. She hated leaving Bart while he was vulnerable but this could be her only chance of returning to the cove without him knowing.

She entered the jungle trail without pausing, aware only of the clammy heat that seized her even in the shade of its lofty boughs. Keeping her eyes on the ground to see where she stepped and humming loudly to herself to bolster her courage, she hurried down the path.

She was unclear what she intended to do when she reached the beach and the grove of palm trees that enclosed it. She pushed to the back of her mind the doubt that her mission was inspired by anything other than concern for Bart.

She recognized the slope where she had fallen and been saved by the Tamil snake boy. She gazed around, wondering if he was hidden in the undergrowth watching her. Hastily, she dismissed the notion, knowing she had nothing to fear but fear itself. Clinging to the branches at the side of the path, she negotiated the muddy slope and continued on her way.

She welcomed the brightness of the sun when she rounded the last bend in the trail and saw the road ahead. A palanquin with its team of bearers was passing and she waited behind a tree until it was out of sight. She peered along the road both ways.

In the distance some foot travellers were walking towards Galle. They were too far off to notice her as she slipped across the road into the palm grove.

She halted and tilted up her head to listen. The busy cheep of the Ceylon babbler birds as they hopped in a small flock from trunk to trunk distracted her. She strained her ears to hear beyond their shrill chattering. Gradually, she distinguished a rhythmic tapping coming from a tree closer to the beach. She looked up. The sky was webbed by palm fronds, the coir ropes of the toddy tappers spun between the tree trunks.

With her heart thumping loudly, she moved towards the tapping sound, shielding her eyes with her hand against the sun. She scanned the tops of the trees in vain for the sight of a man clinging to the ropes or tapping his knife into a palm's yellow spathe.

27

She listened again. The sound of tapping was faint and it came, not from the tree tops, but from closer, almost at waist height.

'My goodness!' she exclaimed aloud. There was a flash of red close to her cheek and she stepped back, startled by the sudden movement.

A woodpecker with vivid crimson feathers alighted on the sloping trunk of a palm tree in front of her. It tap-tapped its beak vigorously against the tree in a search for insects.

She bit her lip with disappointment and walked through the grove to the edge of the beach. She hesitated, torn by her desire to find the mysterious toddy tapper, and her anxiety to return to the villa to be at Bart's side when he woke.

The shimmer of someone gliding across the sand with the sun behind him, attracted her attention. A cold knot of fear formed in her stomach as she waited for the silhouette to resolve itself into Kumara, the man she was seeking.

She clenched her hand until her nails stung her palm. She remained rooted to the spot as the dark and indistinguishable shape moved towards her. She wanted to run but she stayed for Bart's sake. She was convinced the toddy tapper knew why he was attacked.

'Miss Raven!' The voice was velvet-smooth with a trace of light-hearted surprise.

A cloud drifted across the blinding globe of the sun. She blinked as the man stepped forward and she saw him clearly.

'You!' The tension in her welled over and she sank in a gentle swoon at his feet.

CHAPTER FOUR

It was the black swirl of the sun as she stared into it that caused her to lose balance. She revived instantly as hands eased her to a sitting position with her back resting against the trunk of a coconut tree.

Her first sight on opening her eyes was of the spreading star of palm fronds high above her head, and of a cluster of pale gold and green coconuts hanging at the star's centre. She glanced at them, anxious lest one should fall on the man standing over her, shielding her eyes from the sun with his body.

She was intrigued to notice the sun outlining his spindly thighs through the thin fabric of his white sarong. He lacked the tough, impressive build of the toddy tapper. His hair was too carefully combed and his expression too well-mannered to trigger in her the thrill of being helpless in the hands of a simple native.

'Tissa!' she murmured, feeling disconcerted. 'What are you doing here?'

'I am asking myself the same question about you, Miss Raven.' The headman frowned solicitously. 'Shall I get some water?'

'No, no.' She held out her hand for him to help her to her feet. 'I'm all right.' She gathered her dress and shook the sand from it, trying to regain her composure. 'I was taken by surprise . . . the heat.'

'The sun is not kind to a fair skin.'

'I needed some fresh air . . .' She waved her hand to indicate to him that it was of no consequence. 'After what happened to Bart. To think . . .'

'I understand.'

He had clear, observant eyes and she felt guilty under his scrutiny. But as the strength seeped back into her limbs and she manoeuvred so she could see through the palm grove to the road where people and palanquins were passing, she regained her confidence.

29

'You haven't told me why you're here,' she said sternly, hiding her embarrassment by adopting the role of an aggressive plantation mistress.

He smiled disarmingly. 'I am on my way to Galle. On an errand for Bloodheart.'

'I shall ask him if that is true. As soon as I return to the villa.'

He looked crestfallen. 'Surely you do not doubt me?'

'I find it very strange –' She stopped herself just before divulging her own reason for being there. 'Those ropes,' she said, hoping it sounded like a casual enquiry. 'What are they for?'

'The toddy tappers are using them to perambulate between the trees.' He followed one pace behind as she moved towards the road.

By walking away from the beach, she hoped to distract his attention so he would not realize the purpose of her questions. 'Toddy tappers?' She feigned a gasp of surprise. 'I have never seen one. Are there many hereabouts?'

'A few.' He sounded puzzled. 'You will find company on the road, Miss Raven, to escort you to the river. There will be a bullock cart at the ferry landing which will take you back to the villa.'

'You are kind,' she said, bestowing on him a smile that was supposed to dazzle him into forgetting their conversation. 'Do you know those toddy tappers? I should like to meet them. It must be very dangerous work.'

'I know them all.'

'I've heard my husband speak of one,' she said loftily to disguise her lie. 'His name is Kumara. Do you know that one?' She watched Tissa carefully as he considered the name.

He shook his head. 'There is none called Kumara. You must be mistaken.'

'I'm sure I'm not. That was the name Bloodheart mentioned.'

'No, Miss Raven. I would know him if he exists.'

His frowning face and serious eyes convinced her he was speaking the truth. He clearly took it as an affront to his integrity that she should suggest there was someone in the district he did not know.

'What about a snake boy?' she asked as a final test. If he denied knowledge of him too, then he was surely trying to hide something from her.

'You mean Ram?' Tissa laughed. 'He's a hard one to find but I know him. He lives in the jungle with his old father. They come from Jaffna, in the north. You see, I do know everyone here, whether they are plantation workers, fishermen, toddy tappers or newcomers. That's my business as headman of the settlement.'

'And there is no Kumara?'

'No,' he said, smiling at her with an openness that showed him incapable of deceit. 'There is no Kumara.'

Raven pondered Tissa's remark as she walked along the road and engaged in idle conversation with other travellers. The road was bordered on both sides by tall palms leaning towards the sea. On her left, the palms thinned out until they were replaced by brushwood at the edge of the jungle that was the plantation boundary.

She peered at the tops of the trees but didn't see a single toddy tapper. Her companions on the road were residents of the area and she made oblique enquiries from them about a robust young toddy tapper with commanding features and impassioned eyes. No one had seen or heard of such a person.

The road to Matara ended at the lagoon where canoes provided ferry transport to the other side. Along the bank of the river that flowed into the lagoon, Bart had constructed a road to the plantation. Bullock carts plodded along it, carrying supplies from ships anchored in the lagoon, and bringing down casks of rum for transporting to Galle.

Raven rode on one of the carts, sitting at the front with the bullock driver. She was blind to his embarrassment at her presence and barely noticed the discomfort of the ride as the bullock tottered up the hill.

Her thoughts were on Kumara. She had not dreamed the strong hardness of his lips on hers. The clutch of his firm hands around her waist squeezed her still.

For some reason, the toddy tapper must have told her a false name. That was why he was unknown to Tissa. Perhaps he was not even a toddy tapper, although he was dressed as one in his loincloth of indigo blue. The way he shinned up the tree showed he knew about jungle craft.

She recalled the mockery in his voice when he spoke her name. It chilled her with apprehension. He had known who she was, so he wasn't a stranger. He was powerfully built and agile and the man who attacked Bart was strong and quick too.

A sudden jolt by the cart caused her to gasp but it was dismay that inspired her cry. *Kumara and Bart's assailant were the same man.*

31

He must have come deliberately to the beach to harass her. He had taken advantage of her when she was vulnerable and thought she was alone. Her confusion made her pliable to his embrace. In reality, the toddy tapper was a vile and cunning rogue.

She pursed her lips determined to tell Bart about him. She would explain how he molested her on the beach and ran off when Bart called her name. She was too distressed, she would say, to mention it before.

He was obviously Bart's attacker. *Goodness!* she thought to herself. She could even guess why he had come: to steal the elephant pearl.

The crack of the driver's whip across the back of the bullock straining to pull the cart up the hill, roused her to action. She frowned at the driver for the slow progress they were making.

'I could walk much quicker!' she snapped, grasping her skirt in her hand and jumping off the moving cart. She strode up the hill, intent on reaching the villa as soon as possible.

The road wound through trees to the sugar-mill, an imposing complex of grey granite buildings built by Bart's Caffre slaves. There was a grinding shed where the canes were crushed and a boiler house where the squeezed juice was boiled until it crystallized into sugar. The distillery where Bart's famous Bloodheart Rum was produced adjoined it. Opposite was a storehouse containing casks of rum ready for delivery.

Raven hurried past the mill with barely a glance at the buildings that were the source of Bart's wealth. During the long season of cane cropping, the fires burned all day and the sweet and heady aroma of crushed cane and boiling sugar hung over the plantation like a monsoon cloud, affecting them all.

Now the mill was quiet. A few Singhalese workers squatted on their haunches in the shade of the buildings. They greeted her shyly as she passed and then fell to gossiping among themselves. The sound of their chattering followed her when she turned away from the mill to take the path across the plateau of sugar-cane to the villa.

An insistent hissing sound issuing from a clump of young canes buzzed in her ears. She halted and glanced at the long ribbons of leaves rustling in the breeze. She tried to trace the source of the noise, aware that anyone concealed in the tangle of canes would be invisible from the path unless he wanted to be seen.

She caught sight of a flash of brown, darker than the golden cane stalks. 'I see you!' she called sharply. 'Come out!'

The hissing changed to a gurgle of laughter and then there was silence. She peered into the canes, her curiosity roused, but she saw nothing. She was impatient to reach the villa. It overlooked the canefields like a tall ship in the middle of a vast, surging ocean of gold and green.

'Very well,' she cried at the sugar-cane. 'If you don't come out, I shall go.' She was intrigued by whoever was hiding in the cane but when no one emerged, she continued her walk.

There was a chuckle behind her. She turned quickly, her heart racing. At the edge of the canefield, a youth squatted on the path. He had a covered basket at his side and his face was split with an enormous grin.

She gasped in surprise and hastily stepped away from him, staring anxiously at his basket. She remembered him from her walk in the jungle. 'Have you got a snake in there?' she asked nervously.

The youth continued to beam, unconcerned by the tremor in her voice.

She took a deep breath and clenched her fists, ashamed at herself for being so foolish. The youth had helped her once and obviously meant no harm. She prayed he would keep his snakes hidden.

'What do you want, Ram?' she asked, taking control of herself.

The youth nodded gravely at the sound of his name. He put one hand on the cover of his basket. Raven edged further away. He looked at her reproachfully and gestured for her to stand still.

She held her breath as he opened the basket and plunged his hand in. He removed something from inside and clasped it in his fist. He shut the basket, leaving the snake inside.

He offered his hand to Raven, opening his fist.

She drew closer to him and looked at what nestled in his roughened palm. It was a ring. 'Ram, it's beautiful.' She plucked it quickly from his hand in case he tried to withdraw it.

In the centre of its solid gold band was a smooth, honey-yellow and apple-green stone. Turning it in her fingers, she was startled to see a silvery line, like a streak of light, flash across the stone where it caught the sun.

'It's a cat's eye,' she said aloud, gazing on the gem that was reputed to bring protection to its wearer.

She recalled having seen a ring similar to the one she held in her hand, only a few days before. She frowned. 'Where did you get this, Ram?'

33

The youth guessed her question and pointed to a spot on the path.

She looked up at the villa and a *frisson* of fear tingled her spine. She was standing close to where Bart had been attacked. The ring must have been dropped by his assailant.

She turned back to Ram. She was not really surprised to see he had disappeared silently back into the sugar-canes, taking his basket with him.

She slipped the ring onto her middle finger; it was too big. The stone sparkled with an allure she found irresistible so she closed her fingers around it, securing it in her palm. As she resumed her walk to the villa, she wondered where she had seen such a ring before.

The answer dawned on her slowly, as though she was reluctant to accept it. She recalled the hand that had traced the curve of her hip, sending shivers of wanting through her body. That hand had worn a ring; it had brushed against her skin and she had observed its glint like a cat's eye. The ring was the toddy tapper's.

Bart's wound healed slowly. Raven knew his temper would get worse the longer he was confined to bed, so she busied herself in the house, close to hear his call, but away from his frustration which he vented on the houseboys. She hid the ring in her needlework box where she saw it every day.

She was unable to bring herself to tell Bart about Kumara. Now she had proof that the toddy tapper was his assailant, she wanted to keep the secret to herself. It was the link that she hoped would bring the handsome young man to her again.

She was puzzled how her attitude towards Kumara changed from mood to mood. At times she was appalled at herself for harbouring information that could help Bart trace his attacker. At other times, she was thrilled by her knowledge and longed to see him again so she could tell him that she shared his secret.

While Bart was recovering from his injury and still wore the bandage, he slept on a cot in the dressing room. It was at night, when she was alone in her bed, that thoughts of Kumara returned to torment her. In her heart she knew she owed it to Bart to tell him who his attacker was, yet still she kept the secret to herself.

She was hurt by what Mammy Sobers said about Bart taking his real pleasure with whores and native wenches. A small seed of resentment was planted in her heart by that remark. Unwittingly, she nurtured it with her loneliness during the long hot nights she lay listening to Bart sleeping on the cot in the adjoining room.

She was drifting off to sleep, cocooned by the four-poster's muslin drapes closed around her, her whole body engulfed in tides of weariness and despair. She had lain alone for five nights, Bart's irritability draining her until she felt hollow and grudging towards him. She gave herself to sleep willingly, welcoming it like an old friend.

She thought the touch on her shoulder was part of her dream. She sighed drowsily at the light pressure of a finger caressing her flesh. She was only roused into wakefulness when the mattress yielded at her side and hard thighs clashed against her own.

'Bart?' she questioned the enveloping darkness, unable to see him.

His sensual, deep-throated chuckle disturbed her. 'Do you expect another?' he chided softly.

'I was asleep. You frightened me.'

'A wife who is afraid of her husband needs comforting.' His arm snaked around her shoulders and pulled her to him.

The gesture was too sudden, shattering her dreams. She tensed, resisting him out of shock.

'What, am I not man enough for you?' he joked. His hand groped between her legs, preparing her for the brief thrust that constituted his insensitive lovemaking.

She shuddered. 'Bart . . .' She placed her fingers against his chest to restrain him and felt his heart beating beneath the soft mat of hair.

She weakened, responding instinctively to his unspoken demand. 'I love you,' she said breathlessly, trailing her hand down to his lean, taut stomach.

'Aye,' he said gruffly and brushed her hand away.

She remembered Mammy's words of advice to act restrained. It was difficult to do when she wanted him. She longed to encircle his waist with her legs and to smother his cheeks with kisses. Instead, she froze, reminding herself that Bart was performing a duty, not making real love.

When he tried to force himself into her, she wriggled away. She wanted his caresses, to be part of his pleasure and not merely a receptacle for it. Love should be a game for them both to enjoy.

'Are you sick?' His harsh voice grated on her ear.

'Are you sure you want to do this, Bart?' She hoped she sounded loving and not resentful. 'Your injury –'

'It's my ear that hurts, not my –' He rolled away from her and laughed, perhaps sensing her distress.

'Oh, Raven, don't you know I want you? I need you. It's been agony lying on the cot, listening to you murmuring in your sleep.'

She frowned, glad he could not see her in the dark and guess her anxiety. 'What do I say?'

'Nothing I can understand.' The tension had gone from his voice and he sounded relaxed and happy. 'I love you, Raven.' His hand reached out for her and her fingers were seized in his and squeezed.

Her body trembled with wanting. This was a new mood; Bart seemed more loveable, more human. She lay at his side, not daring to touch him in case she spoiled the magic.

His nearness caused her loins to moisten as he traced a pattern up the inside of her arm. Rapture when his fingers closed over the soft globe of her breast made her gasp. He stopped instantly and withdrew his hand.

She was distracted by his departure just as she was dissolving with a melting sweetness. She held her breath, wanting him to touch her again.

Slowly his hands skimmed the sides of her body, down to her hips. She bit her lip lest any cry would drive him away.

'Relax,' he whispered, the softness of his breath tingling her ear, sending shivers of ecstasy down her spine.

She felt her breasts crush against the hardness of his chest when he pulled her to him. Waves of desire throbbed through her. She buried her face in his neck and sighed.

Slowly he raised her head with his hand, his lips waiting. His kiss began gently until his moist, firm mouth demanded more.

She yielded to his rage of passion, stirred by his hands fondling her deliciously, growing stronger as she wilted beneath him.

Her mouth burned with fire when his lips left hers, and kissed a path down her neck to her breasts. She wound her hands tightly around his waist and pressed herself to him, confident that at last she would know the full force of his demanding manhood.

They moved easily together in rhythm that sweetly drained her doubts and fears. She exulted at his male strength poised on the verge of possessing her.

'Bloodheart!'

A hammering on the door shattered her mood of fulfillment just as his mounting passion approached its peak.

36

He sprang from her, leaving her gasping as the door flew open. Daisy burst into the room.

'Bloodheart!' she cried, the lantern shaking in her hand, throwing grotesque shadows over the two of them where they lay in shock side by side on the bed.

Raven struggled to hide the pulsing of her body. She reached for a sheet to cover them both.

'De mill, massa!' Daisy bellowed with fright. 'Come quick!'

Bart leaped out of their bed and seized his breeches, leaving Raven forgotten behind him.

'What's the matter with the mill,' he said, grabbing Daisy by her arm to make her calm down.

'Oh, massa! It does bc on fire!'

CHAPTER FIVE

Raven lay in lonely silence as the wailing of Daisy and the sound of Bart shouting for his boots receded. The door slammed shut on her and the chamber reverted to darkness with only the glimmer of a glass-shaded candle giving light. She clung to the pillow in frustration, pain squeezing her heart at Bart's brutal departure.

'The mill!' She repeated Daisy's words aloud to herself.

A fire at the mill could destroy everything Bart held dear. Her disappointment at being abandoned at the peak of her ecstasy was unimportant compared with the disaster threatening Bart. She felt a sickening twinge of guilt at her selfishness in resenting his abrupt departure.

She sighed deeply in an attempt to chase away her peevish mood. She envied Bart his ability to switch from one emotion to another without a flicker of effort. Her body still throbbed with his presence, a residue of rapture glowing within her. She could not cut off passion to leap from the bed and dash out into the night like he did.

She rose slowly from the bed, her limbs weak. She moved about the room in a daze, opening drawers and cupboards aimlessly, wondering what she was doing. The urgency of the moment whirled around her; it was too fast for her to grasp.

She stopped trying to find a dress that was suitable and hurriedly slipped on the first one that came from her wardrobe. Its bodice was low cut and its skirt full. She just had time to fasten it when there was a tap on the door.

'Miss Raven?' Nimal glided into the room. He was carrying a lantern which he held at shoulder level, its light embracing them both. 'Are you all right?'

'Yes.' She smiled at him with relief. 'Thank you for thinking of me.'

'Miss?' He frowned at her remark.

'How is the fire? Is it bad?'

'I am seeing the flames from the verandah. The master told me to stay here with you.'

'He did?' She ran a brush through her hair, smoothing out the tangles of her long, black tresses. She felt hot in the stifling atmosphere of the chamber. Nimal stood close behind her with the lantern so she could see her reflection in the looking glass. Her glance was perfunctory; she was not concerned about how she looked, only about what she should do.

'Who else is in the house?' she asked, glad to have Nimal to talk to so she could organize her thoughts.

'Malika is with the children. Jagath is staying with her. Mammy Sobers and Little have gone to the mill.'

'Mammy has?' Raven was ashamed that the old Negress had gone to Bart's aid before she did. She threw down her hairbrush and hurried out of the chamber.

The view from the verandah made her pause. The sky in the east over the river was tinged with orange. The roofs of the mill building were outlined against the night by the flames that danced around them.

She was seized with dread that Bart might be in danger, and experienced a spasm of fear that all he strived for was being destroyed. Lifting her skirt high above her knees, she ran down the path towards the blazing building.

Darkness enveloped the canefields and she ran on blindly. Nimal trailed after her, clutching a lantern. Its faint light was enough for her to follow the path until, as she drew nearer to the mill, the flames showed the way.

The boiler house was on fire. The slender shapes of natives from the settlement bobbed around it in the bright darkness.

She pushed through them, forgetting politeness and the manners expected of her, as she searched for Bart. The heat from the fire struck her face with the force of a slap. She stopped at the edge of the crowd.

Bart was at the mouth of the blaze, flinging water on the flames. When his pail was empty, he dashed away, grabbed another as it was filled from the river, and returned to pour it on the fire. The flames were beating him; his attempt to douse them was futile but Raven admired his courage and longed to help him.

She ran across the gap to Bart's side, feeling the flames reaching for her skirt. She picked up a pail filled with water and struggled with it towards the blaze. The heat seemed to scorch her brain;

blindly she hurled the water at the fire, banging her knuckles on the pail's wooden rim.

A numbing sensation tore through her as angry fingers dug into her flesh and pulled her away. She stumbled, caught her feet in her skirt, and fell backwards.

'What the hell are you doing?' Bart's livid face glared down at her. He grabbed the pail and gave it to a native to fill at the river.

'Go back to the villa!' He swung away, not waiting to hear her reply, nor to help her to her feet.

'I was trying to help you,' she shouted after him. Her cry was snatched away by the flames and lost in the confusion.

People were running around the mill yard in panic, falling over each other and adding to the chaos. The flames crackled loudly, drowning their cries.

Bart stood with his back to her, a foolhardy, desperate figure defying the flames by himself. She was hurt by his rejection, wondering if he really understood what he meant to her. She wanted to share his problems, and fight by his side. She blamed his rough rebuff of her on the shock he must be feeling.

She rose to her feet, swallowing her pride. Her bodice of lace was besmirched with ash and her hair was wildly adrift around her shoulders. She looked for Nimal but he was nowhere to be seen.

Half-clothed natives swarmed around the yard, their dark skins glistening with sweat in the light from the flames. Some were carrying buckets while others lugged large copper vats and whatever else could be salvaged from the burning building.

Unnoticed by Bart, she crept away from the muddle of people, withdrawing to a darkened corner of the yard where no one could see her. Her eyes were on Bart, her thoughts mingled with sorrow at the pain he must be feeling. His beloved mill was being destroyed in front of him while he was powerless to stop it.

The flames took hold of the wooden rafters of the roof, eating at the doors and shutters and consuming everything within the building. Bart still raced backwards and forwards with pails of water, trying to limit the spread of the fire.

She marvelled at his dogged determination. His stubbornness was frustrating and pointless; he was in danger every time he approached the blaze. He could do no less, and she loved him for it.

Alone in the corner, she began to notice the activity around the yard. There was a pattern to what at first seemed to be chaos. Tissa was calm in the centre of a whirlpool of people, directing men and women to fight the blaze and supervising the removal of items of value. They were not paralysed by panic as she imagined. Her help, perhaps, had been unnecessary.

She sighed, her thoughts turning to how the blaze started. Was it accidental or had someone deliberately set fire to the mill?

Before she could answer her own question, a movement in the opposite corner of the yard caught her eye. She took her eyes off Bart and stared into the darkness. There seemed to be a shape there that was different from the shadows of the jungle and the gloom of the stone wall of the storehouse. It was solid with a life of its own, creeping like a crouched animal in the flickering half-light.

She was seized with alarm at the shape's furtive progress. The light from the flames was insufficient for her to see clearly. She had the impression as the shadow merged with the darkness of the jungle and disappeared, that what she had been watching was a familiar figure.

A spark on the ground became a glow, spreading through the darkened corner of the compound. The huge wooden doors of the storehouse and its thick granite walls were visible behind it.

At first, Raven thought the glow was from a flambeau someone had dropped in front of the building. Her heart lurched as she saw it grow to a thread of fire that seemed to have been spun around the doors.

Within seconds the huge doors were outlined in flames. The wood was dry and burned like kindling as the fire was fueled by rum vapours. Inside the building casks full of rum were stored for sale in Galle. When the flames reached them, everyone in the yard would be in danger.

Raven's anger at the arson she had witnessed galvanized her. She dashed over to the burning door. The flames were eager, mocking her with their brightness. She rushed at them, her skirt raised, stamping on them as they danced across the flagstones. With her bare hands she beat at the sparks gnawing at the door, frantically trying to smother them.

She cried out in despair. She was helpless against the zest of the fire and its determination to devour the storehouse. Yet she had to try. Her hands were raw and her feet scorched through her shoes.

'Help me!' she called in vain, praying that someone in the crowd would hear and come to her aid. The flames were growing taller than she was, catching at her hair as she flung herself on them. 'Oh, please help me!'

She was alone in her battle to save the storehouse, and she was

41

losing. Not even Bart had seen the danger. She ignored the heat and fought on while the flames, angered by her interference, turned their talons on her. They stripped her skirt and devoured it as though it were paper. Searing pain stabbed her thighs and she screamed.

A blow struck her face, blinding her and forcing her backwards away from the fire. She was dripping wet, her hair streaming with water. Another gust of water hit her cheek, drenching her with its cooling flow, streaming over her shoulders and running down between her breasts.

More water splashed over her, soaking the tatters of dress at her waist and dousing the flames leaping at her. She wiped her eyes but they smarted with the water and she was unable to see as a firm hand led her away.

'The fire!' she shouted blindly. 'We must put it out. There's danger!'

'Dere, dere,' a voice wheezed as though unperturbed by her cries. 'We must save you too, or you goin' be sizzled like a burnt pancake.'

Beyond the deep, calming tone of Mammy Sobers who was clutching her fiercely so she couldn't break loose, Raven heard crisp commands spoken in Singhala. When her eyes cleared she saw a line of *salagamas*, men as well as their bare-breasted women, forming a human chain up from the river bank. Pails of water were being passed along it rapidly from hand to hand.

She squirmed around in Mammy's plump embrace to look at the fire. A shirtless man was at the head of the chain, directing two men where to throw the water. Boys were snatching the empty buckets and racing back with them to the river. Men who previously were scampering around the compound adding to the confusion, were beating at the flames with bundles of brushwood.

The man who commanded them turned as Raven gazed on him with awe. His lean face gleamed in the flames' wild light and his dark eyes smouldered with a fire of their own.

He glanced briefly at her, seemed satisfied she was safe in Mammy's arms, and returned his attention to fighting the blaze. His hand, as he raised it to point out a new patch of flames, sparkled with a flash of light.

'Mammy!' Raven's voice croaked as she struggled to shrug off her hold and run to the man. 'That's him!'

*　　*　　*

42

'It's over now.' Bart's voice echoed with tenderness as he lovingly guided her out of the mill compound.

'You were very brave. The storehouse is saved because of you.' His arm around her waist squeezed her and she snuggled with contentment into his protective embrace.

The night had passed in a blur. Wrapped in Mammy's arms she had watched the blaze being brought under control. In the darkness it was impossible to distinguish one native from another although she had tried to follow Kumara, the toddy tapper, with her eyes when Mammy would not release her to run to him.

Mammy had pressed a cup of liquid to her lips and she drank it thirstily, without thought. After that, the raw soreness of her hands and the pain from the burns on her legs hurt her less. Mammy covered her with a blanket. Although she fought against it, an overpowering weariness caused her to sleep until Bart, jerking her to her feet, revived her.

'What about the boiling house?' she asked, remembering through the mist of confusion befuddling her mind that Bart had tried to save the mill by himself.

'The flames made it seem worse than it is,' he said, the softness of his breath fluttering over her ears. 'The natives organized themselves into a bucket chain. It was soon doused. A new roof and doors and we'll be ready in time for the sugar harvest.'

'How did it happen –'

'Hush!'

He bent towards her, brushing his lips against her cheek, touching off a tremor of feeling that chased the weariness from her body. His firm fingers clasping her below her breast reassured her more than the caring tone in his voice.

The blanket over her shoulders covered her nakedness where her dress was ripped and burned. It added to the warmth seeping through her, sweetening her like trickling honey. She blinked, wondering where he was leading her.

The mill and the throng of shouting natives were behind her. The only light was the deep silver grey of the sky beyond the tousled tops of the coconut palms and the darkened boughs of the jungle trees.

The resonant hooting of an owl formed a soothing accompaniment to the shrill whistles and warbles of night creatures disturbed by their progress through the trees. Beyond the sound was the gentle splashing of the river lapping its banks.

'I stink of the fire,' he said before she could ask him where they were going. 'You could do with a bath to refresh you too, by the looks of you.'

'Bart!' She dug her fingers in his waist to tickle him. 'What a thing to say.'

'Aha!' His smile radiated through the darkness. 'Coming to life again, are you? Mammy said she'd given you laudanum to calm you.'

'She's an interfering busybody.'

Bart's reply made her ashamed of speaking so candidly. 'She cares for you, Raven, as much as I do. That was a crazy thing you did, trying to put out the fire with your bare hands.'

'No more crazy than what you were doing.' She tilted her head up expectantly. The caress of his lips on hers was muted, as though he was unsure of her invitation. She paused, wanting to linger in his embrace.

'The river!' he said, suddenly pulling the blanket from her shoulders and flinging it on the grass.

She stood uncertainly, dazed by his impulsive gesture. He was removing his shirt and yanking down his breeches in a single frenzied movement. She followed his example and cast off the strips of cloth that were all that remained of her dress. Her body tingled in the night as she stood naked beside him.

'Are you hurt?' he asked, raising his hand to her breast and stroking it.

'No.' She smiled at him as the happiness of being at his side cushioned her past despair. She reached for his waist. 'Are you?'

His carefree chuckle filled her with joy. He caught her hand in his and led her down the bank into the river. The cold water chilled the passion welling within her and she gasped when the water lapped her legs.

She clutched at his hand as he moved away and was forced to follow him into the river's race. The water splashed at her thighs, and then leaped for her breasts as she stumbled on a stone and fell in.

His hands held her firmly, pulling her to her feet. 'How cool it is!' he cried, relishing the water washing away the dirt on his soot-blackened body.

She laughed with him and let his hand go as she became accustomed to the current. She dipped her head under, feeling the water tug at her hair, cleansing it in its flow. She felt pure and

44

strong as she accompanied him back to the river bank, her hand holding him around his waist, her fingers trailing down over the tight muscular dome of his buttocks.

'Bart . . .' she said when they sat side by side on the blanket, their feet dangling in the water. 'There is something I must tell you.'

'Later.' He reached for her shoulders and swung her over to him, placing his lips vigorously on hers.

She wanted to protest, to be allowed to finish what she had to say about the toddy tapper. She beat her fists against his chest, trying to push him away. Her resistance inspired him.

He tightened his embrace, lifting his lips from hers. 'Raven,' he said before she could speak. 'I love you.'

He forced her backwards until she was lying beneath him on the blanket. She tried to fight him off but his kiss lingered on her mouth and his tongue prized her lips apart. She opened her mouth and drew him in, drinking in the delicious nectar of his kisses and abandoning herself to the might of his embrace.

He took her with a white hot heat that seared her more than the flames of the burning mill. His strength engulfed her and she became a woman reborn in his arms.

Hours passed as they lay together. Dawn slipped into the sky and the birds heralded the new day with an eagerness that matched her own. She woke to find him smiling down at her with delight. His bronzed and rugged features were softened by the dawn's early light, and she wondered how anyone could dare harm or challenge him.

'Bart,' she began again, needing to tell him she had seen someone set fire to the storehouse, and that she knew who was his assailant.

'Yes?' he asked lazily, his voice mellow with contentment.

She paused, wondering if she should shatter that rare moment of bliss. She saw again the glinting eyes of the toddy tapper as she was about to utter his name. Kumara had saved her, and put out the fire.

Her mind flashed with an image of him waving his hand to indicate where the blaze was worsening. She gasped, recalling suddenly what the sparkle was on his finger. He had been wearing his cat's eye ring!

'What is it?' Bart asked gently.

She smiled at him, trying to keep the relief from her eyes. If Kumara had not lost his ring, then he could not have been the one

45

who attacked Bart on the path by the villa. Someone else must have started the fire.

'Nothing . . .' she said, wriggling her shoulders, grateful that he could not read her thoughts.

'Nothing?' He pretended to be disappointed. 'Is that all you have to tell me?'

'Yes.' She sat up, overwhelmed by his nearness and her hunger for his body. She leaned over him, letting her nipples brush against the hair on his chest. 'Nothing more than . . . I love you.'

She kissed him, then raised her lips to add, as a chill of foreboding shuddered through her, 'I shall always love you, Bart . . . whatever happens.'

CHAPTER SIX

Bart touched the stub of his ear gingerly. The wound had healed and he was relieved at the absence of pain. The sight of it was what worried him. It was a constant reminder that someone held a grudge against him, and was prepared to strike at any time.

He smoothed his long wavy hair, the colour of a field of golden sugar-cane, over the stump to hide it. His cheeks and chin were rough with the blond beard he was growing to disguise his lopsided appearance. Raven complained the beard tickled her when they kissed; it had not cooled her ardour.

He turned from the looking glass, aware of her eyes on him. A warm, reassuring smile lingered in the rosy fullness of her lips. Her dark eyes, as hauntingly beautiful as black satin, sparkled with merriment.

He was filled with an urge to stride over to the bed and sweep her into his arms, squashing her ripe lips with kisses. Instead, he remained by her dressing table, arching his eyebrows in a question.

'It doesn't show,' she said, divining his concern. 'You look very dashing. The beard suits you.'

He searched her eyes for a hint of mockery. Her smile was encouraging and he swelled with pride under her gaze. Before, he had cared little for his appearance. Now, with his left ear robbed and reduced to a twist of wounded flesh, he was conscious of it as a deformity. She seemed not to mind, but how would people react in Galle?

'Will you be away long?'

Her question taunted him. He glanced at her to see if she was probing. He hated to be interrogated about where he was going and what he had done. There were certain matters, business and private affairs, that it was unfitting for a wife to know. Her smile was without guile, almost apologetic; it disarmed him.

'I'll be back before nightfall.' He paused thoughtfully. 'Is it any use me asking you to remain in the villa?'

She wrinkled her nose and shook her head.

'Very well.' He sighed, secretly proud of her irrepressibility. Despite the occasional upset to his esteem caused by her free-spirited behaviour, she was an ideal planter's wife. She could manage the slaves and had developed a strength and stamina at odds with her delicate, English beauty.

Bart had fallen in love with her the very first time he saw her walking in the Street of Moorish Traders. She was aloof then, unperturbed by the jostling of the crowds and by the chaos around her. He was enchanted by the wild tossing of her head, her fleeting smile and the sense of strong-willed determination concealed beneath her gracious charm.

'There could be danger if you go out alone,' he reminded her, moving across the chamber to her side. 'It would be foolish to take chances.'

He bent down to kiss her farewell on her cheek, only to find her lips on his. He savoured the embrace, pulling away when her fingers toyed with the loose tendrils of hair at the base of his neck.

Her eyes pleaded with him. 'Bart . . .'

'I'll be all right.' He dismissed her concern with a scowl of annoyance. 'I must see your father and report what's been happening.'

'You ride alone?'

'I'll be armed. The road is busy. Have no fear.'

She bit her lip, betraying her anxiety with her silence.

He turned away abruptly, embarrassed by his reluctance to leave her. He was the one in danger, and they both knew it. She would be hurt if anything happened to him. Her concern was like a shackle.

It was a new feeling for him to accept that, with Raven as his wife, he had allowed himself to become half of a pair instead of a solo pioneer. He shut the door to the chamber without looking back.

Mammy Sobers was waiting for him on the verandah, dressed in a scarlet array of flounces and frills even at that early hour. Garth, his son, sat on the edge of a chair, wide eyed as he stared at him over the rim of a dish of coffee.

'Now, Bart,' said Mammy sternly, 'don't you say nothin'. I goin' see she behave.'

He grinned, feeling foolish at the old lady's shrewd insight into his thoughts. 'What about you, Mammy? Will you behave too?'

'Whoo!' She threw up her hands with glee, her throaty chuckle startling his son. 'Dere ain't one of dem spindly-shanked coolies wid 'nough bamboo to misbehave wid!'

'I'm pleased to hear that. Whatever next?' His frown did not deter her delight that he was leaving her in charge of the villa and everyone in it.

'Be on the lookout for strangers. Send Jagath to call Tissa if you see anyone who doesn't belong on the plantation.'

'Be off wid you!' she said, rising from her seat as though she was going to box his ears.

He hurried off the verandah to where Jagath was standing with his horse. He patted the animal's neck and, when he calmed, swung up easily into the saddle. He paused to check his pistol was at his waist and his knife was strapped to his leg, hidden by the shaft of his riding boot. He turned to wave at Mammy.

The sight of Raven in her nightrobe, her lustrous dark hair cascading over her shoulders and breasts, brought a lump to his throat. She was staring at him intently, as though trying to retain a picture of him in her mind.

Garth shouted at him, straining at Mammy's hand to run out into the courtyard. Malika emerged from the parlour, holding a struggling Kirti in her arms while Ranita, his niece, clung to her skirts. He saw Nimal in the shadows standing meekly beside Daisy who towered over him like an Amazon. This fuss at his departure struck him as unnecessary. He smiled wryly at Raven, kicked his heels into the horse's flank and cantered away.

At the mill, he stopped to speak to Tissa, instructing him to send a gang of his best men to the canepiece in front of the villa courtyard, ostensibly to weed it. They were to keep alert for any strangers and act as guards without Mammy or Raven realizing the real purpose of their presence close to the house.

It troubled Bart to leave his wife and the children unprotected, except by slaves and natives, but there was no alternative. Although some white settlers had begun to arrive in the colony, there were none he could call on to stay in the villa during his absence.

He made a cursory inspection of the rebuilding of the boiling house being done under Tissa's supervision. The work was progressing well and the damage would be repaired in time for the cane cutting season which would soon be upon them.

It was a tiresome task and an expense he hadn't anticipated. Fortunately, there were enough hands eager to work for the privilege of being allowed to stay in the settlement and grow their own crops in *chenas*, plots of land they cleared in the jungle.

Riding down the plantation trail beside the river on his way to the Galle road, Bart returned the greetings of the natives who bowed their heads with respect as he passed. He was still puzzled about the fire at the mill. Was it one of these apparently humble locals who had done it?

Whoever fired the buildings must have known he had the resources to recover. His mother's death had left him rich. There was no mortgage on the plantation and he had paid off his debts. There was credit with his agents in London, even though the sugar shipped there had not been of sufficiently high quality to sell for a profit. His rum production was successful and his brew highly sought after by the British garrison in Galle.

Perhaps, he thought as he recalled Raven's bravery in saving the casks of rum and the storehouse from the fire, it was that rum that caused the hostility towards him. The favoured drink among the Ceylonese was arrack, the brandy distilled from toddy taken from coconut flowers.

The area from Bentota on the west coast coming south down to Galle and running east along the coast past his plantation to Matara, was renowned for its toddy. Possibly he had unwittingly offended an arrack *mudalali*, a local entrepreneur and trader who dealt in arrack, by cutting into his profits with the success of his rum sales?

Was it simple commercial rivalry that inspired the attack on him and the arson at the mill? He wiped his brow with his hand, self-consciously patting his hair over his ear. There were so many possibilities.

He would have been impressed if Tissa had uncovered some information on his visit to Galle. Despite the headman's insistence that he knew his people and everything that happened in the settlement, there were secrets even Tissa did not know.

Bart saw a clever mind, albeit a devious one, behind the attacks. Someone of influence – and wealth to pay sufficiently to silence wagging tongues – was responsible for the plotting against him.

He had pondered the problem for days. It distracted him. He felt a sense of relief to be going to Galle. He would discuss the events with Collector Radley and visit Madam Gudde. His spirits lifted although he was still uncertain how the whores in her bordello would react to his changed appearance.

He fingered the stubble on his chin and glanced apprehensively around him as he reached the road. On the banks of the lagoon, ferrymen waved, shouting their greetings of 'Bloodheart' with enthusiasm. They were simple people, appreciative of a man's mettle. He had no enemies among them.

He watched a man detach himself from the group, swing onto his horse with the grace of a natural horseman, and trot over in his direction. He was dressed in the style of a man of consequence, his kingfisher-blue coat and gold breeches dazzling in the morning sunlight.

He was hatless, his onyx-black hair flowing in a mane of curls to his shoulders, giving him the appearance of a dandy. His lean, agile figure, his clean-shaven features and compelling eyes, completed the picture of a well-born, local youth who was accustomed to giving orders, not to receiving them.

'Good morning, Bloodheart!' The young man saluted him with the familiarity of an old friend. 'Shall we ride together?'

His heartiness offended Bart. 'Do I know you?' he asked coldly.

'Lord, no!' the fellow retorted, unabashed by his attempt to put him in his place. 'But everyone knows you.'

'Indeed?' Bart replied curtly, pursing his lips and hoping by his silence to indicate his displeasure at the stranger's company. His hackles prickled when he felt himself being scrutinized by the man's probing eyes. He was uncomfortable and touched his ear with embarrassment, at the same time urging his horse to a gallop.

The road had broadened since he first journeyed along it over a decade previously. It was a foot trail then, used only by travellers wending their way to Matara where the British had established the Collectorate for the entire area. In 1815, the first Collector to be stationed in Galle was appointed by Governor Brownrigg and the pattern of commerce along the road changed.

As Bart developed his plantation and the settlement on its borders grew, the trail's usage increased. Over the years it had become a well-trodden highway, a palm-fringed avenue accessible to bullock carts and elephants as well as horses and palanquins.

It was a pleasant ride when the road was free of pedestrians and, seeing his way clear ahead, Bart jabbed his heels to make his horse gallop faster. He was annoyed when he glanced to his left and saw that the stranger was laughing as he effortlessly kept pace with him.

They cantered side by side, neither giving an inch, for a mile. Then Bart saw ahead of them a venerable Bo tree whose huge girth took up the centre of the road, blocking it except for a narrow path on each side. Bullock carts and palanquins were obliged to negotiate the tree with care. The gaps on either side were too narrow for him and the stranger to pass through the same one together.

Bart saw this as his chance to shake off his unwelcome escort. Instead of heading for the gap on his side of the road, he tugged the reins so his horse would make for the gap on the stranger's side of the tree. He planned to edge him off the road, out of his way.

To his delight, the young man seemed blind to what he was doing. The two of them galloped pell-mell towards the Bo tree, their horses' hoofs thundering on the road's hard mud as they strained to race each other to the narrow pass.

Too late, Bart realized the stranger was not giving way. He was beating him at his own game, forcing Bart's horse back into the centre of the path. Since he couldn't overtake the young man, he was the one who was likely to collide with the tree.

'Yield, sir!' he shouted as the wild chase brought him dangerously closer to the enormous Bo tree.

A flash of teeth from a devilish grin and a glint from impassioned eyes that sensed victory were the youth's only response. Bart tugged his reins desperately.

The horse veered to the right, galloping through the gap and missing the tree by inches. He arrived at the other side neck and neck with the stranger.

Gradually Bart slowed his horse's reckless pace. To his annoyance the young man did the same, as though waiting for him. His arrogant chuckle set his teeth on edge.

'Who the devil are you?' he demanded, wondering how he could wipe the smirk off the man's face. His disgust at having his bluff called outweighed the admiration he should have felt for the young man's pluck.

The youth casually pushed his hair away from his face. His stock, an ostentatious blue that matched his coat for brightness, was barely ruffled.

Bart's outrage diminished quickly; he knew he was to blame. The sun caught a light in the stranger's eyes, revealing a cold and lethal calmness. Bart was shocked by it, and wondered how he had misjudged the young man.

He was certainly dressed like a fop, one of the spree-loving Burghers whose improvidence had yet to reduce him to penury.

On the other hand, his complexion and dark-ringed eyes denoted a Singhalese background, perhaps a scion of one of the wealthy land-owning families near Matara. But that did not explain the brutal cruelty he glimpsed behind the young man's mask of elegance.

'I am K. S. Pathirana,' said the youth, standing up in his stirrups and half-bowing. 'I trust you are not angry with me. I was told you enjoy a jape. Your reputation as a man of courage, of compassion too, does you justice.'

He spoke English without the trace of a Singhalese lilt or even a Burgher cadence. It was a living language for him, not learned from schoolbooks or a tutor's desk. He was as at ease with it as Bart was.

'Mr Pathirana,' said Bart, sounding pompous to disguise his shame at his rudeness to the young man. 'You have done me an honour. It behoves a man well to exercise his skills in competition. Perhaps I am growing complacent in expecting victory as a right.'

Pathirana smiled his agreement as though happy with Bart's self-assessment. He turned away and resumed his progress along the road at a gentle pace. Bart was disturbed again by the man's arrogance, his calm assumption that he would follow him.

He glared his resentment at Pathirana's broad back, noting with disquiet that despite his dandyish dress and mannerisms, his stance in his saddle was alert. Every muscle in his body seemed poised for the unexpected.

'You intrigue me,' Bart said candidly, throwing out a challenge. 'You know a lot about me. Tell me about yourself.'

'With pleasure.' Pathirana smiled blandly yet his eyes avoided meeting Bart's. They were searching the palm trees behind Bart's back as though watching for possible attackers.

'What would you like to know?'

'For a start, young fellow, where did you learn your English?'

'From my mother.'

'From your mother?' Bart sighed, piqued again by the youth's conceit. He seemed reluctant to speak about himself despite professing it a pleasure. 'So where did your mother learn?'

'From her mother, I suppose.' Pathirana's laughter implied Bart's question was beneath his dignity. 'I am sorry,' he relented. 'My mother was English, like yours. I went to school there. Rugby.'

'By the devil!' Bart's oath amused the young man but his sniggered reaction only served to rile Bart. He was about to give vent to a lecture on good manners when he saw how foolishly he was behaving.

He realized the youth was better educated than he was. He would be an engaging companion. Apart from Raven's father and the officers at the barracks in Galle, he knew no one he could converse with on equal terms. Living with natives and slaves and giving orders instead of requests as man to man, had taken its toll on his tolerance.

'Forgive me,' he said, touching his ear. 'You must find me churlish. I've never made the acquaintance before of someone of your standing . . . from Ceylon.'

Pathirana's eyes glittered. 'Do not be confused by my manners or speech, Bloodheart. It is not difficult even for a quick-witted child to learn the graces that British gentlemen aspire to. You will find Singhalese culture is less facile for foreigners.'

Bart shied in his overture of friendship. He assumed, obviously wrongly, that Pathirana's background of English public school gave them something in common. The man's mockery of British traditions warned him to be more reserved.

He lapsed into silence, keeping his thoughts to himself as Pathirana rode watchfully beside him. He resolved to ask Collector Radley about this enigmatic young man, half-Singhalese warrior and half a St James's Regency buck.

'We have reached the fort without incident,' Pathirana announced to Bart's surprise when the battlements of Galle were in sight.

They were riding through the *cadjan* thatched huts of the native quarter. Bart's absorption with his problems had made the journey pass quickly.

'I shall leave you here,' the young man said with a cheery voice. 'We'll meet again.'

'Oh, yes . . .' Bart was startled. 'I thought you were going to the fort.'

He shook his head. 'I have business elsewhere. You'll be safe here.' He whirled his horse around and galloped back along the road.

Bart stared after his swiftly disappearing figure. He realized then that the young man had accompanied him solely to see he arrived in Galle without mishap.

Why, he wondered, was K. S. Pathirana concerned about him? And who was he, anyway?

CHAPTER SEVEN

'Pat-y-rahna?' Thomas Radley drew out the syllables of the name with derisive exaggeration. He snorted scornfully.

'Never heard of him. You don't believe the beggar, d'you? Just a cunning schemer trying to wheedle something out of you. English public school indeed! Utter rot, Bart. I'm surprised a man like you was so easily fooled.'

'Fooled?' Bart touched his ear, the palm of his hand scraping against his incipient beard.

He watched his father-in-law fork a slice of juicy ham into his mouth and stuff a piece of bread in after it. He chewed noisily, reaching for his glass of burgundy and water to wash it down. Bart sipped at his own glass of wine; he had declined the Collector's offer of breakfast and sat with him at the table as the only way to speak to him before he began his official duties.

'I wasn't fooled. He struck me as odd but plausible, which is why I asked you about him. Especially after the other incidents.'

Mr Radley continued to eat heartily. He had grown fat in his post. During his years running the bureaucracy in Galle he had learned how to survive with minimum effort. Bart's opinion of him had always been low. Marriage to his daughter had not changed his mind.

'I hope this isn't going to lead to trouble, Bart.' Mr Radley belched and pushed his plate away. A houseboy darted forward nervously and carried it off.

'I don't want any problems in my district. We've settled down nicely after the uprising three years ago. You befriended a Kandyan prince then, Bart. Now you've found a coolie who pretends he's an English public schoolboy . . .'

Bart tensed as the Collector laughed at him reproachfully. For Raven's sake, he kept his temper, his hands clenched into fists on his knees under the table where Mr Radley couldn't see the sign of his anger. His wounded ear burned and he bit his lip at the Collector's casual dismissal of his report.

'Are you not concerned about Raven?' he asked icily, freezing Mr Radley's chortling.

'Raven?' The Collector swept his hand over his brow, rubbing ham grease into his bald pate and into the lank grey locks that fringed it. 'What's she done?'

Bart pursed his lips at his father-in-law's lack of understanding. He wondered if slow-wittedness and a determination to ignore facts were the qualifications that won him his post.

'Raven's done nothing!' He almost shouted with exasperation. 'She could be in danger. Somebody has a grudge against me, so aren't you worried about her?'

'What do you want me to do?' Mr Radley threw up his hands in despair. He leaned back in his chair and gazed across the table, eyeing Bart scathingly as he answered his own question.

'Tell the garrison commander to send soldiers to guard you in your plantation?' He shook his head brusquely.

'Bart, I can't do anything that will excite people. The governor would have a fit. He'd send a clique of busybodies down from Colombo to investigate and I wouldn't have a moment's peace. Don't do anything rash, I beg you. Just go about your affairs quietly. Be nice to the native bigwigs and this affair will blow over.'

Bart rose from the table, pushing back his chair sharply so it scraped on the red tiles of the floor. The sound jarred the orderly silence in the Collector's dining room. His assistant, an English clerk with beads of perspiration on his long nose and an expression of being perpetually harassed, hovered at the door with a list of the Collector's appointments for the day.

'I'll do as you say,' Bart muttered between his teeth, restraining himself from telling his father-in-law what he thought of him. He deliberately ignored his outstretched hand and turned his back, marching from the room and shoving aside the hapless English clerk.

There was a stir of anticipation among the petitioners waiting in the garden for the Collector when Bart strode out. He blinked in the sunlight, pitying the people who came every day to solicit the Collector's help. All of them would be fobbed off with some excuse, a reference to regulations or an appeal to be a good chappie and run along.

Bart had no patience for officialdom. He could never have

56

started his plantation if he abided by regulations. His suggestion that independent British settlers develop the colony met with official discouragement. He had seized his two thousand acres in defiance of Registrar Van Dort, earning the man's enmity. He had succeeded and Van Dort was dead.

It needed action to be successful, not mindless toadying to bureaucratic convention. He wanted to shout at the people waiting patiently in the garden, that they were fools. They allowed themselves to be duped into conforming to the system imposed by British clerks and administrators.

Several people rushed over to him, pleading and begging, waving pieces of paper, trying to get him to listen to their petitions. He brushed them away angrily, annoyed that he was in the same position as they were. The Collector denied him any help yet told him to be nice to people.

His temper was fueled by the heat, a humid warmth that clung to his skin, soaking his clothes with perspiration. He pulled off his jacket, untied his stock and hung them over his arm. His shirt was damp with the sweat off his back and his hair was limp with moisture. Although the sky was a perfect blue and cloudless, the atmosphere was sticky with the humidity that presaged a storm.

His ill-humour was foolish, he realized as he outdistanced the more desperate of the petitioners who still cried after him. He slowed his pace and gazed around him, trying to forget his anger.

The Collector's bungalow was set in a garden and formed part of the bastion that overlooked the sea. A breadfruit tree, said to be the first in the island and planted by the Dutch who introduced it to Ceylon, grew in the garden. It was a pleasant location, removed from the enervating heat of the fort's dusty red streets.

The town owed its glory to its natural harbour. It was built on a promontory and its fortified walls served to protect the bay to the east. His plantation was beyond the headland that guarded the other side of the huge bay.

Historically, Galle was an entrenched settlement in the lowland territory of the Kandyan kings. The Portuguese wrested it from the Singhalese in 1587 and erected the first fortification, a wall, three bastions and a fortalice to guard the harbour.

Then Galle was the most venerable emporium of foreign trade in the universe. It had been the resort of merchant ships since the earliest dawn of commerce. Persians, Arabs, Chinese and Malays were traders in the town before the Portuguese.

Galle was the *Kalah* at which the Arabians in the reign of Haroun Alraschid met the junks of the Chinese and brought back gems, silks and spices from Serendib to Bassora. It was the *Tarshish* of the Bible, the great eastern emporium where ships from Tyre and Phoenicia carried on trade.

Bart climbed the grass embankment to the ramparts that encircled the town. From the battlements he had a view across the sea to the distant hills. The house that he had built despite officialdom was hidden in the jungle of the mountains bordering the old hill kingdom.

The harbour's bustle attracted his attention. Among the vessels at anchor were the dhows of the Arabs, the petamars of Malabar, the dhonies of Coromondel and the grotesque sea boats of the Maldive and Laccadive islanders. Most remarkable were the double canoes of the Singhalese, darting with surprising velocity amongst the shipping.

The harbour was circular in shape, protected on all sides, except at its entrance, by the hills of the hinterland. Although it had been in use since time immemorial, its waters were treacherous.

In Portuguese and Dutch times, the pilots who guided ships were forbidden on retirement from leaving Galle in case they divulged its secrets to an enemy. Over a score of submerged rocks lay in wait for mariners who attempted an approach without a pilot.

The harbour's name was reputed to be derived from the Singhala word, *gal*, meaning rock. Bart believed another story; that it came from *gala* meaning cattleshed. In the legendary epic of Ramayana, King Ravana was supposed to have used the area for keeping his cattle. The promontory would have made a good corral for herding cows.

The fortifications were completed by the Dutch who took possession of the town after severe fighting in 1640. The ramparts with their pepper pot observation towers were built by Negro slaves from granite blocks that came to Galle as ballast on ships. The Dutch transformed the fort to a town of gabled houses with *stoeps* or verandahs, lofty ceilings and massive pillars.

Turning his back on the sea, Bart's gaze from the ramparts took in the narrow streets and the red clay pantiled roofs of the houses. Little had changed in the walled town with its ceding to the British twenty years before.

Water drawn from the sea was still carted to dampen the dusty network of streets that crisscrossed the town. Only the names had been changed from Dutch to English: Morische Kramer Straat had become the Street of Moorish Traders.

Bart ran down the grass-sided embankment, resolved to take his problems – as did many young men – to Madam Gudde.

Several of the Dutch inhabitants and the descendants, known as Burghers, of the original Dutch population remained in Galle after the British take-over. Some were driven by the loss of privilege and income into a life of genteel poverty. Others were absorbed into the bureaucracy, compounding British protocol with Dutch dourness.

Others, like Madam Gudde, survived by their wits. Bart had known Gretchen Gudde since his arrival in Galle in 1809 and regarded her as a friend. She was a formidable woman, long past the youthful good looks that had made her famous. She had never married and lived as chaperon to a school of girls of dazzling beauty and professional charms.

He sauntered down Hospital Street and turned right by the Aurora Bastion into the road the British dubbed Pedlar Street. He preferred to think of it as the Street of Moorish Traders. The Moors' boutiques, small shops that were also their homes, over-flowed with bolts of gaily coloured fabrics, sparkling gem stones and intricately carved tortoiseshell trinkets.

There was an air of mystery about what went on in the depths of their porticoed one-storey houses. To Bart, the Muhammadans were a secretive people whose women were shrouded and never walked alone, and whose men followed age-old rituals that excluded outsiders.

Half-way down the exotic bazaar that formed the street, on its southern side, was a long white-washed wall with broken glass and iron spikes set into its top to discourage intruders. A heavy wooden door, with a grille at head height, was the only means of entry into the garden and mansion secluded from curious eyes behind the high wall. Bart stopped before the door and pounded on it with his fist.

A man with more self-respect than Bart would feel ashamed to be seen begging for entrance to Madam Gudde's bordello in the bright sunlight of mid-morning. The town's more circumspect citizens and the British soldiers waited until after dark.

From nightfall to dawn were the hours of the bordello. Even then, the eyes that forever watched behind the shutters of the Moors' houses never missed anything. Secrets were the currency of the bazaar and of the bordello. Bart hoped he would be able to learn the identity of his attacker from Madam Gudde.

He banged on the door again. 'Wake up!' he shouted, losing patience.

The sound of grumbling and the jangling of keys prepared him for the opening of the grille. The screen behind the wrought iron grating slid back noisily and a black, sleepy-eyed face peered out.

'What yo' bangin' dis door for?'

'To gain admittance, you fool! Open up.'

'Ain't none of de girls 'wake yet.'

'Don't you know me?' Bart frowned with exasperation at the sullen face. 'Tell Madam Gudde that Bloodheart wants to see her.'

The Caffre stuck out his lower lip and shook his head glumly. 'Wait here.'

The grille closed in Bart's face. He was puzzled by the Caffre's insolence and his refusal to be impressed by his name. He was probably a new acquisition.

Madam Gudde liked to use well-endowed black youths with her girls in the shows she arranged for special customers. Since she bought Caffres for their bodies rather than their charm, he would have to tolerate the surly youth's rudeness in keeping him waiting.

He glanced along the street, shifting to the side of the door to take advantage of the slight shade provided by the high wall. People of all description and nationalities thronged it, haggling with the traders, shouting at one another, or simply shoving their way from one end of the street to the next. The mixture of costumes and races drew his attention.

There were Europeans in their white morning undress, shaded by japanned umbrellas, who were visiting the town on their way to Colombo. Around them surged Moors, Malabars and Malays; there were Caffres, Parsees and Chetties from the Coromondel coast, with their extraordinary head-dresses and prodigious ear-rings.

Native Buddhist priests with their shaved heads and saffron robes drifted through the crowd. A chief in his official uniform with jewelled buttons, embroidered belt and ceremonial sword paraded past the boutiques, reminding Bart of Pathirana with his swagger of self-importance. The noise, the stench and the heat were becoming unbearable.

'Thank god, boy!' Bart shouted when the door finally opened

and he was let through. The Caffre, naked except for a loincloth, merely shrugged his broad shoulders and pointed to a seat. He indicated with a grunt that Bart was to wait in the garden.

It was pleasant under the shade of the *suriya* trees, a large hibiscus whose broad umbrageous leaves and delicate yellow flowers imparted a delicious coolness. Even the noise of the street beyond the wall seemed muted. But Bart refused to sit.

He was accustomed to being received by Gretchen Gudde without delay, not treated like a lowly client and made to wait. He paced up and down the lawn, keeping to the shade of the trees. At night, the girls sat there on benches under coloured lanterns, waiting to be chosen by the bordello's customers.

He was glad the girls were still sleeping and fingered his ear stump shyly. There was a grunt from the entrance to the mansion. He looked up to see the Caffre beckoning him.

'Bart, this *is* a surprise!' Gretchen Gudde walked across the curtained parlour with her arms outstretched. She hugged him to her ample bosom and he kissed her dutifully on each cheek.

While he was still grasped in her embrace, she signalled to the Caffre to close the door. The only light in the room came from the chink in the shutters that overlooked the inner courtyard.

'I didn't expect your custom so *early*, Bart. Do you have problems with your wife?' Madam Gudde settled herself on a chair with the false daintiness of a fat lady trying to hide her weight.

Her pendulous breasts and the folds of flesh of her sagging body were shielded by her robe. Her face had spread with age, showing the ravages of decades of gin drinking and the pleasuring of men for money. She was never seen in daylight and chose to sit in a darkened corner of the room that escaped the brightness of the morning.

'Gretchen,' said Bart happily. 'If every man had a wife like mine, you'd have no clients for your girls.'

Madam Gudde sniffed. 'Will you join me in a gin?' She reached for the bottle on the table close to her chair. Her chubby arm was too short and she raised her eyes for assistance from the Caffre who was leaning against the door. He didn't move.

'Allow me.' Bart strode over to her and handed her the bottle and a glass. 'I won't join you though.'

'All my girls are sleeping,' she said as she poured the gin, filling her glass. 'That's where I should be. In bed. With someone strong and lusty like you.' She gulped at the gin.

He moved away in alarm, wondering what kind of man would

61

patronise the raddled old woman. 'You never change, Gretchen,' he said to excuse his hasty retreat.

She belched. 'Of course I do, Bart. I grow old. Fat. Ugly. I can read what's in your eyes. I have my moments, though, Bart Taylor. When a sailor arrives here after months at sea, his belly swilling with rum and his loins afire . . . if the lights are dim, oy! oy!'

She took another swig from the glass and chuckled. 'What brings you here so early, eh?' she asked suddenly.

He looked around the room, trying to distinguish if the shadows and ponderous mahogany furniture, almirahs and ornately-carved love seats and couches, concealed an eavesdropper. He nodded at the Caffre scratching his crotch as he lounged at the door to the garden.

'What I have to say is for your ears alone.'

'Oy! oy!' She gurgled with pleasure. 'A naughty suggestion, Bart?' She mocked him in her hoarse, rasping voice. 'Don't worry about the Caffre. He's not as bright as he looks.'

Bart nodded in agreement. 'Why do you have such a sulky brute around you, Gretchen. Aren't you scared for your girls, even for yourself?'

She snorted gleefully, her jowls shaking and a curious glint entering her red-rimmed, bloodshot eyes. 'The buck's gelded. No balls, but you should see the muscles on him. He's my protector.' She snapped her fingers. 'Nato, come here. Let the master feel your arms.'

'No, Gretchen.' He sank down on a chair, disgusted at the idea.

The Caffre lumbered into the confined space between the two of them. Gretchen ran her hands eagerly up his trunk-like thighs, fondling his buttocks and wheezing delightedly to herself.

'He could throttle a man with one hand.' She glowered at Bart as she spoke, causing him to shift in his chair with embarrassment. The Caffre faced him, a dark scowl on his face that was definitely threatening.

'Can't you dismiss him, Gretchen. Why do you need protection with me here?'

He watched as Madam Gudde nodded her head and the huge black man sauntered from the parlour without a word. He breathed a sigh of relief when he was gone; he felt an evil shadow lifted from him.

He leaned forward and told Gretchen in a low voice about the attack on him and the arson that followed. He asked her if she had heard anything suspicious, any gossip that would indicate who was behind it.

'You know all the secrets about the Burghers and British settlers, Gretchen, and about the wealthy natives too. Someone of consequence is doing this.'

Her reply disappointed him. 'Is this why you roused me from my bed?' she complained. 'I've no interest in your affairs.'

'I didn't say you have, but you must have heard *something*.'

'I haven't.' She pulled herself up in her seat and perched on the edge, reaching for the gin bottle, clearly indicating that she considered the conversation at an end.

'I have one other question, Gretchen,' he said, raising his voice to attract her attention. 'There's a young man in the district you've surely heard of. Maybe he's one of your clients. He's as strong as your brutish Caffre, handsome and intelligent to boot, with a colour of burnished gold. He dresses like a dandy, with arrogance to match. He *says* he's half-English.'

He watched Gretchen's eyes closely for a flicker that would show if she knew Pathirana. Instead, she gulped noisily at her gin and belched, wafting alcoholic fumes over him.

His puzzlement at her unhelpful attitude erupted into alarm when he saw her staring over his shoulders and he felt the presence of someone standing behind him.

'Have you met my son?' she said with a grim chuckle.

He leaped to his feet and swung around, facing the gloom of the shadows behind his chair. He tensed, a flicker of apprehension alerting him for the unexpected.

The shadows parted and a tall man stepped forward, his hand outstretched and a chill smile of greeting on his face.

'So you are Bloodheart?' the man said in a guttural voice of scorn. 'I haf heard so much about you.'

Bart's fingers were squeezed by the man's powerful handshake. He responded with a tight grip of his own and the man's eyes glazed over with satisfaction.

'Forgive me,' said Bart hastily to disguise his surprise. 'I didn't know you had a son, Gretchen.'

He studied the man as closely as he could in the dim light of the parlour. His features and colour were European with none of the coarsening effect of the tropics.

'I haf arrived only recently,' the man said with a heavy accent. 'I vas raised in Holland.' His face was fleshy, like Gretchen's, with tiny, shifty eyes. His clothes were shabby and his hair dishevelled.

63

Bart was unimpressed.

Suddenly the man pushed past him. He reached over and snatched the gin bottle from Gretchen's hand. 'You haf had enough,' he said roughly.

Bart felt like an interloper. In all the years he had known Gretchen Gudde, listened to her advice and patronised her girls, he had never heard her speak of a son. She seemed to loathe the ill-mannered man.

'You go now, heh?' he said, waving the gin bottle in Bart's face. 'My mother is tired.'

He moved towards Gretchen to bid her farewell. The man blocked his way. Nato emerged from the shadows and stood at his side, a menacing grin spreading across his face and his hands bunching into fists. Bart hesitated.

'Please think of what I asked, Gretchen,' he called, seeing her huddled on the edge of her chair.

She nodded without looking at him.

'If you hear anything –'

'Ve vill tell you.' Her son beamed at him unctuously. 'Yes, ve vill.' He seemed to relish Bart's discomfort and waved at Nato to show him the door.

Despite the disquiet that gnawed at his mind, and a suspicion that both Madam Gudde and her overbearing son were hiding something from him, he allowed Nato to escort him from the bordello without protest.

CHAPTER EIGHT

Bart's time in Galle was short since he needed to return to the plantation before sunset. He made calls on the merchants who stocked his rum to seek new orders and to ask discreet questions. There was a growing demand for the Bloodheart brand of rum. If the fire had succeeded he would have been unable to meet it.

He also visited the shipping agent and arranged passage for Mammy Sobers to take Garth to England. Apart from his desire to give his son an English education, he wanted to reduce his worries by sending him away from Ceylon. Although there was no threat to the boy, he was apprehensive about what could happen.

He was tired when his business was concluded, and his throat was dry from the dust of the streets. His horse was stabled with the hostler in the native quarter, just beyond the fort gate. As he headed down Rope Walk Street towards the gate, the bell in the old Dutch belfry tower tolled three times. He would have time for a drink before setting out for the plantation.

He followed the road that ran along the side of the ramparts and turned into Church Street. Few people walked the town at that hour because of the heat. He was glad to step into the shade of the long verandah of the mansion occupied by officers of the British garrison. Formerly the huge old Dutch-built house was the head-quarters of the Dutch military.

It commanded a view of the ramparts and the sea beyond. The spreading branches of gnarled flamboyant trees kept the porticoed verandah cool.

He was a regular visitor to the mansion and relaxed in one of the long-armed chairs that lined the verandah. He swung his legs up and locked them over the extending arms, sinking back with a sigh into the coconut fibre webbing of the hammock-like chair. A steward brought him a rum and water which he sipped with a growing feeling of satisfaction as he succumbed to his fatigue.

'Bloodheart, old boy! You look worn out.'

He opened his eyes and grinned at the officer who had spoken. 'Rum has a remarkable restorative power, Captain Walker. A few minutes rest and I'll be fit for the road home.'

'What, not staying the night?' Captain Walker sat in the chair beside him and nodded his head enthusiastically. 'A visit to Madam Gudde's will do more for you than a glass of your fine plantation rum.'

'I was there this morning.'

'You old goat!'

Bart chuckled and drained his glass. He sat up and stared across at Bob Walker. The officer was a hearty sort, the kind of friend a man could depend on in a sticky situation. He wasn't very bright but his bluff good nature made him an agreeable companion.

'You misunderstand me,' said Bart considerately. 'I went for some information.' He outlined the recent events to the Captain, including his encounter with Pathirana.

'Damned odd.' The officer's fresh young face was guileless, hiding nothing. 'I'll keep my eyes and ears open, of course. Would you like me to bring some men on patrol? A show of force will put the wind up the natives.'

Bart shook his head, warmed by the Captain's support. 'I hope it won't be necessary. I'll soon find out what's behind it. I expected Gretchen Gudde to have heard something. Have you met her lout of a son?'

Bob Walker laughed. 'Curt is his name and curt by nature. He pretends he's tough but he isn't. His mum still runs the show. She won't let him touch the girls, says it's bad for business.'

'This morning she looked positively intimidated.' He frowned. 'The fellow snatched the gin bottle away and said she'd had enough.'

'Probably wanted it himself. I bet the moment you left she was lambasting him with her tongue for taking advantage of her.'

'I'm pleased to hear it. He unsettled me.'

'He unsettled us all until we got to know him. Cries like a baby when he's well-oiled. Harmless fellow.'

Bart fingered his ear, his eyes wandering and taking in the view of the street. A hasty movement by the trunk of a flamboyant tree caught his attention. He peered at the tree steadily, wondering what was disturbing him.

'I must leave now,' he said, draining his drink. 'Raven's alone at home. I want to be there before nightfall.'

'I'll come your way on my next patrol.' Captain Walker stood up with him and clapped his hand on his shoulders. 'Scare the daylights out of the buggers.'

'Raven will be pleased to see you.' Bart smiled, thinking not only of Raven but of her father's reaction. He studied the flamboyant tree again while Bob Walker bid him farewell. He was convinced someone was hiding behind it.

He ran down the steps into the road. A palanquin was being borne along at a steady pace past the mansion. It blocked his view and he cursed under his breath as he was forced to wait for it to pass.

Its team of bearers chanted rhythmically as they poled themselves along with the handles of the palanquin's litter on their shoulders. A gang of children gambolled around them, enjoying the excitement. Some of them ran into Bart, not noticing him waiting to cross the street. He shoved them away and dashed over to the tree.

There was no one behind it although he was certain there had been. He stood behind the tree's trunk and peered out; it gave a perfect view of where he had been sitting on the verandah. Someone could have spied on him with ease.

He glanced down the road towards the Sun Bastion. There was nothing suspicious in the couples who strolled in the sun under parasols, nor in the children playing on the grass embankment below the ramparts.

He walked towards the road that turned off to the fort gate by the Dutch church. The bell tower was opposite the church and it began to ring as he approached it. He counted four; he would have to hurry.

A flash of bright blue caught his eye, then it vanished. He ran to the corner. People filled the road to the fort gate and he scanned the crowd carefully.

He saw the marigold robes of Buddhist priests, the pink of ladies' saris, and the black cowls of Muhammadan women walking in pairs. There was the scarlet of soldiers' tunics and the dust-coated white of servants' sarongs. There was every colour in sight except the kingfisher-blue of Pathirana's coat.

He acknowledged the greeting of the sentries at the gate as he walked through deep in thought. He collected his horse from the hostler, saddled and mounted it with his mind only half-concentrating on what he was doing. Something was puzzling him, causing him to act like a man deranged. The moment he realized that, he blinked and became aware of himself again.

He was riding along the narrow isthmus that linked the fort with the native quarters. He was alarmed that he had travelled nearly two hundred yards in a daze. He had no recollection of the people who had greeted him, nor whether he greeted them in return.

'Damn!' he muttered under his breath, annoyed that his sense of being watched made him ignore normal courtesy. He needed to keep alert for possible danger and not cause offence by his distracted behaviour.

He patted his waist, feeling for his pistol to give him support. It had gone. He looked down in surprise at his belt, unable to believe that someone had stolen it. He slowed the horse and checked in his saddle bag in case absent-mindedly he had placed it there.

He scratched his head. It was too late to return to Galle to see if he had left it at the garrison mansion. The sun would be setting soon and he wanted to reach the villa before dark.

He dug his heels into his horse with a spurt of anger. The animal accelerated into a gallop past the squalid shacks bunched at the edge of the native quarters and took the road along the coast.

The setting sun sent slanting shadows across the road, dimming the light under the trees. Bart was pleased to have the road to himself. He crouched low over the horse's neck and urged it to go faster.

The wind was streaming through his hair, blowing away the foolish notions that the heat stirred in his mind. He shrugged off the suspicion and doubts that plagued him and concentrated on the joy of riding.

The horse's powerful body throbbed beneath him as the animal stretched its legs, as pleased as Bart to be cantering freely along the open road. Bart drew closer to its head, his heels tucked in, and became part of the horse.

He relished the speed, aware that the animal was racing faster than it had ever done before, but unconcerned by it. There was a madness about the beast that he attributed to its pleasure to be given a free rein. He shifted in the saddle and, as he did so, felt it slipping away from him.

The horse veered when he grasped its neck for support. He kicked his feet from the stirrups and clung to the animal with his thighs.

The saddle fell off from under him, crashing to the ground. The horse stumbled over it, regained its balance and sped on.

Bart clung to its neck, clutching at the bridle, desperately trying to slow it down. He felt his grip weakening. He tensed, waiting to be flung off the charging animal. He glanced ahead to choose a spot where the undergrowth would cushion his landing.

A thunderous pounding of hoofs at his side overtook him. A blur of kingfisher-blue and a flash of dazzling white teeth met his eyes. A hand was outstretched towards him as gusts of grass and dirt flew around him.

'I'll catch you,' the man alongside him shouted. 'Jump!'

He obeyed the command instantly, pushing himself away from his horse with his feet. For a split second he was suspended in the gap between the two animals hurtling along the road. An arm seized his waist and pulled him onto the back of the other horse, steadying him so he didn't topple straight off. The horse slowed to a halt.

'Pathirana!' He gasped, slipping gratefully to the ground. He staggered, aware of a wave of fear washing over him. 'I'm . . . grateful . . . to you . . .' he panted.

The young man's dark eyes swept over him briefly then he scanned the bush on either side of the road. 'Wait here,' he ordered, wheeling his horse around and galloping away.

Bart dusted himself down, watching the haze behind his own horse as it disappeared into the distance. He was shaking and took several deep breaths to regain control of himself. He didn't want Pathirana to see lest he think he was scared.

'The strap was cut.' Pathirana tapped the saddle he had retrieved from the side of the road. 'You were lucky not to be thrown off.'

'I suppose it's a coincidence that you happened to be passing?'

'Why not?' Pathirana swung down from the horse and held the saddle out for him to inspect.

'I'll hide it in the bush,' he said when Bart shook his head in disbelief. 'You can send a boy for it later.'

He watched Pathirana dive into the undergrowth at the road's edge. The flapping of his kingfisher-blue coat taunted him. The young man had probably saved his life, yet his presence on the road at that particular moment seemed highly suspicious.

'Mark the trees,' said Pathirana when he returned without the saddle. 'So you can retrieve it when you're ready. Will you ride with me or shall we walk?'

'I should catch my horse –'

'The ferrymen will hold it for you. Come.' Pathirana mounted his horse and held out his hand to pull him up behind him. 'Ride with me so they don't get alarmed when your horse shows up without you.'

'You show extraordinary concern for my welfare.' He mounted behind Pathirana and held his waist lightly as they moved off. 'I wonder why.'

'Must help a fellow traveller in distress, what?' Pathirana's laugh had a cold edge to it that seemed to mock what he was saying.

Beneath his coat, Bart could feel the taut muscles of his waist; he was like a leopard poised to leap. The youth's eyes darted restlessly over the terrain, eying the road ahead and the coconut trees at the side.

'You were following me today in Galle,' he said without preamble. Pathirana didn't flinch.

'You shouldn't wear such a gaudy coat if you don't want to be seen.'

'I rather like this colour.' Pathirana ignored his remark. 'Appeals to the ladies, and flatters me.' He half-turned, a sardonic grin on his face.

'Dammit!' Bart exclaimed in exasperation at being completely in Pathirana's power. 'Give me a straight answer. Why have you been following me?'

'Look out!'

He instinctively tightened his grip as the horse increased its speed and Pathirana crouched down low. He lowered his head too as the decayed brown branch of a palm tree crashed to the ground only inches behind them.

Pathirana sat up and shrugged. Bart felt the acid taste of bile in his mouth. He decided to save his questions until he was safely back at the house with Raven and the children.

Pathirana accepted his silence and rode with apparent ease yet he was tense and alert for danger. When they reached the lagoon Bart's horse was grazing quietly. He jumped off as Pathirana stopped and ran over to the animal. It whinnied with pleasure at seeing him.

'No sign of injury,' he said as he inspected the horse's legs. 'I'll ride him back to the villa.' He half-expected Pathirana to forbid him to ride so he mounted the animal quickly and set off.

When there was no command or protest, he glanced behind. Pathirana was talking to the ferrymen. He waved, his nonchalance offending Bart.

Very well, he thought to himself, *I don't need you.*

He wanted to quiz Pathirana about his presence on the road and to find out more about him. Yet he was eager to return home and his pride prevented him begging Pathirana to ride with him.

Of course, he was grateful but behind his gratitude lurked a feeling that if Pathirana had not been trailing him he would not have needed rescuing. It was only Pathirana's word that the saddle strap had been cut. Perhaps he himself had fastened it carelessly in his bemused state at the hostlers.

Nevertheless, he kept scanning the trees along the path the way he had seen Pathirana doing. He hailed the workers coming back from the canefields. They returned his greetings humbly.

His knowledge of the Singhalese language was sparse. He had learned to judge a person's mood from his smile, his eyes and the tilt of his head. As far as he could guess, everything on the plantation during his absence had been normal. There was no sense of excitement among the men.

Tissa was waiting for him as he approached the mill. He dismounted and handed the bridle to him. 'Walk to the villa with me,' he said. 'Is Raven all right?'

'Of course, Bloodheart.' Tissa frowned when he noticed the saddle was missing. 'And you?'

'Thanks to a chap called Pathirana. Who is he, Tissa? A young fellow, arrogant and built like a Kandyan warrior yet he speaks English better than me.'

'English is the language of the elite,' Tissa said proudly, pronouncing his own words with care. 'Pathirana is an ordinary name.' He sniffed disparagingly.

'I believe you're jealous.'

'You are warning us to beware of strangers, Bloodheart, yet you have befriended one yourself.'

'He befriended me. Have you heard of him?'

Tissa shook his head. The sun had set and the light was fading fast as they walked up the hill. There was no lengthy twilight in Ceylon; once the sun had disappeared beyond the horizon, half an hour of dim light remained before night embraced the plantation. By seven, the fields and hills would be in darkness.

Ahead of him, Bart saw Raven standing at the edge of the verandah. Kirti was at her side, tugging at her hand to be allowed to run out onto the lawn to greet him. His own son, Garth, stood gravely at her other side, aware of the importance of being the only man in the villa during his absence.

He broke into a run and caught at Kirti as the boy rushed

71

towards him. He lifted him off the ground and gasped with mock surprise at his weight. He kissed the boy and placed him back on the verandah. He patted Garth fondly on his head and turned to embrace Raven.

He was stirred by the passion in her kiss and tried to break away in embarrassment. She clung to him.

'Thank god you're back!'

'Why, what's wrong?'

'I had a premonition . . . of danger.'

'You were right. Do you forget, I have the elephant pearl? Nothing can happen to me as long as I possess it.'

'Do you really believe in that Kandyan superstition?' Her eyes locked on his, sending a message of desire that made his loins leap.

He walked stiffly to a chair and sat down. Kirti dashed over to him and scrambled on to his lap. He laughed with relief.

Nimal moved slowly around the verandah, hanging up lanterns as the darkness began to draw in. Tissa, who had been playing with Ranita, his daughter, took his leave. Malika scooped up Kirti from Bart's knees and bore him protesting off into the house. She was followed by Garth and Ranita. Even Mammy Sobers who was usually so keen to hear the gossip from Galle withdrew, leaving him alone with Raven.

'You planned this,' he challenged her as she handed him a glass of punch and sat in a chair close to his side.

'We need moments alone,' she said in a voice that was husky with wanting. Her hand reached for his and he held it comfortingly. 'I was frightened for you.'

'You had no need to be. I had a mysterious stranger to protect me.'

She laughed, treating it as a joke. 'Who?'

'He says his name is Pathirana.'

'So it is!' a voice uttered from the darkness of the lawn.

They both stared as the man in the kingfisher-blue coat stepped out of the night onto the verandah. He bowed deeply.

Bart felt Raven's fingers tense in his hand. He released her and stood up, striding over to the man and gripping him by his elbow.

'Welcome, Pathirana,' he said, determined not to let the stranger give him the slip. 'Come and meet my wife.'

Raven was staring at Pathirana as though seeing a ghost.

'Darling, what is it,' he said, leading the young man to her.

72

Pathirana's dark eyes flashed a warning that Bart didn't see.

Raven blushed. 'It's nothing,' she said hesitantly. 'I was reminded of someone . . . someone I once knew.'

CHAPTER NINE

Raven lowered her lashes quickly to hide her confusion. At the base of her throat a pulse beat and swelled as though her heart had risen from its usual place.

Bart's new-found friend was standing before her, his head bobbing in an acknowledgement of the introduction. She felt the compelling power of his eyes without meeting them.

'How . . . do you do?' she stuttered, raising her trembling hand.

A bolt of lightning seemed to strike her as he took her fingers and lifted them slowly to his lips. She was transfixed, her heart fluttering wildly in her breast as all her senses tingled with anticipation.

The touch of his lips on her fingers kindled feelings of fire and she reddened. Fortunately for her, Bart was too distracted by his unexpected arrival to notice her heaving bosom and flushed features.

The young man did. 'Raven?'

The familiar sound of his voice brought back the memory of that day on the beach with a shiver of vivid recollection. Her lips tingled in remembrance of his bruising kiss.

'You are more beautiful than I ever dreamed,' he said softly, his eyes holding hers.

Bart clapped him heartily on his shoulders. 'Sit over here, Pathirana.'

Raven was astonished to hear what Bart called him and watched speechless as he led him to a chair. Surely his name was *Kumara*?

She struggled to control her excitement and sat as demurely as she could on a chair that was placed beyond the bright glow of the lanterns. She peeped at the youth surreptitiously while Bart looked for someone to bring rum.

Was he really Kumara? There was the same alertness in his glance that she remembered, the same tremor of amusement on his lips and the same enigmatic depth to his eyes. Yet he looked different.

There was a suaveness where she recalled savagery; his clothes were the height of foppish fashion, not the brief loincloth of a toddy tapper. The timbre of his voice was the same, it thrilled her to hear it, yet the words he uttered were platitudes.

'A delightful location,' he said when Bart returned to his chair. 'You get the mountain breeze and a vantage point over the valley.'

'We like it, don't we, Raven?'

She was startled by his inclusion of her in the conversation. She wanted to be forgotten so she could study the young man for a sign. Had the hint of warning in his eyes been real or did she imagine it? He had given no sign of recognition when he kissed her hand. No extra squeeze or sly wink.

'Raven?' Bart's calling of her name roused her.

'I was far away,' she said with a smile of apology directed at the visitor. 'Forgive me. It is so peaceful here at night. You can almost hear . . . the *sea*.'

'Indeed?' The young man's arched eyebrow gave no indication that he understood her meaning. He turned away from her and listened to Bart's questions.

Raven tried to regain her poise, nodding at appropriate breaks in the conversation. Bart was recounting how Pathirana – as he insisted on calling the youth – saved him when his horse bolted.

She barely heard the story as she contemplated his curly black hair flowing down to the broad span of his shoulders. Her eyes dropped to his muscular thighs where he sat with his legs crossed as though he were in a society drawing room. She watched his fingers flutter when he modestly declined credit for the rescue.

His hands were elegant and slender, long-fingered with tips of pale gold against the darker gold of his skin. They showed none of the strength she remembered when they had gripped her waist and begun to stroke her trembling body.

She caught her breath, stiffling her gasp of realization with her hand. He was wearing the cat's eye ring. He *was* Kumara, not Pathirana.

Her doubt was replaced by a feeling of exultation. She leaned forward to show more interest in the conversation, wondering how she could steal a moment alone with him.

She glimpsed Bart's earnest face and smiled, hanging on to his words. She wanted to know more about Kumara, remembering the passion he had stirred in her that day on the beach.

'It's a long ride to Matara in the dark,' Kumara was saying. 'May I stay the night? I'll sleep on the verandah.'

'Of course!' Bart seemed delighted. His face was flushed and the rum glass in his hand was empty.

Raven marvelled at Bart having unwittingly brought back into her life the very man she sought. All day during his absence in Galle she had looked for an opportunity to take the jungle trail to the beach in the hope of seeing Kumara again.

Mammy had shadowed her like a hawk and the children demanded her attention constantly. It was impossible to leave the villa. Now Kumara was sitting only a few inches from her; his nearness both a comfort and a challenge.

'We have a guest room,' said Bart effusively. 'At the back of the parlour, off the courtyard, next to the nursery.'

'Ah, you have children?'

Raven blushed as Kumara turned his eyes on her. There was a kindness in them, encouraging her to speak. She was numb as her heart pounded and her palpitating breasts strained against the thin fabric of her lace corsage.

'Sons,' said Bart brusquely, answering for her. 'By my first wife. My niece stays with us too.'

'Garth and Kirti,' Raven heard herself saying in a strangled voice that sounded like a stranger's to her.

'I hope I'll have the pleasure of seeing them. Kirti is a royal name.'

'He was named after a Kandyan king.' She felt bolder now she was actually speaking. Kumara was not the uncouth scoundrel she imagined. His charm was infectious.

'He's also called Charles after my mother,' said Bart pedantically. 'She was Charlotte.'

'You must be a very happy family.'

'We are.' Raven smiled, trying to convince Kumara of her sincerity. She needed to squash any ideas she might have aroused in him by her behaviour on the beach.

'My wife is Collector Radley's daughter,' Bart said, interrupting the silence.

She supposed Bart mentioned that to impress Kumara. He was staring at her in a superior way that suggested he knew everything about her without being told. It disturbed her.

For seconds her mind seemed to teeter on the edge of an abyss;

she was shocked that the intimate details of her life might be familiar to him. She sat up straight, pulling back from succumbing to the forceful gleam in his probing eyes.

'I shall leave you two to talk,' she said nervously, rising from her seat. 'I'll tell a boy to prepare the guest chamber.'

'You are kind.' He stood up and bowed his head.

She averted her eyes from the dark gleam and moved away before he could take her hand in his and kiss it again. Bart glanced at her curiously and as she left the verandah, she heard him asking Kumara where he came from.

Somehow she knew the youth's answers would be lies. His friendship with Bart was contrived, a way of wheedling his way into the household. She wondered why . . . what did he want?

She paused in the parlour. Candles burned in the chandelier that hung from the rafters. She was reassured by the sight of the two houseboys waiting by the door for their instructions. The house, the servants, they were her shield; the permanence that Bart brought her. Kumara was a threat to it all.

She gave orders and the boys moved swiftly. Jagath made up the bed in the guest room. She instructed him to sleep outside the nursery on a mat to protect Malika and the children in the night.

Nimal poured two more drinks to serve to Bart and Kumara. She told him to be sure to lock the verandah door when they went to sleep. He was to put his sleeping mat in front of the door, blocking it so he would wake if anyone tried to pass in the night.

She took the extra precautions deliberately. It was usually Bart who worried about such matters yet he might forget. She was concerned for them all, as well as for herself.

She glanced around the parlour. It was simply furnished with only a few items of value. Bart's new wealth had been utilized in expansion of his business and paying off debts, not in adding comforts to his home.

There were two low tables, locally made with inlaid tops, two wooden couches with coconut fibre upholstery, a number of rustic, straight-backed chairs, and an escritoire where Bart filed his papers. She wondered for the first time if he kept anything precious in it. The key was in the lock. She turned it, fastening the lid and withdrawing the key, just in case.

Bart had never told her where the elephant pearl he was keeping for Kirti as his inheritance was hidden. She prayed it was in a safe place where no prowler at night would find it.

There was a drawing of Bart's mother hanging on the whitewashed wall of the parlour. It was a pen and ink sketch of no particular merit or likeness, done by an itinerant artist in return for board and lodging while he awaited a ship back to England. Its remarkable feature was the way the eyes were drawn so they appeared to follow anyone moving about the room.

Raven smiled to herself and tiptoed over to the picture. She tucked the key behind the left corner of the frame, resting the picture back against the wall. 'You'll watch over us, won't you, Charlotte?'

The picture's eyes stared back at her and she knew that she had done right.

Bart's hand was clammy against her flesh. She recoiled from him.

'I'm sorry. Were you sleeping?'

She smiled in the candle light, making space for him in the bed. 'Where is Kum –' She hesitated. 'Your guest?'

The scent of rum was mellow on his breath as he wriggled into the bed beside her. 'Jagath's shown him to his chamber.' He yawned and his fingers crept over her stomach.

She edged towards him, seeking his caress. She guided his hand and placed it over her heart so he could feel it beating. 'I'm pleased you're back,' she said. 'You stayed long on the verandah.'

'He's a very interesting young man.' He shifted his hand, trailing his fingers over her breasts.

His touch set a comforting feeling of reassurance flooding through her. She sighed with pleasure. 'Bart, I was frightened.'

His hand was between her thighs. 'Why?'

'I don't know. I'm still frightened.' She quivered with longing. 'Hold me.'

His fingers pressed into her buttocks, lifting her from the mattress. He rolled onto her. She gasped at the hard feel of his manhood seeking her as the rum fired his ardour.

Her body firmed at his touch only to melt with a gush of love when he penetrated her. Their desperate need was a shared one, their bodies in exquisite harmony with one another.

She flowed at the throb within her and her world was filled with him. Her dread at Kumara's arrival passed.

She cradled him in her arms as he fell asleep, snoring contentedly. She was satisfied too. His demand had matched her own. Although his lovemaking was devoid of the touches of endearment she yearned for, he had stanched her need.

She lay her head against his, feeling the brush of his beard on her cheek, and drifted happily into sleep.

She still held him in her arms when she woke up. The candle's glow behind its glass shade was steady; she must have been asleep over an hour, judging by the flame. She eased her arm from under Bart's neck, wondering what noise had roused her from a dreamless sleep.

She lay listening to the night, to the squeak of polecats in the roof, and the rustle of a cockroach scurrying across papers on the windowsill. There was no unusual sound to account for her awakening.

Perhaps it was the knowledge that Kumara was sleeping in the chamber next to hers that roused her. She held her breath and moved to the edge of the bed, careful not to disturb Bart.

The rhythm of his gentle snores showed he was deeply asleep, exhausted after his journey to Galle and back. She swung her legs cautiously over the side of the bed. The clay tiles were cold to her bare feet.

She walked gingerly to the chair where her night robe lay. She buttoned it high up to her neck, loosening her hair so it fanned out over her shoulders. She was naked beneath the robe, and warmed by it. She sat down while she slipped on her shoes. Bart still snored peacefully within the protection of the bed's muslin curtains.

She tiptoed to the door. It opened easily on oiled hinges and she peeped out into the deserted parlour. The candles of the chandelier were all capped; a lantern burned dimly at the main door. By its light, she saw Nimal stretched out on his mat. Anyone who attempted to leave would have to wake him first.

The door to the courtyard was ajar. She hurried over to it. The night sky, heavy with clouds, obscured the stars and the moon. The courtyard was in darkness except for chinks of light from the nursery and, at its opposite end, from the store room where Daisy slept.

She hesitated at the door while her eyes adjusted to the darkness. The air was heady with the jasmine scent of temple trees, the white frangipani flowers that bloomed in the courtyard's garden.

She moved stealthily across the grass, skirting the trees. She was drawn, not to the door of Kumara's chamber but to the light and the faint buzz of conversation that came from the nursery. She paused when she was close to the room and peered down at the darkness by her feet, searching for Jagath. He should have been sleeping in front of the door.

79

She moved closer until she was touching the shutters secured loosely over the open window. The voices were stronger there, speaking in Singhala. She bent forward to listen.

She recognized Kumara's commanding tones. Malika answered pertly, as though flattered. The third voice was Jagath's.

Her curiosity to know what Kumara was doing in the nursery made her bold and she put her eye to the crack between the shutters. Kumara was bare-chested, naked to his breeches. He was standing with Malika and Jagath around the bed where Kirti was sleeping.

The child's white face looked pale in the lantern's bright light. His limbs, uncovered by the blanket he had pushed aside in his sleep, were the pinkish white of a European, in contrast to the darkness of the trio who stood over him.

Raven felt as if a hand was clawing at her heart. She tried to cry out to make Kumara leave the child alone, but her voice stuck in her throat. Instead, Kumara uttered words of his own.

In response, Jagath hung the lantern on a hook above the child's bed and ambled towards the door. His slowness gave her time to draw back into the shadows under the eaves as the door opened, spilling a wedge of light out into the courtyard.

Kumara closed the door after Jagath had left. He was alone with Malika and the child. Garth and Ranita were asleep behind a curtain at the other side of the room. Raven hurriedly returned her eyes to the crack between the shutters so she could watch everything.

Kumara touched Malika's cheek with his finger. She pouted. He ran his finger down her neck and lifted the long braid of hair from her shoulders. Playfully he let it fall back. She giggled nervously.

A numbness seized Raven and her mind floundered. She burned with a fierce anger that made her weak and clutched at the wall to support herself. She wanted Kumara to leave the girl alone. She could not bear the thought of Malika knowing the same deep pleasure she had experienced in his arms. She blinked.

Kumara was whispering into Malika's ear, his lips passing close to her cheek. She seemed surprised at what he said and her almond-shaped eyes widened. She frowned, pulling away from him, then shrugged her slender shoulders in consent.

You wicked girl, thought Raven, assuming she was surrendering to Kumara's lustful suggestion. Her throat went dry and her body ached as she pressed her eye to the window. If Kumara kissed

Malika she intended to burst into the room and cast them both out of the house.

The sight that met her gaze caused her to gasp out loud.

Kumara was bent over Kirti, raising the cloth that was his sleeping garment. Malika watched him, the trace of a bemused smile on her lips. Kumara pulled the cloth above the boy's knees and slowly drew it up his thighs.

With a sickening realization that the world she shared with Bart was about to be shattered, Raven guessed what Kumara was seeking.

There was no clue to Kirti's mixed blood in his features. His complexion was a rosy pink and all who saw him assumed he was Bart's son. The secret that he was really the offspring of a Kandyan prince and Bart's dead wife had been safe up to now.

Raven's fear of Kumara was vanquished as a surge of loyalty to protect Bart and Kirti overwhelmed her. She thrust open the door of the nursery and bounded in, her arms waving.

'What are you doing?' she demanded. Her eyes blazed with anger as she flung herself at Kumara.

He turned towards her nonchantly, fending her off with one hand while the other let the cloth drop back over Kirti's nakedness. He had seen the black birthmark, the ebony scrotum that proclaimed Kirti's parentage. He smirked at her.

'Merely admiring *Bloodheart's* son,' he said mockingly.

'You knew all the time?' Her despair caused the strength to drain from her.

'It was rumoured.' He lowered his voice and gripped her elbow. His touch paralysed her. 'I'm delighted that what I heard is true.'

'What do you mean?'

'That Kirti, like Malika claimed, has the blood of the Kandyan kings in his veins. The royal line is not dead.'

'Yes, it is!' She pulled her arm from his grip and felt her boldness returning. She stared defiantly at his eyes, ignoring the invitation that glimmered there. 'Why are you here? What do you want with us?'

'Want?'

His suggestive smile made her weaken and she almost gave in to him. He led her out of the nursery as Jagath approached across the lawn with another lantern.

'Shall we walk? There is no moon but the night's balm is soothing. I have something to tell you.'

'I won't believe anything you say. It's all lies. You used Bart to

81

worm your way in here. You pretended to be a toddy tapper so you could use me. You enticed Malika to betray Bart's secret.'

'Raven . . .'

The passion in his voice spoiled her resolve. She gaped at him as his arm wound around her waist, his fingers digging into her.

'You need an ally. You are in danger. Please let me help you.'

She opened her mouth to pour scorn on what he'd said but his lips closed over hers before she could speak. His tongue drove savagely between her mouth. She found herself being transported by his ruthless kiss on a devilish voyage as the darkness engulfed them.

CHAPTER TEN

'Let me go!' she blurted out when he lifted his lips from hers. In her heart she wanted him to hold her still, to lead her to the pinnacle of pleasure that his embrace promised.

He released her waist and she was suddenly alone in the darkness.

'Where are you?' she demanded breathlessly. 'I can't see you.'

By the nursery door, Jagath stood in conversation with Malika. He had placed the lantern on the ground and it threw an enormous shadow that danced up to the roof of the villa. The hanging leaves and willowy branches of the temple trees were transformed into menacing shapes by the light. Against its glow she searched the gloom for Kumara.

'By your side,' he hissed, causing her to leap away from him in fright. His hand closed about her wrist and she was pulled towards him.

She wanted to resist but his touch beguiled her. She knew she should cry out for Jagath to rescue her but Kumara's fingers conveyed a sense of bliss and well-being. He drew her deeper into the darkness in the corner of the courtyard.

'Someone will see,' she whispered, startled by her guess at what he intended to do.

'No one must hear,' he answered.

His voice was muted, its low, deep tones vibrating with a passion that sent a delicious thrill of anticipation spreading through her bosom. She could not see his face, nor his eyes, beyond a darker shadow in the night.

She caught his scent, a maleness mixed with the jasmine of the temple flowers that she was crushing under her feet as she walked with him. His breath carried an agreeable flavour of almonds, not the blatant smell of rum she associated with Bart.

'Good heavens,' she said. 'My husband –'

'He will sleep.' His voice hissed with the innocence of a snake.

Her hackles prickled with alarm. 'What have you done to him?'
She tried to pull away but his grip was vice-like on her wrist.

'Your love-making was enough. He'll sleep contented until
dawn.'

Embarrassment flooded through her, making her limbs weak
and her cheeks burn. 'Were you watching?' she breathed, puzzled
by the excitement that replaced her shock. His words seemed to
imply a compliment.

He ignored her question. 'We don't have much time unless you
want Malika and Jagath to get the wrong idea about what we are
doing here.'

'The wrong idea . . . ?' She was tormented by confusing
emotions. 'I thought you wanted . . . me.'

'Is that why you came so willingly?' His laugh was husky and
riddled with mockery. 'Ah, Raven, you haven't heard a word I
said. *You are in danger.* I can help you.'

She reeled as though he had slapped her, the sting of his scorn
ringing in her ear. He tugged her arm and she stiffened.

'Listen to me!' His voice changed to a threat. 'I said you are in
danger. You are.'

'That's a lie,' she gasped. 'You've been leading me on, playing
with me like I'm a silly goose. Do you know what wild fire you've
ignited in me? Your very touch' – she tried to jerk her arm free –
'does strange things to me. You're wicked, you're a sorcerer in
disguise. What devil's powers do you have? *You're* the danger, I
know it!'

Her tears took her by surprise, welling out in a gush of
frustration. She wanted to sink to the ground and bury her head in
her hands but his firm grip still held her. She shook with sobs,
crying for herself, longing for Bart to save her.

She felt a hand stroking her shoulders with a gentleness she
didn't believe possible from a man whose other hand fettered her
wrist like a manacle.

She surrendered to his touch and rested her head on his bare
chest. Her shaking calmed at the fascination of feeling the beat of
his heart against her cheek. The aroma of his body was exhilarating. Her mouth brushed against his nipple, already moist with her
tears. Her lips parted and she was filled with a sensation of peace.

'You can trust me.' He eased her head away from him, lowering
his lips to whisper in her ear. 'I am your friend.' His breath tingled
her cheek. 'You need me.'

She wavered, trying to comprehend what he said. A war of

emotions waged in her because her heart refused to believe what her mind told her. She was completely in his power and he was taking advantage of her. Yet he was also offering her a hand of friendship, not the fickle love of a seducer.

'Release me,' she said. 'I can't think properly when you hold me like that.'

Her hand was freed. She took a deep breath. The night's chill sobered her. Under her robe her nude body quivered. She glanced across at Jagath who was peering in the dark in her direction.

'He'll say nothing.' Kumara's voice was hard with authority. It roused her.

'What is this danger you talk of?' she demanded, forcing herself to act normally, despite his nearness.

'Someone, I don't know who, is threatening Bart. I saved his life on the Galle road, and I saved the mill.'

'It is Bart who is threatened, not me.'

'You are his wife, his weakness. He is tough but he will be weak if you or the children are attacked.'

'Why are you interested?'

'Kirti is said to be the son of my kinsman. Tonight I confirmed by his birthmark that our family rumour is true. I am pledged to protect the child now I've found him. I will help you and Bart too.'

She listened to his words, uncertain what to do. He sounded convincing. Bart himself had sworn to Kirti's father, Prince Gamunu, that he would foster the boy. He had accepted the priceless elephant pearl to seal the agreement.

'How do you know about Kirti?' she asked suspiciously.

'Prince Gamunu told us before he died. He is his chosen heir. If ever the Kingdom of Kandy is restored, the throne is his.'

Raven smiled in the darkness at the youth's delusion. 'The British have conquered Kandy. Even the uprising didn't change that.'

She heard her remark dismissed with a soft cluck of annoyance. 'There are those who believe the kingdom will be revived. Some of them want Kirti, some of them don't.'

His tone caused her to shudder. 'What do you mean?'

'There are rival claimants. If his rivals discover the rumour is true, like I did, that Bart's son is really Gamunu's, he will be executed.'

His words stabbed her, tearing at her insides. It was as she feared. This man's arrival in their home pressaged disaster for all she and Bart valued.

'You are lying!' She turned away from him in despair and began to walk back to the nursery. Jagath was holding up the lantern, straining his eyes to see her. Malika grasped his arm as though begging him not to interfere.

'If I am lying, how do you explain the attacks on Bart, the fire at the mill –'

She stopped before she reached the rim of light. Her mind was clear now. She waited for him to come to her side. 'Why did you tell me your name is Kumara? Bart calls you Pathirana.'

His laugh gusted in her face and she flinched. 'My name is Kumara Santa Pathirana. What lie is there in that?'

She gazed at him, her mind a crazy mixture of hope and fear. If he was speaking the truth, she and Bart needed his help. If it was lies, why was he frightening her with his evil fantasies?

She walked into the light, noticing the glimmer of relief that passed across Jagath's face. He turned away discreetly. Kumara followed her.

When she turned to give him her answer, she saw his face. A muscle flicked angrily at his jaw. His eyes were narrow and his mouth thin with displeasure. She was aghast at the rage ill-concealed in his tense features. His voice in the darkness had given no clue to the fury sparked off by her questions.

'Forgive me,' she said, lowering her lashes to hide her discovery of his weakness. 'I was wrong to doubt you.'

'Of course.' His expression relaxed and his eyes twinkled flirtatiously. 'Now will you do what I say?'

'It depends.' She smiled provocatively, her knowledge giving her the power to resist his charm.

She had discovered that he angered quickly when his word was doubted. Anger made the strongest man weak. It was useful to know if ever she needed to defend herself against his compelling fascination.

The morning dawned with a fine mist filling the valley and a haze hanging over the sugar-canes. Birds chirped and whistled busily. Coucals, a bird like an English pheasant, clucked as they skulked at the field's edge foraging for insects. Cocks crowed in the settlement, blending with the chatter of the natives as they prepared for the day's labour.

For Bart, the day began as usual when he sat on the verandah, blinking himself awake and sipping a bowl of hot, black un-sweetened coffee. Raven joined him.

When she came to the villa as his wife, he wanted her to sleep as late as she liked in the mornings. She had different ideas. She rose with him at dawn to plan their day together.

Jagath was waiting on the verandah for Bart to be roused properly and give him his orders. Daisy, who had served the coffee, lingered to contribute her suggestions about what she and Little wanted to cook for dinner.

It had taken time for Raven to defeat Daisy's natural bossiness. The routine of the household after her arrival was established only gradually. Now there was no doubt in the minds of the slaves that Raven was the mistress. She was not going to be bullied by any of them.

'Daisy!' she said as the housekeeper pouted sulkily behind Bart's back. 'I saw the lantern burning last night in the storeroom. Do you have a paramour?'

'Mistis?' Daisy's mouth fell open with surprise.

Raven smiled, pleased with herself. She had been worried that Daisy would make a comment about seeing her in the courtyard with Kumara. Before Bart discovered from her, she intended to tell him her version.

'I'm sure the master wouldn't approve of strangers in the storeroom without his knowledge.'

'What?' Bart stirred, obviously not hearing what she said. He was still gazing thoughtfully at the mist, watching it lift slowly from the canes and drift off into the jungle as the breeze whispered down the valley.

'I was restless last night, Bart,' Raven explained, using the story she had concocted with Kumara.

'I went for a walk in the courtyard.' She paused, waiting for Bart to react.

He was still drowsy, or distracted by his survey of the sugar-cane. He barely heard what she said. It was going as she planned.

'Daisy's lantern was lit for her paramour.'

'No, mistis. I done burn de candle all night. I ain't have no para-mour lamp.'

She hid her smile at Daisy's misunderstanding because she wanted to appear severe in case the slave *had* seen her. 'Why weren't you asleep?' she asked sternly.

'I was, mistis!'

'Didn't you hear me calling you?'

'Lawd, no. I ain't hear nothin'.'

'Very good.' Raven permitted herself a smile. 'Perhaps I was mistaken.' She paused, knowing how to mollify the slave. 'Why don't you arrange dinner today? You and Little could prepare one of your specialities. I'll be too busy to come near the kitchen.'

Daisy's swagger as she sashayed off the verandah showed she regarded her honour as being restored after the doubts cast on her probity.

Raven observed how Jagath watched the exchange with interest. His English was poor but his humble and obliging manner made him intensely loyal. She was satisfied that he would say nothing to Bart about her conduct in the courtyard the night before.

She sighed and sat back in her chair, confident she had diffused the crisis before it could begin. Bart would never know. She sighed again and became conscious of him watching her quizzically.

'You're in an anxious mood this morning.'

'I told you. I didn't sleep well.' She chose her words carefully. 'Will you spend the day in the house with us . . . with me and the children?'

He put the empty coffee bowl down on the table and stood up. Jagath stepped back nervously at his display of energy. Hope flared in Raven's mind that she had sparked off the reaction she wanted.

'Impossible!' he said. 'I've been looking at the cane.' He pointed at the canepiece as though she hadn't noticed it herself. 'It's ripe. We must start cutting while it's juicy.'

'Don't go today, Bart. You were away in Galle yesterday. Once you start harvesting the cane, we'll only see you in the evenings. You'll be too worn out to play with the children. You should spend more time with them as Garth's going to England in a few days.'

'How can I?' He spread his hands wide in exasperation. 'I have to be at the mill.'

'I thought Tissa was capable of running it himself.' She kept a straight face so he wouldn't guess what she was trying to make him do.

'He is. Oh, Raven!' Bart turned to look at her. He bent down and held both hands in his, letting her see his sorrow.

'Don't you understand? With what's been happening lately, we must be extra vigilant. If there was someone to help me, someone I could trust, I could spend more time here with you.'

She felt a twinge of guilt at trying to manipulate him.

'An Englishman?' she suggested. 'Couldn't you hire someone in Galle? Surely there are prospective settlers you could meet at the

88

quay. Daddy told me plenty of Englishmen arrive on every sailing.'

'Maybe they do, Raven.' He released her hands and leaned against one of the columns that supported the deeply-pitched roof of the verandah. The sun's rays were beginning to seep through the shade trees at the verandah's side. The heat increased as the mist wafted away.

He mopped his brow, showing his concern for her. 'Those Englishmen wouldn't be good here. How do they know who is friend or foe? Besides, they'd wilt in this heat, and they certainly couldn't handle the natives.'

'Yes,' she said, sounding resigned. 'I suppose I must manage with the children by myself.'

'Pathirana is here. He'll be company for you this morning.'

She deliberately looked a trifle anxious. 'Can we trust him? We know so little about him.'

'Don't worry! I had a long chat with him last night. I misjudged him at first. What I took to be arrogance is shyness. He's met people I know in London. I must write to them when I get time.'

'If you say so, Bart.'

'Of course he's all right. He's a perfect gentleman and tough to boot.' He fell silent suddenly, then spun around. 'Dam'me! Perhaps he can stay for the cane harvest? He could give me a hand and I'd get more time to be with you.'

Raven preened herself behind her smile of delight. She had achieved what Kumara had asked her to do: persuade Bart to invite him to stay on the plantation. Only by living in the villa, he had explained, could he help protect them.

'It's a good idea,' she murmured, careful not to sound too enthusiastic and make Bart suspicious. 'I doubt if he'll accept. He's far too intelligent to waste his time here.'

Bart frowned at her criticism. 'He told me he wants to start a plantation of his own on family land in the hills beyond Matara. What better way for him to learn than to stay with us for a while.'

Raven kept silent and lowered her eyes. Now the idea was planted firmly in Bart's mind she would let it take its course. The thought that Kumara would become a permanent guest in the villa filled her with apprehension.

Because of her encounter with him the previous night there was now a genuine bond between them. She wondered how long it would be before that bond was forged into a link that neither of them could escape.

The days that followed Kumara's engagement as Bart's deputy were anxious ones for Raven. She understood the need for Kumara to be circumspect in his dealings with her, but she did not anticipate the brutal coldness in his eyes whenever he looked at her. He was cruelly correct in his behaviour, even when they were alone on the verandah and Bart was far off in the fields.

Under his influence, the routine of the household changed subtly, demoting Raven in status. Somehow he diverted the chain of command so that her orders to the slaves were checked with him first.

Daisy, who had protested at this intrusion into the running of the house, succumbed as swiftly as the others to Kumara's charm. She wriggled and giggled in his presence and sought him out to seek his approval whenever Raven asked her to do something special.

Raven was amazed when he even managed to win over Mammy Sobers.

'He de only coolie I meet who have sense.' Mammy explained to her when she and Kumara were on the verandah. Bart had arrived late from the mill and was eating his supper in the dining room.

'That's because I love England,' Kumara replied glibly.

Raven sensed it was a lie designed to placate Mammy. She had been complaining about having to take Garth to England to school. She was due to sail the next day.

'I'd give anything to be you tomorrow,' Kumara continued. 'With your splendid looks and fortune you'll have a wonderful time in England. You'll have to be careful, though. You'll have dozens of young blades propositioning you.'

Mammy's huge body shook and she wheezed with happy laughter. Raven found Kumara's flattery so obvious, she wondered how such a formidable old lady was sweetened by it.

'I dare say you're right, young man.' Mammy simpered with delight, the dimples deep in her plump cheeks. 'Be sure you take good care of my Bart and Mistis Raven while I gone.'

'Rely on me, Mammy.' Kumara pinched her cheek and her eyes watered with pleasure. Raven smiled with relief that the old lady had forgotten her grumbles about the voyage.

Bart strolled onto the verandah with Garth. The boy was being allowed to stay up late for his last night. In his hand, Bart held a sealed jug of rum. Garth carried glasses which he handed out to Mammy, Kumara and Raven, saving one each for his father and himself.

'What's this?' Raven raised her eyebrow.

'A toast. It's a new jug of rum I brought from the mill.' Bart broke open the red seal and passed around the group, pouring rum into each glass. He smiled at Garth.

'Only a dram for you, son. You'll not drink Bloodheart rum again until you return. You'll be a man then and all this will be waiting for you.' He waved his hand and the jug in an arc to include the plantation beyond the verandah.

A prickle of fear ran up Raven's spine at his words.

'I'll give you a toast,' Bart said, raising his glass.

The others followed suit and prepared to drink except for Mammy who took a quick swig from her glass instead of waiting. Kumara sniffed suspiciously at the rum.

Bart looked around the group, waiting until he had their attention. 'On the eve of my son going to England,' he began expansively, 'I want to say –'

A crash interrupted him. Kumara's chair fell over as he lunged for Mammy and knocked the glass from her hand. 'Don't drink that!' he cried.

'I done so a'ready!' She looked at him with startled eyes, the yellow in them slowly disappearing as her head lolled back and the whites bulged out beneath drawn lids.

'Oh lawd . . .' she gasped, then stopped, a trickle of black vomit billowing on her lips.

Raven jumped from her seat. 'Mammy!' She rushed over to her as Kumara pulled at the tassles on her dress, trying to unfasten her bodice to give her a chance to breathe.

'It's too late,' he said grimly. 'She's dead.'

'Dead?' Bart sniffed his own glass of rum. An expression of horror creased his face. He flung the glass angrily out into the night.

'It's poisoned!' he groaned, snatching Garth's glass from his hand and smashing it to the floor.

'I've killed Mammy!'

CHAPTER ELEVEN

Raven knew instinctively what to do. 'Get Daisy,' she shouted at Kumara, jerking him away from Mammy by his shoulder. 'Hurry!' she added when she saw his dark eyes widen with astonishment at her command.

She gave him a push in his chest. 'Daisy!' she repeated. 'Hurry!'

Her urgency seemed to amuse him. He drew away from Mammy's lifeless form with a shrug of compliance and sauntered off the verandah. Bart was standing behind Raven with his arms around Garth, hugging the boy to him as he whimpered with shock.

'Do keep quiet, Bart!' she snapped at him. 'I can't hear if her heart's beating.'

'I killed her.'

'No, you didn't.' She wiped away the vomit with her handkerchief and put her ear to Mammy's chest. 'I'm not sure if she's dead.'

'Kumara said –'

She stood up and glared at him. 'He could be wrong!' Her temper softened at the sight of his anguished face. 'Please take Garth to the nursery. Daisy will know what to do.'

As soon as he had gone, she unfastened Mammy's dress. She imagined she could feel her enormous body expanding when she loosened the stays. She didn't want to accept Kumara's verdict but the sight of Mammy slumped in the chair without breathing offered little hope.

'Damn!' she muttered, borrowing one of Bart's favourite oaths to give vent to her vexation. She struck Mammy a sharp blow on her chest, wishing she could beat her back to life. She was worried about Bart's reaction, knowing the guilt he felt.

Daisy bustled onto the verandah, followed by a grinning Kumara. She moved away and looked at Daisy hopefully. 'She only took a sip of the rum,' she said.

'Serves her right for being greedy.'

'Kumara!' Raven turned her eyes on him, dismayed by his callousness. 'This is woman's work. Go to Bart. Find out where he got the rum. Maybe the whole batch is poisoned. Do something instead of gawping at Daisy like she's a witch.'

She turned to see what Kumara was staring at. Daisy was hoisting Mammy to a sitting position, smacking her on her back and rocking her backwards and forwards. More vomit trickled out of her mouth and down her chin.

'Water, mistis, lots of it.'

Raven glared at Kumara and was pleased when he did what was required of him without protest. He hurried away instead of ambling and within seconds Jagath brought a pitcher of water.

'It's all right.' Kumara's voice came from the doorway. 'I've tasted it.' He snorted with scorn. 'Mustn't poison someone who's already dead!'

'She ain't dead yet!' Daisy snatched the pitcher from Jagath and poured water directly from it into Mammy's half-open mouth. She continued to rock her backwards and forwards in a frantic effort to revive her. She was rewarded with a slurry of vomit and water gushing out and seeping into Mammy's red velvet dress.

A rattling sound began in the depths of Mammy's throat. It grew louder, gradually becoming a voluble grumble. 'Oh lawd . . .' Her words disintegrated into a fit of retching as she discharged the residue of the poisoned rum from her stomach.

Raven glanced at the doorway in triumph. Kumara had gone. 'Look after her, Daisy,' she said and hastened into the house.

Bart and Kumara were sitting opposite each other under the picture of his mother on the wall. Bart's head was in his hands and he was moaning softly to himself. Kumara jumped to his feet, relieved to see her.

'She's all right, Bart.' She walked straight over to him and put her hands around his shoulders. 'Mammy's not dead. She'll be all right.'

He raised his head and blinked at her. 'It's . . . it's a miracle.'

'Is it? I don't believe that poison was meant to kill her, or any of us.'

'What gives you that idea?' Kumara sounded peeved.

The tone of his voice puzzled her. As she gazed at him she wondered if he could really be trusted. The sight of his lean body, his muscular limbs in tight breeches, and his darkly flashing eyes still held their fascination for her. Everything about him proclaimed a tempting sensuality she yearned to know.

Most of the time she was under his spell, in awe of him and content to be so. It was only in the moments when her natural impulsiveness reasserted itself that she shook off his influence and began to doubt.

'What do you think?' she challenged.

He was speechless. His eyes glinted angrily and his mouth tightened. She was reminded of a wild animal suddenly cornered and about to lash out. The knowledge that she had upset him and penetrated his cold mask of mockery was intoxicating.

'Surely you have some theory?' Her smile was as wickedly taunting as any he had flashed at her.

He scowled and turned away, his shoulders hunched. Instantly she knew she had goaded him too far. How could he speak his mind in front of Bart?

She wept inside at her stupidity, wondering if – for the sake of a cheap jibe – she had lost him. She wanted to leave Bart's side and rush over to him, seize his waist and force him to face her. He would see then that her eyes burned with a desire for him that was stronger than ever.

'What's going on?'

Bart's question startled her. She put out her hand and touched him nervously on his shoulder. 'I don't know,' she said in a small, meek voice.

'Someone poisoned the rum,' said Kumara, his authority restored. He paced across the parlour, thinking aloud, addressing his remarks to Bart.

Raven watched him wonderingly, hoping for a sign.

'We'll go to the mill and find out how. It's my guess it's a single jug that was planted there without you knowing.'

'It was the only jug.' Bart held Raven's hand.

She let it lie limply in his grasp although she found his touch reassuring after her fright.

'Did Tissa give it to you?'

'It was on a shelf where we put the sample flasks. I assumed it was from the new distillation.' Bart hesitated, his eyes on Kumara as he walked from one side of the parlour to the other. He turned to Raven and squeezed her hand.

'That's why I thought I was responsible for killing Mammy. It seemed to be my fault.'

'I understand.' She stroked his arm. 'Shall I go? You want to discuss it man to man with Kumara.'

'Stay!' Kumara's gruff command chilled her and she gaped at him. Bart pulled himself upright and looked concerned.

'I repeat what I asked you earlier. Why do you think the poisoned rum was not for us?'

'I didn't say that.' She was pleased to be acknowledged by Kumara again, but bridled at his thick-headedness. 'The rum was not *intended* to kill Mammy, or any of us. It was to frighten us.'

'It did that all right.' Bart grinned ruefully.

She was grateful for his support even though he sounded patronizing. Kumara looked genuinely puzzled. She explained in a low, modest voice so he wouldn't be offended by her astuteness.

'It follows the pattern. Bart *could* have been killed when they cut off his ear, but he wasn't. The mill *could* have been completely destroyed but we had time to save it. Bart *could* have been thrown from his horse but he's a good horseman. We *could* have been poisoned but the dose was too light to do more than cause vomiting.'

As if to confirm what she said was true, Mammy burst into the parlour. Daisy was holding her arm but she shook off her support and stood in the centre of the room, her arms akimbo. Her bodice was loose; her dishevelled appearance reducing the impact of her indignation.

'Bart Taylor, I pleased I leavin' here! Dat rum de worse you ever produce.' She wagged a plump finger at him. 'You want to be rid of Mammy. I goin' 'fore you kill me proper.'

Raven giggled, triggering off Bart's own laughter. Even Kumara joined in.

'Dis ain't no laughin' matter!' Mammy yanked up her bosom, saw her bodice was adrift, and shut her mouth. She glanced at them all reproachfully but they were too pleased to see her alive to stop laughing.

Raven left Bart's side and held Mammy lovingly in her arms. She kissed her. 'We'll miss you,' she said, a tear quivering at the corner of her eye. 'Come back soon.'

Raven had her own ideas about the odd things happening at the plantation. Bart and Kumara took precautions to protect them all and she followed their instructions obediently, despite her misgivings. Garth and Mammy sailed for England without incident which reduced Bart's anxiety, knowing his son was beyond threat.

At the same time, Bart decided that Ranita should go to the settlement to live. She was close to Tissa, her father, and spoke Singhala better than English. Tissa had built himself a fine home on a rise overlooking the native settlement and had space for her.

Raven was relieved to see Ranita leave the villa. She was a selfish, brooding girl given to rash outbursts of pique if she wanted attention. She was only pleasant when she was with Tissa, matching his placid nature with a dutiful serenity. The villa was more peaceful without her.

Raven regained control of the household she had unwittingly surrendered to Kumara. Instead of concern about their security, he became obsessed with Kirti. He saw danger to the child lurking in every corner of the villa. He tasted the boy's food before it was served, tried the child's juice and, to Malika's chagrin, took the boy to sleep in his own chamber at night.

Bart was content with the arrangement. He told Raven he could protect himself; it was the child who was at risk. Since Kumara was a kinsman of the boy's father, it relieved him of his obligation to raise Kirti as his own son. He believed, like Kumara, that the attacks on the plantation were the work of disaffected Kandyans out for revenge.

Raven kept her thoughts to herself. She was encouraged by Kumara's interest in the young boy. *Bloodheart royal*, Malika called Kirti. Since he was a prince's son, Raven found it fitting that a princely man, like Kumara, should be his tutor.

She was satisfied his affection for the child was genuine. She sensed his cold and calculating manner mellowing because he was taking care of Kirti.

This pleased her because it made him more human. Instead of sparring when they spoke, a mutual respect entered their conversations.

She still thrilled if she caught a glimpse of him when a shaft of sunlight shone on his ruggedly handsome features, transforming him into her idea of a Greek god. Or when he stretched his limbs in his skin-tight breeches, unaware that her eyes were on him.

The tremor of passion was never far from the surface when they spoke. If he touched her she would retreat to the privacy of her chamber until her limbs stopped trembling and her heart resumed its normal rhythm.

They had acknowledged, without speaking of it, that their lives were inextricably linked for a time. She thrived on the suspense that gripped her whenever they were alone together.

Kumara's certainty that Kirti was the reason for the attacks on Bart was a challenge to her. He was not infallible. She was consumed with an urge to prove him wrong. It wasn't that she hated him and wanted to oust him from the villa. It was the opposite.

If she could beat him at his own game, it was a kind of possession of him. It was possession only of his spirit; possession of his body being out of the question. She loved Bart; Kumara was a contest.

She became as much like an animal as Kumara was, lying in wait for prey. She was handicapped by not knowing what, or whom, she was looking for, and by not being allowed to leave the villa alone. Her only clue was the cat's eye ring at the bottom of her needlework box, and her memory of the silhouette of the man sprinting from the mill blaze.

She dwelt on the possible reasons someone would have for plotting to frighten Bart. She was sure that his death was not the object of the attacks. She wondered too about the mentality of the plotter. If he knew Bart well he would know the name of Bloodheart was apt.

The more Bart was subjected to pressure, the braver and more determined he could become. Therefore, she reasoned, the person behind the campaign against him was a stranger, unfamiliar with his personality.

She hated to admit that Kumara was right, yet his suspicion seemed the soundest. The Kandyan enemies of Kirti's father couldn't be expected to know that Bart was tougher than he looked. They would expect him to be intimidated by their scare tactics. So maybe Kumara was correct, the assailants *were* trying to get at Kirti.

Her speculation and anger peaked when Bart announced at the dinner table that he was abandoning the cane harvest.

'Why?' she asked in amazement, knowing how important it was to him. 'You're only half way through. There must be five hundred acres of cane left to cut.'

He sighed, slumping forward in his chair, defeat written over his weary features. 'It will never be cut, Raven. The natives are leaving.'

She looked at him askance. If he didn't cut the cane there would be a shortage of sugar. He would have insufficient to ship to England and none for distilling into rum. Cane was labour intensive, many hands were needed to harvest a field within a day when

97

it was at its best. If the cutting took too long, the cane became over-ripe or dried up and spoiled.

'Tissa's never had trouble finding hands before.'

'He says none of the natives will work. They're leaving the settlement.'

'Why?' She stiffened, drawing back her shoulders defiantly. A sudden insight gave her confidence. Kumara, at the other end of the dining table, appeared unconcerned.

'They say they're not safe here. They say the plantation is cursed.'

'What has happened?' She reached out and touched him, hoping he would share his disappointment with her. She felt a sense of relief when he placed his hand over hers and his opal blue eyes turned sorrowfully on her.

'Small things. One of the boys fell into a sugar vat and was boiled to death. Another had his arm trapped in the millstones. I had to chop it off. Someone else sliced his own leg in two in the field with his cutlass.'

'Accidents are commonplace in the cane season.'

'Coming after the fire . . .' He sighed again. 'They're scared, they're leaving.'

'I know what's behind this,' she said excitedly. 'Someone's planted the idea in their minds. They've never been frightened before. They're fatalists. They don't run away.' She pleaded with Kumara with her eyes for support for her view.

'You are probably right, Raven.' He smiled smoothly. 'If someone is making them leave, how can Bloodheart stop them?'

She was angered by his superior attitude. 'By showing them it's not true. The plantation *isn't* cursed. He *must* make them stay.' She turned on Bart as fury welled within her. 'Can't you compel them to work. Do something, instead of giving up.'

'I'm not giving up, Raven.' The tiredness vanished from his eyes under her gaze of outrage. 'If they were slaves I could take the whip to them. They are free men.'

'They have the mentality of slaves. They're used to tilling the soil under a master's command.' She couldn't help noticing the glow of appreciation in Kumara's eyes at her outburst. 'Have you ordered them to work?'

'Without an army of slave drivers, what can I do?'

'Give me a whip and I'll show you.'

'Bravo!' Kumara clapped his hands and she withered under his gust of satanic laughter. 'Your wife has the makings of a Tartar, Bloodheart.'

'She is thinking of the plantation.' Bart looked at her proudly and she was buoyed by his defence of her. 'Sugar is our livelihood, Kumara.' He was suddenly pensive.

'Perhaps it's justice,' he continued after a pause. 'For some reason, the canes are dry this year. The sugar is very inferior. I was wondering if it is worth shipping to England at all. I've never made a profit on the sugar I've sent there. It can't compete with the West Indies crop.'

'You must harvest the rest!' She refused to share his pessimism. 'You can use it for rum. Every cane in the fields means money and labour were utilised to grow it. Is that to go to waste? Have all your sacrifices been in vain?' She glared at him with an unladylike grimace.

'Just because a few superstitious natives are too idle to work!' She jumped from the table in her rage and stormed out of the dining room. Kumara's rich chuckle resounded mockingly in her ears.

She was infuriated by Bart's complacency and Kumara's derision. She admired both men for the same reason: their strength and manliness. Yet both of them seemed flawed.

Was she the only one to see clearly what was wrong? The natives were running away because of the campaign to harass Bart. He must stop it. If he didn't, she would!

She passed through the parlour in a cloud of rancour, enraged by the two men who stayed at their seats in the dining room. The door through the parlour to the verandah was locked. Kumara and Bart had forbidden her to go on the verandah after dusk because it was impossible to see who might be lurking outside in the dark.

The key was in the lock and she turned it, opening the door defiantly. She ignored Nimal who wanted to stop her, his sarong snapping at his ankles as he hurried to block her way.

She stepped out onto the verandah and slammed the door in his face. She locked it, regretting her rudeness but she was angered beyond reason by the crassness of Bart and Kumara.

She swept over the tiled deck of the verandah, her skirt catching the card table in its wake and toppling it over. The crash strengthened her resolve. She would tell the natives a thing or two, and get them working, whatever Bart did.

The silence as the echo of the falling table died away disturbed her. She leaned against a pillar to recover her breath and control the shaking of her hands. She hated defying Bart.

A noise in the garden made her pause. She gulped, shutting out the roaring anger in her ears to concentrate on the sound.

She stepped back from the verandah's edge, terrifyingly aware that the noises she heard were not in her mind but on the path coming up from the mill. There was a jangling of horse bridles and the stamp of marching feet.

She gasped, clasping her hand to her mouth to still her shriek of fear. A troop of men seemed to spring from the darkness, filling the garden in front of the villa.

Behind her, Bart and Kumara were banging on the locked parlour door. She turned to let them out but it was too late. The men were at the verandah step.

CHAPTER TWELVE

'An army you wanted, an army you've got.'

Kumara stared at her, incredulity bright in his eyes. Bart was more prosaic. He laid a calm hand on her arm before greeting the men milling in front of the verandah.

'Who are they?' hissed Kumara behind his back.

Raven ignored his question, letting him stew in his doubt. Seconds before, she had been poised on the verge of terror until the scarlet of tunics and the pink of mottled white faces were revealed in the dim light from the now opened parlour door. As fast as it had seized her, her fear evaporated and the arrival of the British soldiers filled her with hope instead.

She looked up at Kumara's perplexed face and smiled coyly.

'Captain Walker!'

Bart's eager greeting made her turn from Kumara to watch as he embraced the officer with obvious delight.

'Forgive my delay in receiving you. Our door lock jammed.' Bart glanced at Raven. 'This is so unexpected.' He waved his hand around the verandah. 'You're very welcome, come in!'

She smiled at his enthusiasm and swept past Kumara to the parlour. 'They're from the garrison at Galle,' she whispered, feeling sorry for Kumara's confusion.

'Don't worry, they'll not harm Kirti.' She left him standing in the doorway waiting to be introduced as she went to instruct the houseboys to bring lanterns.

The arrival of the soldiers was a godsend, the solution to the native reluctance to work. Bart was too overwhelmed at their coming to think clearly. She expected him and Kumara to reject her idea. In case they did, she would act on it herself.

Someone had started a rumour that made the natives abandon the cane cutting. She proposed to start a rumour that would make them return.

After the servants were roused, the lanterns lit, and Nimal and

Jagath had carried bottles of rum and glasses out to the verandah for the soldiers, she sat in the parlour and considered her scheme.

'Jagath,' she called softly when the boy hurried towards the verandah with a tray of devilled *cadju* nuts, spicy warm cashews from the kitchen. 'Let Nimal serve that. I want you to go to the settlement.'

He gawped at her and, for once, she was pleased about his poor understanding of English. As long as he got the gist of her message, he could be relied on to add his own embellishments.

'You see the soldiers,' she said patiently, waiting for him to nod his head. She beckoned him closer.

'Do you know why they have come here?'

He frowned, puzzled by her question.

She sensed his worry about why he was being taken into her confidence. She lowered her voice. 'I'll tell you a secret.'

He fidgeted, almost jumping from his skin when she laid her hand on his arm.

'Do you have friends in the settlement?' She took a firm hold of his wrist. 'This is important!'

He nodded again, too tongue-tied to speak but his eyes were alert.

'The soldiers have come for your friends,' she said, lying blithely. 'Anyone who misses work in the canefields tomorrow will be hunted down and arrested. They will go to gaol in Galle. No work, gaol.' She emphasized her words with a squeeze of his wrist.

He shifted his feet uncomfortably. When she released his hand, he rapidly untied and re-knotted his sarong in a nervous reaction to her closeness.

'It's a secret,' she repeated, hoping she could rely on him being sufficiently impressed to spread the rumour.

'I don't want the soldiers to gaol your friends. Go to the settlement now and warn them. They *must* work in the canefields tomorrow, and *every* day. If they don't, the soldiers will hunt them down. Do you understand?'

The look of terror on his face showed he did. He nodded shakily.

'Good.' She smiled. 'Don't let the soldiers catch you.' She held up a finger. 'No work, gaol,' she repeated as he backed out of the room.

She leaned her head on the ornately-carved wooden arm of the couch and sighed. She had done her best. Strangely, she was free of qualms about her lie. What she was doing was for Bart, and to show Kumara that Bart was going to survive.

She glanced up. The picture of his mother was watching her. There seemed to be a glint of approval in the old lady's eyes.

She stood up and tossed her head, inspired by the challenge of helping Bart without him knowing. Her lustrous black tresses shimmered in the flickering flame from the candles in the chandelier, slowly settling to frame her face.

She composed her features into the expression of a meek and dutiful wife that the soldiers would expect, and glided out onto the verandah.

The evening was a lively one. The captain was intimidated by Kumara sitting with them as an equal until the rum loosened his tongue. He soon succumbed under the influence of Kumara's smooth charm and became quite hearty.

He had brought a letter for Raven from her father. Probably to impress Kumara, he presented it to her with all the pomp and flourish of delivering an official document.

She excused herself reluctantly from the jolly atmosphere on the verandah and took the letter to her chamber to read. The soldiers were noisily setting up camp in the small meadow behind the stable. She heard them even with her shutters fastened. Their boyish good humour was a tonic.

She stared at the letter thoughtfully, trying to guess its contents. After breaking its seal, she placed it on her pillow to read when she was in bed.

She had never been close to her father. She came to Ceylon because of his unexpected promotion from being a long-serving adjutant in the governor's office to the new post of Collector of Galle. She lived four restless years as the housekeeper and hostess of his official residence until Bart rescued her.

Bart was all she expected him to be. She could not blame him for his slowness in tackling problems. There were times when a woman, by her very nature, saw things clearer than a man. She had always been curious and impulsive. Bart himself had said she would be fiercely loyal to the man who possessed her, and an ardent friend or ruthless enemy to others.

She lay down on the bed, sleep dragging at her eyes. She picked up the letter and unfolded it, wondering why her father had written. The words, in his precise clerk's hand, swam before her eyes. Blinking away her tiredness, she read the letter slowly.

It was typical of her father; it said nothing. There were enquiries

103

about her health and welfare and a complaint about the monsoon heat and the duties he was obliged to perform in Galle. It ended by wishing her well.

She tossed the letter aside more puzzled than before about why he had bothered to write. She felt mildly sorry for him, having no company except the hapless Englishman who was his assistant.

She sat up suddenly as an idea struck her. She groped for the letter among her bedclothes. She scanned it again. Yes, it provided the excuse she needed. She settled down to wait for Bart, the letter lodged under her pillow.

He was weaving slightly when he entered the chamber. His cheeks were flushed above the spread of his beard and his hair was in disarray. She was warned by the signs of his drunkenness to be careful when she broached the matter in her mind.

'I'm so happy,' she said drowsily. 'It's wonderful having Captain Walker and his men here.'

'What?' His eyes narrowed as he focused on her. 'I thought you'd be put out having them rowdies around.'

'It's entertaining.'

He scratched his head and sat down to pull off his boots.

She didn't speak for a few moments, giving him time to undress. He was quick to take umbrage when he was drunk. The slightest wrong move by her, or wrong word, could set him off in a tizzy. On the other hand, he could also be perfectly malleable, chuckling with delight and agreeing to whatever she wanted.

'I do hope the soldiers will be all right in the meadow.'

He grunted. 'Why shouldn't they be?'

'Poor Captain Walker!' She giggled. 'I don't suppose he likes having to bivouac on the hard ground. You should ask him to stay here.'

'I did,' he answered grudgingly. 'He's passed out on the couch in the parlour. You're not cross?'

'I'm pleased.' She laughed again, encouraging him to laugh too. 'He's a nice man, a good friend to you.'

'You used to object to my spending time with him and the other officers in Galle.'

'I was a silly young girl then. Now I'm your wife.' She gazed at him through lowered lashes and smiled warmly.

He flung his breeches aside and staggered over to the bed. The mattress slumped as he bounced on it.

She turned her back to him to avoid inhaling the odour of rum. His hands closed over her breasts as he wrapped himself around

104

her. She curled against him and he grunted with contentment. In a few minutes he would be asleep.

'I've read the letter from daddy,' she said softly.

'What does the old boy want?' He nuzzled her neck with his nose.

'He's very lonely.' She squirmed when his beard tickled her. Her bottom rubbed against his thighs. 'I suppose I should visit him, but I don't want to leave you.'

'You can't go,' he said, chuckling to himself as his fingers fondled her nipples and they hardened to his touch. 'Too dangerous.'

A surge of wanting engulfed her; she wriggled to keep her mind on what she had to ask. 'I could go with the soldiers when they return. There's no danger staying with daddy. He'd be so pleased.'

'Why should I please him?' He gnawed her ear.

She pushed closer, overwhelmed as his hand descended between her thighs. She was moist when his finger found her and began to delve into the warmth of her being.

'To please me . . .' she uttered breathlessly, abandoning herself to him.

Galle was a riot of colour. The monsoon clouds had been blown away, taking with them the enervating dullness that pervaded the town. People were sprightly as they walked the streets in the breeze wafting in from the sea.

Crowds thronged the stalls and boutiques or strolled the ramparts giving the fort an air of gaiety. The brightly-hued saris and *comboy* waist cloths of the women vividly matched the colourful raiment of the men dressed at their best.

Raven was enchanted to be in Galle after an absence of several months. Although it resembled a chaotic oriental bazaar instead of the island's main port, its dirt and commotion were like civilisation to her after being confined to the villa.

Fields of sugar-cane that stretched as far as the eye could see were no substitute for the vibrancy of town life. Even the smell of the fort's underground sewers when the tide was too low to flush them clean, and the aroma of charcoal fires and sweating crowds was preferable to the cloying stench of boiling sugar that permeated her clothes and hair at the villa.

She walked the streets in a daze in the company of Mrs Redmount, an officer's wife awaiting a ship back to England. They were trailed by a bored escort of two armed and uniformed soldiers.

Part of the agreement she made with Bart before he gave his consent for her to visit Galle was that she would never venture into the streets without a chaperon and an escort. Captain Walker had guaranteed to see she obeyed his instructions.

She regarded Bart's concern as ill-placed. She was worried for his sake. Her fascination with Kumara did not blind her to the devilry that lurked beneath his dashing charm. With her absence from the villa, Kumara would be alone with Kirti . . . and with Malika.

Raven had enlisted Daisy as her ally before she left, instructing her to observe Kumara carefully. If she saw signs that he was up to mischief she was to inform Bart. She disliked the idea of Kumara having the freedom to pry into Bart's papers because no one was there to prevent him. She checked that the key to the escritoire was safe in place behind his mother's picture before she left.

The worry of what might happen between Kumara and Malika she pushed to the back of her mind. She was a jealous person and hated the pain of seeing someone she desired being loved by another. As far as she could tell, neither Kumara nor Malika were interested in each other. She prayed their relationship would remain that way.

The crush of people in the Street of Moorish Traders and the display of fine dress materials and gems on sale in the boutiques diverted her from her worries.

She had left Bart boasting a renewed confidence in his mastery of the plantation. The soldiers had patrolled and – to his amazement and to Raven's secret satisfaction – the natives all returned to the canefields. The cutting was progressing with a vigour, the mill was in full production and the quality of the sugar was improved. He was in a jubilant mood when she left for Galle.

She shared his optimism. Spending time in the bazaar was not the idle pursuit it seemed. She had a hunch that the answer to Bart's problems was in Galle. She set herself the task of finding out.

Her father had believed her when she explained she came to Galle for a change after the loneliness of life on the plantation. He gave her a free hand to wander through the town with her escorts. In his distant manner he welcomed her presence and conversation at his table in the evenings. She kept the real purpose of her visit to herself.

106

While she fingered bolts of dress fabrics in the boutiques, she was alert for any snippet of gossip that would yield a clue. Yet wherever she went she heard only respect and admiration for Bloodheart. She persevered, despite Mrs Redmount's grumbling at the time she spent with the merchants without buying anything.

'First I must know the prices,' she explained with a smile to win the older woman's sympathy. 'The Moors expect a buyer to make an offer, not ask the price. Haggling is important to them. I don't like to be beaten.'

'You're treating this as a game,' Mrs Redmount sniffed with disapproval. 'I've been watching you. You've no intention of buying anything. Every day here and there, asking questions, pretending to bargain. My feet are worn out following you, and as for these two boys . . .' She gestured at the soldiers sweltering in their flannel tunics.

'Do forgive me, Mrs Redmount, I had no idea. Please let the soldiers escort you to your hotel. I will be quite all right by myself.'

'Captain Walker did say I was to stay with you . . .' She wavered.

'It's nonsense, isn't it, Mrs Redmount? Men think we are incapable of managing without them. What harm can possibly befall me here in this public place?' She indicated the crowds in the street.

'Do look, there are Europeans everywhere, ladies as well as men. I want to browse a little more. I don't mind if you have to leave me.' She smiled. 'We won't say anything to Captain Walker. I shall go home directly I've finished. It's only three minutes walk to the Collector's bungalow.'

Mrs Redmount looked at her gratefully. 'I do have a dinner party to dress for. Are you sure?'

She nodded to reassure her as she waved her on her way. She scarcely had time to sigh with relief at her chaperon's departure when she caught a glimpse of a gem-filled interior as the door of a Moor's house swung open. The sight sent a shiver of anticipation rippling through her.

She waited for a gap to open in the crowd and crossed the street to the house. It's narrow porticoed verandah was crowded with Muhammadans in their lace skull caps and white outfits of baggy shirts and floor-length cloths. They were passing gems from palm to palm accompanied by the low murmuring of the ritual of a sale taking place.

They made way for her without interrupting their bargaining and she walked up to the closed door leading into the house. Someone opened it for her. There was a stir among the men in the room at her arrival.

A voice hailed her angrily until someone behind her uttered an introduction in an unfamiliar tongue. The consternation in the room died as she was identified as the Collector's daughter.

'What is your pleasure, madam?' A young man in a skull cap rose up from a group squatting on the floor. He had a black beard etched around his jaw and clean-shaven cheeks.

His teeth flashed as brightly as the gems on the mat at his feet and in the glass cupboards that lined the walls of the room. The murmuring of the gem dealers resumed. The Muhammadans were more interested in commerce than in the whims of a visiting white lady.

She opened her reticule. 'I have found this,' she said, producing the cat's eye ring that she had kept for weeks in her needlework box. She offered it to him.

The man's eager smile faltered. He took the ring and walked to the open window at the back of the room. He held the ring to the light then beckoned her to join him.

'You see,' he said in the crisp tones of an expert, 'the silver streak. This is a cat's eye.'

'Is it?' She pretended to be impressed. 'I'd like to return it to its owner. Can you help me find him?'

The man's eyes clouded with disappointment. He plunged his hand into the pocket of his loosely fitting shirt and produced a soft leather pouch. Opening the palm of his hand, he poured the contents into it. Eight gems, each the honey colour and size of the stone in the ring, glowed against his palm.

'Many are the men who favour rings with such fortunate stones, madam.'

'Perhaps you can help me from the gold of the ring,' she said timidly. 'Surely it was made in Galle? It's such beautiful work.'

'Oh yes.' The man barely glanced at the ring. 'This is my father's work.'

'Then he will know for whom he made it!'

The young man was silent and studied her face keenly. The drone of the dealers sitting on the floor and the cries of the crowds meandering in the street outside disguised the loud thumping of her heart.

She tried to hide the excitement from her eyes and assumed an expression of helplessness. 'If you tell me the owner's name, I would be able to meet him and return the ring.'

The man frowned and stroked his beard then abruptly turned away from her. He hurried across the room and disappeared through a doorway to the interior courtyard.

She would have liked to follow him but sensed that unless she was invited she would have to stay where she was and wait. She was privileged to have been allowed to enter the house at all.

The young man returned as suddenly as he left. The ring was still in his hand. 'My father wonders if madam would like to buy this ring?' His face spread with the oily smile of a salesman.

'Why should he wonder that? It's not his to sell.'

'My father values his workmanship highly. He too would like to see the ring restored to its rightful owner.' He waved the ring tantalizingly in front of her eyes. 'Has madam an offer to make?'

'Do you know the name of the owner?'

The man's eyelids flickered imperceptibly.

Raven smiled and joined in the game. 'I am too humble to offer for your father's great talent. His workmanship is exquisite, his skill inspired by genius. I could offer only for a whispered name whose teller would remain my secret.'

She leaned close to the man and breathed a price in his ear, shamelessly taking advantage of his embarrassment at her nearness.

'I did not hear what you said,' he murmured.

She doubled her offer, letting her words sizzle his ear. His hand closed over hers and squeezed the ring into it.

'The man you seek is not as other men.' His black eyes impaled her. 'He is a slave . . .'

'His name?' She protested as he propelled her out of the room and onto the verandah before she realized what he was doing.

'I would rather save you from yourself than tell you that!' He thrust her bodily into the street, muttering an incantation that made her feel she had defiled him.

CHAPTER THIRTEEN

'Slavery,' said Collector Radley, relishing the chance to air his knowledge, 'exists in Ceylon in a form more benign than in the West Indies.' He sat back on his chair and steepled his fingers under his chin, gazing across the dining table at Raven.

Dinner was over. Seeing her father was in a good mood, she asked him about slavery. Two days had passed since her visit to the gem merchant and she was no nearer finding the ring's owner.

Her shame at what the young Muhammadan thought of her had changed to wry amusement. Her boldness obviously shocked and confused him. In a way, it was touching that he wanted to save her from an involvement of which he disapproved.

How do I find the slave? she asked herself. She knew nothing about slaves. They were not kept in chains and lashed along the streets of Galle by drunken whipmasters. She asked her father about them in desperation.

'How do I know who is a slave?' she blurted out, interrupting his chain of thought.

He waved her question aside. 'Slavery in Ceylon began as an attribute of race. The laws of caste consign some to bondage, doomed to toil from birth. The only obligation on the part of their masters is to maintain them in health, succour them in sickness and apportion their burdens to their strength.' He beamed in a self-satisfied manner and rose from the table.

'Shall we sit outside? The night is cool.'

'So a slave is of low caste?' she mused aloud as she followed him, understanding now why the Muhammadan disapproved of her search.

Mr Radley settled himself in his armchair and snapped his fingers. A houseboy stepped forward with a decanter of cognac and placed it on the table at his side. He poured himself a generous measure, savoured its bouquet with deep satisfaction, and sipped it. He returned his attention to Raven's questions.

'Slavery is not confined to the lower classes. Insolvents are made slaves by their creditors. Even the children of freemen by female slaves followed the status of their mothers until recently when the government emancipated them.'

'But who is a slave?' she asked impatiently, repeating her question at the risk of upsetting her father's digestion.

'Slaves serve the Kandyan chiefs,' he said in oblique acknowledgement of what she asked. 'They swell the train of their retinues and have specific domestic duties assigned to them, such as laying out a corpse after death. In the Tamil districts of the north, slaves labour in the fields and are rewarded with a small proportion of the produce. Amongst the Singhalese, slavery is domestic rather than praedial.'

She saw him glance at her doubtfully, trying to fathom the reason for her question.

'Slavery is very mild in Ceylon, Raven. Don't trouble yourself with abolitionist sentiments. I don't want any problems with radical ideas.'

'Daddy!' She smiled demurely. 'I wouldn't dream of it. I was only wondering who are slaves in Galle.'

'In Galle?' He frowned. 'Ah!' His eyes lit up. 'There are the Caffres, not the natives. I mean the Africans who scavenge the streets at night and toil in the port. They are government slaves. They're treated quite properly, I assure you. There's a Caffre church to keep them Christian.'

'Are there any slaves who are . . .' she paused, wondering how to phrase her question. 'Who are well known, famous for something, a special talent, perhaps, that could bring them riches?'

Mr Radley pursed her lips irritably until a second sip of cognac relaxed him. 'In Galle, the majority of slaves are owned by the Dutch Burghers. Since the British arrived and stopped their monopolies, most of the Burghers are so poor they rent out their slaves just as they do with their bungalows.'

He pinched his nose thoughtfully. 'Only wealthy Burghers like Madam Gudde can afford slaves such as you mention. She has a Caffre who's famous for what he does in her *tableaux vivants* . . .' The image distracted him and his voice trailed off.

She was intrigued beyond measure about what the Caffre did but had sense enough to refrain from asking. Instead, she took up her sampler of embroidery from the table at the side of her chair and picked at it.

111

Ideas chased through her mind. She recalled Bart's friendship with Madam Gudde. The lady had even attended their wedding.

'I think I will go to my chamber,' she said with an outward show of serenity. 'I'm feeling tired.' She kissed her father's bald head and left him contemplating his snifter of cognac.

As soon as she reached her chamber she flung open the door of the almirah and rifled through her dresses. A plan had sprung into her mind that was so obvious she was astonished she had not thought of it before.

'Madam Gudde knows everything,' she muttered to herself as she pulled out a white dress, rejected it as too chaste, and reached for a primrose yellow one instead.

While she changed her clothes she gave thought to how she could leave the bungalow without her father knowing. There was a way and it was risky. If she was challenged by a sentry, she hoped her disguise would fool him.

The yellow dress had a low-cut bodice of lace that emphasized the deep plunge of her cleavage. It was new, especially made for her to wear as a surprise for Bart. She pulled back her shoulders and stared in the looking glass, wondering if she had the courage to wear such a revealing gown in public.

She reached for her box of powder, paint and beeswax. At home on the plantation she rarely used make-up. Her skin was clear and the country air gave her all the colour she required. Tonight, however, she was going to be someone else.

She applied the make-up generously, changing her face with its virtuous sheen to that of a painted, red-lipped houri.

She fizzed with excitement at what she was daring to do. The only way to see Madam Gudde was to go to her bordello. If she were seen entering that infamous house, her reputation would be ruined. If she were disguised as a whore, no one would give her a second glance.

Her idea was to visit Madam Gudde, ask her some questions and be back at the bungalow within the hour. What harm could possibly come from that?

She spun around in front of the looking glass and was amazed at the transformation. It was perfect. She decided she needed more jewellery and took the cat's eye ring from her reticule. She slipped it on her index finger as it was too big for the others.

She practised a coquettish pout in the mirror and giggled with delight at the result. She even felt wanton. She sat down to calm herself and brushed her hair, going over the plan in her mind.

Her father was still on the verandah. She could hear him discoursing loudly with Mr Medley, his harassed assistant. There was no one in the drawing room when she hurried across it and opened the door to the garden.

A lantern illuminated the wall of the house and she took a deep breath and darted out, seeking the shadows under the temple trees. Soldiers patrolled the ramparts at the end of the garden. When none of them shouted an alarm, she made her way through the dark to the door set in the high garden wall.

It was secured from inside. Her heart pounded as she withdrew the bolt and eased the door open. She peered out. A sentry was on duty to patrol the outside of the compound and prevent intruders entering. He was out of sight.

She slipped quickly through the doorway and closed the door behind her, wedging it with a stone at its base so it appeared to be locked. With a gulp of relief, she hurried up the lane beside the house.

She hesitated before crossing Hospital Street because of the people who were walking there. She pulled her bonnet around her ears and raised her shawl to cover her mouth. When there was a break in the parade of people she scurried across the road into the darkness of Front Street. It was a short distance from there, down Rope Walk Street, to the Street of Moorish Traders.

The darkness gave her confidence and she slowed down to experiment with a sluttish walk. She fluttered her eye lashes at an imaginary man and tried to put herself into the character of a whore. *Good gracious*, she thought with a stirring of alarm, *what do I do if a man believes I am a prostitute*?

Fortunately, she reached the wall of the bordello without being accosted. It was there the danger lay. A lantern threw a bright light on the doorway and anyone knocking for admittance could be seen by passers-by.

She swaggered up to the door and banged on it, keeping one hand on her hip and her head cocked defiantly in the stance she assumed a Jezebel would adopt.

The grille in the door slid open, its sudden noise sending a stab of fear to her breast. 'What d'yo' want?' a gruff voice demanded.

'Madam Gudde,' she whispered, simpering for the gateman's benefit.

'Who yo' are?'

The question surprised her. She asked a question of her own to give her time to think. 'Why do you want to know?'

113

The gateman guffawed. 'Yuh husband may be here.'

She arched her eyebrows, feeling the beeswax stretch on her skin. 'My name is . . . Nell. I have no husband, only lovers . . .' She tried out her strumpet's smile and the gateman seemed impressed. He unbolted the heavy wooden door and let her in.

She found herself in a garden lit with lanterns of different colours, red and amber lights flickering in the frangipani branches. She tried to keep the surprise out of her eyes at the sight of the gateman.

He was huge, his black body glistening like polished ebony where oil had been rubbed on his skin. He appeared to be naked. She dared not glance at his loins to see.

'Sit here,' he said with a leer that added to her discomfort.

She was aware of the interest she aroused in the people in the garden. She forgot she was supposed to be an experienced whore and stared with open-mouthed curiosity at her surroundings.

Three girls sat together on a bench. They were dressed in gawdy coloured negligés made of diaphanous material that revealed every curve of their bodies. A man sat in a corner with a woman on his knees, his hand cupped over her breast where it protruded from her bodice. Another man reclined on a *chaise-longue* while two women knelt on the grass at his side, one with her lips on his, the other massaging his thighs.

Raven blushed and averted her eyes. Her courage almost failed her. She thought of Bart and what Mammy had said about him visiting this place. It made her angry and her outrage revived her.

She shrugged off her shawl, unlaced her bonnet and let her hair tumble around her bare shoulders. The pale mounds of her breasts rose and swelled from her lace corsage.

She heard the swift intake of breath of the girls on the bench and knew she had made three enemies. Their jealous stares heartened her. She twisted her face into a warped smile, confident now because she had hoodwinked them into thinking she was a rival whore.

A man was striding towards her from the house. She arranged her false expression into a suggestive puckering of her lips and winked at him. He stopped in front of her with his legs planted apart, thrusting his body lewdly in her face. She tried to keep from trembling at the sight of his bulging breeches.

'Vy do you vant to see my mother?' he demanded.

114

'I'll tell her myself!' She tossed her head so her hair shimmered. She was amazed at her own effrontery but the man's cocksure attitude set off a rill of dislike flowing through her veins.

'Then you must come vit me.'

The man's eyes were small and bloodshot. They swelled with lust as she rose to her feet and walked, remembering to exaggerate the swaying of her hips, towards the house. Her progress across the lawn was accompanied by hisses from the three girls and honks of bawdy appreciation from the men.

'Where is Madam Gudde?' she asked, trying to make her voice sound husky so she didn't betray her breeding with her cultured accent.

She needn't have worried. The man and the Caffre slave were too engrossed by the white orbs of her bosom and the suggestion of nubile curves beneath her dress to consider she was anyone but a woman of easy virtue.

'Step in there,' said the man, opening the door of a side room. 'You can vait in private. She is . . . er . . . busy.'

She stepped in without a second thought. The door closed behind her and she got the impression that the Caffre was waiting outside. The room seemed to be an apartment on its own since it was separated from the main house and there was no connecting door.

She was startled by the presence of a bed in the room. She calmed herself by reasoning that was what she should expect in a brothel. If she had known she was being ushered into a bed-chamber, she would have refused. But that would have led them to doubt her disguise.

There were no chairs so she sat on the bed, marvelling at how whores lived. The room was sparsely furnished. A candle burned on a rickety table. There was a wooden chest of the kind men took on a voyage in one corner and clothes were scattered around it. A pile of rags and a mat rolled up by the door seemed to be the sleeping kit of a slave.

A hint of worry burst through her shield of confidence. It dawned on her that she was not in a whore's room at all. This was a man's chamber with a man's bed and his slave's meagre possessions on the floor. She was about to leap up from the bed in panic when the door opened.

'Vell, my dear,' said the man, stepping into the room. The Caffre closed the door behind him. 'Vy don't ve get to know each other vile you are vaitink?'

He took two strides and he was on the bed beside her. His arms reached around her shoulders and yanked her to him.

She saw his face, pockmarked and blotched with the effects of hard drinking, loom over her before his lips squashed against her mouth.

She struggled to breathe as her nose was blocked by the blubber of his cheek. Her arms were trapped at her sides and she could do nothing to resist. She prayed for the dreadful embrace to end.

'Vat!' he exclaimed as he paused to take a breath himself. 'Is that kissink?' He pulled her to him again, crushing her bosom against the stiff front of his brocade jacket.

She was faced with the threat of his fleshy lips bruising her mouth, or exposure. 'Wait!' she said, summoning strength and pressing her hand against his chest. 'I must see your mother.'

'Aftervards. She von't let me touch her girls but I haf found you myself, heh?'

'No! I'm not a whore!'

'That is good!' He chuckled dryly, his bulbous face shaking with evil glee. 'Then I von't haf to pay you.'

'You don't understand. I'm here on a mission.'

'Then I am the one to fulfil it, my dear. My name is Curt. Ve shall be friends, heh?' He lunged at her again, grabbing her breast with one hand and placing the other in the small of her back. He brought his head close to hers and opened his mouth like a crocodile about to take a bite.

She felt herself falling backwards on the mattress and kicked out helplessly as he clambered on top of her. Her struggles only served to encourage him. He pulled up her skirt and let her legs kick freely.

'Vat a beauty you are. A vild cat!' He grinned when her foot struck the side of his chest. He gripped her ankle effortlessly in his hand and reached over until he caught the other one.

She sat up, trying to prevent him spreading her legs apart. He butted her in her stomach with his head. It was like a cannon ball and she fell back, winded by the blow.

He launched himself on her with a gurgle of triumph. She was spreadeagled beneath him, stuck under the heavy weight of his huge, thrusting body, unable to move.

'Now ve make love, heh?'

His hand clawed up her thigh, leaving weals of pain where he pinched her flesh. His fist closed over her womanhood and he drooled with pleasure as he fingered her.

116

'Vat a juicy vench you are, my dear.'

She shrunk at his touch, longing for the bed to open up and swallow her. Instead, she was ruptured by the agony of his finger prodding her while he pounded against her, wheezing and panting like a millhouse boiler.

'Vait!' he said, easing his hand out. He fiddled with his breeches with one hand while the other rested on her breast, pinning her to the mattress. He snuffled as he opened himself. 'Now you are goink to haf some lovink!'

She was vaguely aware of someone entering the room. The pressure on her chest eased as Curt turned to see who it was.

'Ma Gudde tell yo' come at once, Curt.'

She opened her eyes and saw the Caffre grinning evilly at her. Being left alone with him would be worse than being with Curt. She bit her lip to stop crying out.

Curt pulled himself off with reluctance and stood up, fumbling to fasten his breeches. 'I'm comink,' he grumbled like a spoilt child who knew he would be beaten if he delayed.

He glanced down at her, gloating at the sight of her smooth bare thighs. 'You can stay here vit Nato,' he said.

Her fear at being left alone with the half-naked giant shone from her eyes despite her effort to feel brave.

Curt sneered at her. 'Don't vorry, my dear.' He sniggered. 'This slave's not as other men. He can't take vat is mine. He haf no balls.' He buttoned up his coat and hurried from the room.

She watched him go as the import of his words struck her. *Not as other men*. The Muhammadan's phrase echoed in her mind. She sat up quickly before the Caffre could take over where Curt left off.

She clasped her hands in front of her breasts, surreptitiously slipping the ring from her finger.

Nato advanced towards her, his long muscular arms reaching out to hold her in his grasp.

'This is yours,' she cried, jumping from the bed and holding the ring out for him to see. She brushed down her skirt, smarting at the searing pain in her limbs.

He halted, blinked, and stared at the cat's eye stone.

She thrust it at him like a man teasing a dog with a bone. His brow furrowed and she felt she could see his brain trying to figure out what she was doing with his ring.

'Take it,' she cried. 'It is yours, isn't it?'

'Yes!' He leapt for her.

She stepped aside and flung the ring into the darkest corner of the chamber as he stumbled and sprawled across the bed.

Pausing only to scoop up her bonnet from where it lay crushed on the mattress, she ran from the room.

CHAPTER FOURTEEN

The ratoons, the new shoots springing from the sugar-cane after cropping, were like emeralds sprinkled over the darkly rich soil of the plateau. The cleared canepieces sparkled with green in the morning dew while the fields that remained to be cut waved with their ribbons of gold in the breeze.

Bart drew deep contentment from riding the tableland of his plantation at sunrise; he was proud of what he had created out of the jungle.

He halted his horse and waited while a gang of natives filed past him, heading for a field at the edge of the plateau. The men's task for the day was to cutlass the ripened cane while the women bundled it and loaded it on bullock carts for delivery to the mill.

They avoided his hard-eyed stare and quickened their pace when they saw him watching. He continued down the path, satisfied with the day's turnout of workers.

The danger that the fields would remain uncut had passed. There was an urgency among the natives that had been absent before. In Barbados, on his father's plantation where he was raised, African slaves cut and milled the cane under threat of the lash.

Drivers patrolled the fields with whips to touch them up on their backsides if they slackened. Those slaves were imports without a home and a common tongue. Their independence had been destroyed and they laboured mindlessly to their bondmaster's whim.

The men and woman who worked for him in Ceylon were different, conditioned by caste for a life of toil. There was no compulsion, beyond habit and their belief in the inevitability of their lot. They were easily swayed *en masse*.

Because of Tissa's influence this had worked to Bart's advantage. If he tried to coerce them by whipping in the manner of Caribbean planters, they would have fled.

The natives attached themselves to the plantation without him asking. They were of the *salagama* caste, traditionally involved in peeling cinnamon. Under the Dutch, they prospered, then the British removed their privileges.

Rather than be reduced to the same level as lower castes, and because they sensed the decline of the cinnamon trade and were intrigued by his solo attempt to start a plantation in the jungle, a few of them drifted to work with him. Others followed until Bart found he had unwittingly become dependent on them.

He spurred his horse to gallop down the path to the mill. His reliance on the *salagamas* was nearly his undoing. If he had lost them as seemed likely before the timely arrival of Captain Walker's soldiers on patrol, his plantation would have been finished. *No slaves, no sugar, no income* was the planter's maxim often repeated by those fighting abolition in the West Indies.

He was trapped, and he knew it and it was the bane of his contentment. If Tissa or the *salagamas* realized his dependence on them and thus their value to him, he would be at their mercy, especially at harvest time.

Once the grinding stones were churning and the boiler fires lit, a constant supply of cane from the fields was needed to ensure there was no delay that could spoil the production of sugar.

He entered the mill yard, brushing his thick mop of hair back from his brow to drive away his sombre thoughts. The fires were being lit under the large copper vats using trash, the sugar-canes squeezed dry by the mill stones, as fuel.

Tissa was overseeing the routine with his lieutenants while scores of natives bustled around the yard in noisy confusion.

'I see everything's all right,' shouted Bart in response to Tissa's wave of greeting.

To his disappointment, Tissa continued to gabble away in Singhalese. He hoped he would have time to chat with him. The truth was that Bart could *not* see anything was all right.

The activity in the compound baffled him. It seemed completely disorganized. He had taught Tissa how to run the mill and to make sugar. Then Tissa devised his own routine more suited to the native temperament for apparent chaos.

Out of the noise and dust and heat and disorder came the crystal granules of sugar, ready for shipment. It irked Bart that he had lost control of the process and his own presence wasn't needed.

Yet it was. Just by being in the mill compound while the *salagamas* scurried around, he was showing his support for Tissa's authority. Tissa was his link with them, the reason why they worked.

It would be impossible to command them without him. It added to Bart's ire. The plantation was his, yet its success was dependent on factors over which he had surrendered control.

Disgruntled, he left the mill compound and spent the morning riding around the plantation. It was the same every day since Raven's departure for Galle a week earlier. He expected her absence to provide a chance for him to return to his old ways. He was wrong.

Before he married Raven he ran the plantation in partnership with Tissa. His previous wife had no interest. Raven was the opposite. She was obsessive in her devotion to him and the plantation. She wanted to share in every thing and gradually he succumbed to her influence, deriving a greater pleasure from her companionship than from being at the mill compound with Tissa.

Now he saw the price he had paid. Without Raven, he was adrift. He was unable to return to his old habits. Tissa was too busy to confer with him. He had no desire to seek the company of whores as he did when he was married to Jessica.

He realized with a shudder of regret, that the recklessness of his youth was tamed. He had lost his heart to Raven and his authority to Tissa.

'Dammit!' he said aloud, staring ahead of him across the shorn fields. 'Is this what I want?'

The creak of the bullock carts ambling to the mill, and the drone of bees swarming around a queen at the edge of the jungle, was his only answer. He fingered his stubbled ear then let his hand drift over his chin, stroking his beard.

He blamed his mood on Raven. His loneliness and brooding was caused by her absence in Galle.

He was reluctant to admit his pleasure at the complacency she had brought to his life. To do so would be to accept that he was no longer the dashing pioneer of a decade before. There were still challenges to be faced.

Being preoccupied with his lonely rumination, he didn't notice the person creeping up on him until his horse abruptly shied. The rude jolt startled him out of his mood; he steadied the horse while he gazed around.

He had wandered to the jungle's edge and paused in the shade of its lofty trees. In front of him stood a youth who was watching him reproachfully.

Bart forced a hearty laugh to hide his shock. 'You young devil!' He leaned down from the saddle and extended his hand to ruffle the youth's hair. 'You caught me unawares that time, Ram.'

The youth dodged out of his reach and bowed his head gravely. His serious face showed he was not playing a game.

'Catching snakes, are you?' Bart knew Ram spoke very little English. He was fond of the ragamuffin because he had once cured him of a snake bite. 'Beats me what you do with those serpents.'

He noticed Ram was without the basket he usually carried. His thatch of dark hair was cut short, as black and as bristly as a chimney sweep's brush. His sole garment was his madras-patterned loincloth wrapped tightly around his thighs to give him freedom of rapid movement through the bush. His tough young body glistened where snake grease was smeared on his copper-coloured skin.

From his stern expression, Bart sensed criticism of his careless-ness. He was foolish to roam close to the jungle without being more alert.

'Is there danger here, Ram?' He waved his hand at the long grass by his horse's feet. 'A cobra?'

Hearing a word he understood, Ram relaxed and grinned slightly. Then he pointed in the direction of the villa, moving over to Bart and tugging at his leg. He uttered some words in Tamil that baffled him.

'I don't know what you're saying, Ram.' He shrugged his shoulders and gazed over the tops of the tall stems of sugar-cane. The villa was nearly a mile away on a bluff above the plateau. It was obscured by the shade trees surrounding it.

Ram patted his knee insistently.

'Dammit, I wish you could speak English.' Bart frowned at the youth's inability to express himself. 'I'd like to get you out of that jungle and send you to school. Would you go? Learn English?'

He dived at the boy, holding him firmly by the scruff of his neck. 'What is it, Ram?'

Again the boy pointed at the villa. Then he made a chopping motion in the air with his hand.

The unexpected gesture startled Bart and he let him go. Instead of running off, Ram tapped his knee again.

'Do you mean they're chopping cane by the house?' Bart was bewildered. Ram wanted him to see something yet instead of leading him there, he kept on pawing him.

'Get out of the way,' he said, losing patience with the charade.

He endeavoured to move but Ram clung to his boot and stirrup, a pleading look in his eye.

Gradually it dawned on him what he wanted. 'You want to come too?' He grinned wryly. 'Why not? At least you're someone to talk to, even if you don't understand what I say.'

He held out his hand and Ram leaped onto the back of the horse with the agility of a jungle cat. He sat at ease behind him.

'Where to, Ram?' He indicated with his hand the different parts of the plantation. 'The river, the mill, the mountains?'

Ram patted his shoulder and pointed again at the villa, chattering excitedly in Tamil.

'Very well,' said Bart. 'We'll go home.'

Perhaps it was the effect of riding all morning in the hot sun, or his melancholy mood, or simply that his vigilance was dulled by having nothing to do. Whatever the reason, he assumed Ram was in need of companionship too, instead of realizing that he was trying to warn him of something.

He chatted amiably, enjoying Ram's company, pointing out the different canepieces and explaining how to tell when the cane was at its best for cutting. Ram only nodded, urging him to ride faster.

They approached the villa from the west, from the opposite direction to the mill. Bart had made a complete circuit of the lower reaches of the plantation. He looked around for the cane cutters that Ram had described with his pantomime.

'There 're no men here,' he said with a laugh. 'I believe you just wanted the ride.'

Ram grasped his shoulder and pointed to his left, behind the villa. There was a spinney beyond the hut where Romulus and Mark, his two Caffre garden boys, lived. A large cabin built especially for Mammy Sobers stood empty a few yards away from the wood.

'Mammy's in England,' said Bart, still not appreciating what Ram was trying to show him. 'So's Garth.'

The youth drummed on his shoulder until Bart halted the horse outside Mammy's old cabin. He slipped quietly to the ground and held his finger to his lips for Bart to keep silent.

He frowned his puzzlement as Ram took the reins out of his hands and tied them to the railing of the cabin's porch. He beckoned Bart to follow him.

He dismounted with a sigh of exasperation. He had no doubt now that Ram had lured him to the spinney to show him some monstrous snake he had caught. He obviously considered it important because the reptile was so close to Mammy's cabin. The old cook would have had a fit if she knew.

To humour the youth, he followed him into the undergrowth, crouching down in the way Ram showed him. He edged along slowly, catching the branches in his hand that Ram held aside so his face and clothes would not get snagged by them. When he tried to ask Ram what this was all about, Ram's fierce glare and urgent clamping of his hand to his mouth, persuaded him to keep quiet.

At last, his suspicion was aroused. He wondered if he was being enticed into a trap. What previously he thought was a game was deadly serious to the snake boy.

Ram's face was taut with concentration. He stopped, pushing his hand against Bart's chest, forcing him down into the bush. Sweat trickled down the small of Bart's back and his leg began to go numb with discomfort at his awkward position.

Ram tilted his head on one side, listening carefully. His eyes narrowed and then he nodded, satisfied at what he heard. He touched Bart's good ear, pointing to the screen of foliage in front of them. The sound of a tree being struck, like a toddy tapper at work, was all Bart could hear.

'One of the slaves cutting wood,' he whispered. Ram's black frown made him regret having spoken.

Slowly, Ram parted the bushes in front of him, forming an opening in the leaves. He peered through it, watched for a moment and then shifted aside so that Bart could put his eye to the hole.

At first, he could see nothing. The spinney was a patch of jungle that Bart, on a whim, had left isolated when he cleared the bush around it for his canefields. Its trees were tall, bedecked with vines and orchids; their branches a tangle that formed a canopy keeping out the sun.

As his eyes adjusted to the shadowy gloom, he saw a small glade ahead of him. A sudden movement under the trees wrenched his heart with fear.

Hurriedly, he fumbled for his pistol. He nearly cried aloud with the excruciating pain as Ram's hand gripped his shoulder, paralysing him with his fingers clamped on a pressure point. He stared at Ram in despair.

Ram frowned sympathetically, his eyes compelling him to keep quiet. He indicated that Bart should look through the screen of foliage again.

He did.

Kumara was standing in the glade, a sword in his hand. It was raised in the air, poised at the pivot of a swing that was about to descend. Kirti stood before him, a smile of bliss on his innocent young face.

'He'll kill him!' Bart hissed, struggling to tear his shoulder free from Ram's crippling hold on it.

Ram shook his head, scowling ferociously at him for speaking. He jerked him back to the gap so he was forced to watch.

Kumara stood with the sword held high above his head. He was stripped to his waist, facing away from Bart. Muscles rippled across his back as his arm fell slowly, slicing the sword downwards.

The child's eyes were transfixed by the blade. He gaped as it whistled close to his head, but he didn't flinch. The sword quivered when it struck the earth at his side.

As Bart watched, the exercise was repeated with Kumara sweeping the sword within a sliver of Kirti's cheek. The child blinked but remained motionless.

Kumara praised him in Singhala and Kirti grinned with pride. He bent down and scooped him up with one hand, hugging him to his chest. He laughed encouragingly and Kirti gurgled with delight.

Ram's fingers released Bart and he rubbed his shoulder to restore the circulation. He continued to watch the strange spectacle in the glade, blaming himself for what was happening to his stepson.

He had been warned by Daisy that Kumara took the child out of the villa for hours every day. He assumed Kirti was safe. It was a welcome break for Malika, and the child had no one to play with since the departure of Garth and Ranita.

As he spied on them, he saw Kirti pick up a sword of his own, fashioned out of wood. It was smaller and lighter than Kumara's, although it was almost as big as he was. He struggled to hold it, his tiny face creased with determination.

He pointed it at Kumara, lunged, withdrew and lunged again. Kumara parried the sword gently with his own blade and stepped back. The child rushed for him, feinted with a skill learned from practice, and struck Kumara on his chest.

Kumara burst out with loud laughter, tumbled backwards and flung his own sword on the ground.

Kirti jumped on him with a shriek of childish glee. 'I've killed you!' he said in English.

'No, my little prince.' Kumara hoisted the boy above him as he

125

lay on the ground. 'Do not jump on your opponent like that until you've slit his throat. He could rise up like this and kill *you!*' Kumara jumped to his feet, cuddling the child.

'I wish . . .' said Kirti as he was placed on his feet on the ground.

'What do you wish?'

'I wish there was a charm so no one could kill me.'

'There is.' Kumara lowered his voice. Bart had to move closer in the undergrowth to hear.

'Bloodheart has it.'

'*Tata?*' said Kirti wide-eyed. 'Then I tell him I want it.'

'Yes.' Kumara's voice took on a tone of obsession. 'Ask Bloodheart for the *gaja mutu*. Ask him to show it to you.'

'*Gaja mutu?*'

'The elephant pearl of your ancestors. If Bloodheart asks who told you of it, say Malika did. Don't say I asked.'

'Why not?'

'Because it is a secret.'

The child repeated the Singhala words again, his eyes narrowing. He understood about secrets.

'Bloodheart won't let you keep the *gaja mutu*.' Kumara squatted down and faced the child. 'He'll say he's saving it for you. So watch where he hides it.'

'Why?' The child's inquisitiveness wasn't deterred by Kumara's attempt to hypnotize him.

'Do as I say, Kirti. For your inheritance.'

Bart started at the touch on his shoulder. Irritably, he waved Ram away.

The youth was beckoning him, urging him to leave the spinney. Bart wasn't ready. He needed to know why Kumara was training the child in swordsmanship and how he planned to steal the *gaja mutu* if he could discover where it was hidden.

With a flash of insight that rocked him with dismay at his own gullibility, he saw Kumara as the scourge of the plantation. Kumara was the cobra that the snake boy wanted him to catch.

He obeyed Ram's summons and crept after him out of the wood and back into the open by Mammy's cabin.

'Good boy,' he said gratefully. He led the horse by its bridle wondering what he should do about Kumara. He was deep in thought as he skirted the outside wall of the villa and walked slowly to the verandah at the front.

'Would you like some refreshment?' He turned with a drinking gesture to Ram but the boy had disappeared.

He stroked his beard, blaming himself again for his preoccupation that made him careless about what was happening around him. He whistled to Romulus, the slave tending a nearby flower bed, and told him to take his horse to the stable. He stepped onto the verandah with a sigh.

As he entered the cool atmosphere of the parlour, a shape loomed out of the shadows, rushing towards him. He raised his hands to defend himself.

A heart-rending sob of anguish swelled in the air. He dropped his fists in surprise and Raven fell against him, tears coursing down her checks.

CHAPTER FIFTEEN

Raven had fought for a long while before she yielded to the compulsive sobs that shook her. She had strived to be tough, pretending that the abasement she suffered at the bordello was a trifle compared with Bart's woes.

She had waited calmly in the gloom of the parlour. It was the sound of his voice and the firm fall of his step on the verandah that brought the tears of remorse to her eyes. She gulped hard but couldn't stifle the low, tortured sob when she ran to him.

He gathered her in his arms and she buried her face against the corded muscles of his chest. His hand stroked her back, sliding up from her shoulders and under her long tresses until it rested on her neck, his fingers fondling the fine tendrils of hair. His touch was unbelievable in its tenderness.

She swallowed, biting back the tears, ashamed at what he would think of her.

He exerted a gentle pressure to make her walk. She let him lead her across the parlour to their chamber, clinging to him possessively with both hands around his waist.

Her eyes were tightly shut and her breath came in short, gasping puffs as she tried to regain the composure he expected of her. The warm, zesty odour of his body, hot after hours of riding, filled her nostrils, reassuring her that she was safe.

Suddenly she was lifted into the cradle of his arms. She could feel his uneven breathing on her cheek as his lips swept along the course of her tears. He laid her on the bed and sat on the mattress beside her, his hand holding hers in a loving grasp of compassion. Her eyes flickered open shyly.

The sight of his sombre face, a muscle of concern clenched along his jaw, caused her to shiver with shame at what had happened. His hand squeezed her and she felt some of his strength flowing into her. Unspoken questions sparked from his troubled eyes yet

128

the first word he uttered in a voice mellow with caring was simply her name.

'Raven.'

She managed a wan smile, ashamed of her weakness when she tried so hard to be brave. 'I'm sorry, Bart . . .' she whispered, lapsing into a pensive silence as her love for him overwhelmed her.

'You're safe now,' he said, swinging his legs onto the bed, laying his muddy boots on the coverlet. He rested his head on the pillow beside her. Placing his hand on her waist, he drew her to him. His eyes soothed her with kindness.

'Tell me, why the tears, Raven?'

The touch of his finger under her chin stirred a sigh from her parted lips. She smiled apologetically, wanting to move away.

His finger and thumb gripped her jaw and he peered into her eyes, trying to read the anguish that swirled in their depths.

'Tell me, Raven,' he ordered, harshness entering his voice, fired by a suspicion that some harm had befallen her.

'I didn't mean to cry,' she said, assuming a blitheness she didn't feel. 'I was so pleased to see you.'

'You have an odd way of showing your pleasure.' He released her chin and frowned.

She hated to lie to him. 'I *am* pleased to see you, Bart. I was cross, though. That's why I cried.'

'Cross?' His doubt changed to incredulity.

'Yes.'

She knew if she criticised him, she could deflect his curiosity. She was not ready to tell him what had happened at Madam Gudde's.

'I was waiting for hours for you to come. Instead you were riding aimlessly around the plantation with that urchin snake boy. I waved to you but you ignored me.'

'I didn't see you!'

His gasp of wounded innocence hurt her because she wasn't cross with him really.

'Ram and I were on an urgent matter. If I'd known you were coming today, I would have ridden to meet you.'

She pouted.

'How did you return? Who escorted you? Why didn't you send for me?' He sat up on one elbow and eyed her attentively.

She was relieved his questions avoided the real cause of her distress. 'Oh, Bart,' she said, forcing a smile and reaching out to run her fingers through the hair on his chest. 'I know it's my fault. I should have sent a message. Aren't you pleased to see me?'

'Of course I am.' He stopped her hand's progress under his shirt, but he did not push it away. 'You can't know how much I missed you.' He raised her hand to his lips and kissed it tenderly. Then his fingers tightened.

'How did you come home? You could have been in danger.'

She blinked. If he knew what had happened at the bordello, he would go mad. 'There was a party of gem merchants going to Matara. I rode with them.'

'On a horse?' He sounded shocked.

'They had a spare palanquin. A bullock cart brought me from the ferry.' The last part of her story was true. She dared not tell him she had slipped through the fort gate at dawn and walked the road alone. Her despair was due to exhaustion as much as to shame.

'You should have waited for a proper escort.'

'I was eager to see you. Now you know why I was upset when I didn't meet you until now.'

He seemed distracted. He asked no more questions and lay back on the bed, cradling his head in his hands linked behind his neck. He stared up at the tester, lost in thought. It gave her time to compose herself.

On the long walk back from Galle she had realized how lucky she was to escape without being identified. Her fleeing from the brothel in a distraught state did not arouse suspicion since Curt's reputation of cruelty to women was well known.

She had managed to reach the bungalow's garden and the safety of her room without being challenged. If anyone saw her, they assumed she was what she was pretending to be.

She had cried herself to sleep, trying to expunge the feel of Curt's fingers from her loins. The bruises were like blue fingerprints on her pale flesh. She ached from his brutal touch and slept fitfully. At dawn she rose, left a note for her father, and began the journey back to the plantation.

Now that she lay with Bart beside her on the bed, she wondered whether to tell him what had happened. She was disgusted with herself for breaking down and weeping in his arms. She had thought she was strong.

She wanted to tell him that she had discovered Curt and Nato were behind the attacks on him. Yet before she could tell him that,

130

she needed to concoct a story that was convincing because he was sure to ask how she found out.

She was surprised when he rolled over to her side and placed his hand on her breast. She glanced at him enquiringly, fighting back the rapture rising in her heart.

He parted his lips in a smile of promise, an intimate glint of desire shining in his eyes.

She swallowed tightly, stirred by her reaction to his touch yet fearful he might discover the bruises on her body. Her heart fluttered wildly as his hand slipped beneath the fabric of her dress and his fingers traced a circle around her nipple.

She tried to edge away. 'It's daylight, Bart . . .'

'A week, Raven! Without you it was like a year.'

His pleading eyes conquered the good sense that was behind her disquiet. She wanted him and he was persuasive, scornful of her reluctance to return his embrace. His face, despite his beard and his rugged manliness, was boyish and eager. There was a wistful yearning in his expression.

She was moved by his candid confession that he missed her. Obviously he had not taken his pleasure with a field wench as Mammy warned was his habit.

She writhed uncertainly when his fingers unfastened the bodice of her gown. Although his touch sent her soaring with a delicious sense of excitement, she was a-tremble lest her nakedness betray her in the sunlight streaming into the room through the open shutters. To stall his desire would rouse his curiosity; besides, she wanted him too much to deny his hard, demanding body its need.

His tongue teased her nipples and his mouth pressed a series of slow, shivering kisses from her breasts to the soft hollow of her neck. He raised his face and placed his open lips on hers.

She drank in the sweetness of his kiss, its balm restoring her after the dreadful violence of Curt's cruel lips. Her body stirred with a frenzy that shattered her attempt at caution. When his hand began to drift from the bare flesh of her bosom to pull up her skirt and expose her thighs, she shifted with panic.

'Wait,' she breathed in his ear, countering his mastery with a command of her own.

As he reached out to draw her back to him, she slipped off the bed and stood up. He was startled by her sudden movement and opened his mouth to speak.

She smiled him to silence and walked with her breasts

131

uncovered, their pink globes full and proud, to the window. She paused deliberately, letting him feast his eyes on her near-naked body in the sunlight before she pulled the shutters closed and returned in the safety of darkness to his side.

She caressed him lovingly while his hands explored her. When she winced at his touch on the contusions left by Curt's mauling fingers she disguised it by murmuring her love in his ear.

He was enchanted, not noticing her flinching at the soreness nor seeing the tell-tale bruises in the dark.

Flowing with his thrusts, she welcomed him into her body. The pleasure they shared was pure and explosive, smothering her in an avalanche of ecstasy that drove the shame of Curt's onslaught from her mind. Instead, the overwhelming love inspired by Bart's raw act of possession of her body, unleashed a new and awesome emotion: a blistering hatred of Curt that would not be quelled until he was destroyed.

She was aware of Bart's eyes on her but was unable to fend off her exhaustion. She drifted into sleep, undisturbed when he left the bed and opened the shutters. The impact of the sun on her eyes made her roll over to hide her head in the pillow. Bart smoothed down her skirt where it was rucked up to her hips then sat in a chair beside the bed.

Her sleep was short and dreamless. She awoke minutes later completely refreshed. Her first sight was of him. His face was full of strength, shining with a steadfast and determined energy. It made her proud, and she resolved to make him proud too.

She opened her mouth to tell him about Nato and the ring. He forestalled her by speaking first.

'I know who is trying to intimidate us.'

She was astonished to hear his words echo her thoughts. Her hand flew to her legs and she brushed her skirt down below her knees. She felt a twinge of panic that he had somehow discovered what Curt and the Caffre had tried to do to her.

Caution governed her response. Instead of telling him that she knew too, she sat up, shook her head so her tresses fell over her shoulders, and fastened her bodice. She smiled wryly at the state of the bed.

'It is Kumara,' he said.

'Kumara!' She hadn't thought of him since her return. 'How can it be?' she blurted out without thinking that her surprise would upset him.

'I have proof. I saw him in the spinney. He is training Kirti in swordsmanship. He told the child about the elephant pearl. His aim is to steal it.'

'Have you accused Kumara to his face?' She was puzzled. Although she had her reservations about him, she knew Kumara was not responsible for the attacks on Bart.

'I'll trap him!' he said, irritated by her question. 'I'll be ready for him.' He rose from his chair and walked purposefully up and down beside the bed.

'You must be on your guard, Raven. Kumara is a plausible fellow. I've seen him ogling you. You're an innocent. He might try to take advantage of you.'

She stifled her retort and instead smiled with a sweetness that concealed her amusement at his attitude. 'What will you do if he does?' she said meekly.

He stopped pacing the room, his opal blue eyes clouding with resentment at her question. 'I shall kill him, of course.' There was an unspoken threat to her in his voice and he spun on his heels and stalked from the room.

She knew that somehow she must warn Kumara. She leaned over to the bedside table and hit the plunger on the brass bell. The response was an immediate tap on her door and Nimal glided in. He stood by the bed and listened obediently to her instructions.

During the hour she had to wait for water to be boiled for her bath, she lay on the bed and pondered what to do.

Jagath and Nimal carried in cauldrons of hot water and poured them into the bath tub. They brought buckets of cold water and, under Daisy's supervision, mixed the bath to the right temperature. When Daisy deemed it was ready, she chased out the two houseboys, closed the chamber door and beckoned Raven over.

Raven surrendered to a helplessness as Daisy undressed her. The housekeeper was a practical, caring woman with a tendency, learned from Mammy, to bossiness. Usually Raven shrugged off her scolding. This afternoon, when she stood naked in front of her, she was embarrassed by Daisy's eyes studying her body with a possessive air.

'Lawd, missy,' Daisy said with disapproval. 'You ain't showin' no sign yet.'

She stepped hurriedly into the bathtub, hiding her bruised thighs with her hand. She sank into it, letting the water cover her body up to her shoulders where it dampened the strands of her hair.

133

'Whatever do you mean?' she asked shyly, guessing that she was about to be trapped into one of Daisy's convoluted conversations.

Daisy lathered her zealously, ignoring her squeals of protest when her hand scrubbed too roughly. 'Yo' been married long 'nuff to be pregnant, missy,' she said, rubbing the soap vigorously around her breasts. 'I can't see no sign yet.'

Daisy's fingers swooped and delved between her legs, causing her to shriek with pain.

'Not so hard!' She twisted under the water's surface, trying to keep her thighs hidden from the slave's inquisitive eyes.

'Ah-hah!' Daisy reacted with enthusiasm. 'Yo' an' Mas Bart love de t'ing too much! What dat?' Her soapy fingers slid to her groin and Raven whimpered shrilly at her abrasive touch.

Daisy caught her by her legs when she tried to wriggle away. She lifted her up so her head slipped under the water.

Although Raven struggled, splashing water all over the floor, it was too late. Daisy saw the fingermarks that were bruised like a slave brand on her inner thigh.

'I does ax myself why you bathe today, missy,' Daisy said reproachfully. 'Now I know. Yo' make Mas Bart vexed!'

'You talk too much!' It was pointless trying to assert her authority over the slave while she was being lathered and scrubbed. A bucket of cold water was tipped over her with gusto. She choked, squeezing the water out of her eyes.

Chuckling, Daisy wrapped a towel around her and helped her from the bath. She hugged her before drying her briskly. 'The master can be playful sometimes, missy. Don't yo' worry.'

It never occurred to her to ask Daisy how she knew such intimate matters. She no longer wilted with exhaustion. She glowed under Daisy's brutal but effective massage and stood ready to defy anyone.

Daisy pulled the towel from her unexpectedly and gazed at her body. This time Raven didn't try to shield herself with her hands. Instead, she sauntered around the chamber, flaunting her nakedness, thinking Daisy was jealous of the trimness of her hips, her lithe slim waist and her finely rounded breasts.

'Lawd, missy!' Daisy clucked with disgust. 'Yo' don't have child bearin' hips. Dere ain't no flesh on you to birth a whelp.'

'I'm not a Caffre!' she shouted, provoked by the slave's criticism. She reached for her gown. 'Help me with this.'

Daisy held the dress, muttering to herself. 'Coolie does like deir women wid more meat on dem dan yo' have.'

134

With the dress covering her bruises, Raven felt less vulnerable to Daisy's scathing tongue. 'How very interesting,' she said sarcastically. 'Have you become an expert on Singhalese men as well as on English?'

Daisy snorted with scorn. 'Dem coolies in de fields ain't no match for my Mark,' she said, referring to the Caffre garden slave who was her mate. 'Is de buck in fancy britches dat have de taste for plenty lovin'.'

Raven paused in her strokes as she brushed her hair before the looking glass. She had difficulty following the slave's meaning and Daisy's breezy laughter robbed whatever she said of its importance.

'What buck in fancy breeches? Are you referring to Kumara?' She was angered that he might have propositioned the slave.

'De very same. He tell me himself he like his wenches buxom. Dat mean,' Daisy said with the enthusiasm of the convert, 'wenches big like me.'

Raven tried not to laugh. Daisy's words cheered her, revitalizing her spirit as much as the bath had toned up her body. 'I'm sure he adores you, Daisy,' she said with relief, realizing it was only Kumara's outrageous flattery that charmed the slave.

'Tell me,' she added, lowering her voice to make it seem like they could share a secret. 'What do you think of Kumara?'

'He does be my kind of buck.' Daisy preened herself.

'Did he do anything odd when I was away?'

She looked crestfallen. 'No, missy. I give him every chance but he don't do no odd at all.'

Smiling at the misunderstanding, Raven tried again. 'I asked you to watch him for me. Didn't you see him looking around where he shouldn't? Did he ask you where the key is for the escritoire?'

'No, missy.' She shook her head resolutely and Raven was convinced she wasn't lying. 'He tutor an' train Kirti to be a man. He tell Malika de boy goin' learn to fight an' defend himself proper.'

Raven nodded and laid her brush down on the dressing table. She was satisfied. 'Where is he now?' she asked, making it sound like a casual enquiry.

'He restin' in his room. Malika have Kirti for the time.'

'And where's Bart?'

Daisy's eyes rolled, seeing the purpose of her questions. 'He dozin' on de 'randah, missy,' she said in a voice husky with conspiracy. 'I see he don't disturb.'

'You stay here and clear up!' she snapped, sweeping from the room and leaving Daisy staring after her open-mouthed.

From the parlour she could see Bart stretched out in his deep-pitched verandah chair with his feet raised and hooked over its long arms. His head was slumped on one side in sleep, an empty glass of rum on the table beside him.

She warmed with affection for him but instead of going over to his side and waking him with a kiss, she crossed to the other end of the parlour and opened the door into the courtyard.

It was deserted in the hot sun of the afternoon, although the shutters of all the rooms were open. She walked in a leisurely fashion towards Kumara's chamber. She paused outside the door, wondering whether to knock on it or to leave the questions she wanted to ask him until another time.

She bit her lip with uncertainty. When she heard Kirti's playful shout from Malika's room, she began to walk away from Kumara's door.

It opened suddenly and his arm shot out and grabbed her wrist. She gasped with surprise as she was dragged into his room and the door shut behind her.

His hands seized her waist and pulled her to him. He lowered his face and his lips pounced on hers with a hot and demanding kiss.

When he raised his head, he held her away from him. 'That's what you came for, isn't it?'

She slapped his cheek with such force her hand stung from the blow.

'At last, our Raven unsheathes her talons!' His laugh raked her. 'I wondered when you'd show how sharp are your claws.'

136

CHAPTER SIXTEEN

Raven spluttered, bristling indignation. Kumara was looking at her with a sardonic expression. She stared back at him, dismayed by the hostility of his cynical leer. Backing away, she collided with the closed door. The impact released her from his spell.

The fury that threatened to erupt fizzled out and she laughed boldly in his face. 'I came to warn you,' she said. 'Now I will go for Bart and he will –'

'Will what?' His tongue lashed her with its harshness. 'Kill me?' His eyes glinted. 'Raven . . .' he said, stepping towards her with his arms outstretched.

'Don't touch me!'

'You want me to hold you, to kiss you, to *take* you!'

'No . . . I don't!' She shouted to convince herself.

The door was hard at her back and she pressed against it. He stopped inches from her and his lips curved into a smile that no longer mocked her. His hands fell to his sides and he seemed to be waiting for her to speak.

'You don't. . . ?' he asked softly, atune to her distress. 'Have I misjudged you, Raven?' His hand rose and he placed his finger under her chin, raising her face so her eyes met his.

She felt herself slipping under his spell again.

'What happened to you in Galle?'

Relief flooded through her at his question. 'How did you know?'

He caught up her hand and led her to the bed. He made her sit on it while he took the only chair in the room and placed it opposite her. He sat with his eyes, now mellow with concern, on hers.

She couldn't understand the mercurial change in his attitude, one moment filling her with loathing for him, and the next inspiring her to confess her hidden secrets. She was vaguely aware of being used by him, of being played by a virtuoso who knew every sharp and flat of her mind's melody.

Under his prompting, the details spilled out. Strangely, after she told him about Curt and Nato, their assault on her lost its horror.

'I am proud of you.'

'I wanted to be strong, but I wasn't.'

'You are, Raven, more than you realize.' He rubbed his cheek ruefully where she had struck him. 'I deserved that slap.'

She coloured with embarrassment. 'I thought you would hate me.'

He turned away abruptly and stood up, walking over to the window that was open to the outside of the house. There was a view of the mountains beyond the jungle and he stared up at them, his proud profile caught in silhouette against the light. There was an air of isolation about his tall, lithesome figure; a hint of facing destiny in his stance.

'You're thinking of Kandy, aren't you? Everything you do is calculated towards one end, your victory.' She walked over to his side. 'Perhaps you don't hate me but you certainly don't love me. I'm nothing to you. You'll use me to further your ends then you'll leave.'

His face crumbled; when he turned to her there was a vulnerability in his eyes. She reached out and touched his arm. Standing on tiptoe, she brushed her lips against his cheek.

His hand gripped her shoulders and he twisted his head away from her lips. The fire returned to his eyes.

'Yes,' he said crisply. 'I am thinking of Kandy, my little Raven. Have you sunk your talons in me? Is it my flesh you will dine on some day?'

'I wish you no harm.' She shrugged off the foreboding that swirled in the room around them.

'Good, because I am human too.' His lips tightened and he turned on his heels and strode to the door. 'Perhaps you should return to your husband.'

She was so stunned by the swift re-erection of his defences around himself, she did not move. When the door remained closed, she realized she had caught him bluffing. He had mistaken her confusion for defiance, and he hated to be defied.

'I spoke hastily,' she said. 'I did come to warn you.'

'Indeed?' His lips curled superciliously.

She ignored the sneer. 'Bart is convinced you are the one threatening him. He saw you training Kirti in the spinney.'

'I know.'

'How can you possibly know?'

'Because I sent Ram to bring him there.'

She hesitated, blinking with bafflement.

He grinned boyishly as though taking pity on her. He moved away from the door and led her back to the window. He pointed up at the mountains.

'Bloodheart is a great man, Raven, so he has enemies. Perhaps they come from those far hills of Kandy, perhaps they come from lowland Galle. Yet he seems unconcerned. If he believes I am the threat, won't that make him more alert to danger? Better to believe I want the *gaja mutu*, and Kirti, than to leave them unprotected.'

She was puzzled and more than a trifle nervous. His vibrancy intimidated her. He stood menacingly close to her side yet his eyes appealed for approval.

'It's a mistake to make an enemy of Bart,' she said, fearing the truth of her own words. 'He lies like a sleeping leopard but his claws are more savage than any raven's talons.'

'Then I have succeeded.' Kumara grinned again. 'Now you both doubt me and are prepared to defend what is yours.'

She looked beyond him through the window across the canefields to the jungle and the hills around Galle. 'Curt and his Caffre, Nato, are the enemy.'

'Have you told Bloodheart?'

'He believes it's you. He'll suspect I'm trying to protect you if I say anything.'

'If you are speaking the truth, perhaps Curt and his Caffre are in league with my rivals to eliminate Kirti.'

'If?' She snorted with pique. 'Do you *doubt* me?'

He rubbed his hand over his jaw thoughtfully. 'There was a Caffre at the mill the night of the fire. I saw him running from the storehouse when I arrived. I thought he was one of Bloodheart's slaves.'

'That must have been Nato. I saw him too.'

'I suppose he could have cut through the saddle strap.'

'And started the rumours that encouraged the natives to abandon the canefields.' She gasped with excitement. 'Do you doubt me now?'

'I never did.'

His smile was meant to reassure her with its charm. Instead its very shallowness set off an alarm.

She thought over the conversation and how she had been confused by his motives. Despite the bond restored between them and the glimpse she had of his weak side, there still lingered a suspicion in her mind. Was he sincere behind his smooth charm and flatterer's tongue?

She smiled back at him alluringly, using a weapon from his own armoury of charm. Her body vibrated with a new life. She would use him the way he used her, to get her revenge on Curt and Nato.

She tossed her head, delighting in the buoyancy of her spirit. 'What will you do?' she asked with the calm assurance of seeing herself as the victor.

'Wait.'

Her flush of confidence faltered. 'That's Bart's response. You have to do *something* . . . quickly.'

'Why? Think of it. Whatever they want, they haven't achieved it. They'll try again.'

'I am thinking of it. My limbs burn where Curt's fingers dug into me. I see his fat, obscene stomach wobbling in front of my eyes. Nato's surliness threatens me still.' She turned on him. 'If you are sincere, you'll help avenge me.'

He smirked. 'Am I your *husband*, Mistress Raven?' He opened the door and bowed her out of his room.

Raven listed the people who could help her in her campaign to destroy Curt and Nato. Her father's name was at the top. He could bring official justice to bear, but for what crime? For molesting a whore? There was no proof of anything.

Captain Walker's name came next. Doubtless he was a *habitué* of Madam Gudde's bordello himself, possibly a drinking crony of Curt's. He would require an explanation if she asked for his help, and he would be sure to tell Bart.

She wondered briefly if she could ask the Muhammadan gem merchant. He would be susceptible to her charms and probably had contacts who would carry out some deed of revenge. What deed? If it was to be an attack on them, she could hire ruffians herself, or send Bart's own Caffres, Mark and Romulus, to do the job.

She had few friends in Galle to whom she could turn. Some of the military wives were acquaintances. Her whole life had been wrapped up in Bart since the day she saw him. Yet Bart, like Kumara, was content to wait for events to take their course.

Days of tension in the villa followed and they filled her with unhappiness. She was disappointed that the two men who were most important to her did not try to settle their differences.

Bart was bent on goading Kumara to strike the first blow. He challenged him in everything he did, letting him know he distrusted him. Kumara showed his greater self-restraint by keeping his temper in check and ignoring Bart's taunts.

Raven was on edge, dreading the moment when Kumara would succumb and lash out at Bart. In a fist fight between the two, she expected Kumara, who was younger and more cunning, to win. Strangely, despite the animosity between them, both continued their daily routine as though nothing were wrong.

Bart patrolled the plantation, letting the natives see him so they didn't shirk their duties. Kumara tutored Kirti, teaching him Singhala and Kandyan lore.

Raven was desperate to bring matters to a head so Bart and Kumara would forget their rivalry and concentrate on getting even with Curt and Nato. She racked her brains at what to do. Her list of possible helpers was exhausted, unless she added Ram and Daisy. It was difficult to see how they could help her. She could not converse with the snake boy and Daisy's governessy attitude put her off.

She studied the housekeeper carefully, watching her performing her duties. Nimal and Jagath were usually in awe of Daisy, jumping whenever she addressed them and seeming affronted by her hectoring manner. Yet during the days that followed her return from Galle, Raven detected a subtle change in her.

When Daisy served coffee on the verandah at daybreak, her eyes no longer watched Bart attentively. She accepted Raven's instructions without demuring. She ambled through the villa with an abstracted air, passing up opportunities to grumble at Nimal and Jagath. Something was wrong with her.

At first, Raven attributed the difference in Daisy's behaviour to the climate. It could be a beautiful, sunny day with clear skies and brightly singing birds yet instead of feeling happy, a person could be stricken with misery and despair.

It was the weather; stormy clouds hovered beyond the horizon causing melancholia to pervade the atmosphere. Daisy, being an African, was bound to be affected by nature's moods.

So was Raven. She strolled through the gardens of the villa at her wit's end. It was late afternoon and the heat of the sun had died down. The sky was clear with an ethereal golden light suffusing the atmosphere, a sign of rain in the hinterland.

When she saw Romulus squatting on the lawn, removing weeds with the point of a cutlass, she approached him. 'Will there be a storm tonight?' she asked for the sake of something to say.

141

Romulus was the youngest of the slaves. He was from Mozambique, dark skinned and wiry haired. Bart had owned him since he was twelve and his loyalty was unshakable. He was proud of the strength in his slight, compact body and had no dread of shame or punishment.

He looked at her quizzically. 'Yo' de judge of dat, missy.'

His insolence startled her. She drew herself up and was about to chide him when she saw Mark sitting under a tree, his head lolling back against its trunk. His eyes were closed.

'Good heavens,' she said, distracted by the sight. 'Why isn't he working?'

Romulus shrugged his shoulders without answering and returned to rooting out weeds from the lawn. Raven left him; an idling slave was worse than a cheeky one.

Her shadow fell over Mark as he lay in the grass, his broad chest rising and falling with the regular rhythm of sleep. He was from Madagascar with a lighter colour than Romulus, stronger and older with a thick waist and bulging thighs.

She watched him uneasily, puzzled at catching him asleep. He was an affable giant with a roguish eye and a liking for amusement. Looking around for something to prod him with, she saw nothing practical so she kicked him gently in his waist.

She was a little nervous while she waited for him to leap up and make his excuses. He stirred languidly without surprise, his eyes still closed as he stretched out his hand. When he connected with her leg, he seized her ankle and tugged. She lost her balance and toppled on him with a shriek.

'Oh lawd, missy!' he cried, scrambling to his feet and helping her to stand up. 'I does think you does be Romulus.' He pawed at her dress frantically trying to brush off the leaves and twigs, panicking at what he had done.

'Yo' a'right, missy?' he asked, his eyes pleading for forgiveness.

She was irritated by the sight of the big man acting frightened. 'Of course I am. For heaven's sake, Mark, stop fussing. You're worse than Daisy. Why were you asleep?'

'I ain't sleepin', missy. I so worried, I too sick to sleep, or to work.'

She searched his face for a hint of a lie. He had a high sense of humour and would delight in deceiving her. His eyes were dull, the whites a gloomy yellow without their customary sparkle.

'What ails you? Have you told the master?'

'Missy . . .' He bowed his head. 'Bloodheart don't want to know my troubles.'

'He certainly won't want to hear from me that you've given up work to mope under a mango tree.'

'It's not my fault.' The big man was close to tears. 'Missy,' he put out his hands to touch her then withdrew them hastily. His mouth opened and a great sigh escaped from his lips.

She recognized his anguish. 'What is it, Mark?' she said in a softer tone to encourage him to speak. 'Tell me. Perhaps I can help.'

He flashed her a look of deep gratitude. 'It's Daisy, missy. I love her.'

'Love?' She had not expected Caffres to have the same notions about love that she had. It was their origins. They came from the jungles of Africa, not the sophisticated background of civilized society. She thought of Mark knowing love as an animal instinct, not as an emotion that was a source of joy or depression.

'That's very noble of you, Mark,' she said, realizing how little she knew of the people around her. 'I'm sure she loves you too.'

'No, missy.' He shook his head forlornly. 'She have another.'

Jealousy! Raven was intrigued that this half-naked colossus who throttled wild animals with his bare hands, could be weakened by a woman's infidelity. There was more to Daisy than she credited.

Recalling Daisy's mooning behaviour as she went about her duties, she could see Mark was speaking the truth, however odd it seemed. 'Who's this other man?' she asked, faintly worried that it could be Kumara.

'A Caffre.' He lapsed into silence.

Her first reaction was relief that Daisy had shaken off her partiality for Kumara. She wondered who the Caffre could be. 'It's impossible,' she said when she had thought about it. 'Romulus is the only other Caffre here.'

'I done see him meet with her at night.'

'Where?'

'In de spinney by Mammy's cabin.'

'Are you sure?'

He nodded unhappily. 'She don't lie wid me no more. De Caffre bewitch her.'

'She's been inattentive in her chores lately,' Raven agreed, puzzled by Mark's revelation. 'I shall ask her who this man is.'

If Daisy really had found a new mate, Bart would have to buy

143

him or sell Daisy to the Caffre's owner and find a new house-keeper.

'Don't tell her I tell yo',' he begged. 'If she know I love her, she ain't go'n give me respec' no more.'

Raven left Mark without a reprimand and hurried back to the villa. She went straight to her chamber and rang the bell. Nimal hurried in, alarmed by the unexpected summons because it was a break from her usual routine.

'Send Daisy to me,' she instructed him as she removed her bonnet.

'She is having a sleep.' He looked worried. 'She is saying we are not to wake her.'

'*I* am the mistress, Nimal. Tell her to come at once.'

She settled herself on the couch with her back to the window. The shutters were open and although it was nearly sunset, the light was sufficient for her to see Daisy's face when she questioned her.

She picked up a sampler of embroidery and stitched at it absent-mindedly while she waited. The hint of a secret romance intrigued her, especially as it was the bumptious Daisy who was smitten.

'De coolie say yo' want me?' The sullen voice announced Daisy's arrival.

She raised her head from her sampler and smiled. 'Yes, Daisy, I think we should have a chat.' She gestured at a chair placed opposite her. 'Sit down.'

Daisy's eyes were puffy with sleep and her lower lip protruded sulkily. She blinked in the light from the window.

From Bart, Raven had learned the best way of securing a slave's cooperation was to approach matters obliquely. If the slave gained a clue about what reply was required, he would give it so the questioner felt pleased. *Yes is peace* was the willing house slave's motto.

She wondered where to begin. 'With Mammy gone to England, Daisy, you are a woman of considerable importance.'

Daisy's eyes widened and she nodded her head, reluctant but pleased that her status was acknowledged.

'I know how fond you are of Mark,' Raven continued, pressing home her advantage now Daisy was amenable. 'A woman of your position should take a husband. I am sure the master would agree to your marrying Mark.'

She waited for the reaction as her words penetrated Daisy's brain. She was disappointed when there was no flicker of response

144

in her eyes, although her hands twitched. She wondered who Daisy wanted to hold.

'Would you like me to ask him?' she said, forcing her to an answer.

Daisy nodded glumly.

It wasn't the reply she expected. 'Are you pleased?' She was puzzled how to get Daisy to answer the question she did not want to ask. 'He is the man you . . . er . . . love, isn't he?'

Daisy shifted in her seat without replying.

'Good gracious, Daisy. What's happened to your tongue? I thought you'd be overjoyed.'

'I does be, missy!' She gave vent to a low howl of despair as she slipped forward from the chair and threw herself at Raven's feet. She banged her head on a tile as though she wanted to smash it.

'Daisy!' Raven scrambled off the couch and sank on her knees beside her. She took her head in her hands and held her to her bosom. Daisy's pain gouged a wound in her own heart.

'What is it?' she whispered, holding her tightly until the heaving of her shoulders calmed and her moaning eased.

'Yo' does be so kind, missy.' Daisy mumbled, pulling away from the embrace. She wiped her tears on the hem of her pinafore and stood up, helping Raven to her feet too. She was taller than Raven with strong arms that she folded across her chest. Her mouth twitched and she seemed to arrive at a decision.

'Dere does be 'nother buck, missy. He ain't like Mark. He does be fancy and he bring me presents.'

'Do you love him?' Raven was pleased with herself for extracting the confession.

'We ain't love yet, missy.'

She hid her amusement behind her sampler and turned to face the window. 'I said you're a woman of importance, Daisy. A man might try to *buy* your . . . friendship, because of your position.'

'He talk nice,' she said. 'He does be 'portant too.'

'Really?' She turned to face Daisy again, trying to hide her curiosity. 'Who is his owner?'

'A gen'leman in Galle.'

'What is the man's name?' she demanded, losing her patience.

'He don't tell me.' Daisy giggled, suddenly struck with shyness. 'I know de buck's name.'

She sighed, ready to dismiss Daisy. 'You must tell this Caffre to present himself to the master. He will decide what to do.'

Daisy looked scandalized. 'I don't want to marry de buck!

145

'Sides, he tell me keep quiet 'bout him. He ax me questions an' he give me a ring wid an eye like a cat's. But I ain't partial to him –'

Raven's heart lurched. She gripped Daisy by her shoulders and shook her. 'What's his name?' she cried so loudly the Babbler birds scavenging below the window flew off with cheeps of alarm.

She heard Daisy's answer through a fog of fear. 'He does be called Nato, missy. Nato.'

CHAPTER SEVENTEEN

The night of the full moon, Poya day, is of special significance in Ceylon. Whether through Buddhist veneration for it or because of the island's geographical location, the moon's brightness when it is full outshines the lacklustre version seen in England. Raven marvelled at it from her hiding place on the porch of Mammy's cabin.

When she thought of the full moons she had seen in England, she recalled only distant discs of light shining faintly through a shroud of clouds. An English moon lacked the impact of the great silver orb suspended above the sea, throwing its eerie light on the plantation, making even the mundane sugar-cane seem spectral.

She had ample time to contemplate the moon and feel its spell. That there was a magic in it was beyond doubt as she glanced at it boldly, comparing it with the pale moon she remembered from her childhood. People warned against staring at the full moon for fear of becoming deranged. She felt inspired when she looked at it.

She sat motionless on a chair placed in the shadows of the porch's roof where the moon's probing light would not reveal her. She had been waiting an hour since climbing from her bedroom window and creeping along in the shadows at the side of the villa to the cabin. The brightness of the moon showed her the way; she regarded it as her ally.

She was sitting on the porch waiting for Nato. No one knew she was there. Bart, Kumara and Daisy believed she had retired early to bed with a headache.

The moment Raven had heard Daisy reveal that the Caffre's name was Nato, she knew this was the chance she sought. Her mist of fear had vanished to be replaced by a fervour that guided her, regardless of the consequences.

Her first reaction was to summon Bart and let him hear Daisy's tale for himself. Instead, she delayed so she could think of her own way to make use of Daisy's infatuation with the Caffre.

It was clear to her that Nato was using Daisy to gain information for some diabolical mischief. He was probably acting on Curt's instructions. She could only find out from Nato himself.

It would be a triumph for her if she could get Nato to confess directly to Bart. That way, her foolishness in going to the brothel would remain a secret, known only to herself and Kumara. It was a brilliant scheme.

She decided, instead of telling Bart what she had learned from Daisy, to enlist Kumara's help to entrap Nato.

From Daisy, she discovered the Caffre planned his next visit on the night of the full moon. She extracted the information casually, without alerting the housekeeper to what she intended to do. Kumara was eager to help, the cruel light in his eyes kindled by the chance to catch Nato.

'This is what I've been waiting for,' he told Raven. 'Now we can discover what they're up to.'

She did not tell him of her part in the scheme. She had begun her vigil on the porch in communion with the moon's full glow to make sure she was not robbed of her chance for revenge.

The creak of the back door of the store room opening was like the crack of a rifle shot in the stillness of the night. Raven peered into the darkness looking for Daisy. Until then she had seen only the flitting of bats outlined against the moon as they wheeled in front of the porch.

Daisy glided across the grass in front of the cabin with a purposeful air. She wore a red gingham-check cloth bonnet and a gown that she had inherited from Bart's dead wife. The effect was incongruous. She was dressed more smartly for her moonlight tryst than she was to serve in the villa.

Raven was pleased she had not told Daisy of her plan. She could observe the housekeeper as she really was. From her elaborate dress and bouncy walk, she appeared more anxious to impress Nato than she had admitted.

She was heading straight for the spinney, confident that she was unobserved, lulled into a false sense of security by her excitement at the meeting.

Raven enjoyed the irony. How disappointed Daisy would be, she thought, when she discovered that Nato was not, in the words of Curt, 'as other men'. Her step would be less jaunty if she knew her Caffre admirer had been castrated.

Raven followed her with her eyes, too scared to move from the chair in case it scraped on the porch's wooden floor and made a noise. Nato was nowhere to be seen. She watched Daisy disappear into the embrace of the shadows reaching out from the spinney.

The moon followed her too, its light penetrating beneath the spinney's overhanging branches to illuminate the lower half of her gown. Raven noticed her feet were bare, caught by the moonlight when she raised one leg and rested it on a boulder.

She shared Daisy's impatience as her foot tapped restlessly on the boulder. She glanced around the garden, peering at the darkest crannies for a sign of the Caffre. She felt trapped, sitting immobile on the chair. Gingerly, she rose from the seat and moved with slow steps to the porch's rail.

A movement in front of the cabin startled her. She held her breath and the shadowy hulk of a man emerged a few feet in front of the cabin. He faced away from her, his head alert as he sniffed the air and listened. When he saw Daisy's foot spotlighted by the moon, his shoulders quivered.

He moved away, stalking to the spinney with the stealth of a leopard. He was barefoot, his breeches tight to his shins like a second skin, a loose shirt covering his massive trunk.

Raven bit her finger anxiously, hoping Kumara had seen him. She gazed around, wondering where he was hidden. The two principals were in place, about to meet, yet he seemed to be late for the performance.

'Nato!' Daisy's yelp of surprise echoed through the night. 'Yo' scare me comin' out de trees like dat.'

Raven heard a grunt of reply and the slobbering smack of a kiss. Daisy's squawk of protest deepened to a hum of satisfaction.

'Boy!' she said after seconds of hot silence that stirred the blood in Raven's veins while she wondered what was going on. 'Yo' sure in de mood tonight.'

'I see yo' like a moon goddess, Daisy.'

Nato's bass voice triggered off an explosion of hatred in Raven. She gripped the porch railing and glared across the darkness, willing the Caffre to drop insensible to the ground. It hurt her that Daisy was as keen as mustard for his kisses and too ruttish to see the truth behind his imposter's patter.

The two shadowy shapes under the trees joined for an interminable time of snuffling and sucking noises, grunts and groans. Raucous sighs from Daisy proclaimed her animalistic enjoyment of Nato's kisses.

Raven was disgusted. She suspected Daisy of showing-off to

149

impress him. She wondered if Nato was roused and how he would be able to satisfy Daisy's ardour.

She was relieved when the two of them emerged from the sahdows and sat on a boulder, brightly lit by the pearly glow of the moon. Nato held his arm around Daisy's shoulders fondling her breasts as he talked. His low voice carried over to the cabin enabling her to hear every word.

'Yo' find de t'ing?' he asked, lowering his mouth to Daisy's cheek.

Daisy squirmed at his touch and wriggled her shoulders. He nibbled the tiny lobe of her ear.

'It ain't easy,' she gasped. 'Bloodheart does be very secretive.'

'Yo' say yo' know everyt'ing 'bout him.'

'I do.' She stiffened and withdrew her lips.

'Den why yo' take so long to find de t'ing? Don't yo' want me?'

'Yes.' She giggled girlishly.

The sound made Raven furious at Daisy's stupidity.

'Find out where he keep de t'ing. I goan come take it one night. Bloodheart ain't goan 'spect yo' 'cause he 'ssume it does be Kumara. Den when de time right, yo' join me in C'lombo. Dey have plenty Caffres live like buckra masters dere. Yo' goan have yuh own housekeeper an' coolie boys.'

His lies were so transparent, Raven was amazed how Daisy could be fooled by them. She wished Bart was with her to hear what Nato said.

She released the porch railing and clenched her fists, frustrated because she wanted to rush out and crack their skulls together. Daisy had deceived her; a glib tongue and a lecher's lies showed how shallow her loyalty was.

Nato was taking full advantage of the moonlight and the charm it worked on Daisy. He kissed her again, seeming to devour her lips with his.

Despite her disgust at the sight, Raven's blood raced and she watched the shadowy show with morbid curiosity. She saw Daisy's head tilt back and her body slide down until her back rested against the side of the boulder.

Nato knelt in front of her, pushing her skirt and petticoats up to her hips. He spread her legs apart and eased her knees wide so she was half crouching on the ground. When he grunted, Daisy raised herself off the grass with her hands.

Raven shuddered at the sight. Daisy was facing her while Nato had his back to the cabin. She dreaded what was going to happen

150

but she was unable to turn away. The clouds drifted from the moon and its light shone down on Daisy waiting with her legs wide open.

Nato gradually lowered his head until it was lodged between Daisy's raised thighs. He pushed forward, burying his mouth in her loins. His head rose and fell with a quickening rhythm as Daisy thrust and bucked to meet him.

A low rumbling moan escaped Daisy's throat, soaring into the night, mingling with Raven's startled gasps of fascinated horror.

She clapped her hand to her mouth to stifle her excitement, but the faint sound drifted over to Nato. He cocked his head, his pink tongue protruding from his mouth like a cat's.

Kumara, who had crept unobserved from the spinney to the boulder where the two of them lay, leapt at that moment. He had in his hand a fishing net, the circular kind with lead pellets to weigh it down in the water. He flung the net at Nato, billowing it open so it would fall around the Caffre's shoulders.

Nato sensed the attack coming and rolled aside just as the net fluttered down. It caught Daisy in its mesh. She began bawling, setting the dogs barking and roosting birds squawking with her shrieks of fright.

Nato jumped from the ground as Kumara dived for him. He kicked out and caught Kumara a blow under his chin with his foot. It felled him to the ground. Raven screamed.

Nato raised his foot to stamp on Kumara's neck with a force that would break it. He never connected. Kumara's hands gripped his ankle; he heaved and tossed him on his back. Pouncing on him with his fists striking his face, he endeavoured to pummel him unconscious.

This was not the way Raven planned it. Kumara had boasted he could capture Nato easily and she believed him. Neither of them knew his background.

Nato was raised in the toughest savannah in Africa, a killer with his bare hands of three tribal enemies before he was twelve. By the time of his manhood ceremony, he was acclaimed throughout his tribe for his skill as an assassin. His neutering by a white man when he was sold into slavery, added to his anger.

Kumara pounded his face with his fists as he lay unmoving.

Raven edged to the porch's steps to join Kumara and lend her kicks to his merciless punches. She paused, puzzled by the sudden rearrangement of the shadows.

Nato, who ought to have been beaten senseless, suddenly raised his great arms and almost casually pushed Kumara off him, pitching him into the air like a stone from a catapult. He yelled with surprise. Raven retreated to the back of the porch, her delight changing to horror.

Kumara landed awkwardly, then staggered to his feet to chase after Nato. The Caffre was unconcerned. He tugged leisurely at the fish net wrapped around Daisy. In her panic, she had become helplessly entangled in it.

His gruff laughter at her predicament terrified Raven in case he decided to attack her. She was mesmerized by the power of his gaze as he stared into the porch's shadows, looking straight at her.

Kumara struck him in his face. He shrugged off the blow and then turned his cheek, inviting the next one. When Kumara tried to strike him again, he jerked his head aside. Kumara toppled forward under the momentum of the missed punch. He was stopped by the edge of Nato's open palm chopping into the side of his neck.

'Kumara!' Raven shrieked as he went down. Her cry drew Nato's attention. She heard him grunt and then saw him take a step in her direction.

She forgot that he couldn't see her clearly in the moonlight and was unlikely to recognize her as the whore who had tricked him in the bordello. He took another unhurried stride towards her.

Her scream roused Kumara. With a wild battle-cry of anger, he scrambled onto Nato's broad shoulders. He clung to his throat with one hand and punched him under his heart with the other.

He held fast, despite Nato's bucking and twirling, trying to shake him off. Gradually, he tightened his hold on Nato's neck. Raven listened anxiously until she heard Nato gasping for breath.

At last, she thought, feeling weak with excitement. When Nato sank to his knees with Kumara still grasping his throat, and his gurgling changed to a deathly rasping, she squealed with pleasure.

Her heart swelled with gratitude for Kumara and she felt she would love him for ever for saving her. She listened eagerly for Nato's death rattle when he slumped to the ground in front of the cabin.

A shot blasted out close to her head. She was lifted by its force from her feet and flung against the back wall of the porch. She went limp as she slid down the side and collapsed like a discarded marionette in a heap on the floor. She was winded, stunned by the scorching path of the shot, and dazed by the spatter of orange and green stars that was all she could see.

Above Daisy's screams, Nato's grunts and Kumara's cry of anguish, she heard Bart's stentorian voice ordering everyone to lie still. There was a sudden rush of air close to her ear and a panting that receded into the darkness.

She blinked to clear the light from her eyes. Bart was ordering Nimal and Jagath to bring lanterns. Slowly she rose to her feet. She supported herself against the cabin wall, breathing deeply, disturbed how close she had come to being shot.

The silvery light of the moon deepened to amber when the boys hurried over with lanterns. The sight that met her eyes made her stomach churn. Bart was standing in the centre of the lawn, by the boulders, with Daisy at his feet. She had ceased to struggle under the net and lay whimpering, her shoulders shaking with sobs of fear.

Across the steps to the porch, one arm reaching up to her, his eyes closed and his body unmoving, was Kumara. Blood spurted from a wound in his side.

Raven's scream froze in her throat as she stared around the glade looking for Nato. He had escaped. Bart had shot the wrong man.

Book Two

Kumara
1822

CHAPTER EIGHTEEN

Christmas is a nostalgic time in the tropics for someone used to the winter's cold, holly, mulled wine and the hearty fare of the festive season in England. Although it was her sixth Christmas in Ceylon, Raven missed the bracing cold and the cheering melodies of carol singers. Christmas Day fell on a Tuesday and to her it was like any other day of the year; hot, humid and languorous.

She brightened the house with sprays of poinsettia, its crimson leaves forming colourful stars in the gloomy corners of the villa's large rooms. She persuaded Daisy to cook a special meal and they dined on baked ham and chicken and salted beef washed down with burgundy and water. Bart, to whom a European Christmas was as foreign as it was to the Singhalese and the slaves, joined in to humour her.

He even offered to accompany her to church in Galle despite his disapproval of formal occasions. He needed to visit Galle so he could confront Madam Gudde about the behaviour of her Caffre slave.

Raven declined; she would not leave Kumara until his recovery was complete. It was another two weeks before his wound healed sufficiently for her to be satisfied.

From the moment she saw him lying on the steps of the cabin and thought him dead, she knew she loved him. The shock of that moment changed to a tortured joy when he opened his eyes and smiled faintly at her through his pain.

Jagath and Nimal had carried him off to the house. She stayed with him, holding his hand in hers, willing him to live. Blood from his wound seeped into the red of her robe and darkened it. She vowed she would never leave his side until he was fit; if he died she would mourn for the rest of her life.

Her relief at discovering he would live muted her anger at Bart for his reckless shooting. There was little time for recrimination in the turmoil that followed. She was frantic to stanch the bleeding

157

from Kumara's side and shared with Malika the task of binding Kumara's wound as he lay, a deathly sallow colour, his features taut with agony, on the bed.

Tissa was dispatched to bring the army doctor from Galle while Bart hovered around demanding an explanation, insensitive to the distress he was causing Raven. Daisy was seized with hysterics and when she was released from the fishing net rushed wailing to her quarters where it took Little hours to calm her down. No one thought of chasing Nato.

In the days that followed, first Raven then Kumara, as he grew stronger, recounted to Bart what they had heard the Caffre telling Daisy. Daisy, when she was assured by Raven that she would suffer no punishment, told the same story in her own convoluted and outraged fashion.

Bart discussed it many times with Raven in the privacy of their chamber.

'Now do you believe Kumara was not involved?' she had asked him, desperate for his reassurance that his attitude to Kumara had changed.

'Yes, yes,' he had answered, waving away the question with embarrassment. 'I fired to wing the Caffre. He was smart to swing around so Kumara took the shot instead. You should have told me what was happening.'

'You should have fired in the air.'

As Christmas passed and Kumara recovered, Raven's spirits rose. That the Caffre had asked for 'the thing' proved it was Nato and not Kumara who was trying to steal the elephant pearl. The question of what to do about Nato was left unresolved until Kumara was fit enough to leave his bed and walk to the verandah.

His injury, despite the copious loss of blood, was only flesh deep. He amazed Raven by his lack of bitterness at what had happened. He chatted with Bart as amicably as ever, his charm never faltering. She wondered if he really forgave Bart. Bart never apologized and acted unperturbed by the incident.

When she watched the two of them sitting on the verandah, a flagon of rum on the table between them she was frightened.

Bart with his craggy, tanned features and blond beard stirred her with his quiet self-confidence; he was a pioneer blessed with an innocence and faith that he was right. Kumara, in contrast, was a lean, bronzed godling who sat with regal bearing, thrilling her with the passion and strength coiled within his erect, youthful body.

The two men frightened her because she feared that one day she would have to choose between them.

'I must go to Galle,' Bart announced. 'I believe you're fit enough to protect Raven while I'm away.'

Raven hid her excitement behind her fan at the thought of being alone in the villa at night with Kumara. She glanced over its rim to find Bart's eyes on her.

'I shall ask Tissa to sleep here too,' he said. 'In case . . .' His words hung in the air like an accusation.

'Yes, please do,' she said quickly. 'I wouldn't want Kumara to be alone with only Kirti for company. Even though he appears to be fit, the doctor said he must rest.'

'And you?' asked Bart with a trace of irony in his voice. 'Won't you be company for him too?'

'How can I be when I'm coming with you?'

'To Galle?' Bart frowned at her to indicate his objection to her plan. 'I have to raise with Madam Gudde the question of her Caffre. There is no need for you to come with me.'

'You offered to take me to Galle at Christmas!' She challenged him with her eyes.

'That was for a special occasion.'

'My desire to see my father is no less than it was then. I am coming, Bart. Kumara, as you say, will be all right here with Tissa. They can guard the house and valuables while we are gone.' She smiled at Kumara and was gratified by his nod of agreement.

Despite Bart's show of reluctance, she believed he was pleased that she refused the opportunity of being alone in the villa with Kumara. It impressed her that at least a flicker of jealousy burned behind Bart's impassive façade.

Elaborate preparations were made for the journey since they would be travelling together. The palanquin was brought out from the stables and cleaned, its drapes washed in the river and re-hung with care. Tissa selected a gang of eight bearers to carry it.

Raven protested at this indulgence but Bart insisted his wife must travel in style instead of on horseback or by bullock cart. They were to be attended by four tough-looking Singhalese from the settlement armed with staves, more for show than for effectiveness.

Raven was delighted at the prospect of visiting Galle, especially when she saw an opportunity to exact revenge on Curt without Bart knowing her real reason. She made some arrangements of her own and was ready at dawn on the morning of the trip.

Kumara and Kirti were on the verandah to see them off. She kissed Kirti on both cheeks before turning to Kumara and extending her hand to him.

His grip set off an intense feeling of fondness rushing through her body. She could do nothing to show how she felt with Bart watching from the palanquin. Instead, she held her head aloof while Kumara brushed her fingers with his lips.

His touch inspired her even though the roguish glint in his eyes mocked her warm affection.

'Be careful, Raven,' he said softly, holding her hand moments too long for propriety. He released her and escorted her to the palanquin, bowing his head to Bart. 'I wish you success in your mission, *Bloodheart*.'

Raven wondered if Bart noticed the teasing note in Kumara's voice. He let Kumara help her into the palanquin while he checked the entourage. As they were about to move off, Bart's exclamation of rage made her raise the curtain and peer at him anxiously.

'Ram, what are you doing here?' Bart demanded of the snake boy who sidled out from behind the bougainvillaea bushes and joined the retinue.

The youth was wearing a clean check cloth extending like a sarong to his ankles under a white loose-fitting shirt that covered him from his shoulders to his thighs. His spiky hair was smoothed down in a semblance of tidiness. He was grinning nervously at Bart without speaking.

'Let him come with us,' Raven pleaded before Bart could turn him away. 'He's never been to Galle.'

Bart glanced at the reed basket slung over Ram's shoulder. 'If you wish. As long as he hasn't got any cobras with him.'

Ram's eyes brightened and he touched the basket, shaking his head.

Raven nodded conspiratorially and beckoned him to walk at the side of the palanquin as Bart gave the command for the procession to begin. She peeked through the curtains at Kumara. He was crouched on the verandah on the same level as Kirti encouraging the child to salute as they moved off.

The bearers trotted along at a steady rhythm, chanting to keep up their speed. Inside the palanquin, Raven relaxed on the cushions, fretting at having to travel in such ladylike splendour when she preferred to ride with Bart.

The motion of swinging from side to side while she bounced along suspended from the shoulders of the bearers, and the stifling heat of the morning, made her sleepy. Shielded by the silk curtains from the gaze of the entourage, she lay in drowsy warmth, allowing her subconscious thoughts to surface.

She was puzzled by Bart's composure at recent events. His lack of remorse at shooting Kumara instead of Nato was uncharacteristic of him. She thought of him as sensitive and caring despite his reputation for reckless daring.

In bed his loving had not changed. She experienced such exquisite fulfillment in his arms she considered she was bound to him by love for ever. Why, then, she asked herself, did she feel such a strong bond of affection for Kumara?

The devilish glint in his eyes as he kissed her hand in farewell came back to mock her thoughts. At times he blatantly toyed with her emotions, and yet he had reached for her when he lay bleeding on the cabin's steps. He was the opposite of Bart in temperament, burning with an irresistible passion that stirred a desire in her equal to the love she had for Bart.

She dreaded – and yet longed for – the night when he would take her. Then she would have to decide whether to go with him or stay with Bart. She could not contain the wildness of her soul to become the mistress of one man while she was the wife of another.

She was so concerned about both of them, her mind was in torment and she passed the journey gripped with anguish. For Bart she wanted a resolution to his problems and the sweetness of revenge against Curt. For Kumara, she wanted whatever it was he was seeking as he brooded in exclusive majesty in the shelter of their lonely plantation home.

The shouting of boys running alongside the palanquin and the inquisitive cries of foot travellers warned her that they had reached the native quarters and would soon be entering the fort.

She pushed her dreams about Bart and Kumara to the back of her mind and readied herself to meet her father. She had brought a cake she had baked herself as a belated Christmas gift. She expected more than that would be needed to sweeten the dour old man when he heard Bart's complaints.

Their reception at her father's home was what she expected. He was not slow to voice his objection to their arrival even though they had sent a message three days in advance to warn him. In his mind, Collector Radley linked Bart with trouble. Raven's own behaviour in disappearing without a word before dawn at the end of her previous stay made him suspicious of their reasons for visiting him.

'To wish you season's greetings, daddy,' Raven proclaimed to reassure him. 'For the New Year!'

'The Singhala and Tamil New Year begins in April,' he said gloomily. 'Like everything else in this country, they want it all ways. Every holiday whether Buddhist, Hindu, Muhammadan or Christian must be celebrated. That means I have to don full rig and perspire in the company of half-naked natives without shoes nearly a hundred times a year just to impress on them the omnipresence of British authority.'

His grumbling continued throughout the day, effectively dis-couraging Bart from broaching the matter of Madam Gudde's Caffre. In the evening, when they returned to their chamber leaving Mr Radley still placidly carping, Raven asked Bart what he was going to do.

'I shall go direct to Gretchen Gudde. Your father won't take any action even if we have a case against Nato.' He spoke belligerently, as though he expected her to try to dissuade him.

'What a good idea,' she said, catching him off guard by her agreement. 'I shall come too.'

He gawped at her across the chamber where he had paused by the door prior to going out. 'You can't! It's . . . er . . . well, it's not a place for respectable ladies.'

'I know what it is. If I come with you no one will assume you are visiting Madam Gudde's for an immoral purpose.'

He bristled. 'What do I care for what people think!'

'I care.' She smiled to soften her words. 'We arrived here with such pomp everyone in Galle knows you have your wife with you. I don't want them also to know you frequent a bordello while your wife stays at her father's house. What respect can they think you have for me?'

'Does it matter?' He spread his hands in exasperation. 'I'll be gone only half an hour. Clients at Gretchen's stay there all night.'

She bit her lip to banish her dismay and reached with deter-mination for her bonnet. 'I was the one who heard Nato cajoling Daisy. I shall tell Madam Gudde myself.'

Bart's eyes were like monsoon lightning, a flare of anger spark-ing in his stormy glance. She stared back at him despite the unhappiness that raged through her for having to defy him. Her heart swelled with a deep feeling of adoration for his tolerance when he brusquely nodded his consent.

'Very well,' he said, opening the door with an abrupt twist of the handle. 'You shall come. Perhaps after this you will be less inclined to interfere. Your reputation, I can assure you, will be in shreds by the morrow.'

'My conscience will be intact,' she answered, tying the ribbons of her bonnet as she followed him out.

She struggled to keep up with his long strides down the darkened streets. He only slowed when he turned into the Street of Moorish Traders. Coconut lanterns and flambeaux lit the street from the verandahs of houses where Muhammadans were gathered, even at that late hour, in desultory discussions of business deals.

She felt countless pairs of eyes watching her and Bart with interest. Glancing behind, she was relieved to see they were being followed by Ram, exactly as she had instructed him in secret that morning.

Bart's knock on the bordello door was loud and defiant, echoing down the street. The murmur of the Muhammadans in the gem merchant's house ceased. When the grille was drawn back Bart pressed his face to the latticed screen and leered. The door opened instantly. He ushered Raven through then paused as she beckoned Ram to enter with them.

'Let him come, Bart,' she hissed sternly, compelling him with her eyes to consent. His shrugging of his shoulders showed he had abandoned hope of understanding her. His response made her bold.

'Good evening, Nato,' she said to the Caffre holding the door, hiding her hatred of him in her tone of icy politeness. 'We have come to see your mistress.' She led the way through the garden to the house ignoring his attempt to prevent her.

'Rave –' Bart's entreaty was lost as he gulped into silence, realizing how foolish he would look in front of the watching whores if he commanded her to wait and she refused. Instead, he hurried after her in her wake, Ram following behind. It was just as she planned.

The big jowly hulk of Curt lumbered out of the gloom, blocking the doorway into the house. 'Vat do you vant –?' he began to ask but stopped in amazement as Raven pulled off her bonnet and shook out her hair so it swirled and shimmered, dazzling in the lantern's golden glow. He gawped at her, bereft of speech.

She hoped Bart would attribute Curt's surprise to his being enchanted with her beauty. That he recognized her was obvious from his bulging eyes and the squawking sound that issued from the back of his fleshy throat. She shoved him aside with her elbow

163

before he recovered his wits, and strode into the bordello's parlour.

She was on unfamiliar territory now and momentarily overawed by the richness of the brocade and velvet hangings in the room, the heavily shaded lanterns and the vermilion hues of the parlour's half-light. She looked at Bart for help, expecting him to be pleased that she had gained an entrance for the three of them to Madam Gudde's presence.

The lady herself rose unsteadily to her feet, propping herself up on the arms of her chair. She glowered at them from a face that was painted like a Christmas decoration; crimson lips, rouged cheeks and eyelids of silver and blue. Her dress of emerald green taffeta into which she was just about squeezed completed the garish effect.

She belched, swaying uncertainly as she opened her arms to welcome Bart. He rushed forward to stop her falling and found himself swept into her embrace. He was clutched to her breast and kissed resoundingly on both cheeks before he emerged with paint and powder smeared on his face and coat. He turned bashfully to Raven and presented her.

She kept her distance from the grotesque figure of Madam Gudde, appalled at the woman's drunkenness. Her heart sank at the thought of getting any sense out of her. Bart had been right, she should not have interfered.

'Whoo!' Madam Gudde exclaimed, falling back on to her chair with a suddenness that shook the room. 'Have you come to leave your wife here where she belongs? Curt will be pleased.'

Raven hoped Bart would blame the rudeness on Madam Gudde's inebriated state. He seemed distracted by her actions. Her hands were reaching to paw him and he had to step back sharply to avoid being grabbed in his crotch.

'It was my wife's idea to visit you, Gretchen,' he said, dodging her grasp. 'We have something to tell you about your Caffre.'

'And about your son,' said Raven resolutely, ignoring the fat old lady's antics. 'Your son and your Caffre are engaged in a campaign to harass my husband. The pair of them attacked him on the plantation, set fire to the mill, tried to poison him and threw him from his horse.'

Madam Gudde stopped fidgeting and focused her tiny, shifty eyes on Raven. She hawked with noisy relish into the spittoon at her side, deliberately splashing spittle onto Raven's gown.

'Take your *trollop* out of here, Bloodheart!' she said with a sneer. 'You are not welcome any more. Unless you want me to tell her a few things about you?'

Raven fought back the flush of anger surging into her cheeks. She didn't want to hear about Bart's infidelity. 'I have proof of these charges!' she said in a voice that matched Gretchen's in raucousness. 'I heard your Caffre enticing my housekeeper to steal the elephant pearl from our house.'

Madam Gudde seemed to swell. 'Elephant pearl?' She exploded with an obscene bellow of laughter. 'Elephant's balls are what that Caffre needs.'

Bart grinned sheepishly and waved Raven to silence. 'Gretchen,' he said coldly to make her stop laughing. 'Nato was heard asking our housekeeper to steal something for Curt. We assumed it's the *gaja mutu*.'

Madam Gudde shook her head and the effort set her whole body trembling like a bowl of jelly. 'Bart, your wife is not the innocent you think she is. Ask Curt. Why does she bring these lies to me?'

'They are not lies!' Raven's disgust added strength to her accusation. 'We have a witness.' She paused and studied Madam Gudde, suddenly realizing her wobbling drunkenness was a sham. 'You know what we're talking about!'

'Of course I don't.' Madam Gudde flapped her flabby arm and Curt and Nato came to her side immediately. 'This woman is annoying me.'

'Wait!' Raven's shout halted Curt as he advanced on her. 'Ram!' she called to the snake boy who stood forgotten in the shadows of the room.

He dashed forward, grinning mischievously and holding out his basket in front of him.

'Vat's dat?' asked Curt, his brow puckering as he sensed danger.

'*Nalla pamboo rendoo.*' Ram opened the lid of the basket.

'Two cobras,' said Raven with relish.

Curt and Nato hastily backed away behind Madam Gudde's chair. The old woman herself clutched her breast and heaved, too terrified to speak.

Ram knelt down at her feet and laid the basket on the floor, whistling softly to the cobras to lure them out.

'Now,' said Raven with a giggle of delight at the beginning of her vengeance. 'I want you to explain why you've embarked on this feud against Bloodheart.'

CHAPTER NINETEEN

The cobra is a sluggish creature with a hooded head that flares open when it is disturbed. Its poison is deadly and yet it can be reluctant to bite unless provoked. Snake lovers, like Ram, tame cobras and keep them as domesticated pets, letting them go in and out of the house at pleasure and in common with the rest of the inmates.

There are four species of cobra: the *raja* or king; the *velyander* or trader; the *baboona* or hermit; and the *goore* or agriculturist. The snakes that slithered from Ram's basket were of the rare variety fancifully designated the 'king of cobras'. Their heads and the anterior half of the body is so light a colour that at a distance it seems like a silvery white.

Raven stepped back involuntarily, fighting the nausea rising in her throat when Ram coaxed the snakes out. He touched one of them tenderly then enclosed his hand around it, offering it to Madam Gudde.

She drew her knees up to her chest, squirming as far back in her chair as possible. She slobbered and her body jerked with spasms of terror. Curt gawped at Ram from behind the chair while Nato searched with his eyes for something to stand on if the snake got near him.

Raven glanced at Bart, relieved to take her eyes off the horrible sight of the two pale mottled serpents swaying at Ram's whistled command.

Bart remained motionless, watching Ram alertly. In his hand was his knife, ready to defend himself if Ram lost control and the snakes decided to strike at him instead of Madam Gudde.

'Hold them, Ram,' Raven whispered, overcoming her own revulsion of the slippery creatures.

He seemed to understand her words for he kept the snakes occupied. They were entranced by his whistling and his weaving hand passing to and fro in front of their eyes.

'He will release them if I tell him,' said Raven, drawing back her shoulders and tossing her head to emphasize her authority. 'They are as deadly as they look. Ram has only to let one *accidentally* fall on you while he is displaying his skill as a snake charmer, Madam Gudde, and you will be on a swift descent to hell.'

'Put them avay!' cried Curt in a voice unnaturally high-pitched with fear. 'They might get loose.'

'Yes, they might . . .' Raven smiled smoothly, 'Do you admit you sent your Caffre to the villa to seduce our housekeeper?'

'I haf my reasons.'

'What reasons?' Raven noticed Curt seemed mesmerized by the swaying snakes. 'Was it to steal the elephant pearl?'

'No, no, no.' Curt flapped his hand and then dropped it to his side in dismay as the movement roused one of the snakes and it raised itself off the ground, opening its hood at him.

'For the title deed!' Gretchen Gudde spat the words out in desperation.

Bart was amused. 'The deed for my plantation? Why do you want that?'

'It's not your plantation,' said Curt. 'You swindled it from Marcus Van Dort.'

'Nonsense! It was deeded to me by the governor.'

'By rights it should haf gone to Marcus Van Dort.' Curt whined unhappily, the snakes depriving him of the joy he could be expected to feel at confronting Bart. 'I mean to haf it for myself,' he bleated unconvincingly.

Bart's guffaw of scorn upset one of the cobras and it swung its head to peer at him through alert and livid eyes.

Ram whistled furiously and waved his fingers to regain its attention. He looked pleadingly at Raven as if begging for permission to put the snakes away before they got beyond his control.

She ignored his unspoken request and faced Madam Gudde. 'Why should your son want our plantation?' she demanded, showing no sympathy for the old woman's quivering panic.

Madam Gudde gasped, opened her mouth to speak and closed it again. She could not see the snakes, only the movement of Ram's hand as he tried to charm them. 'It is his,' she said on her second attempt. 'Bloodheart robbed it from Curt's father.'

'Dammit!' Bart moved forward impulsively at the lie. Raven tried to restrain him.

One of the cobras rose up in the air and Madam Gudde saw its head swaying close to her knees. She screamed.

Ram gathered up the lazier snake and coiled it back in the basket. His eyes were on the livelier one as he tried to hypnotize it to obedience.

The snake was rattled by the activity around it. It swayed viciously, its hooded head peering at Madam Gudde's fat ankles then at Curt and Nato cowering behind her.

Raven realized Ram was having difficulty. She kept her hand on Bart's arm to give herself assurance as much as to detain him from doing something rash.

'Who is your son's father?' she asked, trying to understand Curt's involvement.

'Marcus Van Dort himself!' Gretchen Gudde uttered the name like a curse. 'He left everything to Curt, including the land where you have the plantation. Curt has a title deed.'

'It's forged!' Bart shouted.

'I haf come to Ceylon to claim my land, Bloodheart.' Curt wiped the sweat from his brow with the back of his hand.

'That's why you want to steal Bart's title deed,' said Raven, understanding the scheme at last. 'You would destroy it and present your father's forged one instead.'

'That's why you've been harassing me!' Bart took a slow step backwards, drawing Raven with him. 'To make me give up the plantation and leave Ceylon so you could claim it.' He patted Raven's hand.

'Ram,' he called softly. 'Collect up the snakes. We have stayed long enough. I want fresh air!'

His calm acceptance of Curt's unscrupulous scheme infuriated Raven. She stared at Curt, loathing him for everything he represented. He was a fat toad of a man, out to destroy her and Bart because of his greed. He wasn't fit to live!

'Ram!' she called between tight lips. He took his eyes off the snake to watch her.

On the table behind her was a glass of gin, left there by Madam Gudde when they burst into the room. She snatched it up and flung it to the floor. It broke and the gin splashed over the snake, distracting it from Ram's influence.

Raven darted over to Ram's side, kicked over his basket and upset the other cobra. She seized him by his arm and pulled him with her as she rushed for the door.

Bart held it open, grinning hugely. Madam Gudde's screams

rent the air and Curt and Nato shouted, jostling each other for space as they scrambled for the table top. On the floor below their feet the two cobras writhed angrily.

'You could have been bitten!' said Kumara, looking shocked. He regarded her with disapproval but Raven knew from the silky tone of his voice that he was impressed by her tale.

She related the events at the bordello to him as soon as they arrived back at the villa. Bart was at her side on the verandah where Jagath was serving them drinks. Kirti played in a corner watched by Malika.

They had left Galle early that morning. The brothel was in an uproar. Whores and their clients had fled naked into the street the previous night to seek safety from the rogue cobras.

Madam Gudde had remained paralysed in her chair as the snakes wormed and wriggled their way menacingly around the room. They were dazed by the commotion and missed the chance of striking at Curt and Nato before they bolted.

'We heard about it afterwards from one of the girls,' explained Raven, giggling at the memory of Curt Van Dort's face when she had thrown the gin to encourage the cobra to bite him.

Kumara frowned. 'What happened to the snakes?'

'Ram wanted to fetch them this morning before we left, but I wouldn't let him.' She felt a glow of wellbeing spread through her at what she had done.

'You mean there are two king cobras loose in that brothel?' Kumara's serious expression changed to a grin of amazement. It sent a thrill up her spine.

'I must be careful when I go there for a whore,' he commented blandly, crushing her delight when she pictured him in such a vile place.

'I hope Madam Gudde has to close her establishment!' She shut her mouth firmly and glared at him.

'Raven,' said Bart, raising his glass to his lips and drinking to revive himself after the journey from Galle. 'You surprised me. You're lucky no one was killed. You could have been charged with murder.'

Smacking his lips with satisfaction, he drained his glass and placed it on the table. He stroked the point of his beard with his thumb and forefinger. 'Gretchen will have no more clients, or whores, until the snakes are caught. We're even now for the trouble she caused me.'

'Even?' Raven gave way to the outrage sweeping through her. 'How can you say that? They've confessed to trying to steal your plantation from you. They'll not stop just because Ram's snakes scare them for a few hours.'

'Curt didn't succeed, Raven.' He rose from his chair, smiling at her with his eyes. 'It's over. He'll give up now we know his scheme.' He bent down and kissed her, the brush of his beard against her cheek distracting her from her anger.

She glanced at Kumara, using a question to conceal her embarrassment at having him watch her being embraced so intimately by Bart. 'Do you think it's over?' she asked sceptically.

Kumara leaned back in his chair and stretched his legs out in front of him, causing her to wonder if he knew the effect the sight of his robust limbs and tight breeches could have on a woman.

She averted her eyes hastily and looked around for Bart. He was standing with his back to her, his hand on a verandah column, gazing thoughtfully across the lawn. His broad shoulders and stalwart frame reflected his unflappable nature. Her heart beat a little faster as she thanked God for his presence. He would protect her from herself as well as from others.

Kumara raised an eyebrow, piercing her with the keenness of his glance. 'After what you did, Raven, Curt and his mother will want revenge. They have been humiliated and made the laughing stock of Galle. Burghers like fun but not when they bear the brunt of it.'

Bart slapped the column with the palm of his hand, the sound expressing his contempt for what Kumara said. 'A bully is a coward. Curt will ship back to Holland now his scheme is exposed.' He jumped down from the verandah.

'I'm going to the mill to see Tissa. We need more rum to fill the orders I collected in Galle.' He waved at Raven cheerily and strode off down the mill path.

Raven sighed and stood up. 'I need a rest after all that excitement.' She was uncomfortable at being on the verandah with Kumara. His eyes were watching her probingly, as if he were trying to understand a secret side of her personality she didn't know herself.

'I'm going to my chamber,' she said emphatically.

He beamed at her from his chair without making an attempt to get up. A lock of hair fell over his brow and he flicked it back, his long index finger tracing a line down his clean-shaven cheek and coming to rest under his chin.

Raven felt the caress was meant for her. Her cheek twitched in reaction. She gathered up her skirt and hurried off the verandah.

She was about to cross the parlour to the chamber when something made her pause. She looked up at the portrait of Bart's mother and squinted at it. The eyes of the drawing stared back and she imagined the formidable lady looked unhappy.

She noticed the frame was crooked and went over to straighten it. Slipping her fingers under the left hand corner of the frame, she felt for the key to Bart's escritoire. It was not there.

She lifted the picture away from the wall. Two geckos, pallid from the lack of sunlight, scurried out from behind the frame and raced across the wall. They caused her to drop the picture in fright.

It swung on its nails, Bart's mother's image tilting drunkenly. She steadied it as something slipped out from behind the frame and fell with a clatter to the floor. She stepped away nervously, sighing with relief when she looked down and saw it was the missing key.

As she knelt to retrieve it, she saw something else had been dislodged when she shifted the picture. It was a small leather sachet with a drawstring, the kind used by European jewellers for gems of great value.

She glanced behind her. The door to the verandah was closed and she was alone in the parlour. Hurriedly, she returned the key to its hiding place, on the left side of the picture, wondering who had replaced it on the right side.

She kept the leather purse enclosed in the palm of her hand as she walked, concealing with difficulty the excitement rising in her breast, towards the chamber door. She was on tenterhooks that Kumara might enter the parlour and tease her, or Daisy might come rushing in for her to deal with some foolish complaint.

She managed to reach her door without interruption. She pushed it open, entered the chamber and shut and locked the door behind her.

She walked over to the window, still clasping the soft purse in her hand, and peered out. The sun was subdued, frills of hazy white clouds framing the sky. The shadows from the trees surrounding the house were soft, merging into the mellowness of the morning.

There was no breeze and the still air emphasized the languor of the atmosphere. When she was satisfied that no one was spying on her, she moved away from the window to the bed.

171

She sat down on it, her stomach clenched tight with apprehension as she opened her hand. The pouch seemed to be burning her palm and she let it roll onto the bed. For seconds she stared at it, half in dread, half in anticipation. Her lips were dry and she licked them cautiously, convincing herself that what she was doing was right.

With trembling fingers, she unknotted the drawstring. She felt she was prying into someone's privacy as she tipped up the purse and watched the contents tumble onto the crimson coverlet. Her exhilaration slumped as she gazed in disappointment at the dull, lacklustre bead that nestled in the coverlet's fold.

It was an anti-climax. She had expected a gem that shone, radiating a magnificent power and living up to its fame as a priceless heirloom. Instead, the spherical object was yellowed with age; uninspiring and seemingly unworthy of the veneration placed in it.

Picking it up gingerly, she polished it with a corner of the silk coverlet. Its colour remained the same yet she could almost see it glowing. She blinked, a feeling of courage seeping through the bones as she touched the bead. She knew instinctively that the ivory in her hand was indeed the fabled *gaja mutu*.

She gazed on it lovingly, filled with a respect for the elephant pearl and its ancient history. It was warm in her hand and she was no longer nervous of it; somehow it was part of her and she knew fate had placed it in her protection. It had certainly not been behind the picture when she hid the key there. She pursed her lips, pondering what to do.

The answer came easily. She rose from the bed and opened her jewellery box. She plucked something from it and placed it in the leather purse, refastening the string. She wrapped the pearl in a piece of muslin and laid it carefully among her jewellery, closing the box. She would think later of where to hide it more securely.

She walked over to the door, unlocked it and looked out. The parlour was still empty. She quickly went over to the picture and tucked the leather sachet beneath it. She grinned at Bart's mother, pleased to be sharing the picture's secret.

During the days that followed their return from Galle, she expected that at any moment Bart would discover the *gaja mutu* was missing. However, he remained unconcerned. He was preoccupied, urging the Singhalese to greater efforts in the production of rum.

Bart was happier than he had been for weeks. He treated her and Kumara with a breezy affability. Life on the plantation picked up a jauntier rhythm. Being no longer under suspicion, and fully recovered from his injury, Kumara too was more at ease as he continued with his training of Kirti.

'One day,' he boasted to Bart and Raven, 'this child will be called upon to serve his country. He must be prepared.'

Bart smiled indulgently at his treatment of Kirti, and said nothing.

Kirti lost his baby softness under Kumara's influence. He toughened into a good looking, sturdy child with serious, questing eyes and a fierce determination.

Raven admired the way Kumara was moulding him. She shrugged aside her concern about his motives. She had no wish to be involved in any internecine squabbles among the families of deposed princes and estranged Kandyan nobles.

The lull after the events of the previous year gave them a welcome respite at the villa. She enjoyed the evenings spent drinking and chatting together, engaged in games of *caram* or hands of cards.

She was intrigued by the domestic side of his personality that Kumara revealed when he relaxed his 'man of destiny' pose. He seemed to enjoy himself in trivial small talk on the verandah at night with Bart and herself.

The shattering of her contentment that she feared, came when she least expected it. It was Kumara who raised the matter of the *gaja mutu*, not Bart. He gave no indication of what he was going to ask that would have given her time to prepare.

The question she dreaded most was fired at Bart in the middle of a hand of poker.

'Won't you show me the *gaja mutu*?' Kumara said, placing his cards on the table to win the hand.

She caught her breath and watched Bart eyeing him owlishly.

'If you win the next hand, you can see it.'

'Capital!' Kumara laughed and turned in his chair to wink at her.

She coloured, wondering if he could read the distress in her mind.

'Let's play.' Bart kept his face expressionless as Kumara dealt. He glanced at his cards, placed them face down on the table and exchanged two of them.

Kumara kept his hand. 'If I win, you show me the *gaja mutu*?' he asked as though he couldn't believe it. A pulse jerked in his cheek, betraying his surprise at the bet.

Bart nodded without speaking. Raven tried to guess his hand. If he lost, he would look for the pearl behind the picture and she would have to confess she had removed it. He would feel cheated and angry.

Up to that moment, she gloried in the blissful life they shared without a dispute between them. Bart showed only tenderness and love for her and she responded with full affection of her own. There was trust between them.

She had learned to control the wild passion that tore at her heart when Kumara cast his deeply seductive eyes on her. He made no attempt to hide what he wanted. For Bart's sake, she ignored him.

She was distraught that the turn of a card could wreak havoc on their relationship by revealing her perfidy. When she removed the pearl from behind the picture, she assumed she was inspired by divine direction. Now, as she waited for Bart to show his hand, she saw retribution threatening her instead.

'What do you match my bet with?' Bart's strained whisper broke the silence. She clasped her fan close to her bosom to hide her anxiety.

Kumara's eyes glinted sardonically and he brushed back his hair with a casualness she sensed was feigned. She remembered how he disliked being challenged and wondered how he would react if he lost.

'I'm not playing for the *gaja mutu*,' he said. 'Only for a sight of it. It is your secret. If you win, I will share one of my secrets with you.' He smiled disarmingly.

Raven's anxiety leaped. *What secret?* she wondered. *Would he tell Bart about her?*

'Show your cards.'

Bart's command made her draw to the edge of her seat, biting her lip in mounting panic. She wanted both of them to win. Whoever lost could expose her.

Kumara calmly laid down three kings on the table, followed by two jacks. He sat back in his chair, his eyebrow arched. Raven quailed.

Bart remained for a second without moving. She realized his bluff had been called and he had lost. She rose quickly to get the elephant pearl from its new hiding place to save him from the shock of discovering it was no longer behind his mother's picture.

'Wait!' he said reprovingly.

174

He laid down two queens, the red of hearts and the black of spades, saying as he did so, 'Here is my mother, and here is Raven.'

He looked up at her and she fought to control her swirling emotions as the piercing blue of his eyes seemed to light on her treachery.

'And here,' he added with a smirk, playing the black ace of spades, 'is Kumara.' He added another ace, the club. 'And here is his pupil, Kirti.' He twisted the final card tantalizingly in his fingers.

Only one card from the pack, another ace, could win him the hand and save her from his wrath. He played.

'This is me.'

He laid down the ace of hearts, challenging Kumara with a bleak, tight-lipped smile.

CHAPTER TWENTY

Kumara leaned back in his chair and fit his fingers together. His short bark of laughter lacked humour, warning Raven of his pique at losing.

'Another hand?' he said languidly, reaching for the cards.

Bart's hand fell on his, pinning his fingers to the table. 'The elephant pearl is not some whore's bauble to be wagered over. I'll play no more for such stakes!'

He slapped Kumara's hand off the table and stood up, alarming Raven with his sudden movement. His guilt at gambling over the pearl caused his brow to crease into a frown.

'What secret do you have that could match a glimpse of the *gaja mutu*? It bestows a blessing on all who sight it.' He paused and turned to face Kumara, his brow clearing. 'Or a curse on its possessor's enemies.'

Kumara carefully gathered the cards strewn over the tabletop and stacked them together. His resentment at losing evaporated in the blast of Bart's scorn. Watching him closely, Raven saw him choosing his reaction like she would a dress: something suitable for the occasion.

He decided on a light-hearted approach, an appeasement. 'I must confess there is little enough you do not know already, my friend,' he said with his customary disarming smile. 'Perhaps I can pay you in some other way.'

'What, no secret?' Bart mocked. 'You're supposed to bluff with your cards, not with the stake.' He dismissed Kumara with a wave of his hand. 'It is time to retire.'

Raven heard her cue and moved in a daze. Bart was on edge and it worried her as much as the prospect of Kumara divulging her secret. She had expected Bart to be magnanimous not bitter.

She bid Kumara a hasty goodnight and followed Bart to the door where he stood waiting for her, his face stern. She smiled to mollify him but he didn't notice.

In the chamber, he removed his shirt and flung it carelessly away from him so it fluttered to the floor. She glanced at him nervously as he plunged across the bed, his feet trailing on the ground. He made no effort to remove his boots.

Quietly, not revealing her confusion at his mood, she sat at her dressing table to remove her necklace. She placed it in the jewellery box. She considered for a moment and then decided against telling Bart that she had the elephant pearl. It would only add to his choler.

She longed to speak to him but something about the way he lay deterred her. She accepted that he wanted to be alone with his thoughts and she curbed her desire to tease him to good humour with silly chatter.

She guessed he was thinking about the elephant pearl and the responsibility he felt as its guardian. His mother had died because Marcus Van Dort thought she had it. At times, the pearl seemed to mean more to him than she did.

Before she undressed, she walked softly over to the chamber door and opened it. She wanted to be sure that Nimal had locked the verandah doors and snuffed out the candles. She was puzzled to see the lights still burned and the doors were wide open. She looked back at Bart, wondering whether to disturb him.

His arms were folded across his chest, his eyes closed and his brow racked with the private agony of his thoughts. She tiptoed out, leaving the door ajar.

There was no one on the verandah. She assumed Kumara had gone to his room yet it was unlike him to neglect the villa's security. It was he who repeatedly reminded her to check that the houseboys had fastened all the doors at night. She had never done so before his arrival.

She hesitated at the parlour door, gazing out across the verandah into the darkness beyond the rim of light.

'You wait for him?'

The sadness in the voice, as well as its unexpectedness, made her jump. She gripped the door jamb and turned. 'You frightened me,' she said, gasping with relief that it was Bart and not a stranger who had crept up behind her.

'Are *you* his secret?' He tilted his head on one side and regarded her so forlornly, she wanted to reach out and hug him.

'I was wondering why the doors are open,' she said brightly, hoping to dispel his melancholy. The question upset her because it

177

renewed her anxiety that Kumara might have said something to him that would mar their happiness together.

'Doubtless the doors are open to aid your assignation.'

His remark was cruel and it hurt her. A tear faltered at the corner of her eye. She offered her hands for him to hold, seeking his reassurance that he didn't mean it. He remained unyielding as she grasped him around his waist and placed her cheek against his bare chest.

'Bart,' she said, unable to stop the tears of outrage and despair. 'I love you.'

His hands remained firmly at his side. 'Is that why you gaze out into the night?' he asked grumpily.

She raised her head and stared into his eyes through a mist of tears. 'Yes, Bart, it is. I was thanking God for what we share, for our happiness.'

He blinked, wavering in his doubts. As she bit her lip, embarrassed by her own tears, he patted her reassuringly on her bottom. She returned her cheek to his chest, trying to hide her shame at her spontaneous display of weakness.

He touched the back of her neck, easing her away from his body. He lowered his lips slowly to her face and kissed away a tear glimmering on her cheek.

She opened her mouth to meet his, submittingly willingly to the strength and demand of his hands holding her under her breasts.

The shriek of terror that pierced the night drove through her heart. She clutched at him in fear but he brushed her hands away and ran out onto the verandah. She clasped her bosom, quaking at his abrupt departure even as she marvelled at his ability to leap from embrace to combat without a qualm.

He had already disappeared into the darkness by the time she followed him to the verandah's edge. The single shriek had died and been replaced by a rise in the sounds of the night and a rustling of creatures disturbed by the noise. She hesitated, listening for Bart's shout as he searched for the source of the blood-curdling cry.

Someone rushed onto the verandah behind her and she turned, expecting to see Kumara. It was Jagath, rubbing sleep from his eyes with one hand and clutching his sarong with the other. His appearance roused her to action.

'Hold a lantern,' she said, remembering the night Bart was attacked. She tried to keep her voice steady to quell her alarm that Kumara might be the new victim.

Walking into the garden behind Jagath, she prepared herself for the worst. If it was Kumara she resolved not to give way to weakness again. She would shed her tears in privacy where Bart would not see the extent of her grief.

'I am hearing something by the stable.' Jagath broke into her thoughts.

She held her skirt higher so she could walk faster. She refused to cower to her apprehension, determined to be calm at whatever sight confronted her.

'Bart?' she called cautiously as she approached the stable. Her voice was overwhelmed by the startled whinnying of the horses. 'Bart?' she called again.

'Boy, bring that lantern here!' Bart ordered sharply, his voice coming from close to the door of the stable. 'Raven, wait where you are!'

She hesitated as Jagath hurried from her. The lantern's glow lit up the cobbles of the yard in front of the stable. She followed slowly, keeping to the edge of the circle of light so she could see what was happening. Bart was on his knees by someone who lay in the stable doorway. The neighing of the horses was deafeningly loud, tinged with fear.

'Kumara?' she uttered under her breath as Bart raised the shoulders of the person on the ground. Jagath stood over him, the lantern shaking in his grip. Bart let the body flop back to the cobbles and she knew he was dead.

Bart stood up and spoke to someone out of sight behind the stable door. She watched in amazement as a man emerged from the stable holding a lantern of his own. She ran forward impulsively, crying his name.

'Kumara!'

Bart looked at her quizzically and she broke her stride, appalled that she had been unable to control her outburst, despite her resolution to be firm. She approached the two men slowly while Jagath knelt and touched the body at their feet.

'I thought it was Kumara who was hurt,' she explained lamely.

'Not *him*!' Bart's bitterness was like a slap in her face.

'I heard a noise.' Kumara's voice was bland, unperturbed by Bart's suspicion of his presence. 'The boy was killed while I was coming here. He must have interrupted them.'

Raven's relief at seeing him alive distracted her from identifying the body that Jagath was holding tenderly in his arms. She moved to Bart's side and touched his arm before she looked down. The

179

boy's head lolled forward, his long hair smothering his face. Jagath smoothed it back. It was Nimal.

She frowned with anger instead of sorrow at the death of the houseboy. 'Why? What did Nimal do?'

'It's like Kumara said.' Bart answered gruffly. 'Don't go in the stable. The horses have been hobbled, their fetlocks sheared through with a sharp knife. I'll have to destroy them all.'

'Someone of immense strength has done this,' said Kumara handing his lantern to Raven and lifting Nimal's broken body from Jagath's grasp. The boy was light and his spindly shanks dangled down from his sarong.

'His neck has been snapped. It must have been done by a giant.'

'Nato?' Raven was aghast at the thought.

Bart stroked his beard, his eyes on Kumara, noticing the ease with which he held the dead boy in his arms. 'Anyone trained to kill could have done that,' he said pointedly. 'But only a man used to horses could have got near enough to cut them without being kicked. Is Nato a horseman?'

'I'll take Nimal to the villa.' Kumara's voice was unnaturally subdued. Raven wondered what was on his mind.

'I'll come with you,' she said quickly. The shrieking of the wounded horses was making her jittery.

Bart took the lantern from her without a word. She looked away as he drew his pistol and entered the stable.

She was silent, walking up the path to the villa behind Kumara and Jagath. The muffled sound of Bart discharging his pistol into the heads of his beloved animals was drowned by the shrillness of the horses' frantic neighing. She was stunned with despair at the futile carnage.

When they reached the villa, Kumara lay Nimal's body on the verandah and disappeared back into the night. Jagath ran off to the settlement to inform Nimal's friends. Malika and Daisy kept vigil over the body, waiting for Nimal to be carried off to the settlement for cremation.

Raven sat alone in the parlour, her thoughts jagged and painful and almost more than she could bear. Nimal's murder meant the torment had begun again; none of them were safe.

When the door opened, she looked up anxiously as Kumara strode in. 'Where's Bart?' she demanded, disappointed he wasn't with him. 'Is he out there alone?'

Kumara's smile was deep with compassion, his eyes devoid of their usual flippancy. He sat at the opposite end of the couch, far from her legs which she hastily withdrew so they were hidden by her skirt.

'Tissa is with him,' he said gravely. 'And some of the *salagamas*.'

'What are they doing?'

He permitted his frown to lighten. 'Making a lot of noise. Hunting ghosts.'

'You find that amusing?' She was glad of Kumara's presence. He kept her alert as she was never sure if he was teasing her or sharing a secret joke.

He looked rueful. 'Sudden, violent death is seldom amusing. Bart and Tissa are wasting their time. The assailants have vanished; yes, like ghosts.' He seemed relieved that she perked up in his company.

'Can I get you a drink?' he asked, preparing to rise.

She shook her head. 'Why would Nato hobble the horses?'

'Nato?' He smiled benignly as if dealing with a deranged child. 'I don't know.'

'You don't believe it was Nato, do you?' Her swift challenge set him back on his haunches.

He placed his hands firmly on his knees, his expression turning grim. 'Forgive me,' he said. 'In my concern at your distress, I forgot your astuteness.'

He was teasing her again but she said nothing, only watched his eyes for a trace of deceit.

'Nato may have been present. There were others. The bullocks at the mill have been maimed too.' He returned her gaze boldly.

'Who are they?' She waited impatiently for his answer. There was no clue in his eyes, now bereft of the concern he had shown her when he sat down. They were dark and unfathomable, unblinking as she accused him with her own glance.

'Bart thinks you're involved. Why were you at the stable when he arrived there? He knows you're a good horseman. Perhaps you're a killer too?' Her tongue was running away with her and she was powerless to stop.

'I thought the secret you would have told him was about me. So did Bart. Was it something else? Are you secretly in league with Curt and Nato to drive us away from here?'

'Raven!' He threw back his head and let out a great peal of laughter.

Instinctively, she knew she was wrong. If there was any truth in

181

her charges he would have felt threatened and reacted angrily. She knew his moods.

'I don't think laughter is appropriate,' she said huffily, referring with a nod of her head to Nimal's body stretched out on the verandah deck.

'You're right.' For a moment he looked serious then the teasing laughter returned to his eyes. 'So Bart still doubts me?'

'You being at the stable before him struck him as odd.' She pouted.

'As I said, he's hunting ghosts.' He leaned against the back of the couch and crossed one leg elegantly over the other, looking like he was at ease in an English society drawing room.

His nonchalance infuriated her. 'Answer my question!' she snapped. 'If Nato didn't do it, and you didn't, who did?'

His eyes glinted. 'Ever tenacious, Raven,' he mocked. 'We can rule out your *bête noire*, Curt Van Dort. He is too clumsy to move fast in the dark. That doesn't mean he isn't involved, perhaps in the planning.' He uncrossed his legs and leaned forward.

'You see, it has the hallmark of Curt's wanton cruelty. Crippling all those animals so Bloodheart has no means of transporting his rum to market, of making his livelihood. He will lose orders, his business will flounder, the plantation fail.'

She agreed it made sense in its perversity. 'Have you told Bart?'

'If I do, he'll suspect me all the more for interpreting Curt's scheme. A man smells his own fart before others do. Better for him to arrive at the answer himself than believe I invented it, or smelled my own fart.' He brushed back his hair with a worried gesture.

'What's wrong?' She was touched by this sign of uncertainty in his normally confident manner.

'If this was Curt's scheme, who carried it out? Bart was right. Nimal's killer is no stranger to combat.'

'I saw you trying to throttle Nato like that.' The words tumbled out before prudence made her hold her tongue. 'So did Bart.'

'Others have the ability,' he answered casually, waving her observation aside as though it was of no consequence. 'I am going to ask Little to make some coffee.' He rose to his feet. 'I must see if Kirti is safely asleep.'

She was not taken in by his changing the subject. Instead, she kept her suspicions to herself when Bart returned much later.

He was worn out from trudging through the canefields, chasing ghosts and shadows. He smelled of blood and horses and damp vegetation as he lay on top of the coverlet in his breeches and fell soundly asleep beside her.

Three hours later he was awake. The sky showed shafts of dawn seeping over the plantation from the east where the mountains merged with the clouds. Cautiously, he moved off the bed but Raven woke immediately.

She lay without speaking, letting him wash in the basin of cold water without interruption. When he began to dress, she rose from her side of the bed, slipped her robe over her shoulders and padded from the room.

He did not ask where she was going. After the months of their marriage they were used to each other's moods and needs. She walked through the dining room to the kitchen and woke Little who was asleep on the floor.

She threw some wood on the fire while Little dragged herself to her feet. A pot of coffee was on the hob and it was soon boiling. She poured its strong dark, unsweetened brew into two bowls and carried them on a tray through to the verandah.

Bart looked up gratefully from his chair as he pulled on his boots. She couldn't help glancing to the spot where Nimal had lain the night before. Bart sipped at the coffee, blowing on it to cool it.

'I am going to Galle,' he said, sipping again. It revived him. 'I shall have to walk so I'm leaving early.'

'To report Nimal's murder?' She sipped her own coffee slowly.

He nodded. 'This could be the beginning of another uprising by the Kandyans. They have immobilized us. If your father won't take official action, I shall invite Captain Walker here with his soldiers. I expect to be back by noon.' He rose to his feet.

She placed her coffee bowl on the table and moved over to him, flowing with love. Despite the times when she found his impassiveness exasperating, she was fired now by the gleam of defiance in his eyes. His rugged jaw was set with determination and an unquenchable vigour flamed in his stance.

She reached up and held his shoulders, kissing him on both cheeks, and on his lips. She did not expect him to respond but he embraced her briefly, holding her tightly to his body. That touch meant as much as a night of his loving. She drew away and wiped her eyes.

'Take care,' she whispered.

'You must stay in the house until I return. Keep Malika and the child with you. Tissa will be here before sunrise.'

'Kumara?' she asked softly, not wanting to rouse his anger.

183

He gripped her around her waist and looked at her with a glance that possessed her, penetrating to her very soul. 'You have no fear of Kumara,' he said confidently. 'Neither have I.'

She had to step away from his tense, hard body to stop swooning into his arms. When the passion passed and she had her emotions under control, she raised her eyes to thank him for his faith and the strength it gave her.

He was gone, disappearing into the darkness that was changing gradually from its evil gloom to a grey dawn.

She wished he had company through the jungle to the Galle road. He was in danger as well as Kirti, the household staff, and herself.

She carried her bowl of coffee into the parlour, closing the verandah door and locking it. Already she missed Nimal for his dedication to his duties. She sat down on the couch. It was too early to wake Kirti. He was sleeping in Kumara's chamber and Kumara would be tired after the events of the night.

She had left the door into the courtyard open and watched idly, without really paying attention, as the dawn brightened and the shadowy forms in the courtyard garden became temple trees, crotons and hibiscus bushes.

Malika was at her side, calling her name before she was aware of it. She smiled at her drowsily.

'You surprised me,' she said. 'I must have dozed off.' She blinked, trying to understand what the girl was saying.

'Kirti?' she sat up, alert now as she realized Malika was blurting out the child's name between her sobs of anxiety. 'Gone? Where to?'

'I am not knowing, m'm,' she said, clutching at Raven's robe.

She felt a wave of panic slap her bosom. 'Isn't he with Kumara?'

'I am not knowing, m'm,' Malika repeated helplessly. 'Kumara is gone too.'

184

CHAPTER TWENTY-ONE

Reluctantly Raven faced up to what should have been obvious to her from the moment she heard Malika's words. Kumara and Kirti had disappeared. Her sense of disbelief at being betrayed prevented her from seeing the situation clearly. She made Malika accompany her on a fruitless search through every room in the house, demanding from Daisy, Little and Jagath if they had seen Kumara and Kirti leave the villa.

Jagath was sent to search the spinney in case Kumara was teaching the child his warrior skills before breakfast. With Daisy, she walked the perimeter of the lawn, heedless of Bart's instructions not to leave the villa. She called Kirti and Kumara by name in vain. She considered every possibility except the one she dreaded most.

'Perhaps they went to Galle with Bart?' she asked Tissa hopefully when Bart's headman arrived at the house and was told the news.

Tissa shook his head glumly. He stood before her with his hands at his sides, his dazzling smile and bright eyes shrouded with concern. Although he was slight in appearance and no taller than she was, the serene beauty of his features concealed a toughness. His hair was long, pulled back from his brow and swept into a bun in the style of a native of consequence. Beneath the white of his shirt and waistcloth, he was lean and muscular, exuding a masculine pragmatism that forced her to accept the impossible.

'Kumara has kidnapped him,' she said, refusing to surrender to the despair that hovered over her heart. 'Damn him!'

Tissa's eyebrow quivered and she felt the impact of his unspoken reproach.

'We trusted him,' she explained to excuse her unladylike oath.

Sitting down on the couch, she placed her head in her hands and dug her fingers into her eyes to stop the tears of frustration that welled there. There was silence in the parlour. Malika, Daisy,

Little and Jagath were watching her, all waiting for her to decide what to do.

Anger at being duped by Kumara chased away the horror of the situation. She jerked her head back and glared at the five of them. 'We must find him!' she said, thinking of Kumara, not of the child.

'I'll send a man to Galle to inform Bloodheart.' Tissa wheeled around and stalked to the door. 'When he returns he will organize a search party.'

'No.' Her voice was hard with decision. Tissa froze in the middle of the room and scrutinized her with troubled eyes.

'We can't wait for that. We must go now.' She jumped up from the seat and began issuing orders to Daisy to prepare food and drink for an expedition.

'Bloodheart said you are not to leave the house. I am to guard you.' Tissa spoke with quiet authority.

She tossed her head, her hair swirling angrily about her shoulders. 'You may guard me if you wish, Tissa. To do so, you will have to follow me wherever I go.' She glared at him.

His smile softened her resentment, and he bowed, a twinkle in his eye. 'You will have to search for him in the jungle. They have probably gone to the waterfall. It is a difficult trail.'

Impatiently, she waved aside this attempt to deter her by humouring her. 'Are you coming?'

'There will be the bush to cut, perhaps wild animals to repel.'

'Daisy,' she interrupted him again. 'Tell Mark and Romulus we are going hunting. They are to bring cutlasses.' She turned to Jagath. 'Take a message to Ram to come at once. If we have gone before he gets here, he is to follow.'

She allowed herself a faint smile of scorn at Tissa's bemused expression. 'There is a blackguard to track down and a child to restore to his home. Are you the man to show me the way to this waterfall, Tissa, or am I to rely on the Caffres?'

Tissa was offended by her brashness, as she knew he would be. 'My place is at your side. You have Bloodheart's spirit.'

She took the remark as a compliment, and it gave her an idea. She hurried to prepare herself. The activity stopped her dwelling on Kumara's treachery in stealing Kirti. Instead she let her fury goad her on.

She ransacked Bart's almirah for clothes to wear. She donned his breeches and with some adjustments made them fit. She had riding boots of her own that would serve. One of Bart's shirts and a jerkin completed her outfit. As a final touch, she added a gold necklace and attached a heavy pendant to it that nestled out of sight between her breasts.

Glancing in the mirror she saw she would have to do something about her hair to stop it being snagged by every branch overhanging the trail. She found an old cloth cap, like one Little wore in the kitchen. She spent far too much time arranging her hair so it was secure under the cap.

She took a final look in Kumara's chamber, where Kirti slept on a truckle-bed at the foot of his own larger one. Nothing looked disturbed to indicate Kirti had put up a struggle. Kumara's clothes hung in the wardrobe, his books on a shelf.

It showed his cunning, she thought, to run off leaving everything behind. Yet what use would fancy clothes and books be in the mountain fastness of the renegade Kandyans?

The shutters of the room's windows were open. She wondered if Kumara had taken the child out that way to make sure no one would see him. He must have prepared the boy for weeks for his kidnap, pledging him to secrecy and telling him that it was a game. He had taken advantage of the confusion of the night to slip away.

She even remembered him saying he was going to Little for coffee and then to check to see Kirti was safe. *The guile of the man!* Her anger surged back and she marched out to meet her escorts on the verandah.

Romulus and Mark rolled their eyes at her appearance until she stopped their grins with a black look born of her wrath. Ram was waiting, his basket strapped to his bare back. His presence gave her confidence and she acknowledged his bow with a grateful smile.

Despite what the Caffres thought of her appearance, she found wearing Bart's breeches was exhilarating. She had freedom to move like a man. She enjoyed striding over the verandah towards Tissa.

'Is everything ready?'

'It's a long climb,' he cautioned, starting off casually into the yard.

His attitude provoked her and she pushed past him, striding out angrily along the path to the river. Romulus hurried to overtake her, swinging his cutlass from side to side to demonstrate how he would chop down anything in her way.

The sun was cresting the hills, its rays diffusing the pink edges

187

of puffy clouds in the dawning sky. She had scant appreciation of its beauty as she began to feel the heat. After a hundred yards of swift walking, her body was trickling with perspiration. She blamed Bart's clothes for their unsuitable design. She could not, like him, open her shirt to her waist.

'Is it far to the waterfall?' she asked Tissa diffidently. He had caught up with her and walked easily at her side.

'About two hours climb, maybe longer. The trail is through the jungle, by the river. It will be overgrown.' He shrugged.

'If we had horses . . .' The realization spread through her, filling her with horror and greater anger at Kumara's duplicity. 'That's why they maimed the horses!' She was stupid not to think of it before. 'Kumara *was* responsible for that!'

'Horse couldn't climb that trail.' Tissa's tone was apologetic. 'It's rocks and boulders.' He pointed up to the hills. 'The waterfall is up there, hidden behind a vast outcrop of rock, like a screen. It can only be seen from the sea, or when you are beside it.'

She digested the information slowly, becoming uncomfortably aware that Tissa's attempt to dissuade her from making the journey was wise. It was with relief she entered the shade of the path beside the river. Her feet were pinched by her boots, the breeches clung to her skin, rasping against the inside of her thighs, and sweat made Bart's shirt heavy and airless. She longed to rest.

'How do you know Kumara took this path?' she asked petulantly, hiding her discomfort, her eyes on Romulus leaping ahead.

'I guessed.' Tissa answered with a flash of teeth in a brilliant smile. 'I was right. See.' He touched a handful of twigs that were snapped off where someone had brushed against them. 'This was not cut by Romulus. They passed this way.'

'Why are they going to the waterfall?' She continued walking while she talked, spurred on by willpower and her refusal to let Tissa see she was weakening.

'It flows over the entrance to a cave. The cave opens into a passage through the mountains that leads to the hinterland of the Kingdom of Kandy. Bart calls it Kingdom Falls.' His reverent tone was intended to make her feel intimidated.

'I *will* get there,' she said to dispel his doubts. 'I am going to find Kumara.'

'And Kirti.' He smiled sadly. 'They will be in the Kingdom by now.'

'There is no Kingdom of Kandy!' she said crossly, seizing the chance to put him in his place. It took her mind off the agony of

188

continual walking. 'The king was exiled to India. There is one Ceylon, and it's British!'

'There are heirs to the Kingdom,' Tissa said darkly. 'They are not British.'

'You've been listening to Kumara and his talk of revolution. Kirti isn't going to be king. When he's old enough, he'll go to school in England. He'll be British.'

'If we find him . . .' Tissa lapsed into a silence that was forbidding in the gloom of the jungle.

She thought the trees would provide shade from the sun as it rose in the sky and blazed down on the plantation. There was plenty of shade from the broad leaves. In fact the sun barely penetrated the creepers, intertwined boughs and lofty branches of the jungle's luxuriant vegetation. Instead there was a humidity, a damp and wearying heat, that made every step an effort.

As the path deteriorated to a game track for sure-footed, four-footed beasts, and climbed ever upwards sometimes surmounting sheer faces of rock, Raven drew on reserves of energy she never knew she had. She scrambled up the rocks using her bare hands, shredding her nails and chaffing her skin. She climbed bravely and was rewarded by a change in Tissa's attitude. He smiled to encourage her, clearly impressed by her tenacity.

She was panting and soaked to the skin by her sweat, her heart thumping loudly and her feet numb with pain when she paused for breath at the summit of a steep outcrop of rock. Romulus and Ram had disappeared ahead; Tissa and Mark kept her company. She gulped, her eyes glazed, only her vexation at Kumara keeping her going.

'It's very odd,' said Tissa conversationally, patting his hair. There was not a trace of dirt or sweat on him. 'Kumara has left a trail of clues for us to follow.'

His words took a few seconds to sink in. 'What clues? I haven't seen any.' She struggled to keep her eyes open and stop passing out with fatigue.

'There have been many. This ribbon was tied to a tree trunk at the fork we have just passed. It showed us which path to take.' He handed her a strip of cloth which may have been torn from Kumara's buff coloured shirt.

'Coincidence!' she snapped, overcome by tiredness. She was annoyed at how unaffected by the climb Tissa looked. The gleam of triumph in his eye, as though he was delighting in her sore feet and bedraggled appearance, added to her temper.

189

'You are imagining it, Tissa.' She wished he would stop gloating at her misery.

'Am I imagining that?' He pointed to a shallow cleft in the rock by her side. It was a small indentation filled with rain water. A trick of the light made the water sparkle like a diamond in the dull grey surface of the rock.

She shifted wearily, not interested in his fantasy but making an effort just to prove that she wasn't beaten. 'What is it?'

She rubbed her eyes and the glitter was still there when she opened them.

Tissa leaned over and plucked something from the water. He held it out for her with a wide smile that urged her not to give up. She took it automatically.

'A ring?' She stared at the object in her hand. 'It's Kumara's!' She half-rose from her seat on the rock. 'He must have dropped it.'

'Or placed it where you would rest and be sure to find it.' Tissa helped her to her feet, his words setting off a disturbing train of thought.

She slipped the ring into the pocket of the jerkin and clutched his hand firmly as he pulled her up another rock face. Her knees were blistered, her legs scratched and her feet swollen, but she knew she had to keep going.

Kumara was teasing her. It was his way. The ring said: *I was here*. Its message was meant to mock her. Instead, she was inspired, her anger and humiliation because of Kumara's insidious wickedness driving her on.

The sound of the waterfall roared in her ears before she saw it. It added to her confusion. She climbed in a delirium, spurred on by her need for vengeance at being hoodwinked by the glib-talking Kandyan.

She no longer saw Kumara as a princely warrior but as an artful cheat. She wanted only a brief encounter with him to rake her jagged nails down his face, scarring for ever that handsome visage that enabled him to prey on gullible people like her.

Her mind raced with excitement, caught up in the rhythm of the rushing noise of water tumbling a hundred feet from the mountains to a whirlpool in the river below. She gaped at the sight, her fever and fury waning at the awesome spectacle.

'Kingdom Falls,' Tissa shouted proudly above the noise.

Spray from the roaring water splashed over her, drenching her hot and sticky body, inviting her to strip off her clothes and stand naked at the crevice's edge while the water spumed over her. She

190

stepped nearer, only to feel Tissa's hands clutch her and draw her back from danger.

She shook her head, revived by the water trickling down her cheeks. She cupped some in her hands and drank it thirstily.

Romulus hunkered down on his haunches at her feet and grinned up at her. She patted his wiry head as she would a playful puppy. Ram stood out of the water's blast, his eyes narrowed as he listened to sounds beyond the roaring of the falls. She was reminded of their mission.

'Where is Kumara now? Are there clues here too?' she asked cynically.

Tissa pointed at the waterfall. There was a ledge three feet wide, like a shelf projecting from the wall of the canyon, running from where she stood to disappear under the waterfall. The spray showering down like rain in a tropical storm obscured her view.

Tissa's answer was drowned by the noise. She watched his lips carefully to understand him as he mouthed, 'In . . . there . . .'

She sighed, baffled by how he knew, and by what she was expected to do. Having to crawl along the narrow ledge with a hundred feet drop to the pool below and a river's torrent in full flood hurtling over her, went beyond her lust for vengeance.

Without warning, Ram darted out from his sheltered perch and slithered down the side of the gorge to the ledge. He poised momentarily to regain his balance then scurried with the agility of a mountain goat out of sight under the great wall of spuming water.

She looked enquiringly at Tissa who shook his head, offering no explanation for the snake boy's behaviour. Mark and Romulus, evidently convinced their bush work was at an end, squatted on a rock and devoured cold pancakes from the provisions prepared by Little.

She was at her wit's end, ready to admit defeat although it shamed her to do so in front of Tissa. At least she had reached the waterfall which he had clearly not expected her to do.

'We go?' she said wearily. 'Bart will be back by the time we reach the villa. We can tell him where they've gone.'

'Wait.' Tissa's curt command jolted her and she looked at him askance. He had shed his fawning manner and his eyes glowed with a fervour induced by the hypnotic effect of the waterfall.

'Rest,' he said, gesturing with his hand for her to sit down away from the edge of the falls.

Now she felt like a puppy herself as she wandered off to join

191

Romulus and Mark. They made a space for her beside them, and she leaned with her back against the moss-covered trunk of a tree. It never occurred to her that she could be in danger from them.

Bart's clothes were drenched on her and clung enticingly to her body, revealing every curve and dip of her beautifully formed figure. She had opened the top two buttons of her shirt, exposing her cleavage. The breeches hugged her thighs tightly and, soaked with spray, did nothing to conceal her shapely limbs. Her hair flowed free of the cap and hung down loosely, damp ringlets fringing her bosom.

She was an innocent, unaware that domestic slaves could be as highly impassioned as English pioneers or Singhalese adventurers. While she was lulled by the presence of Mark and Romulus to protect her and drifted off into a deep untroubled sleep, the two of them exchanged thoughtful glances.

Neither uttered a word. Mark lifted his chin slightly in the direction of Tissa. Romulus nodded agreement. They both waited, glancing from Tissa to Raven's heaving bosom and open thighs laid so tantalizingly before them. Romulus watched as Tissa moved closer to the canyon's edge, his back to them. He frowned.

Mark lifted his hand and made a sign of pushing. Romulus looked from Raven to Tissa and back again. He pursed his lips until they disappeared into his mouth as he considered Mark's instruction.

He shook his head. Instead of doing what Mark wanted, he slid over the face of the rock and quietly adjusted the foliage surrounding them. Tissa's view of them, if he chanced to turn away from the waterfall, was now obscured by bushes and ferns. He kept watch.

Mark slid his hand speculatively against Raven's thigh. His loincloth was bulging and his chest heaved at a faster rate than Raven's. He lay down on the rock beside her, rubbing his thigh against hers. She did not stir.

He rolled over so he was pressing his body against her side. He unknotted his loincloth in a frenzy, pulsing against her damp breeches. She quivered, moaning softly in her sleep.

It was too late now for Mark to draw back. He threw his leg over her, straddling her, his manhood rigid. He poised to place one hand over her mouth to stifle her scream and the other to rip open the pouch of the breeches.

Romulus shouted a warning. Mark flung himself backwards,

missed his footing and toppled off the rock. He grasped at a bush as Raven opened her eyes and sat up.

'What is it?' she asked Romulus, noticing how he was gaping with horror at something beyond her.

She turned in the direction of his startled eyes and saw Mark sliding down the slope below the rock. The bush he clutched to stop his fall pulled away from the moist soil. He scrabbled frantically for another handhold but his heavy body gathered momentum and he smashed through the ferns bordering the gorge's edge.

Raven watched in dismay as he disappeared from view. He was swallowed up by the gusts of water from the falls and crashed down in its wet embrace to the rocks in the river below.

She turned away and saw his loincloth lying at her side. She was confused. She picked it up without thinking and tossed it into the gorge after him.

'Raven!'

The shout of her name soared above the roaring of the falls, filling her first with excitement then dread. She turned reluctantly. A bush blocked her view where Romulus was standing staring wide-eyed into the chasm. She rose to her feet and scrambled past him.

On the ledge, emerging from behind the veil of raging water with a devilish smile on his face as he followed Ram, was Kumara.

CHAPTER TWENTY-TWO

He ran along the slippery, spray-soaked ledge heedless of the yawning chasm that opened only inches from his feet. His eyes were watching her with a mixture of astonishment and pleasure; the brooding darkness of his countenance transformed with delight. Her wrath wilted at the sight of him bounding towards her and she had to steel herself to be impervious to his lying charm.

She clenched her hands into tiny fists and stood rigid in the dampness of the dripping jungle foliage. She tried to halt him with her state of disdain yet he clambered over the canyon's edge and ran to her without hesitating. His arms were spread wide to embrace her and clasp her tightly to his chest. She clung to her anger in a desperate attempt to resist him and retain her hold on reality.

'Raven!'

His cry was sheer joy as he reached her and enveloped her in his strong, demanding arms. His clothes were sopping wet and she felt the moist pressure of his body against hers with a *frisson* of shock at what was happening.

She pounded her fists against his hips to make him release her. He took no notice and forced her head with his unyielding hand to rest against his chest. He patted her shoulders and rocked her in his arms.

'How brave of you to come here!' he said warmly, full of admiration. 'I was expecting Bloodheart.'

'Let me go!' She managed to force her fists between their two bodies and push against his chest. She could feel her limbs weakening as her emotions responded to his nearness. She had to recall her humiliation at his treacherous disappearance to give her the willpower to withstand his touch and his smooth-tongued flattery.

He released her immediately and a hurt look entered his eyes. 'Is something wrong? Where *is* Bloodheart?' He glanced around the glade as though expecting to see him.

'He went to Galle,' she said irritably, annoyed by his concern for Bart. 'Now I've got you in front of me,' she gasped as tears filled her eyes, 'I should push you into the gorge.' She bit her lip to cut off her exasperation.

He was staring at her in amazement, his eyebrows arched and his proud brow furrowed with concern. He raised his hands to hold her then dropped them to his side, apparently perplexed by her remark.

'How could you do this to us?' She blinked back her tears and glared at him with most of her anger intact.

She tried to ignore his pathetic, baffled expression with its mute plea for enlightenment. 'I suppose you thought you'd fooled me nicely. With Bart away, you didn't expect anyone to chase you here.'

'Fooled you?' He grinned helplessly, the kind of expression that tugged at Raven's heart.

She raised her eyes and forced herself to stare back at him with a ferocity that was rapidly evaporating because he seemed to be genuinely bewildered.

'I *wanted* Bloodheart to follow me. I left markers on the trail so he'd find me. I didn't dream that you would come. That's why I'm surprised.' He took a step towards her.

She raised her hand to fend him off. If he touched her she would lose track of what she had to say. 'Why do you want Bart?' she asked, troubled by the truth of his statement; he *had* left markers.

'To help me free Kirti, of course.'

She glanced around for something to sit on. Her fury was being sabotaged by his blatant twisting of the facts to suit his tale. She realized that if she sat down he would be towering over her and she'd feel even more intimidated by him. Yet he looked so boyishly innocent, like a rugged angel with his unclouded eyes and seraphic beauty.

'You kidnapped Kirti!' she accused, trying to sort out her emotions. Was it possible, really possible, that she was mistaken? More likely she was falling victim again to his ruthless allure.

She studied him covertly. He seemed to be stung by her accusation. He swept his hand over his brow, brushing back a damp lock of hair, and turning his troubled eyes bashfully on her.

When he spoke, his voice was soft, a hint of pain instead of his usual mockery giving it a sad timbre. 'Listen to me, Raven, it's not

195

what you think. They took the child in the night. I picked up their trail when I discovered he was gone, and followed them here.'

'Why didn't you call Bart?'

'He was chasing ghosts, remember?' He sighed. 'You really believe I would steal Kirti? Have you understood nothing of me after all these weeks?' He put out his hand for hers but she dodged away.

'Who has taken Kirti?' she demanded, seeking corroboration before she accepted his story. 'Nato?'

'No!' His face twisted in a wry smile. 'That was not the Caffre's doing. There are two of them, Kandyan outlaws. The others have fled already.'

She shook her head with disbelief. 'Where are they now?'

'In the cave under the waterfall. They're resting. Kirti is tired. They believe they're safe. Ram found me where I was keeping watch, waiting for Bloodheart.'

She turned towards the snake boy with a sense of relief. She could trust him. 'Is it true, Ram?'

Ram looked startled at being addressed directly. He turned to Kumara for advice.

'No,' she said when Kumara began to speak. 'I want Tissa to ask him.' She put her hand out to hold Ram by his shoulder, careful not to touch the snake basket on his back.

She made him face her as Tissa spoke to him in broken Tamil. His young face was eager and although she didn't understand him she saw from the frankness in his eyes that he spoke the truth.

She heard him speak about Kirti and she recognized the Tamil word for two, *rendoo*.

'Two men,' said Tissa, 'are guarding the boy. They are both asleep.'

A final flicker of doubt lingered. 'They could be your accomplices,' she challenged Kumara. 'This might be a ruse to bluff your way out now you've been caught.'

'Yes,' he agreed disarmingly, 'it might. You'll see if you go into the cave and wake the two bandits. Before you have time to ask them, they'll kill you.'

'You could have told them to do that.'

He laughed with astonishment. 'Raven, you amaze me anew every day. How you must be scared of me to believe I'd do that.'

'Scared?' She shook her head, feeling weak under the mocking glint of his eyes. 'I'm not sure of anything any more.'

She accepted his embrace this time, drawing strength from his hands as they rested very lightly on her shoulders. He acted as though he was too timid to touch her in case she took offence. It was another sign of his conflicting, yet endearing, traits.

The scent of his body and his wet shirt against her cheek were stimulating. She wanted to run her hands over his chest, pulling off the shirt and massaging him until he was dry. The urge gave her the ability to wonder what would happen next.

She drew out of his arms and sat on a boulder. He squatted on his haunches beside her.

'Do you have a plan?' she asked, referring to the child, not to them.

'If Bloodheart were here I could negotiate. To fight them is too dangerous. Kirti could get hurt. Besides,' he nodded at the waterfall, 'they could easily push us off the ledge, one by one.'

She was puzzled. 'What is there to negotiate? Do they want a ransom for Kirti?'

He looked thoughtful. He leaned forward and picked up a stone, twisting it restlessly in his fingers. 'They've discovered the boy's value. Money would have no appeal.' He tossed the stone from palm to palm.

'The *gaja mutu*?' she said softly.

Respect flashed in his eyes and he gazed at her a little incredulous. 'You are right, Raven.' He flung the stone at the waterfall in impotent rage. 'Nothing else will secure his release.' He was looking at her through fresh eyes.

'Could you return to the villa, Raven? Send a message to Bloodheart to come from Galle. I'll follow the two and leave marks so he can trace me. Perhaps I can win their confidence and open the bargaining . . .'

'Would they really take the elephant pearl in exchange?'

'Their chief wouldn't, but these two are hirelings. They're bound to be greedy.'

She stood up, fired with resolve, her eyes dazzled by the orgasmic rush of the waterfall. She stepped towards the gorge's lip. 'I'm going,' she said, preparing for his challenge.

'To Galle for Bloodheart?' he asked hopefully.

'To rescue Kirti.' She tried not to look down where the water tumbled. The ledge was so narrow, and her feet so sore, she wondered how she would be able to walk it to the safety of the cave.

'Help me, Tissa,' she said, holding out her hand, not wanting to ask Kumara.

Tissa hesitated then suddenly she felt her arms being seized and she was jerked backwards away from the chasm. She stared up at Kumara's sombre face.

Drops of moisture clung to his forehead, softening the severity of his expression. His hand was like a manacle about her wrist and his eyes glittered with a cruel power it would be impossible to resist. She fell limply against his chest, pretending to cower to his will.

'You can't go there!' he said, an amused anger tingling his voice.

'Why not? You did.' She felt his grip tighten and he held her away from him, shaking her by her shoulder with his other hand. She was uncertain whether to interpret his reaction as concern for her safety or worry that he would be exposed as a liar.

He seemed flabbergasted by her intention. 'That ledge is slippery, Raven. You couldn't cross it.'

'I must.'

'Just to see if what I say is true?' He released her wrist and wiped his face with his hand, looking unhappy that she still distrusted him.

It gave her the urgency to proceed, to prove him right, not wrong.

'I want to free Kirti,' she said, growing impatient with his arrogant obstinacy. 'Are you going to help me? I can't speak their language.'

'They won't release him because of your pleas.' He shook his head condescendingly.

She turned away from him with an abruptness that made him shout to Tissa to block her path.

'All right,' he said reluctantly. 'If I come with you, what are we going to bargain with? A promise?'

'This,' she said, pulling at her necklace and smiling tantalizingly at him.

'Gold? Very pretty!' He snorted with derision. 'You could divert their attention, I suppose, while Tissa and I try to overpower them.'

'We are going to negotiate! Kirti's freedom for the elephant pearl.' She dangled the gold chain with its heavy pendant of purple leather pouch in front of his eyes.

He was speechless and for the first time since she met him she saw his face clearly, bereft of guile and charm, almost virginal in its simple youthful astonishment. His reaction amused her.

'Isn't this what you wanted Bart to bring?' She let the pendant

198

fall back between her breasts. 'Am I not his wife to think like him, to represent him?'

He recovered his breath but none of his poise. She was fascinated how naive he seemed. She was flattered to think it was because he acknowledged her talents at last, but she guessed it was the magic of the *gaja mutu* that dulled his brain.

'You've had it with you all the time?' he gasped with open admiration. 'That's what gave you the courage to climb here. And the strength.'

She wished it were so, then her aching feet, tired limbs and utter weariness of spirit would vanish because she wore the pearl around her neck. 'That's superstition,' she said dismissively. 'It's just a bead of ivory that legend has endowed with importance. It does nothing for me.'

His distress at her words made her regret her brashness. 'Well, it will get us Kirti,' she added.

She took a step down to the ledge, supporting herself by a branch that overhung the gorge's mouth. She prayed she would have the courage to continue walking. If she did, perhaps it would be the *gaja mutu's* doing.

She winced as her feet touched the ledge. It was a slab of granite, its jagged crust pitted with shallow pools of water. Tiny crabs scurried across the glistening sheen of its surface. Even as she released the branch to take another step, her feet slid from under her and she felt herself falling.

She landed with a bump on her bottom, jarring her spine. Frantically, she flung herself away from the edge towards the cliff face. She fought for breath as water gushed over her, grateful that the sting of the spray took her mind off the agony of her feet and backside.

Her breeches were split and she felt the cold water from the pool she sat in lapping her thighs. She paused for a moment, daring neither to look down or behind. Above the din of the falling water she could hear someone shouting her name.

Gingerly, she clawed her hands up the cliff face, searching for a grip so she could stand. She felt herself being grabbed roughly under her arms. Hard fingers dug into her breasts, bruising her in their forceful grasp.

She was dragged backwards before she gained control of her legs. She flailed her arms at the man holding her, but he would not let go. She couldn't struggle more in case she plunged both of them off the rock shelf.

She was lifted off the ledge and placed on her feet on the softer terrain of the jungle's muddy floor. She spun around to abuse her rescuer, inflamed by the helplessness she experienced in his brutal clutches.

'What a sight you are, Raven!' he spoke before she understood it was not Kumara who had plucked her from the ledge, but Bart. 'What the devil are you doing?'

'Bart. . . !' She uttered his name tremulously, relief mingling with her outrage at being frustrated in her attempt to get under the waterfall. It may have been foolhardy but she was driven to do it for Kirti, and for Bart.

She became aware of soldiers emerging from the trail and collapsing on the moist soil to rest. Her eyes fell on Ram smiling encouragingly at her as he squatted at the canyon's rim. She smiled back, nodding once to indicate she was all right.

He seemed pleased, although when she turned back a few seconds later to look at him, he had disappeared.

While Kumara explained rapidly to Bart what had happened, she became conscious of her dishevelled appearance. She flinched under the gaze of the soldiers milling around the glade. Bart had brought them and Captain Walker with him.

Nestling into Bart's protective embrace to hide her embarrassment, she listened to Kumara's story. When he reached the point about her negotiating with the kidnappers, she interrupted him.

'I had the idea of bribing them with the *gaja mutu*,' she said, staring at Kumara to compel him to keep quiet. 'I was going to offer myself as a hostage in exchange for Kirti and as guarantee that *you* would bring the elephant pearl.'

'You let her do this?' Bart glared at Kumara, hugging her possessively.

She tingled with the confidence released in her by his grasp. She kept her eyes on Kumara, hoping he would support her lie and say nothing about the pearl being around her neck.

'I . . . er . . .' he began, unconvincingly, wiping his brow with bemusement. 'She's a resolute woman when she's roused, Bloodheart. She was on the ledge before I could stop her.'

A movement by the waterfall caught her eye and she realized where Ram had gone. Bart looked around the glade, becoming aware of the soldiers ogling her.

'I'm going to send you back to the villa with Tissa and Romulus,' he said. 'You're soaked like a drowned rat and you're too provocatively dressed to be here.'

'How are you going to get Kirti?' she asked, ignoring his display of husbandly ire. She calculated that his gratitude at finding her would conquer his anger at her appearance and behaviour.

'That's my worry,' he said, stroking his beard thoughtfully. 'For God's sake, sit down out of the way,' he shouted as she sauntered to the edge of the canyon for a better view of the falls. The soldiers fidgeted as she bent over, revealing the split in her breeches.

'I'm sorry, Bart,' she smiled contritely, pleased that she wasn't being sent home. 'I could help you if you like. Kumara suggested I distract the men holding Kirti. If there's another way into the cave, the soldiers could creep in while I keep the kidnappers occupied.'

Bart gazed up at the cliffs rising sheer for a hundred feet on either side of the waterfall. He dismissed her idea immediately, looking vexed with himself for considering it. She felt guilty at the disruption she was causing when the objective was to rescue Kirti.

She moved over to where Romulus was crouching out of the way of the soldiers, a glazed expression in his eyes. He jumped when she touched him on his bare shoulder.

'Romulus,' she whispered coaxingly. 'Would you walk along that ledge if I asked you to?' She ran her forefinger over his shoulder and down his arm, squeezing him. 'You're not afraid, are you?'

'No, missy.' He blinked and turned his eyes on her with frank adoration. 'I do what you say.'

She smiled gratefully. 'Be ready,' she said. 'Watch the water-fall.'

She indicated Bart, Tissa and Captain Walker standing around Kumara in the centre of the glade discussing what to do. The soldiers were sitting on the rocks, out of reach of the spraying water, easing their aching limbs.

'No one else is watching it.' She clung to his arm and raised her head, whispering in his ear. 'Ram has gone back to the cave. He may need your help.'

She was fascinated by the sight of the Caffre's eyes observing first the four men, then the soldiers and afterwards the ledge and the waterfall. It was easy to follow his thoughts and she waited patiently for his smile of understanding. When it came there was a deeper, unsuspected meaning in his response.

'Mah heart sick for yo', missy,' he said, shaking his head as though he knew what he was saying was wrong. 'Please don't touch me no more. It does boil mah blood wantin' yo'.'

Hurriedly she released him and stepped away. She wanted to rebuke him but the openness of his face and the sincerity in his dark eyes were oddly endearing. She was humbled as she realized she was not so clever that she could read a Caffre's thoughts.

'I'm sorry, Romulus,' she said, tears pricking her eyes. Whatever had happened to Mark she knew now that unwittingly the fault was hers. 'I'll always be your friend,' she said. 'There can be nothing else.'

'Yes, missy,' he said, his broad grin reprieving her.

They listened to the rushing of the falls while Bart expounded his plan of action. Romulus saw the movement first. He touched her arm, rousing her from the trance induced by the sight of the water plummeting to the river.

He stepped away from her, scrambling down the side of the canyon and gaining the ledge with ease. He was barefoot and moved swiftly until he was under the falls, his dark body vivid against the white wall of water.

In seconds he emerged with Kirti in his arms. The boy clung to his neck, his sobs of terror mingling with the droplets of water that broke over his brow.

'Bart!' Raven called, just as he turned and spotted the pair of them.

Captain Walker shouted commands and the soldiers crouched into firing positions to cover Romulus as he crept slowly along the ledge.

'Oh God,' prayed Raven aloud, 'don't let him slip.'

Ram suddenly appeared from the waterfall behind Romulus. He was naked, his snake basket missing from his back. Raven smiled to herself when she saw him, imagining how Ram had let his snake loose near the sleeping kidnappers.

Romulus and Kirti were almost at the canyon's edge where Tissa and Kumara were waiting to pull them clear. In his haste, Romulus stumbled and Kirti fell from his arms.

Kumara leaped out and flung himself along the ledge, catching Kirti by his wrist as the force of the water swept him perilously close to the edge. A man darted out from the cave behind Ram. Before the soldiers could fire, he raised his arm and aimed a knife at Kirti.

Ram dived for the man's legs, knocking him off balance as the knife flew out of his hand. It was deflected by the waterfall and passed harmlessly over Kirti's head. The man toppled off the ledge and Ram scuttled out of the way as the soldiers opened fire.

While Bart cuddled Kirti in his arms, almost weeping with relief, Raven seized Ram. She hugged his wet, naked body with a passion that made him squirm and wriggle with embarrassment.

Gently, Kumara pulled her away and led her back to Bart.

CHAPTER TWENTY-THREE

The sun's fierce glow was unbearable and the cloudless sky a source of misery during the day. The heat was unrelenting from seven in the morning until four in the afternoon, making movement a wretched experience. There was no breeze, except along the sea shore, and the fields of young cane grew in the scorching sun without a ripple of wind to cool them. For Bart it was a sign of good yield at harvest time because, in the night, there was rain.

Raven longed for the balm of night. Although the heat then was cloying, especially just before the rain fell, she was able to move and think more clearly after the sun had set. She no longer sat on the verandah during the day – it was too bright – but sought solace in the depths of the house. At night she was confined to the parlour because of her fear at what might happen next.

After Kirti's capture and rescue, Captain Walker's soldiers had stayed a week. Bart wanted them to set up a permanent post on the plantation. He petitioned the military commander but because the request had to be referred to the governor, it would be weeks before they could do so.

The soldiers hated the heat and cowered all day in what little shade they could find. They left the plantation with relief, Captain Walker extending his sympathy to Raven that they could not stay.

'This is a private settlement,' said Bart in an effort to explain to Raven why their protection was withdrawn. 'I am here on sufferance. The island needs development but it's no longer the policy to encourage independent settlers from Britain.'

'Perhaps you should give up the land to Curt Van Dort then!' The heat made her irritable and she uttered the remark thoughtlessly.

She was sitting with Bart in the parlour. Kumara was with them, reading while Malika and Kirti played at his feet. The doors to the interior courtyard garden were open to catch any breeze.

Bart's reaction, like the atmosphere, was sluggish. 'Is that what you want, Raven? Are you tired of plantation life? I don't blame you, being under threat all the time.'

'We could easily remove the threat.'

'That's wishful thinking. Curt won't just go away.'

She was exasperated by his apathy. 'If you dealt with him and Nato properly, we could lead normal lives again.'

Bart sighed and addressed her as he would a child. 'We have no real proof of their involvement. Captain Walker will submit his report. He blames the Kandyan bandits. If the Governor approves, he'll take official action.'

She tut-tutted with impatience. 'We know Nato was here! He was seen.'

'By a native who might have made up the story to please me.'

'It *is* possible Curt hired the brigands,' said Kumara, putting down his book and rising from his seat. He walked to the open door and raised his arms above his head. His body quivered like a cat's as he stretched.

Raven gazed at him openly since he was in the process of talking to them. She loved to watch him but she knew she must be careful not to upset Bart.

'Curt believes Kirti is *your* son.' He swung around and lounged against the door jamb, his ankles crossed elegantly and his arms folded across his chest. He resembled a poet or an artist at a drawing room soirée with his handsome profile and dark flowing locks.

'What better way of forcing you to submit to him than by using your son as a hostage?'

'You said they were Kandyans who kidnapped him.'

'They were, Bloodheart. Curt is a devilish schemer.'

Bart touched his ear thoughtfully. 'His father used Kandyans, Caffres, anyone he could hire to do his dirty work.'

Raven put down her sampler and stood up impatiently. 'It's the same discussion night after night. When are you going to do something? Nato and Curt are behind it all. We lived peacefully until they arrived.'

'I've told you. We must wait for the Gover –'

'Fiddlesticks!' She lost control of her temper and waved her finger at him. 'You have to take action *yourself*.' A rumbling roll of thunder interrupted her.

Kumara moved away from the open door with a laugh. 'The gods are angry!' he mocked. 'At least the rain's coming so that should cool us down.'

There was a rapid drumming on the tiles of the roof as the rain descended in a concerted fury, rattling noisily through the house. The din of the rain's onslaught made speaking impossible.

She walked over to Bart and offered him her cheek for a kiss. His embrace was perfunctory, his eyes reproachful. She left him and went to their chamber.

The heat, the tension, the feud – something was affecting Bart's attitude towards her. She realized he was preoccupied and forgave him when his ardour faltered.

Because of the heat – or so he claimed – he had taken to sleeping on a mat, native style, on the floor at the foot of the bed where it was cooler. Since every morning she awoke drenched in sweat, she could understand that. What worried her was why Bart's loving had changed from an act of pleasure back to his old attitude of performing a duty.

'The duty of a planter's wife is to bear children for her husband. He is her master,' Mammy Sobers had once told her.

Raven rejected the idea as a slave cliché. Bart had never expressed a wish for a baby. Would he be more caring if she gave him one? The thought intrigued her as she lay in her lonely bed, awaiting sleep.

The answer, if Bart would do nothing about Curt and Nato, was to see that they were dealt with herself. She had tried before without much success. She needed someone, like a paladin of olden days, to be her champion and do as she instructed.

She considered the possible candidates. Kumara was too sophisticated to obey a woman's orders, especially hers. Ram, the only one who had helped her, was too young. She needed someone devoted to her who was tough, muscular . . . and brutal. She smiled as she thought of an unexpected choice.

The following day, while Bart was at the mill and before the sun reached its height, she strolled with a parasol to protect her, in the garden at the front of the villa. Kumara was sitting in the depths of the verandah where the shade shielded him from the sun's full heat. Although he was reading to Kirti, he was keeping a watchful eye on her. She called out that she was going to walk in the garden at the side of the house and he waved in acknowledgement.

She smiled at how easy it was to fool a man simply by seeking his consent and letting him feel he was in charge. She would have to try it with Bart instead of arguing with him. She dismissed both men from her mind as she found a shaded spot beside the house and stood silently watching the Caffre at work.

Romulus was wearing a torn, sweat-stained loincloth that left little to her imagination. When he crouched down to pull out weeds from the flower bed, his sex hung down between his legs, almost scraping the earth because of its prodigious size.

She eyed it curiously, averting her eyes when she realized what she was doing.

She was astonished by its size and wondered how any woman could accommodate him. Since Mark's death, Romulus was in demand by Daisy as well as by Little. It occurred to her that Caffre women were built to large proportions to match their men. Despite her dispassionate view of his physique, she felt an odd stirring of desire deep within her. She frowned to chase it away.

Her purpose in studying Romulus was to see if he would be a contender against Nato. When a Caffre was found dead any enquiry into the circumstance was merely formal. No one was ever charged with a Caffre's murder. She saw Nato's death as the solution. Without Nato as his henchman, Curt couldn't harass them.

'Romulus . . .' she called softly.

He had been aware of her studying him since she arrived in the garden. He remained on his haunches and glanced up with a roguish twinkle in his eye.

'Come here,' she said when he refused to move. She sensed he was playing a game and that she was the prize. It gave her a feeling of recklessness, a thrill she hastily stifled, ashamed of the lusts that swirled within her.

'Come here!' she demanded again, her insecurity giving an edge to her voice.

Romulus rose slowly, exhibiting the swelling in his loincloth without shame. His shining black face beamed as he swaggered across the lawn towards her. She had difficulty keeping her eyes off his crotch; it was like a threat.

She wondered what had unleashed the Caffre's emotions. He used to be a simple, good-natured slave who was proud of the strength in his compact body. He had been with Bart for a decade, working obediently. It was only since the incident at the waterfall with Mark that he had begun to show off, trying to attract her.

'Stand there,' she said, pointing to a spot directly in front of her. She looked both ways to see if she was observed. His eyes flickered with speculation at her glance.

On an impulse, she put her hand on his chest. His pectoral

muscles were as hard as ebony and he grinned at her appreciatively. He tightened his stomach, lowering his eyes, indicating that her fingers should descend.

She removed her hand hastily, quelling the sensual stirring of her own feelings with a shudder.

'I yuhs, missy.' Romulus's voice was husky. 'De spinney . . .'

She swallowed her outrage at his sordid suggestion. If she rebuked him he would get sulky and be difficult to manipulate. His blatant need, like an elephant in must, would serve her well.

She smiled her regret, glancing around her to indicate the danger that they would be seen. 'It's impossible, Romulus.'

He nodded his understanding and shuffled his feet, holding his hand in front of his crotch.

'You are very strong,' she said to flatter him because he was so obviously proud of his body. 'I'd wager you could fight a gelding and beat him.'

He frowned, mouthing the words 'wager' and 'gelding' to himself. He looked at her trustingly for an explanation.

'I'd stake money,' she said, pleased by his reaction. 'I'd *give* you money if you fight a Caffre for me. He's been neutered, a *gelding*, and he's been troubling me.'

'Troublin' yo', missy?' His brow darkened and she knew she had touched a responsive chord. 'Who he is?' He spun around to demonstrate his readiness to batter anyone who troubled her.

'He's from Galle,' she said, delighted that he understood what he must do.

A plan came to her mind quickly. She would write to Nato, pretending the note came from Daisy, and ask him to be at Mammy's cabin the next evening.

'I am to meet him tomorrow night,' she said sadly. 'By the spinney. I'm terrified of him, Romulus. What shall I do?'

'I help yo', missy.'

'I won't be free of worry until he's *dead* . . .' She touched his cheek with her finger and was amazed to see the serenity that swept over his angry features.

'I yuhs, missy,' he said for the second time, bowing his head.

She left with a display of reluctance so he would feel she fancied him, and hurried back to the villa to write the note.

It was Bart's apathy that drove her to such desperate measures. To her it was simple: destroy Nato and Curt and the feud would end. She was angry enough to do anything to achieve that, for

208

Bart's sake. The thought that Romulus might be no match for Nato didn't occur to her.

She asked Malika to write the note. If it was in her handwriting, he wouldn't be lured into the trap. Signed *Daisy*, it read: *Nato, I have the thing. Meet me at the spinney tomorrow night*. She gave it to one of the cart drivers to deliver to Nato at Madam Gudde's.

She could barely contain her excitement the next day. Twice she walked the garden to see if Romulus understood the plan. She told him she would be waiting on the porch of Mammy's cabin. He should hide in the trees. There would be no moon that night so he would have to watch very carefully for Nato.

'Ain't no problem, missy.' Romulus assured her with an eager grin. 'I hear a leopard's footfall in de dark. A fancy town Caffre give himself 'way wid his smell.'

'You have a knife?' she asked, curious how he would kill him. 'You'll have to take him by surprise.'

His eyes glinted merrily and he rubbed his finger over the blade of his cutlass. 'One chop wid dis an' his head fall off.'

Doubt ripped through her mind at what evil she had set in motion, until she recalled Nimal's broken body and the sound of the horses shrieking in agony. She fluttered her eyelashes at Romulus, convinced she was right.

'I see yo' tonight, missy,' he said, touching his crotch suggestively.

'Oh . . . er . . . yes.' She was taken aback by the menace in the flashing teeth of his broad grin. 'Afterwards,' she added, wondering what predicament she was letting herself in for.

When she planned the scene in her mind, she had not thought beyond Nato's death. That Romulus might come to the cabin's porch expecting his reward was too daunting to consider. She worried about it throughout the afternoon. At supper, she was so agitated that both Bart and Kumara commented on her nervousness. She knocked over a glass of wine and dropped a fork on the floor.

'I don't know what's wrong with me,' she stammered, blushing at her clumsiness.

'The weather,' said Bart wisely. 'The heat in the day, the rain at night, being confined to the house. It's unsettling. I'm thinking of sending you to Galle for a few weeks. Malika could go with you. You could stay with your father until this blows over.'

She banged her knees together under the dining table to force herself to keep calm. If he sent her to Galle there would be a chance to get even with Curt as well. 'Whatever you say,' she said meekly.

Kumara gazed at her as he raised a chicken leg to his mouth. 'You are right, Bloodheart,' he drawled. 'Raven is not only skittish tonight, she's preoccupied too. She rarely agrees to do what you tell her without protest.'

She glared at him, hating him for being so smart. Bart would never have noticed anything unusual if he hadn't spoken. 'Is it odd for a wife to do what her husband considers best for her?' she retorted tartly.

'It is, if you are the wife.' Bart gazed at her speculatively, trying to read her mind. 'It makes me wonder what bee you have in your bonnet.'

'You're impossible!' She pushed her plate away, cross with them both. 'Please excuse me,' she said, standing up. 'I'm not myself tonight. I have a headache.' She patted her forehead, trying to ignore the glint of mockery in Kumara's eyes.

'A wife's traditional excuse . . .' she heard him say as she swept from the room. It was unforgiveable of him to side with Bart to ridicule her.

Once inside her chamber, she hurried over to the window and anxiously opened the shutters. The night was black and humid, heavy with approaching rain. She wondered if Romulus was ready in the spinney.

She told him she would be waiting in the porch but now the time had come to go there, her resolve weakened. She was frightened of herself, of the impulsive passion that could drive her to foolishness.

She sat on the bed, breathing deeply, trying to regain her composure. She regretted giving Kumara the chance to mock her. He and Bart had become firm friends. Before, he would never dare to criticise her in front of Bart yet now they shared jokes about her. It was really too bad when she was only trying to help Bart.

She listened for a sound outside the villa that would indicate Romulus was attacking Nato. The rush of rain pelting through the leaves and rattling on the roof tiles startled her. She closed the shutters to prevent the rain entering the chamber, relieved that it provided a reason for her to break her promise to wait on the cabin's porch.

Having pleaded a headache to escape Bart's scrutiny, she was obliged to prepare for bed. It had become Bart's habit to enter the room very late, after she had fallen asleep. He would unroll his mat without disturbing her and go to sleep in his clothes. He always slept with his pistol close to him.

She lay down on the bed and tried to keep awake, listening for sounds of activity that would indicate her scheme was successful. Eventually the patter of rain lulled her to sleep and she didn't hear Bart enter the room.

It was Kumara's voice that roused her. She opened her eyes in surprise and stared out through the curtains enclosing the bed. A lantern glowed on the floor where Kumara was bending over the mat where Bart slept. She listened carefully, pretending to be asleep.

'Bloodheart!' hissed Kumara, shaking Bart's shoulder. 'Wake up.'

'What's wrong?' she heard him mutter in a voice thick with sleep.

'I don't know.' Kumara sounded worried. 'Tissa didn't come for his turn to keep watch on the verandah. He should have relieved me ten minutes ago. I've done my two hour stint.'

Bart was on his feet instantly. 'Keep your voice down,' he whispered. 'Raven doesn't know we're keeping watch all night. She'd worry too much.'

'What shall we do?' Kumara walked towards the door, drawing the light away with him.

'We'll go to Mammy's cabin to wake him,' Bart said. 'He must have overslept, that's why I told him to sleep there tonight so he'll be close enough to call when he's needed.' His voice drifted off into the darkness as he closed the door of the chamber behind him.

Raven rolled out of bed, her heart pumping with nervousness at what she'd heard. A candle burned faintly and by its light she donned her robe, brushing her hair away from her face with her hand.

The rain had stopped and the night was quiet as she hurried through the dining room to the kitchen. Through the open back door she could see the glow of Kumara's lantern where he and Bart stood on the steps of Mammy's cabin.

She felt the rain-soaked grass chilly against her bare feet. Instead of returning for her slippers, she hurried across the lawn, eager to be there when Bart discovered Nato was dead.

She saw them both draw back from the cabin. Kumara's light lowered to the ground. She was spurred on with the ecstasy of triumph and ran to join Bart. He and Kumara were staring at a bloodied body on the grass.

CHAPTER TWENTY-FOUR

'With Tissa dead,' said Bart tenderly, 'you must stay with your father in Galle. I have to take charge of the mill and the field gangs myself. I can't be here in the house to protect you.'

Raven said nothing. It had taken a day to overcome her shock at seeing Tissa and not Nato lying in front of the cabin. She had erupted with hysterics when Bart pulled her away so she would not see Tissa's split head, his tortoiseshell combs smashed and his fine hairstyle oozing blood.

Stricken with guilt, she had surrendered to Daisy's arms and allowed herself to be led off to her chamber. She had been too confused and horrified to accept what had happened. It was a dreadful mistake.

She had thrashed at Daisy when the housekeeper held her down on the bed, and she shrieked dementedly until Daisy forced her to sip a sweet drink. She gagged on it but swallowed; minutes later she felt the fight drain from her limbs as she sank into a drugged sleep.

In the morning, she had kept to her chamber, ashamed to face Bart. Tissa had been his friend since the day he arrived in Galle thirteen years previously. That her idea for revenge had led to his death filled her with a bitter regret for the wrong she had done. She was inconsolable, shaken with shame because Romulus had mistaken Tissa for Nato and killed the wrong man.

'Lawd, mistis!' Daisy had chided her when she set a bowl of coffee down on the table beside the bed. 'Yo' ain't to blame so why yo' take on so?'

She had shaken her head without speaking and waved Daisy away. She wanted to be alone to consider her sin and how she could expunge it. She was damned.

Daisy had swept her into her arms and hugged her to her warm, yeasty bosom. 'It ain't yuh fault, missy,' she crooned, offering her the coffee.

She sipped it reluctantly and the hot liquid eased the dryness left by the laudanum. She twisted from Daisy's grasp, still confused and wanting the slave to go. The coffee revived her spirit and her interest in how it had happened.

'Where's Romulus?' she blurted out, not bothering to disguise her concern about him.

Daisy's eyes had opened wide and she pulled away although she still sat on the bed and kept one arm around her shoulder. 'Lawd, missy, yo' know everyt'ing! Yo' more 'ware of we Caffres dan Bloodheart himself.'

She had looked at Daisy blankly, not understanding.

'Is he I want to marry, mistis.' Daisy beamed and clasped her hands with contentment on her lap. 'When I see him waitin' by de spinney las' night in de rain, jus' moonin' for me, I know he de one. I take him to de store room an' he give me de bes' lovin' I ever have! Only de noise of Tissa screamin' done stop us.'

Raven had watched Daisy with a growing feeling of being out of control of events. 'Romulus was with you?' she said in amazement. 'At the time Tissa was killed?'

'Sure.' Daisy had smiled happily. 'Yo' don't mind, mistis? Please ax Bloodheart to marry we two.'

'Then who killed Tissa?' she asked, ignoring Daisy's request.

'Dat Caffre boy, Nato, of course. Jagath done see him.' She reached in her apron pocket. 'I jus' rem'ber. A boy from de settlement bring dis note yes'day mornin'. He say it have my name on so he give it me.'

Raven took the piece of paper from Daisy's hand. It was the note Malika had written to lure Nato to the villa. It had not been delivered to him.

She sighed, feeling the great burden of guilt lift from her shoulders. Neither Nato's presence on the plantation nor Tissa's death were the result of her ruse.

'Raven, did you hear what I said?' Bart's voice was rich with compassion.

She blinked at him, still reliving her joy at discovering she was not to blame for Tissa's death. 'Forgive me, I was thinking of last night, of Tissa.'

'There's nothing to forgive.' He sounded kind and walked over to touch her lightly on her shoulder where she sat on the couch staring into a void.

'You were shocked. It's my fault. If I hadn't told Tissa to sleep in Mammy's cabin, it wouldn't have happened.'

'It's all right, Bart.' She squeezed his arm, knowing how he felt from her own experience of guilt. 'Tissa wanted to help you guard the villa. You must not blame yourself. He wouldn't.'

The look of tired sadness passed from his features and his eyes glimmered with relief. He patted her shoulder lovingly as he stood in front of her. 'You're right, Raven.' He sighed, touching his ear stump. 'I never dreamed they'd kill Tissa.'

'One native's like another to Curt Van Dort. Life is cheap to him.' She pulled back her shoulders, her grief and shock hardening to a desire for action. 'He must have told Nato to chop anyone guarding the villa as a warning to us. He hasn't given up wanting to make you leave.'

'I see that now.' He shook his head sorrowfully. 'That's all the more reason why you must go to your father's. That's what I told you but you didn't hear because you were grieving.'

'I'm all right now, Bart.' She stood up, considering his idea. She had been wrong to think she could defeat Curt and Nato alone. 'I'm not going to Galle,' she said. 'My place is here with you.'

'You are!' His shout stunned her with its vehemence. 'By the devil, Raven, won't you do one thing you're told?'

She raised her head and looked at him with serene defiance. 'Sometimes,' she said with a hurt smile, 'a wife's husband does *not* know what is best.'

'I'm not going to argue with you.'

'Good, then I shall stay.'

'You won't! Raven . . .' his angry tone softened to pleading. 'These people will stop at nothing. They could try to set fire to the villa, even attack you.'

'Then I suggest you do something about it.'

He flung himself down on the couch in despair. 'I am,' he said shamefacedly.

'At last!' She crossed the room to sit beside him. She was pleased he was stirred into action even though he was reluctant to give her the credit for doing what she had suggested weeks before.

'Kumara is hiring some men. Since the military won't protect us, we must do it ourselves.'

'Protection isn't enough. You have to destroy Curt and Nato.'

'What can we do? We're on our own.'

'You could hire a gang of Caffres to attack them in Galle.'

'That's not my way. We'll set a trap for them. Sooner or later, Curt will grow impatient. He'll come out into the open and

214

challenge me directly. When I have some evidence to show what he's trying to do, I'll take it to Collector Radley.'

'Daddy won't do anything. He doesn't want to spoil his sinecure. You must complain to the Governor himself.'

'About a land dispute and the slaying of two natives?' Bart shook his head. 'I'll be sent back to your father with a flea in my ear and told to follow the proper channels. Curt Van Dort was born here, I wasn't. He's part Singhalese through his half-breed father. The law supports native landowners, not interlopers like us.'

She stared at him aghast. 'That's not fair! You created this plantation. Without you it would be jungle.'

'Fairness is not the law, Raven. Speak to your father, make him see we're in peril. Perhaps he'll do something official then.'

She drew away from his side, a warning tingling up her spine. He was persuasive, his rugged profile softened by his smile of helplessness. His broad shoulders sagged and she reacted to his display of impotence by wanting to hug him. Instead, she jerked back as the jolt of warning stalled her impulse.

'My God, Bart,' she said with an explosion of outrage. 'You almost tricked me! You merely want to get me away from here. Asking me to tell daddy what's happening is an excuse!' She folded her arms and sat at the end of the couch with her back straight. 'I'm not going!'

His face flushed with anger. She was pleased to see the fury return to his eyes because pretending he was spineless didn't suit him. She waited for his rebuke, determined no matter what he said, to stay at the villa with him.

He tried reasoning with her again. 'I will have to sleep at the mill. You'll be alone in the house.'

'Why can't Kumara sleep at the mill and be the overseer?'

'He knows nothing about rum and sugar.'

'Then you know nothing about him! If Tissa could learn, so can he. Anyway, he probably knows more than Tissa already. He knows how to lead men; all the natives are in awe of him.'

'He doesn't want to be a plantation overseer.'

'Ask him! He's indebted to you because of Kirti. He's appointed himself the child's guardian for reasons of his own. He won't leave here unless Kirti does.' She sat back and watched Bart consider her remark. There were times when men missed the obvious.

'Even if I do ask him,' he said grudgingly. 'I still want you to go to Galle.'

'I'll think about it.'

She leaned across and pecked him on his cheek, and was not in the least surprised when he pushed her away.

The men recruited by Kumara to guard the villa were an odd bunch of ageing Kandyan warriors, survivors of the uprising of 1818, and idealistic youths whose ideals were the gold to be earned rather than the royalist cause of the former warriors. They took over the Caffre slave quarters as their barracks. Since few of them spoke English, Raven had little contact with them.

There were ten altogether. Armed with swords and knives, they patrolled the gardens around the villa in pairs on a shift system throughout the day and night. They were fiercesome in appearance with bushy beards, wild staring eyes and saliva so deep a red that their lips and teeth appeared to be covered with blood.

This phenomenon caused Raven concern until Kumara explained it was the outcome of their perpetual chewing of betel.

'Everyone of them carries in his waistcloth an ornamental silver box,' Kumara said when he sat with her on the verandah observing one of his warriors sending a stream of crimson spittle at a gecko sunning itself on the path.

'Inside is a smaller box containing a portion of *chunam*, that's lime obtained by the calcination of shells. The larger box contains the nuts of the areca palm and a few fresh leaves of betel pepper.' He paused and she nodded to show she understood.

'When a chap feels inclined, he scrapes some parings from the nut and rolls it up with a pinch of the lime in a betel leaf. He pops the package in his mouth and chews it. It causes great salivation which is why you see them spitting red, like blood.'

She shuddered. 'It's staining the path rust-coloured. Why do they indulge in such a filthy habit?'

'They eat neither flesh nor milk nor poultry nor eggs, and fish only rarely. Betel adds to their diet. It's spitting that makes it offensive to European eyes. Is it any filthier than inhaling burning dried leaves into the lungs?'

She loved listening to him explaining the peculiarities of traditional life in Ceylon. Since the warriors came to the villa and performed the duties he assigned them, Kumara was more relaxed. He explained they were all kinsmen of his who were obliged to serve him without question and did so willingly.

'They would die for me now if I asked them,' he claimed, thrilling her with his power over them.

She gained confidence from his faith in his motley troop, although it was some weeks before she was sufficiently accustomed to them that she could forget their presence. Each day they were at the villa, the threat of violence from Curt Van Dort receded. She could not imagine he would dare to challenge Kumara's men. If he did, he was certain of a hot reception.

While she viewed the bodyguards as a source of comfort, Bart did not. They annoyed him as much as the threat that necessitated their presence. 'It is impossible to live this way,' he fumed when they were alone in the privacy of their chamber.

She was already in bed and watched him with a flurry of anticipation as he paced the room, pulling off his clothes. It was over a week since he had made love to her. Although he no longer showed his keen sensitivity to her feelings, she preferred even the most selfish of his love-making to none at all.

'It's a small inconvenience to suffer for our safety,' she murmured softly, hoping to soothe his annoyance. 'Kumara is very kind to have arranged for them to guard us.'

'Kind?' His voice was quiet yet held an undertone of icy contempt. 'We are prisoners in our own property. How do we know they're not in league with the others?'

'Kumara trusts them.'

His cold eyes sniped at her from the end of the bed where he was preparing to unroll his mat. 'I don't!'

She quailed before his pent-up fury, uncertain how to diffuse it. The pressure he was under had changed him until he was a stranger to her. She was no longer able to gauge his moods. Anything she did or said in innocence could be twisted by him into a challenge and spark off his anger.

The worry showed in his tightly-knit brow, the tense way he held himself and his frequent tugging at the stump of his ear. Even her silence goaded him.

'You lie there without caring a fig about me. Do you know what I have to do each day to keep this plantation intact?'

'I do care!' she retorted impulsively.

'By the devil, Raven, hold your tongue for a minute.' He flung his mat down on the floor and walked around to the side of the bed. He had stripped off his shirt. His chest with its crucifix of golden hair disappearing below the waistband of his breeches heaved in his simmering rage. His blue eyes darkened like angry thunderclouds.

'I sleep at the foot of your bed to protect you. From the time I awake, Raven, you are constantly in my thoughts. I long to be in the villa with you, to see you are all right.' He dashed his clenched fist into the open palm of his hand in frustration.

'I have to be everywhere, in the mill to see none of the natives sabotage production, in the fields to see the *salagamas* don't shirk their work. I have to do the ledgers and accounts. I have to be vigilant for strangers . . .' He sat down heavily on the bed, bouncing her with his sudden weight on the mattress.

She eased herself up from the pillow and watched him warily, trying to calculate if he wanted sympathy or praise. Her frankness overcame discretion.

'Why didn't you ask Kumara to help you like I suggested?' she said sharply.

'Why don't you go to Galle like I suggested?' he retaliated. 'Don't you see, Raven, it's your being here that's causing me all these difficulties.'

'Fiddlesticks! I'm more protected here than I would be in Galle. You know what I'm like. I'd find some way to get even with Madam Gudde for what Curt has done, reducing you to a pathetic ghost of the man you used to be.' Her breath burned in her throat and she gasped at what she had said.

Curses fell from Bart's lips; his nostrils flared with a wild and passionate fury. She bunched her fists under the coverlet, digging her nails into her palms in alarm at his violent reaction. She had never seen him so enraged and she paled as his words singed her ears.

He spluttered, banging the mattress with his fist, venting a stream of oaths learned from the slave drivers of Barbados. His wrath blinded him.

She was shocked by words she had never heard before but her pique dissolved into sympathy for his outrage. She hesitated to tell him she was sorry until his fury calmed.

'By the devil's ballocks,' he said at last, running out of breath to continue cursing. 'If I seem pathetic to you, you're the cause of it.'

'Me?' she mouthed, clutching her bosom and pouting her innocence.

'If you were in Galle, I wouldn't need Kumara and his brigands to guard you. I have to leave him here to protect you from them. If he's here, how can he help me on the plantation? That's why I'm reduced to what you see before you.'

He stood up and banged his chest with his fist. 'At least I'm still a man, not a ghost.'

She wanted to leap out of the bed and run to him, smoothing back his hair and stroking his chest and shoulders to calm his fury. Instead, she began to weep, despite knowing that this sign of womanish weakness would anger him more because he would assume she was doing it to win his sympathy.

'I'll go to Galle,' she said, 'if you don't want me.'

'Dammit, Raven, haven't you been listening? I *do* want you!' He put both his hands to his brow and staggered back clasping his head as though hit.

'I want you safe, I want you in peace, I want you without all this.' He lowered his hand and gestured lamely at his mat on the floor.

The sudden silence overwhelmed her. She managed to stop weeping before the sight of her tears set him off again.

She watched him hungrily, eaten up by an urge to grasp him to her bosom and succour him. She was confused, overawed by his masterful wrath yet sensing his own need and longing to respond to it.

'I will do as you say, Bart. Anything.'

He waved her to silence and slumped on the bed beside her, laying his head on the pillow. He closed his eyes while his legs dangled over the edge. She regarded him with a desire that set her fingers twitching, eager to hold him.

His chest rose and fell and his mouth fluttered as he exhaled noisily, trying to calm the demon that caused his outbreak of despair. She edged closer to him.

His hand arched up to meet her and without opening his eyes, he placed it firmly on her breast. 'No,' he muttered sternly. 'Let me rest.'

'Bart, Bart . . .' She frowned, knowing she could help him.

He held her off, his arm rigid. She saw each ridge of muscle of his stomach tense like the ribbed surface of a washboard. Suddenly she remembered the power that lay in acquiescence.

'Of course,' she said, withdrawing from him so his hand fell from her bosom to the coverlet. 'You must rest.'

She placed her head on the pillow and closed her eyes, peeking to watch what he did.

For seconds, he remained tense, expecting her to make another attempt to touch him. When she didn't, he let his arm relax, his fingers curling into the coverlet and pulling it idly. She curbed her impulse to seize him and pretended to be asleep.

After several minutes, he shifted his head and looked at her

219

quizzically. The bodice of her nightgown was loose and her nipples peeped above the border of pink lace. She breathed deeply, accentuating the rise and fall of her chest.

'I know what you're doing, Raven,' he said gruffly, the anger drained from his voice. 'I'm sorry you were subjected to my rage about everything. I feel better now I've sounded off.'

'I didn't understand it, anyway.' The warmth of her smile echoed in her voice as she opened her eyes and let him see how much she cared for him.

He grinned back briefly, with no trace of his former animosity. 'Will you go to Galle, Raven?'

'Yes, Bart.' She smiled again but managed to restrain herself from reaching out to grasp him. 'I am tired now. I want to sleep.'

She buried her head further in the soft down of the pillow. She deliberately didn't apologize for her own rash remarks in case he was roused to ire again.

He swung his legs up on the bed. 'This could be our last night together for a while.'

'I suppose it could.'

His breath was hot against her cheek, his sudden nearness searing her with a fire that made her gasp. His lips touched hers and his arms curled around her, crushing her to his chest. He devoured her mouth in a frenzy of his own passion, yet she refused to yield to him despite the chasm of craving opening within her.

'Raven!' he shouted as she broke away from him. 'I want you!'

'I want you too, Bart,' she said, choking back a tear. 'I want your love, your child –' She shrank with terror at the word that had spilled out of her subconscious.

For a moment he hesitated, frowning at her. Then his face filled with joy and he reached for her, his fingers bruising her arms as he pulled her towards him. He smothered her cheeks with kisses.

She was stunned by his arousal, too slow to resist when his hands tore the nightdress off her.

His lips smacked against her flesh, his fury becoming an insatiable desire. His mouth slipped lower, caressing the most sensitive, secret curves of her body.

She soared with an inner peace under his touch, flowing with satisfaction. She yielded to a vibrant, gushing sweetness as he penetrated her and she felt the seed of his manhood taking root.

CHAPTER TWENTY-FIVE

The coastal scenery along the road to Galle enchanted Raven with its tropical loveliness. She observed how the sea's current had scooped the line of the shore into coves and bays of exquisite beauty, separated by precipitous headlands covered with forests and crowned by groves of coconut palms. She made the journey in a euphoria of happiness that heightened her enjoyment of everything she saw.

The cool shade of the palm groves, the fresh verdure of the grass, the bright tint of the flowers that twined over every tree, the rich copper hue of the soil, and the occasional glimpse of the sea through openings in the dense wood; all combined to form a landscape unsurpassed in novelty and beauty.

Her appreciation of the scene was poetic, inspired by her feeling of fulfilment that lingered long after the night of Bart's farewell love-making came to an end.

Her first few days in her father's bungalow were passed in a haze of delight. She wondered why she had resisted Bart's entreaty that she come to Galle. It was refreshing to be able to walk in the garden without attracting the attention of hawking guards. The constant flow of visitors to Collector Radley in his official capacity added a spice to the day that was lacking in the confines of the plantation.

Combined with the stimulus she drew from the change of scene was the knowledge that she had captured Bart's inner essence in her being. It was ironic that at the moment of their separation, she should feel closer to him than she ever did in the chamber they shared.

She did not pine for him although every sunset, in a ritual that acknowledged their bond, she stood on the battlements and gazed across the bay to the headland opposite. Behind it where the sun's rays slanted, was jungle, the plateau of sugar-cane and their home.

She imagined Bart sitting on the verandah watching the same sunset and thinking of her, a glass of rum in his hand, of course,

221

and Kumara playing with Kirti at his side. The child's nanny, Malika, had accompanied her to Galle and some evenings they stood on the battlements together. Raven pitied the girl for not knowing the contentment that she was blessed with.

'Bloodheart will be drinking a rum now and relaxing after his day in the fields.'

'M'm?'

'I can see him in my mind, Malika.' She smiled benignly at the girl, suddenly realizing that Malika was her own age.

She was slight and light-skinned, with dark, sad eyes that were more mournful since her brother's death. She was dressed simply with a white muslin jacket loosely covering her figure and a floor-length *comboy* or waist cloth. Her long black hair was piled into a bun and secured with a tortoise-shell comb in a manner similar to Tissa's.

Malika's resemblance to Tissa was striking, emphasized in the golden light of the sun's setting. Bart's mother had bought the girl from slavery at Madam Gudde's bordello after she had been consigned there by Marcus Van Dort. At twelve, she had been the old Burgher's mistress. Her past was impossible to guess from the haunting beauty of her face, its smooth dusky skin aglow with pale gold undertones.

As she gazed at her, Raven's pity evolved into a love and trust. Perhaps it stemmed from her new-found serenity inspired by Bart's love, and she wanted to share her joy. Whatever the reason, she decided to take Malika into her confidence.

'Do you remember,' she said when they turned away from the sun after watching the green flash as it set into the sea, 'that you wrote a note to Nato for me?' She watched Malika discreetly to gauge her reaction.

Her eyes blinked once at the sun then she turned to face her with a forlorn and impassive stare. 'Yes, m'm.'

Only then did Raven remember her dismay when she believed it was her note that had brought about Tissa's death. 'The note was never delivered to Nato,' she said hastily, ruffled by the memory. She had intended to introduce her confession in a more auspicious way.

'I know, m'm.'

She sighed with relief until doubt struck her. 'How can you possibly know?'

'I retrieved the note from the messenger. Daisy and I decided it should not be sent.'

Raven nodded, preferring not to dwell on this evidence of Malika's disobedience and its comment on her own folly. 'The note was my idea to get revenge on Nato for what he and his master are doing to Bloodheart.'

She paused and invited Malika to sit with her on a bench. She explained briefly the reasons behind the feud.

When she finished, Malika commented sagely, 'Curt Van Dort is both his father's son and his mother's child.'

'Wouldn't you like your revenge on him? For Tissa's death?' Raven smiled to encourage her, certain of her answer.

She was confounded when Malika shook her head gently and with a sad smile said, 'No.'

'Why not?' She was upset at being wrong in her judgement of the girl's character. 'He is an evil man.'

'He is loved by someone, even if only by his mother.'

'He hates *her!*' Raven was piqued by Malika's defence of Curt Van Dort. 'You don't know what he's like.'

'I've seen him in the street. He watches me with the eyes of an excited pig, his tongue dribbling lust down his chin.'

'There, you do know what he's like.'

'No different from other men.'

Raven was about to disagree when she remembered Malika's past as a reluctant whore in the bordello. 'What about Madam Gudde? Surely you hate her?'

'I am trying to purge evil feelings from my soul.'

She was disappointed by Malika's attitude but a twinge of guilt intervened when she wanted to upbraid her. She fell into a thoughtful silence with Malika at her side.

She wondered if she was wrong to pursue her vindictiveness after what had happened to Tissa. She began to envy the Singhalese girl for her tranquillity, considering the dreadful treatment she had suffered.

'Are you upset, m'm?'

Raven sighed, given strength by Bart's imagined presence. 'Malika,' she cried, reaching out and clasping the girl's hand in her own, 'I want to do something, don't you?'

'To help Bloodheart?'

'Yes!' She was relieved the girl understood at last. 'Helping someone could earn you merit as a good Buddhist, couldn't it?'

She felt Malika's hand being carefully removed from her grasp and she smiled ruefully at the clash of their two cultures: Malika's placidity and her own impulsive exuberance.

223

'How, m'm?'

'I need information. I need to know Curt's habits. Who are his friends? Who does he see?' She stopped before she explained why, and put Malika off the idea.

'I can't go near the bordello. I'd be in danger. You might have more success.'

'Collector Radley is going there.' Malika let the words slip casually, not recognizing their importance.

Raven stared into the gloom that had descended swiftly on the garden with the sun's setting. She was disgusted by the news of her father's patronizing the brothel. It was a blow to her self-esteem as well as shattering what little respect she had for him. She was aware of her father's flaws in his grand image of his own importance but had no idea he was a whoremonger too.

'Are you sure?' she asked in a strangled voice.

'All men are the same, m'm,' said Malika, sensing her shock. 'Lust is the weakness of the mightiest as well as the lowest.'

'Indeed?' She stood up, fired with resolve as a new idea entered her mind. 'You've a poor opinion of the British, Malika. Not all men seek their satisfaction in whorehouses. The governor wouldn't be pleased to hear what my father is doing.'

'Why not, m'm?' Malika sounded amused that a man's proclivities could earn the governor's censure.

'Because,' Raven said with a growing feeling of excitement at her idea, 'it leads a man of influence into the paths of evil. He becomes corrupt, open to bribes in return for favours. He is no longer impartial as he needs to be to administer his inferiors.'

'Yes, m'm,' were Malika's final words as she escaped to the servants' quarters while Raven returned to the house.

To aid her plan, Raven expressed an interest in her father's duties. She was delighted when he responded favourably. She learned of his love for routine and regulations and the rigmarole of the colonial civil service. His passion was desk work; he loathed having actually to deal with the natives and solve problems for which there was no established procedure to follow.

'I've done well so far,' he boasted. 'No black marks and I'll retire with a pretty pension. Not long to go now.'

She listened patiently every evening to his dull catalogue of clerical achievements. In the day she discussed the running of the Collector's affairs with Medley, his perpetually perspiring and harassed assistant. She played the part of a dutiful, interested daughter with ease, ingratiating herself with the British officials and army officers, learning all she could about the hierarchy in Galle.

She was helped greatly by Captain Walker whose enthusiasm for gossip rivalled a washerman's. She learned from him about Curt Van Dort's insistence that the plantation was really his and how he was only waiting for Bloodheart to leave Ceylon so he could claim it.

Curt's version was accepted as the truth among the locals. He backed up his claim with his title deed. He was believed because it was not the first time that a foreign settler had usurped native-owned land for his own purposes.

Curt Van Dort cut a gay figure as he swaggered around Galle, tended by Nato in fancy livery bearing a parasol. Being Madam Gudde's son, and the son of the former registrar, gave him the highest prestige among the natives, whether Burgher, Singhalese, Moor or Tamil. His influence was considerable through the secrets he knew from his mother and the obligations owed to him because of his father.

Far from becoming the laughing stock of the town after the incident of the snakes, Curt was transformed into a popular figure. Those in thrall to him enjoyed discovering he had fears like them, while others were sympathetic.

When she glimpsed him strolling the ramparts, whipping off his hat with a flourish to every lady he met, Raven was astounded by the change from the monster she remembered. His flabbiness had taken on the edge of authority and he proceeded through the town with an assumed air of dignity instead of the shuffling gait of a disgraced lecher.

Raven observed the nuances of Galle's social life with the utmost care. She was dismayed by Curt's popularity and her father's profligacy. She regretted it had taken her so long to realize what was happening.

Carefully, she chose the moment to put her plan into action waiting until she was alone in the parlour with her father. He was cradling a snifter of cognac in his hand and reminiscing about his youth as a clerk in Governor Maitland's secretariat.

'You have a record of long and distinguished service to the crown, daddy,' Raven said when he paused to take another sip of cognac. 'You ought to be knighted when you retire.'

'Oh no,' Mr Radley protested mildly. 'Sir Thomas Radley . . . yes, it does have a certain cachet.'

'It would be a shame if news of your private enterprises were to

225

reach the governor. You'd lose so much if you were obliged to retire in disgrace.' She remained aloof as her father choked on his cognac.

His florid face flushed a deeper shade of pink. 'What are you talking about?' he spluttered, clasping his snifter to his chest as though it were a charm to deflect her criticism.

She pulled a piece of paper from her reticule and rose from her chair. As she crossed the room holding it out to him, she was aware of his eyes, already frightened, watching her in consternation.

'This is a list of people, mostly Burghers and Moors, who pay you a retainer or on consignment to overlook customs duties on their imports.'

He snatched the paper from her hand. 'Where did you get this?'

'I compiled it myself, daddy.' She stood over him. 'I have a copy prepared to send to the new governor.'

'The new governor . . . ?' He squawked, collapsing back in his chair. 'This is nonsense.'

'It is illegal nonsense, and absolutely true. What about that cognac you are drinking? That was a gift from Madam Gudde herself to overlook certain taxes.'

'You don't understand about administration, Raven. One has to cooperate to achieve a disciplined community.'

'Are the whores that Madam Gudde supplies for you part of this cooperation? I wonder if Sir Edward Paget, as I believe the new governor is called, would understand – or even approve of – the way you administer the Galle district.'

She smiled archly. 'The governor is a new broom and that, as they say, sweeps clean, even in the colonial civil service.'

She had no compunction for what she was doing to her father. He had forfeited the right to her filial loyalty by his hypocritical conduct and debauchery. Besides, it was for Bart.

She returned to her seat, disgusted by her father's pretence at outrage when he could easily admit his guilt.

'It's all lies,' he said, slapping the paper. 'These people have said these things to discredit me. I am a Collector of Customs, it's the most unpopular official post in Ceylon. They are scheming to ruin my life.'

'Madam Gudde's name is at the top of the list.'

'Yes, yes,' he nodded, wiping the sweat from his brow. 'She's the worst. A greedy, evil woman. She and her son believe they run the town.'

'Why don't you take action against them?'

He blinked. 'What sort of action?' he asked eagerly, taking the bait.

'For infringing regulations, the brothel should be closed down. For non-payment of duty, Madam Gudde should be fined. For providing girls against their will to pleasure British officials, she should be gaoled.'

'I can't,' he wailed desperately. 'It would lead to such a scandal –'

'My report to the new governor would lead to worse.' Raven paused, picked up her reticule and prepared to leave the parlour.

'However, if the brothel were closed down tonight, on your order, and remained closed, it would convince Sir Edward Paget that you are taking action against a confirmed anti-British trouble-maker.' She smiled coyly.

'Then I would not feel bound to inform the governor about your indiscretions . . . or about your dubious methods for preserving order in Galle.'

She swept out of the room in a rapture of triumph as her father crumpled on his chair and placed his head in his hands, muttering incoherently to himself.

Collector Radley showed a mettle Raven had not suspected, although she should have realized that her own courage had its roots in her parents. The Collector, having chosen Raven's solution to keep his transgressions secret, acted boldly. He issued an order declaring Madam Gudde's an illegal gaming establishment and had it closed.

As Raven requested, it remained closed. Mr Radley was ada-mant when Madam Gudde come to protest and ignored her threats. 'A new broom,' he told her, borrowing Raven's cliché, 'sweeps clean.'

Curt and his mother were outraged. Malika repeated to Raven the gossip that they held her responsible for influencing the Collector against them. Raven was overjoyed that they had the wit to work out that she was the victor of their feud with Bloodheart.

She walked the town proudly, pleased with the new respect afforded her and her father by the natives of all races. The house with its high wall in the Street of Moorish Traders stayed closed and shuttered, deserted except for a caretaker.

Rumour had it that Madam Gudde and her son had retired to Colombo, accompanied by some of their girls and attended by Nato. Wherever they had gone, they had left Galle. Within a week of their departure, Bart came to take Raven back to the plantation. She went happily, buoyed by her victory and by Bart's renewed vigour.

The night of her return was as memorable as the night of her farewell.

'Now I know you missed me,' she giggled when they lay side by side in bed, their bodies naked, still moist from a frenzy of lovemaking.

'I was able to do twice as much work in your absence,' he grunted teasingly.

'I was able to do twice as much shopping. You should see the dress fabrics I've brought back, and the combs and gems.'

He beamed, hugging her, his pride at what she had done communicating itself without either of them mentioning it. Talk of Curt and Madam Gudde would have spoilt their mood so she relaxed in his arms, thrilled at being with him again.

'We don't have money for such extravagance,' he laughed. 'You're a poor planter's wife, not a townee belle.'

'People gave me presents.' She smirked. 'They thought I might intercede on their behalf with the Collector . . .' They laughed together and she was warmed by the satisfaction of knowing their love was mutual.

Bart had dismissed the guards in her absence. Kumara was philosophical about it, warning Bart not to underestimate a Burgher adversary. He laughed off the warning, feeling confident that Raven's strategy had destroyed Curt as a threat.

In his light-hearted mood, he proudly showed Raven the plantation, riding newly-acquired horses to inspect the fields where the cane was fast approaching maturity. At the mill, Kumara demonstrated some innovations of his own that made the sugar and rum production easier on the labour force.

'You have become a formidable partnership,' Raven congratulated them, basking in Bart's happiness at having her at his side.

'I've knocked the sophistication out of his britches,' said Bart, punching Kumara affectionately on his chest.

'And I,' Kumara said with a twinkle that stirred a forgotten passion deep within her, 'have polished his rusticity. See how he is no longer uncouth. He radiates a *joie de vivre*.'

'I was immodest enough to assume that is due to my return,' she said, joining in their laughter.

The repartee of their moments together brought back contentment to the plantation. Bart was still of stolid temperament compared with Kumara's devil-may-care approach. The two of them were foils for each other and Raven loved them both, although in different ways.

The tranquil life on the plantation filled her with tolerance and happiness. She retired early every night to her chamber to allow Bart and Kumara time to drink too much and swap preposterous yarns as men liked to do.

She never worried about Bart's lateness in coming to their chamber because she understood his need for male companionship, as well as his concern for the plantation and the natives. She slept easily, knowing that when he came he would slip into bed and take her lovingly in his arms.

As she lay embraced by dreams one night two months after her return to the villa, an unusual noise roused her. She opened her eyes expecting Bart but when she looked around the chamber, he was not there. She guessed the noise had come from a jungle creature running across the roof, so she settled back to sleep.

The sound was more definite when she heard it a second time. Someone seemed to be tapping on the shutter. She listened, puzzled as the noise was repeated again. When it became an insistent knocking, she rose from the bed.

She was lulled by her sleepiness and by the safe, loving atmosphere that filled her days and nights. She opened the shutter without thinking.

For a fraction of a second, she thought the face at the window was an old friend. The black bushy beard was familiar so she didn't cry out at the unexpected sight.

Only when the man's face spread into a mirthless grin and she saw his bloodstained lips and gums, did she shriek. But then it was too late. He was climbing through the window with his sword pointed at her heart.

CHAPTER TWENTY-SIX

Bart laughed at Kumara's joke and looked at him admiringly. Even sitting relaxed in the reclining chair on the verandah, Kumara had a ruggedness and vital power that Bart envied. He was attractive and unscrupulous enough to take any woman, yet he lived a disciplined and chaste life since he came to the villa.

He had won Bart's trust. His personality had proved genuine over the months. However, Bart was aware that Kumara's charm concealed facets of the man of which he knew nothing.

He leaned over and tapped Kumara on his knee. 'I enjoy your talk of the women you have had,' he said, emboldened by his third glass of rum for the evening. 'What now? There is little enough to entertain you here. Two strapping Caffre wenches and the melancholy Malika.'

Kumara's eyes took on a momentary blankness. It was deliberate and annoyed Bart because he wanted to penetrate his thoughts. The enigma of the man was as carefully preserved as the day Bart met him. He gave no clues about himself apart from his humorous anecdotes which Bart suspected were borrowed from others.

His glance brightened and he smirked as he said, 'Romulus has two wenches to service. Do you think I should offer to help him?'

Bart waved the remark aside as frivolous. 'If you had a wife here, Kumara, she would help you with Kirti. Be company for Raven too.'

'Aye.' Kumara's smirk changed to a wry smile. 'And fetter me before my time.' He leaned forward to meet Bart's probing eyes and seemed to relent in his obsession for privacy. 'I have a wench or two in the settlement,' he confined. 'They amuse me enough.'

Bart relaxed. Kumara had taken over Tissa's duties in the manner that Raven had suggested. He had ample opportunity to exploit his position and popularity with the bare-breasted *salagama* maidens.

It was a weight off Bart's mind that he was not fretting for greater satisfaction. He had become used to Kumara's presence both as an overseer and as a friend. He was worried about losing him if he grew bored with plantation life.

'It's the soldiers and bachelors in Galle you should worry about,' Kumara ridiculed. 'With Madam Gudde's establishment closed down, what do they do? Each other?'

Bart chuckled and reached for the decanter, offering Kumara a refill. He shrugged when Kumara declined and poured himself a generous measure.

'It's on nights like these,' he said, feeling maudlin, that I really 'preciate your friendship, Kumara. You're an odd cuss but I've grown 'customed to you.' He sipped the rum and smacked his lips with relish.

'A planter's life is a lonely one, dealing with niggers or natives all day and a wife's nagging and children's bawling all night. No friends. I'm lucky. You're my friend an' you love Kirti more'n I do an' me wife don't nag.' He sagged back in the chair, a smile of boozy contentment spreading across his face.

Kumara tensed, a pulse racing in his neck. His head was cocked, reminding Bart of a mongoose listening to a snake slithering across the grass. His eyes peered alertly into the darkness shrouding the lawn beyond the lantern's glow.

'What the devil's eating you?' Bart taunted.

Kumara's brisk gesture to him to be silent made him jerk forward in his seat, spilling his rum. He was annoyed by the man's disrespect.

'I'm telling you –' he began drunkenly, breaking off to gape when Kumara rose swiftly to his feet and with two strides bounded off the verandah and into the parlour.

Bart grimaced at his rudeness and twisted in his seat to see where he was hurrying off to.

'Kirti!' he heard him call as he disappeared into the courtyard.

'Makes more fuss of him than a mother,' Bart mumbled to himself, settling down to enjoy the remainder of his rum before he went to join Raven in bed.

He sank into a lazy reverie – about Raven, about the plantation, about his dead mother – as he gazed unseeing into the garden. A bat swooped out of the night, gliding towards his head before veering sharply away. He blinked and rubbed his beard, idly watching the shadows of the bougainvillaea bushes where they danced as the lantern flickered over them.

231

One bush seemed to merge with another, its shadow spreading then becoming two separate shadows again. It was a curious sight and he concentrated his tired eyes on it, feeling amazed when he saw the process repeated.

In his befuddled state it occurred to him only gradually that there were people lurking behind the bougainvillaea, gliding from one bush to the other as they crept nearer the house.

He froze. The rum-induced confusion in his mind vanished and was replaced with a dreadful clarity.

He sat up, trying to conceal his awareness of the threat. He placed his empty glass with a painful slowness on the table and eased himself out of his seat. He swallowed, fighting back his apprehension as he turned his back on the garden and walked towards the parlour doors.

'Jagath!' he hissed urgently to rouse the boy dozing on the floor inside. 'Close the doors.'

The boy scrambled to his feet and prepared to go out onto the verandah.

'No,' Bart said between clenched teeth, his voice low. 'Leave the lanterns burning. Close the doors behind me. Quickly now. Pretend there's nothing wrong.'

Jagath stared at him, pondering the command. Bart reached the inside of the parlour and dived behind a door, slamming it shut. Jagath understood the game and did the same thing.

'Bolt and lock it, boy,' he cried, his voice stronger now he was inside the house. He glanced around the parlour. 'Close the shutters too.'

The door to the courtyard was open and he hesitated about whether to close it with Kumara outside. He ought to bring Kirti into the parlour so they could group together in case there was going to be an attack. Why hadn't Kumara warned him of what he had seen before he went for Kirti?

He shook his head at Kumara's odd ways and decided to leave one door unlocked for the time being. Intruders could only get into the courtyard over the roof and he had enough arms and ammunition to repel them.

A shriek erupted from Raven's chamber. It shrivelled Bart's courage with its chill echo of terror. She screamed again, a high-pitched cry that filled the night with her fear, reverberating around the inside of the house with a terrible, blood-curdling insistency.

He lurched towards the door to her chamber, dazed by her panic

232

and by the thought of what might meet his eyes when he entered the room.

'Kumara!' he called over his shoulder, wanting his help as he pushed against the door. It was locked.

Raven's scream was abruptly stifled and an ominous silence surged back into the parlour. He glanced around. Jagath was standing transfixed by the verandah windows.

'Go for Kumara,' he shouted at him, realizing his weapons were all in the chamber with Raven.

'Tell him to come here. You stay with Kirti. Lock yourself in the room and don't open the shutters.'

He was expecting the intruders in the garden to start their attack, now Raven had raised the alarm with her scream. Without his pistols, he wasn't sure what to do. He listened at Raven's door for a sound that would give him a clue what had happened to her.

'Open the door!' he shouted desperately. 'Raven, can you hear me?'

There was a noise of scuffling, of someone falling across the bed. Anger welled in him, replacing his shock.

He hammered on the door with his fists. 'Open up!'

The door was solid mahogany, with large brass hinges. It was bolted inside and locked. There was nothing he could do to force it open.

He turned sharply as Jagath returned to the room. 'What the devil are you doing? Where's Kumara?'

'He is gone. Kirti too.' Malika pushed past Jagath, her voice calm. She stood in the centre of the parlour, drawing her shawl over her shoulders with no sign of fear.

'Shut all the courtyard doors and fasten them,' he ordered, dismayed by her news. 'Kumara should be helping us. Where's Romulus? He's the only other man here.'

'In the store room with Daisy and Little.' Malika sat on the couch with a fixed stare on her face.

He realized her apparent calm was a placid form of panic, an acceptance that what was going to happen was inevitable. Jagath moved to her side and sat with her, grasping her hand.

'By the devil, what am I to do?' Bart turned away from them in frustration and beat on Raven's door again. 'Open up, whoever you are. Don't harm her, she's done nothing.'

'Vat a touchink display of affection!' a voice uttered sneeringly behind him.

He spun around to see Curt Van Dort lounging in the entrance to the dining room. 'Jagath,' he breathed. 'You didn't fasten the doors!'

'No matter, Bloodheart.' Curt stood aside to let Nato pass.

The Caffre grinned mockingly at Bart and walked to Raven's door. He banged a quick rat-a-tat on it, followed by two more knocks.

'You see, Bloodheart, your vife already asked us to drop in.' Curt chuckled dryly as the bedroom door opened and a burly Kandyan warrior released his hand from Raven's mouth and pushed her into the parlour.

Bart reached for her and she ran to him, clinging to him nervously. She was wearing only her nightdress with its lace collar and red ribbon tied under her breasts. He shielded her with his arms away from Curt's ogling stare.

'Are you all right?' he whispered in her ear as her fingers clutched at his waist. She didn't answer.

'Be brave,' he muttered, feeling the need of encouragement himself.

'What do you want with us,' he demanded, glaring at Curt so he wouldn't see how helpless he felt.

Curt ambled around the room, gloating at him and his effort to protect Raven from his eyes. 'I vant vat is mine, Bloodheart,' he said, a hard edge to his voice. 'You haf brought this on yourself by refusink to cooperate.'

'He'll never give in to you!'

Bart was startled by Raven's outburst. He pulled her back into his arms, hushing her to keep quiet.

'What do you think is yours, Curt? My wife and I? Let us go and we can talk. A court of law could decide.'

'You haf been free to go but you stayed. Your resistance to my vish has been annoyink. Mother is very upset at losink her house and her girls.' He giggled. 'Ve talk no more, heh?'

He snapped his fingers and Nato strolled over to the verandah door with another leer at Bart as he passed close to him. He unlocked it and Bart saw there were two Kandyans standing guard outside. Another Kandyan, making four in all, entered from the courtyard when Nato opened that door.

Bart recognized two of them as having been in Kumara's band of guards. That was obviously how Curt had known the layout of the house and been able to enter so easily.

Six men, Bart thought, calculating his chances of defying them successfully. If Kumara was hiding somewhere and could come to his aid with weapons, and if Romulus used his cutlass, there was a chance. Jagath was unlikely to be of use; he was cowering beside Malika, watching Nato and whimpering with fear.

'Vere's Kumara?' Curt asked the Kandyan.

He answered with a glob of red spittle on the tiles which caused Raven to flinch with anger and dig her fingers deeper into Bart's waist.

'He's gone,' the Kandyan said arrogantly. 'With the boy. I am telling you before, he is cunning.'

'No matter.' His gesture of dismissal was brusque. His eyes had a maniacal gleam and his lips a mean thinness in the pockmarked fleshiness of his ugly face.

'I am going after him,' said the Kandyan, brandishing his sword and sending one of Raven's prized ornaments shattering on the floor from its plinth by the door.

'You are stayink here!' Curt's voice hissed with menace. 'The boy is of no interest to me. Bloodheart's vife is a more interestink hostage.'

'I am wanting the boy. That is why I joined you.'

'Vy are you so tiresome? I am payink you for information and assistance. It is better Kumara is not here. You may hold the voman.'

Bart felt Raven tremble in his arms. He gripped her tightly. 'Leave her out of this,' he said, losing hope. 'I'll do what you want.'

'No, Bart!' Raven rasped into his ear, her voice showing her indignation despite her fear. 'You must not give up your plantation.'

'I think he vill, my dear.' Curt beckoned impatiently at the younger Kandyan who was idly chewing betel, a trickle of red saliva frothing on his lips.

'Take her,' he ordered, his face flushing with anger at the Kandyan's impudent slowness.

As the man reached for Raven, Bart thrust her aside so she fell on to the couch across Jagath and Malika. He brought up his knee and felt the man flinch when it connected with his groin.

The Kandyan yelled with surprise and his sword clattered to the tiles as he bent double, clutching himself with pain. Bart heard Curt's chuckle of pleasure at the man's agony and then he was seized from behind.

'Run, Raven!' he shouted. 'Romulus!' He hoped she would understand to seek the slave's help.

He couldn't see what she was doing as a flash of pain blinded him. His arm was twisted behind his back, wrenched out of its socket by brutal force. Another hand held his shoulder, making resistance impossible.

'Yo' trouble me, Bloodheart,' Nato said hoarsely, 'an' I snap yuh head off.'

'He vill,' said Curt, pretending to frown with disapproval. 'He's ruthless.'

Turning his head, Bart saw Raven was being dragged to her feet by the Kandyan. He held her easily in his massive arms, his black beard scraping against her cheek as he hugged her from behind. She was watching Bart, the fear in her eyes replaced with concern for him.

Curt sneered. 'Don't expect help from your slaves,' he said. 'Nato has already locked them away.' He paced the floor in front of them, gazing around in mock admiration.

'Yes, this house vill suit me nicely now my mother's is banned to me.' He put his hand inside his coat and brought out a sheaf of papers which he flourished under Bart's nose.

'I have here some deeds of transfer. You vill sign them and you vill be free to go.'

Raven swung herself up off the floor, using her captor's hold on her as support. She lashed out with her bare feet at Curt Van Dort, knocking the documents from his hand. She spat at them as they fell to the floor, and tried to trample on them.

The bearded Kandyan hoisted her up and her legs kicked wildly against his shins.

'Take her to the cave,' said Curt, losing his patience. 'She's a distraction to Bloodheart.'

The Kandyan walked to the door with Raven struggling in his arms. The other Kandyan, still rubbing his crotch, and with a sullen glance at Curt, joined him.

Bart heard Raven call his name before a hand clapped over her mouth, gagging her. There was no panic in her voice, it was a cry of warning, a rebuke.

He admired her courage although it was pointless. He would sign the deeds so they would release her. He could repudiate his signature afterwards and have Van Dort charged and brought to justice.

He smelled the stale sweat from Nato's body as the Caffre held him. His arm was less painful when he relaxed the pressure. It helped him think.

236

Curt Van Dort obviously knew he would be unable to convince the authorities the transfer was genuine if Bart was alive. It made him shudder at his probable fate.

'Ah, yes,' said Curt, picking up the documents from the floor and wiping them on Bart's shirt.

His breath, a tart smell of sour arrack, gusted into Bart's face causing him to wriggle his nose. Curt took the grimace for defiance and slapped his cheek with the sheaf of papers.

'Ah, yes,' he repeated, gurgling excitedly. 'You are thinkink you vill sign the deed then contest it before the registrar, heh?'

Bart held his eyes unblinking. He was powerless to do anything else while he was embraced by Nato's strong arms, except show Curt that he was not scared of him.

'The registrar is my man.' Curt giggled. 'And so is the Collector.'

'You will never be able to bribe Mr Radley!' Bart said, surprised by Curt's remark. 'When he hears what you've done to his daughter, you'll be jailed. Release her before the Kandyans harm her!'

A sickening feeling churned in the pit of Bart's stomach as Curt looked at him scornfully.

'Mr Radley is beink discharged from the Collectorate. Ve haf influence in Colombo, Bloodheart. A vord in the right place . . . enough! I'm vasting my time here. Your precious vife vill need me to protect her.'

Bart tried to strike Curt a blow with his head. It was in vain. Nato's hold on him was solid. All he succeeded in doing was exciting Curt.

'I haf something special for you.' Curt placed the papers on the table and pulled a slave whip from under his coat.

He jabbed the stock into Bart's crotch. The unexpected burst of pain made him wince, bringing a smile of pleasure to Curt's bloated face.

Bart clenched his teeth with determination, knowing that as long as he refused to sign, his life would be spared. 'You can whip me, but you won't make me sign!' he said, fearing that his weakness was Raven. He could stand whatever brutality they inflicted on him, but if they harmed her, he would sign immediately.

'Ve vill vip, you vill sign, Bloodheart. Take him outside.'

Nato tightened his grip, forcing Bart to walk to the verandah. The two Kandyan guards watched with interest, moving reluctantly when Curt ordered them to take a rope and tie it around Bart's ankle.

He kicked out but was no match for the two of them when they grabbed hold of his legs and held him down. The rope was fastened to his left leg and hung over the central beam supporting the verandah's roof. When he was secured, Nato let him go.

Bart rubbed his sore shoulder and gazed about him in trepidation. In Barbados, he had seen Negro slaves trussed upside down like chickens and whipped mercilessly by their bondmasters. He never imagined it would happen to him.

The rope tightened and his ankle was jerked from under him, sending him toppling sideways onto the verandah floor. He hung on to the rail as his body was raised, feet first, into the air.

Curt lashed at his fingers to make him loosen his grip. He was hoisted up until he dangled head first down from the beam, his hands inches away from the floor, too far off to support himself.

He arched his body so he could raise his head. 'I'll never sign,' he taunted Curt.

The whip smashed across his breeches, stinging him and setting his body spinning on the end of the rope. He was secured to the beam by one leg, his other dangling down. The weight of his body pulled at his ankle as though stretching it. He tried to raise himself to control the spinning.

Curt lashed him again, the long leather thong of the whip smacking against his chest.

'How do you like this, Bloodheart,' Curt called. 'Hurts, heh?'

He gritted his teeth as the whip stung him a third time. Curt's eyes were ablaze with an insane joy as he prepared for the fourth stroke.

Nato reached over and plucked the whip from his hand. 'Yo' ain't lashin' proper,' the Caffre scolded him. 'Like dis.'

Curt's crestfallen face brightened as the whip tore into Bart's buttocks under Nato's skilful application. It ripped into the fabric of his breeches and set him spinning at speed. The next stroke was placed with accuracy across the first, tearing another gash in his clothes and flesh.

Bart was stunned by the pain and the wild revolving of his body. He grappled with his hands to reach the floor.

'Vat a master!' drooled Curt, running his hands down Nato's biceps as he prepared to strike again.

'Get de wench,' said Nato, shrugging Curt's fingers off his arm.

The whip sliced into Bart's flesh, searing him with a blinding, giddy agony. He tried to concentrate on what was being said.

'Vy?' Curt appeared flummoxed by Nato's assumption of command. The whip cracked again and Curt squealed with delight. Bart bit his tongue to stop crying out at the slash of pain.

'If I whip de wench, dis buckra sure go'n sign de papers.' Nato lashed him nonchalantly while he talked and the clothes fell off Bart in shreds, weals of blood etched into his skin.

'Boys!' Curt addressed the two Kandyans. 'Go for the voman. Bring her back here.'

'No.' Nato paused in his strokes and glared at Curt. 'Yo' go for her.' He brandished the whip in Curt's face.

'If dem hill folk go dey go'n run off wid de wench, Yo' ain't go'n get yuh taste.' He prodded Curt in his waist and his deep chuckle echoed around the verandah. 'Neither am I.'

'I'll need a boy to escort me.' Curt brushed the whip stock aside, agitated by what Nato had said. He bustled off the verandah followed by a Kandyan youth carrying a lantern.

Nato flicked his wrist again and the whip sizzled past Bart's ear, tearing a gash in his shoulder through the thin linen of his shirt.

'Don't cut him down,' he heard Curt call from the darkness. 'Let his vife see. I'll get her and ve'll have our fun, heh?'

Nato began to exact his private vengeance on white men, sending the thong biting into Bart's flesh with a rapidity that was dazzling.

Every stroke cut Bart's skin, burning him with the scorching power of flaming charcoal. The ceaseless spinning made him dizzy and he lost control. He puked, the vomit spraying out on to Nato and the Kandyan as he spun around.

'You are killing him,' he heard the Kandyan warrior speak through a red haze. 'Make him say where the elephant pearl is hidden, before Curt returns. We are having it for ourselves then.'

The blows stopped and Bart felt himself being lowered to the floor. He fell face down into his own vomit and lay panting, struggling to stop blacking out as an overwhelming desire to sleep seized him. The Kandyan picked him up by his shoulders and shook him.

'The *gaja mutu*?' he asked gruffly. 'Where is it?'

Bart was dazed, his head still spinning, his flesh itching with fire. Blood oozed from the wounds crisscrossing his body. His resistance was broken. He heard as if in a dream, his mother's voice calling him.

'Behind . . . the . . . picture,' he stammered, answering her.

He was shaken as his body jolted back to the floor. At last he was left alone in peace. He felt his life seeping away through the countless cuts of the whip. His mind reeled and the floor seemed to lurch.

'Yo' fool me?' Nato stood over him, waving the leather pouch that contained the elephant pearl. He held a cat's eye ring in his fingers. 'Dis ain't de t'ing.'

Bart stared at the empty pouch, trying to understand. 'I hid it there myself,' he gasped, seeing his hope of survival vanishing.

Nato picked up the whip and lashed him angrily.

Bart was defeated, too weak to try and crawl under a chair for shelter. He twitched involuntarily with despair as he guessed that Raven had removed the pearl without telling him.

The *gaja mutu* could not save him now . . . he was doomed to die at Nato's hands . . . because of her interference.

CHAPTER TWENTY-SEVEN

Sounds carried easily in the darkness that engulfed the plantation. The snap of the whip whistled through the still night air to Raven's keen ears. She shivered with horror for Bart's sake, unconcerned about what would happen to her.

She prayed he would not weaken out of consideration for her. The plantation, the *gaja mutu*, Kirti – whatever Curt and his Kandyan renegades wanted – were more important than her safety.

The whip snapped like fire crackers on the verandah behind her; she tried to shut the noise from her ears because it meant Bart was suffering and she could do nothing to help him.

The Kandyans each held an arm, forcing her to walk between them. Whenever she stumbled and begged them to go slower, they jerked her forward regardless of the pain in her arms and the agony of her bare feet stubbing against roots on the path.

They were heading westwards, away from the house and the river, through canefields towards the jungle that separated the plantation from the hills overlooking Galle. At first, she tried to impede their progress so she could remain near the villa. She thrashed and struggled against the two grunting, sturdy men, seeking a chance to wriggle from their clutches. If she could escape she would run to the settlement for help.

She was impotent in the men's rough grasp and it annoyed her. She decided to use more subtle tactics and preserve her own strength by walking with the men instead of making them drag her. Her ploy did not fool them into relaxing their grip and she was obliged to run to keep up with them.

She stole a glance at the villa, its golden glow from the verandah lanterns dimmed by the night and the overhanging trees surrounding it. The harsh noise of the whip was muted by distance. She hated to be leaving Bart.

'Where are we going?' she gasped, falling against one of the men as she tripped.

He yanked her ungraciously to her feet. 'You'll see,' he answered with a choke in his voice.

She realized the feel of her near-naked body when she fell against him affected his concentration. He was muttering resentfully in Singhala under his breath.

'I'm tired,' she said, stumbling into the man again so her bosom contacted with his chest. 'Please let me rest. I won't try to escape.'

The man pushed her away with his free hand groping her breasts. He spoke rapidly over her head to his companion. His laugh chilled her blood with its menace but at least they halted.

She collapsed limply, her exhaustion real. For a second she was suspended like a puppet between them until one man grunted and released his hold on her wrist. She sank down to the ground, whimpering softly as the strain on her legs and arms eased.

The Kandyan who kept his grasp on her wrist squatted down beside her. His beard was pushed close to her face. The other man held a flambeau and watched her with the eyes of a hawk. Her nightdress was torn, the ribbon unwound, and in the light from the torch, she felt humiliated by his probing glance.

'I know you,' she said softly to the Kandyan at her side, hoping to win his confidence. 'You're Banda, aren't you?'

He was startled that she remembered his name from when he was one of Kumara's guards.

'I'm sorry Bloodheart kicked you . . . there,' she said pointedly. 'He didn't mean to hurt you; it was because of Curt.' She rubbed her feet with her free hand while the other hung limply in Banda's grasp.

The older Kandyan, the one who had tricked her into opening her window, spoke a warning. Banda replied heatedly, releasing her wrist to gesture with both hands.

For a moment she thought of escaping but instead massaged her feet while the two men argued. They were both watching her and would easily catch her if she moved. She settled down on the path, conserving her energy at the same time fluffing her hair provocatively. The tempo of their argument increased.

From their tone she could guess what they were saying. The older man was Curt's lackey, committed to doing what he had been ordered without question. Banda had other ideas, bolstered by his resentment of Curt. Raven watched him with blatant admiration and sensed him swelling with self-esteem under her glance.

He pulled a silver box from his waistband and snapped it open. He packaged the betel leaf, lime and nut parings casually as the older man reprimanded him.

Raven edged an inch away from them both. Her move brought a torrent of words from the older Kandyan. He drew his sword and plunged it into the hem of her nightdress, sticking it to the ground. His swift reaction cowered her and emphasized her helplessness.

Banda popped the betel package into his mouth and chewed nonchalantly, returning the box to his waistband. He seemed unperturbed by the sword quivering in the ground in front of her. He muttered a few words and hawked onto the path, splattering her nightdress with flecks of red spittle.

She feared the two of them were reaching an agreement. She had hoped that by favouring one, the other would get angry and they would fight, neglecting to watch her so she would have a chance to escape.

'Banda,' she cried with boldness she didn't feel. 'Please tell that oaf to remove his sword. It was a silly thing to do, I might have been hurt. Curt wouldn't like that.'

The old Kandyan looked aghast as Banda translated her words, mocking him at the same time for what she had said. He took a step towards Banda, waving the flambeau threateningly. Banda drew his own sword and the man retreated, seizing his sword from the ground.

Raven jumped to her feet wondering whether to dive into the canes. Her hesitation helped her to think. Instead of running, she moved behind Banda, grasping him around his waist and squeezing him.

'Protect me from that oaf,' she hissed into his ear. 'I have gold. I'll pay you.'

He shoved her away, spitting at her feet as though telling her to stay where the red stain spread in the soil. He turned his back on her to face the other Kandyan who was shouting curses at him and at her.

She watched with acute anxiety, desperate for them to forget her and fight each other so she could slip away in the darkness before they noticed.

The big man lunged, not at Banda but at her. She gasped, impaled to the spot by fear. He thrust the flambeau at her and she reeled backwards, raising her hand to shield her eyes.

He shouted and held the flaming torch towards her again, handle first. She reached out and found she was holding it. He gestured to her to raise it higher so its glow lit up the path and the sugar-cane.

She was perplexed as the man advanced on Banda brandishing his sword above his head. With the flambeau in her hand she could see her way along the path to escape. As she moved, the light wavered and Banda shouted at her to stay.

She was trapped. Any dimming of the flambeau would alert them both to her movements. She watched, awaiting her chance.

Banda, still chewing contentedly, circled around the Kandyan, keeping out of reach of his sword. It seemed to Raven a strange way of fighting because she expected the thrust and parry of duelling fencers, not the ritualistic dance the two men were engaging in.

She moved experimentally towards the canefield on her left. Both of the men growled at her without taking their eyes off each other.

She looked around for a branch at head height in which she could wedge the flambeau. It would give her a few seconds start before they realized she had gone. Another option was to fling the torch at them and rush off in the direction of the villa. There was not enough light from the stars to show her the way.

The swords clanged, exciting her. Banda spat at his rival's feet and sniggered. She wondered what would happen to her if he won.

They circled each other again, swords glinting in the flame. Banda lunged, swinging the blade like a club. His rival dodged and swung at him, the blade passing close to his nose as he stepped aside. The clash of blades rang through the night, disturbing birds and animals in the jungle into hooting and shrieking with alarm.

A plan formed in Raven's mind. Whoever was the victor would expect to claim her. She would wait until he was close then plunge the flaming torch into his face. She hoped Banda would win the fight as he was more arrogant and easier to dupe.

The two men continued to chop and feint, wielding their heavy swords with skilled familiarity. Banda had stopped chewing and his rival was grinning beneath his ill-kempt beard. Their elaborate prancing made her grow impatient for one of them to finish off the other.

Gradually, as nothing happened beyond the clinking of one blade against another, she realized with despair that killing was not their object. She was. They were contesting to see who would have her first.

'Banda!' she shouted as though in panic. Her cry caught him off balance as his rival lunged at him, expecting him to sweep his blow aside.

Distracted by her, Banda faltered for a fraction of a second. It was fatal. The sword smashed into his neck, severing his jugular vein. He collapsed in a pool of blood at the feet of his surprised companion.

Raven charged with the flambeau and pushed it into the man's face. He swung his sword in an arc, knocking the torch from her hand. She screamed in frustration as he caught her wrist, forcing her backwards onto the ground beside Banda.

She lay in his blood as he stood over her, unwinding his waistcloth. The flambeau lay burning at the edge of the sugarcane, throwing eeric shadows into the night around her.

She tried to wriggle away but he trapped her with the point of his sword touching her chest. He ran it almost lovingly from the cleavage of her nightdress down to her navel and onwards between her thighs, slicing through the fabric. She shrunk, fearing the tip of the blade would penetrate her flesh.

He guffawed happily as he flicked the torn nightdress aside and gazed at her nakedness.

She glared back at him, furious with herself for her failure to escape. The sight of the bright red gash of his mouth in the midst of his black bearded face filled her with despair.

He fell on her.

The thunderclap of a shot deafened her at the same instant the weight of his body hit her. A sticky moistness oozed over her and in the light from the fallen flambeau's flames she saw her skin spreading red with his blood.

She wriggled out from under his dead body, leaving the remnants of her nightdress trapped beneath him. Eagerly she turned to greet her rescuer, expecting to see Bart striding up the path with his pistol waving in the air. Instead, Curt Van Dort emerged from the darkness.

'I haf come in time.'

His sardonic drawl paralysed her. She stared at him with disbelief, his lewd chuckling scorching her ears. She covered herself with her hands and, looking at the two Kandyans dead at her feet, she was stricken into action. She knelt beside Banda, frantically tugging at the sword pinned beneath his body.

A hand seized her hair and pulled her by it to her feet. 'Raven,' Curt's voice trilled. 'I haf saved your life. I deserve a kiss!'

She turned into his arms with a yelp of dismay, forced into his embrace. She twisted her head as his lips sought hers and he slobbered against her cheek.

Furious, he gripped her behind her neck and tried to steer her mouth on to his. He pressed his lips to hers, crushing them in his anger. She tasted blood where her teeth bit into the flesh of her own lips.

In desperation, she tickled him under his arms. He drew away from her, giggling. She had a chance to breathe.

'Ah,' he said, snuffling obscenely at her nakedness in the flamelight. 'You vant to play, heh?'

She crouched down over Banda's corpse and pulled at his waistcloth. When it came free in her hands, she wrapped it around her waist, ignoring the clammy stickiness of his blood where it rubbed against her thighs. She became aware of a boy with a lantern behind Curt, gazing at his dead compatriots with alarm.

'Run!' she shouted at him. 'Bring Bart. This monster will kill you too.'

Curt glanced casually at the Kandyan youth dithering on the path. With a snort of contempt, he raised his pistol and pointed it at him. The youth dropped the lantern and fled with a shriek. Curt placed his pistol in his waistband and snickered at Raven.

'You look upset, my dear.'

'Where's Bart? What have you done to him?'

'Me?' He squawked with feigned innocence. 'It is vat he haf done to me that should concern you. Now I take my kiss, heh?' He opened his arms and lurched towards her.

She took a step backwards, clasping the bloodstained cloth around her waist with one hand, the other shielding her bosom. 'Is he dead?'

'My dear, I left him alive. Of course, if he offends Nato . . .'

She took another step back, halted by the flames at the edge of the canefield where the flambeau and the lantern had set fire to the dry stems of sugar-cane. She faltered, her feet becoming twisted in the folds of cloth.

Curt pounced for her and she tried to run. The cloth wrapped around her ankles, binding her and tripping her. She sprawled on the path a yard from the flames.

Curt gobbled excitedly and dropped to his knees beside her. His bulbous nose and unshaven jowls loomed over her in the blaze from the spreading fire. His hand reached out and touched her breast, squeezing her nipple. She shrivelled with revulsion.

'I haf wanted to see you like this.' He leered at her, eyes half-closed with lust. 'You haf lost your pride now, heh?'

She glared back at him, loathing his oily features, his dank hair and the chubby fingers that clawed at her breasts. Strangely, his words inspired her. She had not lost her pride, but her shame at her nakedness had passed. Her body was smeared with so much blood, mud, cane dust and soot from the fire, it no longer worried her.

With a curious detachment, she watched his hands fondling her breasts. She was numbed by his assault and felt it was happening to someone else. Even when he slapped her cheek she didn't stir from her state of shock. A fearful heat was building up within her, stronger than any arousal Bart's touch ever provoked.

'Stand up, girl!' Curt cried, seizing her hand and pulling her to her feet.

She rose without resistance, intrigued by the panic in his eyes. She was puzzled when he draped her arm around his neck and placed his hand in the small of her back, forcing her to walk while he supported her.

'Hurry,' he said. 'The fire haf caught on both sides of the path. Ve'll be trapped.'

She realized then that the heat was not inside her but from the flames devouring the sugar-cane. She stumbled along blindly, leaning against him, aware that something was wrong but unable to decide what it was.

'Ve must cross the stream,' he shouted. 'The fire vill burn itself out there.'

Flames were leaping high in the canes on either sides of the path, lighting their way through the inferno. The fire kept pace with them as Curt urged her to run faster to reach the stream before the flames cut them off.

'Bart,' she cried softly to herself, trying to twist out of Curt's grip. She knew what was wrong; they were running away from the villa instead of back to it.

Behind her, the path was blocked by the blaze. There was no way through either for her to return to Bart, or for him to rescue her.

As ribbons of flames rained down on her naked body, singeing her hair and burning her skin, she ran at Curt's insistence. She sensed he was trying to save her so he could save himself, drawing strength from her company when he would have jellied into panic if he had been caught in the flames alone.

The suspicion that Curt needed her help revived her own interest in survival. His obvious fear of being burned to death gave her an unexpected advantage over him: she was no longer afraid.

'I can't run,' she said, sinking to her knees to delay him.

'You must!' he screamed at her, his frightened eyes lit up by the flames closing in on them. Sweat poured down his face and he was shaking with terror. He yanked her arm, lent phenomenal strength by his panic.

She stumbled after him, because he was going to drag her all the way if she didn't. It was a heady feeling to know he was scared and she wasn't. It gave her back the boldness she had lost when the Kandyan fell dead on top of her.

By the time they reached the stream, Curt was heaving for breath, apparently close to collapse. The stream was a water course dividing the two largest canefields, watering them from its source high up in the hills. Cane grew to its banks on both sides.

Curt ploughed into the water, pulling Raven with him. The flames chasing them stopped hungrily at the stream's bank, trying to leap across and consume the cane on the other side.

The chill of the water on her feet, rising up to her knees as she walked through the stream, was bliss to Raven. She longed to lie down and let it wash away the dust and slime on her body.

Curt didn't pause and she had to follow him up the opposite bank and into a clearing in the cane. She fell at his feet, pretending weariness. He sank down beside her, panting and muttering with relief.

She studied him carefully in the dim glow from the flames, expecting him to take a long time to recover. She wondered what to do. To her dismay, before she could think of anything, he was suddenly exuberant, his panic banished by his successful escape.

He pulled off his coat, removed his stock and lay them neatly by his side. He removed his pistol from his waistband and placed it with his coat, loosening his breeches. He pulled a knife from inside his boot, and placed it with care beside the pistol, where it would be close to hand.

Raven sat upright, no longer pretending to be exhausted. He swung at her with the back of his forearm, catching her jaw a stinging blow that sent her sprawling, filling her eyes with starry tears.

She winced when her chin struck the ground and a flint gashed her cheek. Before she could recover, he clasped her from behind, his hands on her breasts and his body bucking against her rear.

She fell forward, spreadeagled on the flinty mud, and reached out for something to grasp. There was nothing. She fought to shake him off but his lust gave him an overpowering strength.

He held the pistol in his hands, chuckling with glee as he pushed it between her legs. His fingers opened her buttocks, forcing it in. He mounted her, straddling her backside and thrusting himself in, penetrating where not even Bart had entered.

She moaned and flailed, beating the earth with her fists while he snorted and grunted. She arched her buttocks in a desperate attempt to fling him off. He squealed with pleasure as he hammered into her.

Her hands reached blindly over the soil, searching again for something to grasp to deaden the dreadful pain. She touched the pile of clothes and clawed at them, her hand closing over the handle of his knife.

Curt's squealing rose to a climactic shriek when she rippled her thighs and turned to face him. He bellowed her name in triumph.

She smiled and plunged the knife deep into his groin, twisting it and severing his manhood from his body.

CHAPTER TWENTY-EIGHT

'We'll take the child for the pearl.'

Bart's pain was excruciating. Even when Nato stopped whipping him and turned to the Kandyan who had spoken, there was no end to the agony. He panted, willing himself to withstand the torment.

He wanted to defy Nato so he could find Raven and retrieve the *gaja mutu*. It was Kirti's, pledged to *him* for safekeeping, not for Raven to hide herself.

As the image of Raven focused in his memory, he remembered the ecstasy of holding her in his arms. This was not the bliss of death overtaking him but the birth of a determination to survive. He wanted desperately to tame Raven and make sure she would never meddle in his affairs again.

'Stand up!'

The voice was gruff and demanding, hands holding him under his arms and pulling him to his feet. He was dragged inside the house and lowered onto the couch. He kept his eyes closed, not wanting them to know he had decided to live.

'How can he sign Curt's papers if you are thrashing him to death? He can tell us where the child is.'

Nato's sullen grunt showed his contempt for the Kandyan.

'He's unconscious.' The Kandyan's fingers raised his eyelids so Bart gaped at him blankly.

'You, girl,' the Kandyan said to Malika who was crouching in fear in a corner with Jagath. 'Bring water. Hurry!'

'Why yo' fuss over dat buckra?'

'He's valuable to us, Nato. He is bluffing about the *gaja mutu*. I guess the child has it. If we take the child and the pearl, we can trade them to his kinsmen, or to their rivals. What do you gain if Curt gets this plantation?'

Nato scratched his head and pouted, his fat lips protruding sulkily.

'Nothing!' The Kandyan left Bart and prowled around the parlour, studying the contents of the room with interest.

Bart, peering at him through half-closed eyes, was reminded of Kumara. The man was more cunning than he appeared and had won Nato's respect with his persuasive tongue.

'Follow me, Nato, and you are becoming rich. With Curt you are always being a slave.'

Nato shrugged his huge shoulders and sauntered to the door of the parlour where he lounged against the door jamb and stared out into the night. 'Fire,' he said nonchantly. 'Mas Curt burnin' de cane.'

The Kandyan glanced over his shoulder. 'The wind is keeping the blaze away from here,' he said with obvious relief. He turned as Malika entered with a bowl of water and a cloth.

'Bathe his face,' he ordered, looking back at the fire as she knelt at Bart's side.

Malika placed the bowl of water on the floor by the couch and dipped the cloth into it, squeezing water over Bart's face and dabbing it gently. The tender touch of her fingers reminded him that he was not alone. He opened his eyes and smiled weakly at her. She frowned back at him, cautioning him to keep quiet.

She leaned forward, putting her lips close to his ear. Her hand trembled. 'I've unlocked the store room,' she whispered. 'Here, take this.' She pressed some powder into his hand.

The weals on his arm stretched and prickled as he took it, causing pain to shoot through his body.

'Chilli powder,' she hissed before he could ask.

'Is he conscious?' The Kandyan strode across the room and she shrank away in fear, the cloth in her hand. He glanced briefly at him then picked up the bowl of water from the floor and tipped it over his head.

'Wake up, Bloodheart!'

Bart spluttered and jerked up instinctively, but he kept his hand and the chilli powder out of sight at his side. The Kandyan snatched the cloth from Malika and threw it at him.

He wiped his eyes with it and looked around blearily, pretending to be dazed. Nato was on the verandah, captivated by the sight of the flames crackling across the plateau.

'The child?' the Kandyan said roughly. 'Where is he?'

From the corner of his eyes, Bart saw a shadow drift past the open door of the dining room. He moaned as though he didn't understand the question and fell back limply, his head resting on the couch's ornate wooden arm. He closed his eyes, gasping exaggeratedly for breath.

The Kandyan moved closer and bent down, sticking his beard close to Bart's. 'Are you hearing me? Where is the –'

Bart slapped his hand into the man's face, forcing the chilli powder into his eyes.

Chillis of Ceylon are the finest in the world. Dried and ground, they add a fiery zest to any dish. One grain in the eye can smart for hours, a handful is blinding.

The Kandyan staggered backwards with a shout, colliding with Malika as he rubbed his eyes frantically. From behind him Romulus darted out of the dining room into the parlour. He raised his cutlass above his head and brought it down sharply into the Kandyan's neck.

The man screamed and fell to the floor, dragging Malika down with him. She wriggled out of the way as Romulus chopped at him again, cleaving his head from his shoulders, showering her and the parlour walls with blood.

Nato stood by the door, frowning heavily. He beckoned Romulus to come for him, his eyes gleaming. Bart raised himself from the couch and tried to grasp Romulus's arm.

'Go for help,' he pleaded. 'He'll kill you.'

'I go'n kill him, Bloodheart. He only got de whip.'

Nato walked backwards slowly on to the verandah, waving tauntingly to Romulus to follow him. He cackled like a broody hen to mock him, drawing him out of the confines of the parlour to where he could swing the whip effectively.

Bart warned him again but Romulus's ears were filled with voices only he could hear. He ran after Nato who jumped off the verandah and halted, raising the whip to defend himself. Romulus thrust his cutlass at him like a sword, whooping with the frenzy of a fight he expected to win.

Bart heard the loud crack of the whip and Romulus's startled shout. He pulled himself off the couch and tried to stand. Jagath, who was cuddling Malika, left her side to help him.

Every step he took towards the door racked him with pain. Blood dribbled from the whip cuts and soaked through the tatters of his shirt and breeches. He leaned against the door jamb for support. He saw Nato on the lawn casually snapping the whip around Romulus's ears, toying with him.

'My pistol, Jagath,' Bart hissed urgently. 'In the bedchamber.'

The boy nodded his understanding and ran across the parlour to the bedroom.

Nato reduced Romulus from a brave man to a snivelling slave in seconds. Bart felt every cut that scored a stripe on Romulus's hide, feeling his shame and impotence under the flailing lash. Romulus tried to defend himself with his cutlass until the sharp sting of the lash across his fingers made him drop it.

Nato advanced mercilessly behind a barrage of strokes, preventing Romulus picking up the cutlass. He drove him into the bougainvillaea bushes where Romulus quickly escaped into the darkness.

Bart looked around for Jagath, eager for his pistol to shoot Nato while he stood with a self-satisfied smirk in the centre of the lawn. Jagath was standing by the chamber door, shaking his head.

'Raven!' he muttered with despair. 'She's hidden it!' He glanced frantically at Nato to see how much time he had before the Caffre came for him.

Nato was scratching his head, gazing at the grass in bewilderment. Bart looked where Romulus had dropped the cutlass and frowned too. It had disappeared.

Nato spun around, coiling his whip ready for use. He was obviously puzzled by where the cutlass had gone but saw Bart as more important. He crossed the lawn towards him, a murderous glint in his eye.

Bart backed away as Nato stepped up to the verandah. 'Jagath, hand me the Kandyan's sword!' he shouted desperately. It was too late. Jagath and Malika had fled to the bedchamber and bolted the door.

He gazed at Nato with a sickening dread filling his mind, almost robbing him of the power to think. His only weapon was his fist. By luring Nato into the parlour where there were too many obstacles for him to swing the whip, he might have a chance.

'You stupid Caffre!' he taunted. 'You've lost your ballocks and your brain. Come here and I'll show you how white men fight.'

With a snarl of rage, Nato bounded into the parlour. He used the whip handle to jab at Bart as he dodged behind the couch. Bart's foot hit the empty bowl and he snatched it up and flung it at Nato's head. It bounced off and smashed to the floor, barely slowing Nato in his stride. The Caffre dropped the whip and reached out both hands to seize Bart's neck.

As Bart ducked, he saw Kumara creep into the room from the verandah. He was holding Romulus's cutlass.

253

The sight distracted him and made him an easy target for Nato. The Caffre bellowed triumphantly and closed his hands about his neck. Bart crumpled to the floor under the weight of his body, feeling the choking pressure of Nato's thumbs on his larynx.

While he wondered if it was really Kumara he had seen at the door, Nato's fingers suddenly slipped from his throat. The Caffre mewled like a baby. Bart wriggled out of his grasp, surprised to see the cutlass sticking out of Nato's shoulder where Kumara had thrust it.

With a roar of rage, Nato reached behind him and pulled the cutlass out. He threw it at Kumara's head. It missed, soaring past him and smashing into the portrait of Bart's mother on the wall.

Despite the pain of every movement, Bart leaped on to Nato's back, clinging to his waist with his knees and digging his ankles into his crotch. He gripped his hands around his throat as Nato tried to shake him off, charging around the parlour like a wounded elephant.

Kumara retreated to the verandah, laughing. 'Finish the job, Bloodheart,' he called cheerfully.

'I'm hurt!' Bart shouted as Nato crashed into the escritoire and swung him against it.

Kumara grinned, treating it as a joke. The escritoire canted over to the floor.

Bart felt he was going to be shaken off. He raised his hand from Nato's neck and rubbed it against his eyes. There was still some chilli powder on his palm and it added to Nato's confusion.

Angered by Kumara's lack of concern, he summoned a last reserve of strength and dug his fingers into Nato's throat. The Caffre choked, tripped over a chair and sprawled forward on the floor.

Bart hung on, squeezing his fingers into his gullet, throttling the life out of him as Kumara watched, grinning his approval.

'Is he dead?' Bart gasped, pleading with Kumara to help him.

Kumara smoothed back his hair. 'You're on top of him. You should know.'

Bart relaxed his fingers and slid off Nato's back to the floor. 'He lashed me,' he panted. 'I'm almost . . . dead myself.' He rose unsteadily to his feet, supporting himself against the couch.

Kumara brushed past him and walked to the door of the bedchamber. 'Raven!' he called, banging on the door. 'You can come out now. Your husband's killed Nato for you.'

'Where have you been?' Bart demanded, incredulous at Kumara's casual return as though nothing had happened.

'I took Kirti to safety. He's with Ram. Is Raven here?' He gestured at the door.

'No.' Bart stumbled towards the verandah and stared out at the blazing cane. 'The Kandyans took her. Curt went after them.'

Kumara's bluff good humour vanished instantly and he stared aghast at Bart. 'I thought she was safe in her chamber!'

Bart shook his head sadly and sank onto a verandah chair. 'She's gone. In the blaze . . . Save her, Kumara.' Pain and weariness overwhelmed him; he blacked out.

The glow of gold and orange in the sky hovered over Raven where she lay in the balmy waters of the stream. Flames flickered from the dying fire. They lit up the stream in the darkness and she sank within it.

She longed to join the gurgling flow of the water course, becoming part of it and losing herself until she was cleansed. She let the current bear her downstream, her eyes closed as she drifted in its eddies. Her limbs were numb, her mind hazy. She stayed under the water as long as she could before surfacing for a gulp of air.

Wiping the water from her eyes, she gazed in consternation at a shape looming out of the golden darkness, standing on the bank of the stream, regarding her quizzically. She shivered for a moment, thinking it was Curt Van Dort come to life to haunt her.

The shrill squeal of agony when his startled eyes had accused her as his guts spilled on the ground still resounded in her ears. She had run from him then, seeking shelter in the stream while his life ebbed away in agony.

The shape of the man on the stream's bank was silhouetted against the background of the dying fire. He did not move. She imagined his eyes were mocking her. The outline of his body, of his thighs spread apart and his arms akimbo on his hips, increased her torment.

She plunged her head below the water and prayed that he was a spectre conjured up by her weary mind. She wanted, when she raised her head, to see only the burning sugar-cane and the glistening water spuming around her hips. There was no place for Kumara in her shame.

A hand touched her arm and she jerked her head out of the water, spluttering with panic. He was real. His hands caught her, seizing her by her shoulders and gripping here tightly. He sank down on his haunches in the stream beside her, his grasp relaxing, infusing her with a soothing calm.

She looked into Kumara's eyes when he turned his face to the glow from the fire. They brimmed with a tenderness she had never noticed before, not a trace of mockery glinted there.

His head was level with hers, the water gushing around his knees, soaking his boots, breeches and shirt. She bit her lip, feeling foolish under his gaze.

'Aren't you going to laugh at me?' she said timidly. 'You usually do.'

His hands tightened but held her at a distance from him. She saw how his face was blackened with soot and dust from the fire, his locks dishevelled and his brow troubled. She put her hand out cautiously in case he would push her away, and raised her finger to touch his cheek.

'Are you hurt?' she whispered, overwhelmed by concern for him. Seconds before, she had wanted to hide from him, now she was worried about his unhappiness.

'Raven,' he said, startling her with the boldness of his voice. 'Are *you* hurt?'

She shook her head, spraying him with water from her wet hair. She was aware of the strength in his hands and the power of his body. It emphasized her own weakness, crouched in the stream, caught in his arms. Those hands could crush her, his lips devour her. She sighed and struggled to break free.

'Raven . . .' His voice was a whisper now, aware of her fear. 'It's all right. It's all over.'

She tore herself away from him with a broken cry and slipped back into the water, lowering her head below its surface. She let the current wash away her tears and she emerged trembling, wondering if he was still there. He was watching her with his familiar sardonic expression and she felt reassured.

'You know what happened?'

He nodded, indicating without words that he had seen Curt's disembowelled body and understood her pain. She was grateful for his silence and watched bemused while he removed his shirt. He dipped it into the water, bunching it in his hand. He raised it to her face and pressed it gently to her cheeks, wiping away the droplets of water that glistened there like tears.

He dabbed her forehead, soothing her scratches and slowly bathing her face. She parted her lips breathlessly at the nearness of his body. The hair on his broad, golden chest hung with drops of water like diamonds.

He ignored her trembling and smoothed his hands over her shoulders and around the curves of her neck, patting her dry.

She could feel his uneven breath on her cheek and she tensed as his hands slipped lower. With an exquisite gentleness they outlined the circle of her breasts. She laid her head back, her hair tumbling down until her tresses were caressed by the stream's flow.

She relaxed as his firm hand on the small of her back steadied her. His fingers stroking her breasts were replaced by the softer touch of his tongue, tantalizing her nipples as they swelled, marble hard against his mouth.

She rose out of the stream and stood in front of him with water dripping down her thighs. His hands clasped her hips and he lowered his head. She strained to pull away from his teasing embrace, clasping the empty air with her hands, wanting to hold him, wanting to leave him.

He paused, raising his head and drawing her to him. He placed his mouth over hers, devouring its softness. His slow, drugging kiss revived the passion she thought had been extinguished for ever by Curt's vileness.

She walked with him blindly to the bank of the stream and let him lay her down on the grassy slope. She gazed at the stars gathered above her head and felt the heat from the dying fire behind her. She welcomed the warmth after her long submersion in the purifying waters of the stream. The night engulfed her with a soothing peace and she smiled at the darkness.

Kumara was standing naked over her. She gasped when he lowered his body, covering hers. He took her hands, encouraging her to touch him.

She caressed the strong tendons at the back of his neck, while his hands stroked the secret recesses of her body. She thrust herself against him, filled with a fear that he might pull away and leave her.

When she felt the heat of his body coursing down the entire length of hers, she relaxed, knowing at last it was happening. She tingled under his assured touch, his dextrous fingers finding pleasure points she never knew she had. He caused her to vibrate with a desire that shed all her doubts and fears.

He was tender and controlled as he made love to her. Against his rigid body she was like a humming bird, fluttering hesitantly to come to rest until he seized her and held her and took her.

Her breath came in long, surrendering moans. She flowed with torrents of ecstasy, filled with an overwhelming joy at possessing him within her and knowing that, at last, the bond between them was complete.

Dawn was spreading over the canefields when she woke. Her first glimpse was of the smouldering canescape, smoke mingling in the morning mist as the sun's fragile rays filtered through it from the hills beyond the river. It was a curious sight of desolation, heightened by the cloying stench of burnt cane that hung heavily in the air. She blinked, recalled the events of the night before, and closed her eyes again.

Her head was resting on Kumara's arm, using it for a pillow. During the night he had covered her with Curt's frock coat, its peacock green contrasting with the charcoal grey of the charred field. She snuggled under the coat, unwilling to open her eyes to the reality of the morning.

Kumara's long fingers stroked her hair and he blew softly in her ear, tingling her with contentment.

'We must go to the villa,' he said, easing his arm away. 'Bart needs you.'

She sighed and sat up, glancing at him shyly. When she saw the wealth of his smile, she smiled too, feasting her eyes on his face.

As the rising sun's glow caught him in a shaft of gold, his bronzed features were kindled with a radiant, majestic beauty. It was a powerful, bold and handsome face and she thrilled with the knowledge that for one night at least, she had captured the love of this mercurial man.

'Kumara,' she said suddenly. 'Take me with you!'

He rose to his feet, amused by her worry. 'Of course I will.' He held out his hand, helping her to rise.

He had donned his clothes while she slept and his shirt and breeches clung damply to his body. She could see the agitated rise and fall of his chest and knew he was lying.

'You must cover yourself,' he chided, catching the coat as it slipped from her shoulders.

She grimaced when he held it open. 'I don't want to wear that man's coat,' she said sulkily.

'Raven!' He cautioned her with his eyebrow arched and she felt a pang of remorse that she was starting the day by defying him.

'For you . . .' she said sadly, submitting as he wrapped the coat around her. It hung on her like a tent and reeked of horses and woodsmoke and Curt Van Dort. Before she could register her repulsion, he pulled her towards him and kissed her lovingly on her forehead.

When his lips drew away she raised her head and wound her arms in the baggy sleeves of the coat around his waist. She pressed herself to him, raising her lips for a kiss.

His mouth curved with tenderness but he held her away. She gulped back her despair and released him, tossing her hair to show she didn't care. The demonic smile returned to his lips and she knew she hadn't fooled him.

'Are you coming?' he said, starting to walk away, shielding his feelings from her. It gave her hope . . . perhaps some day he would return for her.

'I'm tired,' she grumbled, reducing the magic of that rare moment to the commonplace. 'My whole body aches.'

'So does mine,' he said with a grim chuckle, ignoring her need for sympathy. 'Let's go for Daisy to make some coffee. That will revive you.'

The normal light-hearted tone of his voice almost convinced her their life would continue as though nothing had happened. She walked gingerly in his wake, biting her lip to stop crying out with pain at every step. She longed for him to turn and help her but she was determined not to beg. He wanted her to be strong; she would show him she could bear even the cruelty of rejection.

'Raven!'

The sound of someone shouting her name made her pause. She looked at Kumara wildly, a sudden shaft of terror spearing her heart. His bland smile teased her.

'It's Bart,' he whispered, by his tone conveying more than his nonchalant stance suggested. 'He's bringing Kirti.'

She turned away from him, reluctant to take her eyes off the lean, feline grace of his body. It seemed incredible that a few hours before he had been hers. She tried to banish the yearning from her eyes, not wanting to embarrass him nor alarm Bart. He would admire her if she kept her emotions hidden.

Bart was stumbling as he walked along the track, supported by Ram. Jagath walked behind him, bearing Kirti on his shoulders. As soon as she saw Bart, her heart bled for him. She was not taken in by his brave attempt to appear strong. The awkwardness of his gait shrieked out the pain he was in.

She stared with dismay at Kumara. 'What happened to him?'

'Nato lashed him rather badly.' He smirked. 'He'll recover.'

'You didn't tell me that last night!'

He laughed openly in her face.

She flew at him with her hands outstretched, her nails straining to gouge the satanic glint from his eyes. His hands clamped around her wrists and he held her in a vice-like grip. She kicked at him in vain with her bare feet. His chuckle deepened.

'Still fighting me, Raven?'

'I hate you!' she cried, guilt engulfing her. 'Bart needed me.'

'So did I.'

She shrank from him and he let her go, turning with his shoulders braced to greet Bart. She was stunned and only Bart's shout roused her from her trance. She ran to his arms as he hobbled the last painful step towards her.

'Thank God you're safe,' he said, cradling her to his sore and puffy chest.

The familiar fragrance of his body reassured her and she clung to him, her eyes damp with tears. He winced in her embrace.

She forgot her own anguish and shame as she saw his appalling injuries. 'Oh Bart,' she cried, 'I was coming to you. We had to wait until daybreak . . . for the fire to die out.'

'I know, I know.' He hushed her with a kiss on her cheek.

She pressed her lips firmly on his, not caring about Kumara and the others watching her.

'Bravo!' Kumara's guffaw shocked them both. She released Bart and stood aside, glancing at Kumara angrily.

'You're both safe now,' Kumara muttered, lowering his eyes under her gaze. She felt better at his sign of shame.

Kirti was pounding Jagath's shoulders with his hands, begging to be put down. Bart nodded his consent and Jagath lowered the child to the ground. He ran over to Kumara and wrapped his arms around his legs. Kumara stooped and picked him up, holding him high above his head.

'Where've you been?' Kirti demanded. 'There was a fire and Ram showed me his snake. He's got it in the basket on his back.'

'I know.' Kumara let him slip to the ground and turned to face Bart.

Intuitively, Raven gasped. Kumara's lips tightened at the sound. She reached for Bart's hand and held it tightly.

'You have no more to fear, Bloodheart,' Kumara said diffidently. 'You and Raven can live in peace now.'

'You're going?' Bart's voice was thick with sadness. He held out his hand, not to Kumara, but to Kirti. 'Say goodbye like a man, son.'

Raven caught the sob in her throat as Kumara guided the child forward. Bart shook his hand and then placed his palms together at chest height and bowed his head, Singhalese style. Kirti returned the tribute and walked back to join Kumara.

'Kirti is my natural blood brother, *Raven*.'

She raised her head. His uttering of her name was like a caress. She stared at his sombre face, wondering why his eyes avoided hers.

'We share the same father. It is our destiny to be together.' He turned away from her. 'Thank you, Bloodheart!' He held out his hand to Bart.

'Wait.' Bart gestured irritably. 'There is something else.' He frowned at her. 'The elephant pearl, Raven. Where the devil is it?'

She blushed, ashamed of his rebuke in front of Kumara. She looked pleadingly at the snake boy.

Ram nodded with understanding and lowered his snake basket to the ground. She shrank away, clutching Bart as he lifted the lid.

Ram spoke in Tamil. Kumara tensed and grasped Kirti's shoulder. The child slipped from his grasp and ran over to the snake basket.

A cobra rose up sluggishly, swaying his head. It puffed out its cheeks at the child's approach. Unperturbed, Kirti danced in front of it, waving his arms in a snake-like motion before its eyes. While it was distracted by his movements, he eased his hand into the basket and pulled out a purple velvet pouch.

'The *gaja mutu*,' Kirti said proudly, handing it to Kumara. 'Can we go to Kandy now?'

'Yes, my brother.' He hoisted Kirti on his shoulders and walked away from Raven and Bart, shading his eyes with his hand which Raven thought was strange because the sun was shining from the opposite direction.

She put her hand under Bart's arm and supported him. They turned and walked back to the villa.

'Bart,' she said after a long period of silence when the only noise was the shrill cheep of birds foraging in the burnt canefields. 'I have something to tell you.'

'You don't have to say anything, Raven. I *trust* you.'

'I must.'

261

He sighed and pulled away from her, preparing for her confession.

'You'll learn soon enough.' A small smile of enchantment touched her lips. 'I'm pregnant. In six months we will have a son of our own.'

He looked at her intently and opened his arms, hugging her to him. 'I love you, Raven,' he whispered. 'I always will.'

She gazed over his shoulder into the distance where Kumara and Kirti were disappearing into the jungle. Her eyes were misty and wistful.

'I love you too, Bart,' she said, a single tear trickling down her cheek.

Richard Tresillian,
Galle, Sri Lanka.